W9-CBD-258

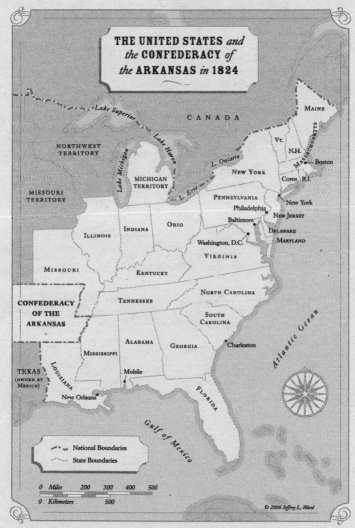

THE UNITED STATES *and* the CONFEDERACY *of* the ARKANSAS in 1824

CANADA

Lake Superior

NORTHWEST TERRITORY

Lake Michigan

Lake Huron

MAINE

MISSOURI TERRITORY

MICHIGAN TERRITORY

L. Ontario

VT.

N.H.

MASSACHUSETTS

Boston

NEW YORK

L. Erie

CONN. R.I.

ILLINOIS

INDIANA

OHIO

PENNSYLVANIA

Philadelphia

New York

Baltimore

NEW JERSEY

DELAWARE

MISSOURI

KENTUCKY

Washington, D.C.

VIRGINIA

MARYLAND

CONFEDERACY OF THE ARKANSAS

TENNESSEE

NORTH CAROLINA

SOUTH CAROLINA

ALABAMA

GEORGIA

Charleston

MISSISSIPPI

TEXAS (OWNED BY MEXICO)

LOUISIANA

Mobile

FLORIDA

New Orleans

Atlantic Ocean

Gulf of Mexico

National Boundaries

State Boundaries

0 Miles 200 300 400 500

0 Kilometers 500

© 2006 Jeffrey L. Ward

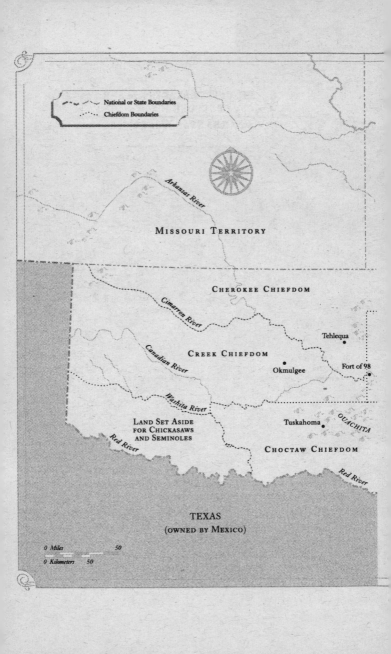

National or State Boundaries
Chiefdom Boundaries

Arkansas River

MISSOURI TERRITORY

CHEROKEE CHIEFDOM

Cimarron River

Tehlequa

Canadian River

CREEK CHIEFDOM

Fort of 98

Okmulgee

Washita River

LAND SET ASIDE
FOR CHICKASAWS
AND SEMINOLES

Tuskahoma

OUACHITA

Red River

CHOCTAW CHIEFDOM

Red River

TEXAS
(OWNED BY MEXICO)

0 Miles   50
0 Kilometers   50

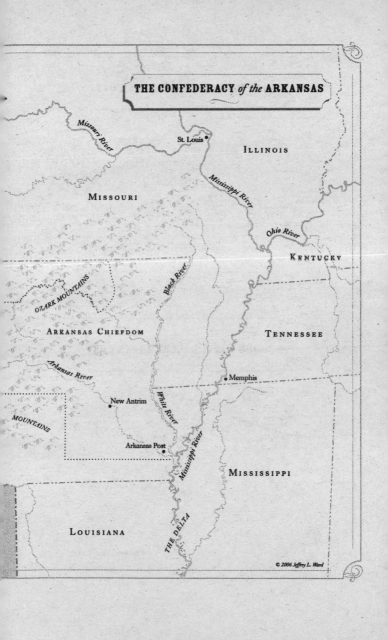

THE CONFEDERACY of the ARKANSAS

Missouri River

St. Louis

ILLINOIS

MISSOURI

Mississippi River

Ohio River

KENTUCKY

Black River

OZARK MOUNTAINS

ARKANSAS CHIEFDOM

TENNESSEE

Arkansas River

Memphis

White River

New Antrim

MOUNTAINS

Arkansas Post

Mississippi River

MISSISSIPPI

LOUISIANA

THE DELTA

© 2006 Jeffrey L. Ward

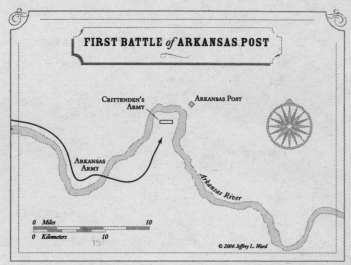

FIRST BATTLE *of* ARKANSAS POST

CRITTENDEN'S ARMY

ARKANSAS POST

ARKANSAS ARMY

Arkansas River

0 Miles 10

0 Kilometers 10

© 2006 Jeffrey L. Ward

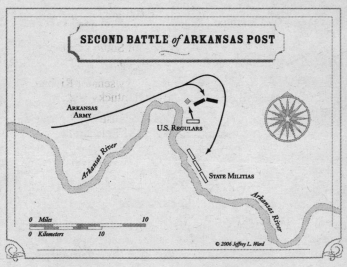

SECOND BATTLE *of* ARKANSAS POST

ARKANSAS ARMY

Arkansas River

U.S. REGULARS

STATE MILITIAS

Arkansas River

0 Miles 10

0 Kilometers 10

© 2006 Jeffrey L. Ward

DRAMATIS PERSONAE

American Characters

JOHN QUINCY ADAMS: U.S. secretary of state; candidate for president in the 1824 election.

ADAM BEATTY: Adviser to Henry Clay.

JACOB BROWN: Major general, commander of the U.S. Army.

WILLIAM CULLEN BRYANT: American poet and newspaper reporter.

JOHN C. CALHOUN: U.S. senator from South Carolina; candidate for president in the 1824 election.

JULIA CHINN: Mulatto wife of Kentucky senator Richard M. Johnson; the marriage is invalid by Kentucky law.

HENRY CLAY: Speaker of the U.S. House of Representatives; candidate for president in the 1824 election.

JOHN COFFEE: A close friend and associate of Andrew Jackson.

WILLIAM H. CRAWFORD: U.S. secretary of the treasury; candidate for president in the 1824 election.

ROBERT CRITTENDEN: Leader of the expedition to seize the Delta from Arkansas; scion of a prominent political family in Kentucky.

EDMUND GAINES: Brigadier general, U.S. Army; one of Jacob Brown's two top subordinate officers.

WILLIAM HENRY HARRISON: Retired U.S. Army officer.

ANDREW JACKSON HOUSTON: Son of Sam and Maria Hester Houston.

MARIA HESTER HOUSTON: Wife of Sam Houston; daughter of James Monroe.

SAM HOUSTON: Special commissioner for Indian Affairs in the Monroe administration; adopted son of Cherokee chief John Jolly; his Cherokee name is Colonneh, which means "The Raven."

ANDREW JACKSON: Senator from Tennessee; candidate for president in the 1824 election.

THOMAS JESUP: Brigadier general, U.S. Army; quartermaster general for U.S. Army.

ADALINE JOHNSON: Daughter of Richard Johnson and Julia Chinn; twin to Imogene.

IMOGENE JOHNSON: Daughter of Richard Johnson and Julia Chinn; twin to Adaline.

RICHARD M. JOHNSON: Senator from Kentucky; married to Julia Chinn, although the marriage is invalid by Kentucky law.

JOSIAH JOHNSTON: Adviser to Henry Clay.

JAMES MONROE: President of the United States, 1816–1825.

PETER PORTER: Adviser to Henry Clay.

SCOTT POWERS: Adventurer; partner of Ray Thompson.

WINFIELD SCOTT: Brigadier general, U.S. Army; Brown's other top subordinate officer.

ZACHARY TAYLOR: Lieutenant colonel, U.S. Army.

RAY THOMPSON: Adventurer; partner of Scott Powers.

MARTIN VAN BUREN: U.S. senator from New York; known as the Little Magician.

Arkansas Characters

CHARLES BALL: General, Arkansas Army.

JOHN BROWN: Abolitionist; a tanner from Ohio who moves to Arkansas.

SALMON BROWN: Abolitionist; brother of John Brown.

HENRY CROWELL: Banker and entrepreneur.

PATRICK DRISCOL: Principal chief, Arkansas Chiefdom. Also known as the Laird of Arkansas.

TIANA DRISCOL: Formerly Tiana Rogers; niece of Cherokee chief John Jolly; leader of the Arkansas Women's Council.

MARIE LAVEAU: Former New Orleans voudou queen; now married to Charles Ball.

ANTHONY MCPARLAND: Captain, Arkansas Army.

CALLENDER MCPARLAND: Soldier, Arkansas Army; cousin of Anthony McParland.

SHEFFIELD PARKER: Freedman from Baltimore; later soldier and then officer in the Arkansas Army.

HENRY SHREVE: Steamboat designer and entrepreneur; business partner with Patrick Driscol and Henry Crowell.

UNCLE JEM: Freedman from Baltimore; later soldier in the Arkansas Army; uncle of Sheffield Parker.

Confederate Characters

DUWALI: Cherokee chief; also known as Chief Bowles or The Bowl.

PUSHMATAHA: Principal chief of the Choctaws.

JOHN RIDGE: Co-owner, with Buck Watie, of a major newspaper in the Confederacy; later an officer in the Arkansas Army; son of Major Ridge.

MAJOR RIDGE: A major Cherokee chief; father of John Ridge; uncle of Buck Watie.

JOHN ROSS: A major Cherokee chief.

BUCK WATIE: Co-owner, with John Ridge, of a major newspaper in the Confederacy; later an officer in the Arkansas Army; nephew of Major Ridge.

British Characters

THOMAS CLARKSON: A leader of the British antislavery movement.

DAVID ROSS: Son of Robert Ross.

ELIZA ROSS: Wife of Robert Ross.

ROBERT ROSS: Former major general, British army; active in the antislavery movement.

WILLIAM WILBERFORCE: Member of Parliament; a leader of the British antislavery movement.

PROLOGUE

The north bank of the Ohio River,
near Cincinnati
APRIL 22, 1824

By the time they had finished making camp for the night, Sheffield Parker was exhausted. They'd been pushing hard for over a week, ever since they'd reached the boat landing at Brownsville in Cabell County and started traveling across country instead of continuing down the Ohio River on a flatboat. A friendly white riverboat man had cautioned them about it. He said they'd been safe enough, passing down Virginia's western counties, since there were hardly any slaves in the area. But from there on downriver they'd have Kentucky on the south bank of the Ohio, and several slave catching parties were active on or near the river.

"We freedmen," Sheff's uncle Jem had protested.

The boatman glanced at their party, which consisted of Sheff and his mother, his sister Dinah and his uncle Jem, and twelve other people from three different families. Several of them were children of one age or another.

"Well, that's pretty obvious. You don't never see runaway slaves in parties this big. But look, folks, it just don't matter—and you got to know that much yourselves. Those slave-catchers are rounding up any black people they can lay their hands on, these days. It's been a field day for the bastards ever since the exclusion laws started getting enforced. They'll even roam into Ohio to do it. They'll grab you and haul you before a tame judge in Kentucky, and he'll bang his gavel and declare you obvious runaways, and you'll be up on the selling block before the day's over."

"We got papers—" Sheff's mother started digging in the sack where she kept their few valuable belongings.

"Ma'am, it don't *matter*." He flipped his hand, dismissing the idea. "Forget about anything you can call 'law,' down there. If you got papers, the slave-catchers will just burn them. Then it's your word against theirs—and any judge they'll be hauling you up before would rule against Jesus Christ in a heartbeat, if he was your color."

He shrugged. "It's a shame and a disgrace, but there it is. Was I you, I'd sell the flatboat and start moving overland. Stay away from the river, as much as you can. Course, that ain't so easy, lots of places. Just be careful, is all."

They'd taken his advice, eventually, after finding someone who was willing to pay them a reasonable price for the flatboat. But it had been hard going thereafter. The road along the north bank of the Ohio was a primitive thing compared with the National Road they'd been able to take as far as Wheeling after they'd fled Baltimore. Sheff had had to carry his little sister for the past two days, she'd been so worn out.

And then it all seemed to come to nothing. Less than an hour after they made camp, just at sundown, Sheff heard a noise in the woods that circled the clearing on every side except the river. A moment later, two white men emerged, with five more coming right after them. All of them had guns, to make it still worse. Two of them held muskets, and all the others had pistols. Nobody in Sheff's party had any weapons at all, except the big knives that Jem and two of the other men carried.

"Well, lookee here, boys. Ain't this a haul?"

Sheff stared at them, petrified, from where he was squatting by the fire. He was sixteen years old. The first eleven years of his life had been the cramped years of a poor freedman's son in Baltimore, but not really so bad as all that. Then the white people started getting crazy after some sort of battle near New Orleans that Sheff didn't understand much about, except it seemed some black men had beaten the state militia over there and moved to the new Confederacy of the Arkansas. Which was way out west; Sheff wasn't really sure exactly where.

White people had gotten mean, thereafter, a lot meaner

than usual. New laws had been passed in Maryland, ordering all freedmen to leave the state within a year. Like most freedmen, they'd just ignored the law, seeing as how they were poor and didn't know where to go anyway. Most states were passing the same laws. Freedmen exclusion laws, they were called. Then the rioting had started, and they hadn't had any choice but to try to make it to the Confederacy.

And now, even that was going to be denied them.

One of the white men with a musket hefted it up a few inches. Not cocking it, just making the threat obvious. "Don't be giving us no trouble, now. I don't want to kill no nigger, on account of it's a waste of money. But I will. Don't think I won't."

One of the other men chuckled and started to say something. But he broke off after the first couple of words, startled by movement to his left.

Sheff was startled, too. He looked over to the far side of the clearing and saw that another white man had come out of the woods.

He hissed in a breath. That was the scariest-looking white man Sheffield Parker had ever seen. And, even at the age of sixteen, he'd seen a lot of scary white men. Especially over the past few months, since the killing had started.

"And who're you?" one of the white men demanded of the new arrival.

The man who'd come out of the woods ignored the question. His eyes simply moved slowly across the clearing, taking in everything. He was holding a musket in his right hand, almost casually.

The sun had set by now, and in the flickering light of the campfire, those eyes looked very dark. But Sheff was pretty sure they were actually light colored. That scary bluish gray color that he'd come to fear and hate more than any color in the world. The color of the eyes of most of the men who had beaten his father to death just a few weeks earlier. Sheff hadn't had any trouble, then, determining the color. The men had done the deed in broad daylight, on a street in Baltimore.

He'd thought they were going to kill him, too, but they'd satisfied themselves with just beating him and his mother. Following which, they'd given them two days to get out of Baltimore, or suffer his father's fate.

They'd left that very night, instead, along with a dozen other survivors from the race riot the white men had launched.

"Who're you?" the white man demanded again. He began to raise his musket.

"Bring that gun an inch higher and you're a dead man," the newcomer said. Turning his head, slightly: "See to it, Salmon. Levi, if any of the others makes a threatening move, kill him."

The seven original white men froze. Partly, Sheff thought, that was because of the sight of two musket barrels emerging from the woods, gleaming in the campfire light. But mostly it was just the way the man had said the words.

Scary, that had been, like everything about him. The words had issued from those gaunt jaws like decrees from a judge—or maybe one of those Old Testament prophets that Sheff's uncle Jem was so partial to. For all the threat in the words, they'd been spoken neither casually nor in heat. Simply . . .

Stated. The way a man might state that the sky was blue, or that the moon rose. A certainty, a given, decreed and ordained by nature.

One of the other seven white men finally broke the paralysis. He hunched his shoulders and spit. "Well, tarnation, sir, who *are* you?"

In a more aggrieved tone, one of the others added: "It ain't fair! We spotted and tracked 'em first. Rightfully, the reward should be ours."

The gaunt-jawed man brought his gaze to bear on that one. "What 'reward'?"

"Well . . ." The other seemed a bit abashed, for a moment. "The reward for capturing runaway slaves, of course."

That finally brought Sheff's mother out of her own paralysis that she'd fallen into the moment the first seven white men had come into their camp. "Tha'ss not true! We freedmen! We was driven out of Baltimore, and we on our way to the Confederates in Arkansas."

One of the white men glared at her and started to snarl something, but the gaunt-jawed man cut him off.

"It matters not, anyway. This is Ohio. We do not tolerate the heathen institution of slavery here." He nodded toward the negroes squatting by the fire. "They are men, and thus they are by nature free. So God decrees. I care not in the least what some sinner claims in Virginia or the Carolinas. Soon enough, his flesh will roast in eternal hellfire."

He took a step forward, his musket held higher. "Begone, all of you."

The seven original white men just stared at him.

"Begone," he repeated.

One of them had had enough. He snatched his hat from his head and slammed it to the ground, then planted his hand on the pistol at his belt.

"The hell we will! I don't know what crazy notions you've got in your head, but we—"

The gaunt-jawed man took another step forward. He was now standing not fifteen feet away from the man with the pistol.

"I believe in the Golden Rule, sir, and the Declaration of Independence. I think that both mean the same thing. And, that being so, it is better that a whole generation should pass off the face of the earth—men, women, and children—by a violent death than that one jot of either should fail in this country. I mean exactly so, sir."

The man with the pistol hesitated. Then he sneered. "You won't shoot."

The musket came up like dawn rising. Not quickly, no. Sheff wasn't sure, but he didn't think the gaunt-jawed man was really what people meant by a "gun man." He wasn't handling the musket awkwardly, but he didn't seem especially favored with it, either.

It mattered not at all. The dawn rises. It just does, whether any man wills it or not.

At the end, the pistol-man seemed to realize it also. "Hey—!" he started to shout, before the bullet took him in the chest and hammered him to the ground.

"Hey!" two of the others echoed in protest.

The gaunt-jawed man ignored them as he began reloading his musket. "If any of them move, Salmon and Levi, slay them."

They didn't move. Even though they all had guns, too, and had the gaunt-jawed man and his fellows outnumbered.

Well . . . maybe. From the corner of his eye, Sheff could

see his uncle Jem and two of the other men in their party reaching for their knives. His mother was doing the same.

Sheff wished he had a knife himself.

Halfway through reloading his musket, the gaunt-jawed man looked up. He was close enough now that Sheff could finally see the true color of his eyes.

Grayish blue, sure enough. That same frightening, cold color. But since it wasn't aimed at him for once, Sheff wasn't so scared.

"All of you," the man said quietly to the six white men still alive and facing him, "were condemned before you were born. God is Almighty and so He decreed, for purposes of His own. I will shoot each and every one of you—shoot you as dead as that one, sirs—and I will simply be the instrument of God's will. So do not think—ever—to say to me 'thou wilt not do it.' Oh, no, sirs. I assure you. I most certainly will."

They were strange words, in a way, coming from a man whom Sheff suddenly realized was quite young. Somewhere in his early twenties, at a guess, although the harsh features of his face made him seem older. Yet, he'd spoken the words like one of the ancient prophets, and Sheff knew that some of them had lived to be hundreds of years old.

"I most certainly will," the man repeated. He was close to being done, now, with the reloading. "Indeed, I shall, the moment this musket is ready to fire again."

He broke off the work for an instant to point with the ramrod at one of the six white men.

"I will kill you first. After that, the others. Those whom my brothers—black as well as white—have left alive. If there are any."

Sheff's uncle rose to his feet. So did the other two black men. Their knives were all visible, out in the open and with campfire light on them.

"Won't be a one, sir," Uncle Jem predicted. "Not if your brothers shoot as straight as you do."

The eyes of the six original white men were very wide, by now.

"Hey!" one of them cried.

"Begone, I said." The gaunt-jawed man didn't look up

from the reloading. "And do not—ever—come near me again."

Sheff almost laughed, watching how they ran away. His mother did, after one of them tripped over a root.

Before they slept for the night, the gaunt-jawed man insisted on leading them in prayer. Then he read from his Bible for a few minutes, until he passed it over to Jem.

Sheff didn't mind. His uncle Jem's heavy voice was a reassuring counter-tone to the white man's. And it wasn't as if they were quarreling over the biblical text, after all.

The next morning, when he awoke, Sheff saw that the white man and his two brothers were already awake. Awake, clothed—and armed.

For the first time in his sixteen years of life, the sight of an armed white man didn't scare Sheff. Even if the man in question was still the scariest-looking white man he'd ever seen.

Once the party were all awake and ready to resume their travel, the man spoke.

"My brothers and I will go with you as far as the Confederacy. To make sure nothing happens like last night."

"It's a far stretch, sir," pointed out Jem.

The man shrugged. "We've been thinking of settling in the Confederacy, anyway. I would much like to make the acquaintance of Patrick Driscol. In a world full of sinners, his like is not often encountered."

Uncle Jem nodded. "We'd much appreciate it, sir. Ever since Calhoun and his bunch got those freedmen exclusion laws passed, it's been nigh horrible for black folks."

"Yes, I know. Calhoun will burn. Not for us to know why God chose to inflict him upon us. No doubt He had His reasons."

By the time they reached the Mississippi, almost two weeks later, Sheff had worked up the courage to ask the man's name. He was the first one to do so.

It helped that a party of Cherokees was there, ready to escort them the rest of the way to the Arkansas Confederacy.

Cherokees were frightening, to be sure, but they weren't as frightening as white men.

Not even all white men were frightening to Sheff any longer. Not even *him*. He was learning to make distinctions that hadn't seemed very clear, back in the freedmens' quarters of Baltimore.

"Please, sir," he said. "I'd really appreciate to know your name."

The man nodded gravely. Then he smiled. He had quite a nice smile, even if it wasn't often evident.

"I wondered when one of you might ask." He pointed to his two brothers. "That's Salmon. The other is my adopted brother, Levi Blakeslee. My name is Brown. John Brown."

PART I

CHAPTER 1

Washington, D.C.
APRIL 25, 1824

"Houston must have known." The president turned his head away from the window, presenting his profile to the other two men. The expression on his face was not condemnatory so much as simply pensive. "Must have known for several years, in fact. Am I right, Winfield?"

The tall, handsome general in one of the chairs in Monroe's office shifted his position. Only slightly, of course. The very fancy uniform he favored didn't lend itself well to extravagant movement while he was seated.

"Oh, certainly," General Scott replied. "Driscol's been building another Line of Torres Vedras in those mountains. The original took Wellington over a year to build—and he had the population of Lisbon to draw on. Even with all the negroes who have migrated to Arkansas the past few years, Driscol doesn't begin to have that large a labor force. And the Cherokees and Creeks are useless for that sort of work, of course. For the most part, at least."

The secretary of state, the third man in the room, cleared his throat. "Perhaps . . ." John Quincy Adams pursed his lips. "The work stretched out over that long a period of time . . ."

President Monroe shook his head. "I thank you, John, but let's not be foolish. *Sam Houston?*"

He chuckled. "I remind you that my son-in-law is the same man who, at the age of sixteen, crossed sixty miles of Tennessee wilderness after running away from home. Then he lived among the Cherokee for several years, even being

adopted into one of their clans. He could find his way
through any woods or mountains in Creation."

The president's tone of voice grew somber. "Even drunk,
as he so often is these days."

Monroe finally turned away from the window. "No, let's
not be foolish. He spends as much time in the Confederacy
as he does here at home, since the treaty was signed. There
is no chance that Sam Houston failed to see what his friend
Patrick Driscol was doing. Nor, given his military experience, that he didn't understand what he was seeing."

As he resumed his seat at his desk, Monroe nodded toward
Scott. "It didn't take Winfield here more than a few days to
figure it out, when he visited the area. And—meaning no
offense—Winfield's not half the woodsman Houston is."

The general's notorious vanity seemed to be on vacation
that day. His own chuckle was a hearty thing. "Not a tenth,
say better! I've traveled with Houston a time or two. But it
didn't matter on this occasion. Patrick provided me with a
Cherokee escort, who served as my guide. He made no attempt to keep me from seeing what he had wrought in those
mountains. Quite the contrary, I assure you. He *wants* us to
know."

A bit warily, Scott studied the president. John Quincy
Adams didn't wonder as to the reason. James Monroe was
normally the most affable and courteous of men, but they
were treading on very delicate ground here. That most
treacherous and shifting ground of all, where political and
personal affairs intersected.

Sam Houston's marriage to James Monroe's younger
daughter Maria Hester in 1819, following one of the young
nation's most famous whirlwind courtships, had added a
great deal of flavor and spice to an administration that was
otherwise principally noted for such unromantic traits as ef-
ficiency and political skill. The girl had only been seventeen
at the time. The famous Hero of the Capitol—still young,
too, being only twenty-six himself, and as handsome and
well spoken as ever—receiving the hand in marriage of the
very attractive daughter of the country's chief executive.
What could better satisfy the smug assurance of a new republic that it basked in the favor of the Almighty?

It hadn't been all show, either. Very little of it, in fact. Allowing for his constant absences as the administration's special commissioner for Indian affairs, Houston had proved to be something of a model husband. He treated Maria Hester exceedingly well; she, in turn, doted on the man. And, thankfully, Houston's notorious womanizing had vanished entirely after his marriage. There'd been not a trace of scandal, thereafter.

His steadily worsening affection for whiskey, which had become a growing concern for the president, was something that Houston kept away from his wife. However much whiskey he guzzled in the nation's taverns—that, too, had become something of a legend—he did not do the same at home. He drank little, as a rule, in his wife's presence; was invariably a cheerful rather than a nasty drunk, on the few occasions when he did; and quit altogether after his son was born.

Even Houston's stubborn insistence on naming the child Andrew Jackson Houston hadn't caused much in the way of family tension. Monroe had made no formal objection of any kind, whatever he might have said in private. In any event, the president was far too shrewd a politician not to use the occasion to defuse the tensions with Jackson that had begun to build. As political tensions always did around Jackson, the man being what he was.

So, despite Houston's faults—and which man had no faults? Adams asked himself; certainly not he—the president liked his son-in-law. So did John Quincy Adams, for that matter, and he was not a man given to many personal likings.

Adams glanced at the general sitting in the chair next to him. So, for that matter, did Winfield Scott. At least, once he'd realized that Houston's resignation from the army and subsequent preoccupation with Indian affairs meant that he was no longer a rival in the military.

Yes, everybody liked Sam Houston. You could not have found a man in the United States who would tell you otherwise. Until they finally discovered that, beneath the good-looking and boyishly cheerful exterior, there lurked the brain and the heart of a Machiavellian monster.

A few months after his marriage, all of Houston's scheming and deal-making had come to fruition later that year with the Treaty of Oothcaloga.

The Confederacy of the Arkansas had been born that day. At first, the great migration of the Cherokees and the Creeks that followed had been hailed across the nation as a stroke of political genius on the part of the Monroe administration. By none more loudly than Andrew Jackson, of course, who had by then solidified his position as the champion of the western settlers. But even Calhoun had grudgingly indicated his approval.

For that one brief moment in time, the so-called Era of Good Feelings had seemed established for eternity. But, in hindsight, it had only been the crest of a wave. On January 13, 1820—almost five years to the day after he and his Iron Battalion had broken the British at the Battle of the Mississippi—Patrick Driscol and those same black artillerymen routed the Louisiana militia in what had since come to be called the Battle of Algiers. The four years that followed had been a steadily darkening political nightmare.

Houston was blamed for that, too, nowadays, by many people. His diplomacy had defused the crisis, long enough to allow Driscol and his followers to leave New Orleans and migrate to the new Confederacy. So, a full-scale war had been averted.

But John Calhoun had never forgiven the Monroe administration for the settlement Houston engineered, and Monroe's approval of it. Servile insurrections should be *crushed* and their survivors mercilessly scourged, he argued, not allowed to flee unscathed—and never mind that the "servile insurrection" had actually been the work of freedmen defending their legal rights against local overlords.

To John Calhoun and his followers, a nigger was a nigger. Rightless by nature, legalistic twaddles be damned. The black race was fit only to hew wood and draw water for those who were their superiors.

A few months after the Algiers Incident, Calhoun resigned his post as secretary of war in order to run for senator from South Carolina. He won the election, very handily, and had been a thorn in the side of the administration since. It had been Calhoun who led the charge in Congress to pass

the Freedmen Exclusion Act, which would have required all
freedmen to leave the United States within a year of manumission. Monroe had vetoed the bill on the obvious ground
that it was a gross violation of states' rights, whereupon Calhoun had given his open support to freedmen exclusion legislation passed by various states and municipalities, and his
tacit blessing to more savage and informal methods of exclusion.

A duel had almost resulted, then, when Sam Houston publicly labeled him—Adams could not but smile, whenever he
thought of the brash youngster's handy way with words—"a
tsarist, a terror-monger, and a toad. Nay, say better—a toad-
stool. A toad can at least hop about. Calhoun is a fungus on
the nation's flank."

"What are *you* so cheerful about, John?" demanded Monroe.

Delicate ground, indeed. Adams stifled the smile.

"Ah, nothing, Mr. President. Just a stray thought that happened to cross my mind."

The look Monroe gave him was exceedingly skeptical.
"Stray thought" and "John Quincy Adams" were not phrases
that could often be found together. Anywhere within shouting distance, in fact. Disliked as he might be in many quarters, no one thought Adams's brain was given to loose
functioning—and he was generally considered the best-read
man in America.

But Monroe let it drop. Instead, he turned his gaze to
Scott.

"What's your military assessment, General?"

Scott shrugged. "The fortifications that Driscol's built in
the Ozarks and the Ouachitas pose no threat to the United
States, Mr. President. They're purely defensive works, and
too far—much too far—from the Mississippi to pose any
threat to our commerce."

Monroe nodded. "Yes, I understand that." Perhaps a bit
acerbically: "I have some military experience myself, you
may recall. What I meant was—let's be frank, shall we?—
what threat do they pose to our army in the event the United
States goes to war with the Confederacy? Or, to put it more
bluntly still, if *we* invade Arkansas?"

Scott looked out the window for a moment. "Assuming

Driscol's in command? Which, of course, he would be, if he's still alive when—if—that time comes." He paused for another moment. "Let me put it this way, Mr. President. Were you, or anyone, to ask me to command such an expedition, I would strongly—very strongly—urge that an alternative route of attack be chosen."

"*What* alternative route, Winfield?" Adams demanded. It was not so much a question as a statement—and a caustically posed one, at that. If the president was known for his affable manners, the secretary of state was not.

Adams heaved himself out of his chair and went to another window than the one Monroe had been looking out earlier. The same window, in fact, that had been the focus of Scott's examination. That window allowed a view to the west.

Once there, Adams stabbed a finger at the land beyond. "Attacking the Confederacy from the south means marching through Texas. That means a war with Mexico, and probably Spain. An unprovoked war with Mexico—and no one except southern slave-owners would accept the premises for such a war as a provocation suitable for a casus belli—runs the risk of embroiling the European powers. The last thing we need. Not even Jackson would support that, as much as he hates the Dons."

He shifted his finger slightly to the north and jabbed it again. "The only other alternative is coming at the Confederacy from the north. That would be *diplomatically* feasible, but as a military proposition . . ."

He shifted his gaze back into the room, to land on Scott. "You're the expert, Winfield. What's your opinion?"

The general grimaced. "The logistics would be a nightmare. You'd have to move the troops down the Ohio to the juncture with the Mississippi. Then—"

"Passing by free states as you went, each and every one of which will be opposed to the expedition," Monroe injected. "They have no quarrel with the Confederacy. Rather the opposite, since many of them are happy to be getting rid of their own freedmen—and without the Confederacy, they can't."

Scott's grimace had never quite left his face, and now it returned with a vengeance. "Yes, I understand that, Mr. President. You'd have to bivouac on the south bank of the Ohio and resupply in Kentucky ports."

The president wasn't about to let up. "I remind you that Richard Johnson keeps getting reelected by the citizens of Kentucky, General. What's he likely to say about that?"

"He'd pitch a fit," Adams agreed. "There's not only the matter of his personal attitudes to be considered, either. Senator from Kentucky or not, living openly with a black woman or not, don't forget he's also the darling of the northeast workingmen—and they're even happier with the freedmen exclusion laws than Calhoun is. Except, not being slave-owners, they don't care a fig about the problem of runaway slaves. Let the darkies escape to Arkansas, and good riddance—and for sure and certain, don't expect *them* to support a war to get them back. Much less volunteer to fight in it."

"I wasn't *advocating* such an expedition, Mr. President, Secretary of State. Personally, I think it'd be sheer folly. But you asked my military opinion, and I'm simply trying to give it to you."

"Of course, General." Monroe's courtesy was back in full force. "Neither I nor the secretary meant any of our—ah, perhaps impatient view of the matter—to be inflicted upon you."

"Yes," Adams grunted. "My apologies, Winfield. I didn't mean to suggest you were a party to Calhoun's madness. Please continue."

Scott nodded. "It would help a great deal, Mr. President, if I had a map to work from. Is there one at hand?"

"I can have one brought, certainly." The president began to rise, but Adams waved him down. "Please! The proprieties must be maintained. The best maps are in my office, anyway. I'll get one for us. Just the trans-Mississippi region, Winfield?"

"Yes, that should do."

Adams was at the door to the president's office. "This will take a moment. There's no point sending a servant. He'll just waste time not finding it and then waste still more time trying to think up an excuse."

It was said rather sarcastically. Adams said many things rather sarcastically. It was a habit his wife chided him about.

As did a veritable legion of other people, including Adams himself. He tried to restrain the habit, but . . .

Alas. John Quincy Adams had many virtues. Even he would allow that to be true, as relentlessly self-critical as he was. But "suffering fools gladly" was not and never would be one of them.

Still, he thought God would forgive him that sin when the time came. As sins went, it was rather a small one, after all. Even Jesus, if you studied the New Testament from the proper angle, suffered from it to a degree.

By the time Adams returned to the president's office, Monroe had cleared his desk of all the materials on it. Adams, with Scott assisting, spread the large map across the surface.

"Good. This will make it all much clearer," Scott said. "Let's begin here, at the confluence of the Ohio and Mississippi."

A long, powerful-looking finger pinned the spot, then slid to the north. "Then, up the Mississippi to St. Louis. At St. Louis—upstream again, you'll notice—you move along the Missouri, skirting the Ozarks to the south. Then . . ."

He looked up, giving the other two men a sardonic glance. "Then . . . *what?*"

"There's the Grand River," Adams suggested, but with no great force. "Eventually."

"Ah, yes, the Grand. Also called the Neosho, I believe. Hard to tell from this map, but it doesn't really *look* all that grand, does it? And do please note that you have to traverse a considerable distance before you can reach any headwaters of the Arkansas. By now, you've gone hundreds of miles upstream, followed by a land march with no means of supplying your troops except with horses and wagons. That's difficult even without enemy resistance being encountered—and we're bound to encounter some. From the indigenes, first—those are the Osage, you know, a fierce tribe—even before we come into Cherokee territory."

He straightened. "I won't say it *can't* be done. It could, certainly, with the expenditure of enough time, effort, and—most of all—money. There's simply no way around it, Mr. President, Mr. Secretary. West of the Mississippi, the main rivers all run west to east, or northwest to southeast. There is no real help there for an army large enough to do the job that tries to approach the Confederacy from the north."

Monroe pushed aside a portion of the map and sat down heavily in his chair. "I understand. The gist of it is that there is no practical alternative, unless one is prepared to wage a long and costly war, to launching a major expedition against the Indian Confederacy except up the Arkansas River valley."

"Yes, sir. The Red River can't serve, not with at least a hundred and fifty miles of it clogged up with fallen trees. The Great Raft, they call it."

"And Driscol, being a very experienced soldier, knows that perfectly well."

"Yes, sir."

"So he designed his fortifications and lines of defense—his version of Wellington's Lines of Torres Vedras in the Peninsular War—in such a way as to channel any attacker up the river."

"Yes, sir. His lines are brilliantly designed, too. Far better than I would have thought, to be honest. I think he must be getting advice from somewhere. Driscol was a sergeant in Napoleon's army, not an officer. And the only sight he would have ever gotten of Wellington's defenses would have been from a distance. Even with his huge army, Massena never made any serious attempt on Torres Vedras."

"How do you mean, 'brilliantly designed'?" asked Adams.

The general turned to face him. "Consider the problem he faces. Even with the recent flood of immigrants coming from the freedmen communities, added to the constant influx of runaway slaves and the settlers sponsored by the American Colonization Society, there still can't be more than some tens of thousands of negroes in that Arkansas Chiefdom, as the Confederates call their respective states. Certainly not more than eighty thousand, I shouldn't think. Add to that perhaps ten thousand whites by now, all told."

"*That* many?" The president's eyebrows were lifted. "Whites, I mean. I wouldn't have thought . . ."

He glanced at Adams. "Again, a smile. Why?"

Adams had also resumed his seat. Now he leaned his short, heavy frame back into it. "I can't say I'm surprised,

Mr. President. Not *every* white man in America shares Calhoun's attitudes."

Nor do most of them come from Virginia gentry, as you do. But he left that unsaid, of course. "There are the missionaries, first of all. A very heavy presence of Quakers, naturally, and they tend to move in entire families. Then, a fair number—call it a heavy sprinkling—of young radicals. Abolitionists, they're starting to call themselves."

Monroe made a face. For all the president's humane nature, which Adams would be the first to allow, the man was still the product of his upbringing. Though a slave-owner himself, Monroe—like his close friends and predecessors Thomas Jefferson and James Madison—considered the institution of slavery problematic at best, and probably an outright evil. Still, any drastic and rapid abolition of slavery was considered impossible, and the attempt to do it, economically and socially disastrous.

Adams, a New Englander, thought it was probably impossible also, for political reasons. But he would have accepted the economic and social disasters abolition might bring, for the sake of the greater political disaster they would avert. More and more, he was becoming convinced that if slavery festered for too long, it would produce, in the end, one of the most horrible episodes of bloodshed any nation had ever endured. And would steadily undermine the foundations of the republic before it got there.

But there was no point reopening that debate here and now, so Adams continued to the next point.

"I imagine that most of the whites there, however, are simply settlers. No different, really, from any western settlers. Scots-Irish in the main, of course."

"I'd think they'd bridle at being ruled by blacks," Monroe said.

The president was a very perceptive man, so the moment those words were spoken, his gaze moved to Scott. "And now *you're* smiling, General. Why?"

Scott coughed into his fist as a way of suppressing his amusement. "You have to be there to understand the thing, Mr. President. Yes, it's true that most of the chiefs—they've adopted Cherokee terminology—are negroes. Still, they're elected—and whites can vote also. They can run for office,

as well, and a disproportionate number of them get elected.
Even the negroes in Arkansas are more likely to vote for a
white man, all other things being equal.

"What's most important, however, is that the *principal*
chief—that's their equivalent of what we'd call the governor of the state—is Patrick Driscol. You can't even say he
gets elected in a landslide, since nobody ever runs against
him."

He coughed again, into a large fist. "They don't call him
that, though, except the Cherokees and Creeks who live in
the province. Of whom, by the way, there are perhaps another five thousand. 'Principal chief,' I mean. I was quite en-
tertained during the weeks I was there, I assure you, to
discover that every white or black man I encountered refers
to Patrick Driscol as the Laird of Arkansas."

The fist couldn't possibly suppress the grin that came then.
"Not to his face, of course."

Adams smiled. Monroe, who knew Driscol personally,
laughed aloud. "I can imagine not!"

After the moment's humor was gone, Scott said: "Perhaps
you remember Driscol's young soldier, who accompanied
him everywhere he went during the war. McParland? The
young deserter whose faked execution I had Driscol stage,
shortly before the Battle of the Chippewa?"

Monroe frowned slightly, dredging his memory. "Oh, yes.
I remember him now. A country boy."

Scott nodded. "Yes. From a poor family in upstate New
York. Except none of them live in New York, any longer.
The entire family—uncles, aunts, cousins, and all—pulled
up stakes and moved to Arkansas several years ago. And
they're no longer poor, either. They're rather prosperous; in
fact, since they own one of the furniture factories that Houston fostered in Fort of 98. Which, incidentally, has become
surrounded by quite a large town. More in the way of a small
city, by now. There are a number of advantages to moving to
Arkansas, for a poor white settler, now that Driscol has established his rule there. For one thing, there's far less danger
from Indian attacks, for obvious reasons."

At Monroe's gesture, the general resumed his own seat.
"A large town—soon, if not already, a small city—protected
by a powerful fortress, which holds the only gate to the rest

of the Confederacy and the Cherokee and Creek lands beyond. Driscol has nothing like the population of Lisbon that Wellington had. But he's still got tens of thousands of men, and he designed those lines so troops could be moved rapidly from one point to another along the high ground. Any invading army will get battered back and forth as they march up the river valley, until they come to Fort of 98. He named it after the Irish rebellion, you understand? The one that brought death to his father and brother, and exile to him. I've seen it at close hand—spent two days studying it, rather, inside and out. Please trust me when I say it's as formidable a fortress as any in the continent."

Scott leaned over. His finger landed forcibly on the Arkansas. "That's the only really suitable invasion route. And Driscol knows it. And he spent some time as a young sergeant in the French colors, staring up at Wellington's Lines of Torres Vedras after having marched across all of Spain. And saw that his commander, Massena, never ordered a full assault. Massena had sixty-five thousand men in that army. How many soldiers will the United States send against the Confederacy of the Arkansas?"

Monroe's reply came instantly. "Not one, so long as I am president."

There was an awkward silence. Pleasantly, Monroe said to Scott: "Thank you for your advice, General. It was very helpful. And now would you give us a moment, please?"

Scott rose to his feet. "Certainly, Mr. President. I'll be in my offices at the War Department, should you need me again today." He turned and nodded to Adams. "A pleasure, as always, Mr. Secretary."

He probably even meant it, Adams thought. Winfield Scott and he got along quite well, as a rule. If for no other reason, because Scott was even less prone to suffering fools gladly.

After the general was gone, the silence returned for a time. Finally, sighing, Adams spoke up. "There is some talk, I believe, that people might want me to succeed you, Mr. President."

"Yes, so I've been led to believe."

Monroe maintained a studied blandness in his expression and tone of voice. It was the firm protocol of the young republic that no gentleman suited to be chief executive in the first place would ever directly express any ambition for the post, as absurd as that apparent indifference might be. Even Henry Clay maintained the posture, though every suckling babe in the nation knew that the Speaker of the House lusted for the presidency as other men lusted for food or whiskey or money or women.

Adams scratched under his chin. "Should that unlikely eventuality come to pass, my answer would be the same as yours. Not one dollar spent to send one soldier against the Confederacy."

Monroe nodded. "Jackson's answer might be different. He's as savage as anyone on the subject of the runaway slaves for whom Arkansas has become a magnet. But he's also far shrewder than most people realize. Even something of a genuine statesman, I think, in his own way. Finally, Jackson takes his honor seriously, and there is his vow to Houston. Which he might—or might not—feel has been satisfied by now."

Houston. Always Houston, it seemed. On Mondays, Adams thought the young man was the republic's greatest blessing. On Tuesdays, its greatest curse. On Wednesdays and Thursdays, he was indifferent to the question, for the secretary of state had many other things in midweek to occupy his mind. By Friday, he was back to blessing the youngster, and on Saturday to showering him with silent curses.

Sunday, of course, was the Sabbath. On Sundays, Adams studied the Bible and tried not to think about the subject of Houston at all. Sometimes he even succeeded.

"Yes, Andrew Jackson," he said. "Impossible to know how he'd react, and what he'd decide. With Henry Clay, of course . . ."

He left the rest unsaid. Monroe, however, did not.

"Clay will do whatever serves opportunity, as he sees it. And since he can't get the presidency without the support of Calhoun and at least the acquiescence of Crawford, that will determine his course."

"He'll call it a great compromise," Adams predicted.

The room burst into momentary laughter, again. The moment over, Adams began rolling up the map.

"Let's hope we never have to find out."

CHAPTER 2

A tavern not far from Lexington, Kentucky
MAY 10, 1824

The innkeeper eyed the big man in front of him uncertainly.

First, because he *was* big. At least two inches over six feet and very broad-shouldered. The heavy Cherokee blanket he was wearing over his uniform made him seem as massive as a bear. He filled practically every square inch of the doorway to the room he'd rented for the night.

Second, because he'd obviously had some whiskey to drink, even though it was only two hours past dawn. The smell of it on his breath was not overwhelming but was still noticeable.

And finally, of course, simply because of who he was.

If there was one thing the whole country had come to know about Colonel Sam Houston, it was that . . .

You never knew. He might do anything.

The innkeeper decided to try reason. "Look, Colonel, you were planning to leave town this morning anyway."

"Not before breakfast," came the feared rejoinder. Stated every bit as reasonably.

"Well, sure," the innkeeper admitted. "But there's a good tavern just six miles down the road. And your boy's already getting your horses saddled."

The big young colonel smiled. "Chester's five years older

than I am. Not as tall, I admit. Still, it seems a bit silly to be calling him a boy."

Who else would even think that way? A black man was always a "boy"—and the colonel's was a slave, to boot.

But the innkeeper wasn't about to argue the point. Not now, for a certainty, when he was trying to keep his tavern from being turned into a shambles.

Where reason hadn't worked, perhaps outright pleading would.

"Colonel . . . Jack Baxter's the meanest man in northern Kentucky. Just take my word for it. Been that way since he was a kid. He'll pick a fight over anything. And, uh . . ."

Houston's smile widened. "And, in my case, he's got real grievances."

"I guess. Depending on how you look at it."

"Well, then!" Cheerfully, Houston came into the hallway, moving the innkeeper aside the way the tide shifts seaweed. "As an of-fi-cial of the United States government, I figure it's my bounden duty to listen to the complaints of a taxpayer."

Over his shoulder, as he moved toward the stairs leading down to the tavern's main room: "He *does* pay taxes, doesn't he?"

"As little as he can," the innkeeper muttered, hurrying after him. "Please, Colonel—"

"Oh, relax, will you?" Houston's soft Tennessee accent thickened noticeably. "I bean't a quarrelsome man. In fact, my mama told me she almost named me Tranquility instead of Sam."

He started down the stairs, not clumping as much as a man his size normally would. Partly because he was wearing Cherokee-style boots to match the blanket he still had over his shoulders, but mostly because he was very well coordinated. The innkeeper had been surprised by that the night before. There were usually impromptu dances in the tavern on a Friday evening. Half drunk—better than half—Houston had still been able to dance better than anyone else. Any man, at least.

"Almost," he added.

The innkeeper was following close behind. " 'Almost' is what I'm worried about, Colonel."

Houston chuckled. "I told you, Ned, relax. Just have Mrs. Akins fry me up a steak."

"No porridge?"

The chuckle came again. "Don't think porridge would do the trick. At all."

By the time Ned Akins scurried into the kitchen, gave his wife the order, and got back into the main room, the worst had happened. He was just in time to see Houston pull out a chair at the table in the corner where Jack Baxter was having his breakfast. A moment later, the young colonel was sitting right across from him.

Houston was smiling cheerfully. Baxter returned the smile with a glare.

It wasn't a very big table, either.

"And I just put in a new window," Akins muttered to himself. Fortunately, the window was a good ten feet from where Houston and Baxter were sitting. Maybe it wouldn't get smashed up along with everything else.

The room had fallen silent. Even packed as it was with men having their breakfast, you could have heard the proverbial pin drop. Most of the diners were travelers passing through on business, not locals. But it didn't matter. Every one of them had heard Baxter's loudly stated threats, should the nefarious nigger-loving traitor Sam Houston dare to show his face. And the fact that Jack Baxter was the meanest man in town could have been surmised by a half-wit, upon fifteen seconds' acquaintance.

Houston turned his head part way around, ignoring Baxter's glare. "Oh, Mr. Akins—I forgot. Be so kind as to tell your wife that I prefer my steak cooked rare. No blasted leather for me, thank you. When I stick my knife into meat, I want to see it *bleed.*"

He turned back to Baxter. "I've got quite the knife, too. Here, let me show you."

From somewhere under the blanket, Houston drew out a knife that looked more like a short sword than what any reasonable man—certainly any reasonable innkeeper—would have called a knife. It was all Akins could do not to hiss.

Two of the customers in the room *did* hiss.

"Had it made for me in Arkansas," Houston continued, his

tone as cheerful as ever. "At the knife shop James Black set up in Fort of 98. I think Rezin Bowie designed it, though. He or his brother Jim, anyway. Can't say either one is exactly a friend of mine, so I'm not sure."

All the while he'd been prattling gaily, Houston held up the knife and twisted it back and forth, letting Baxter—every man in the room, for that matter—get a good view of it. The thing looked as lethal as a rattlesnake.

"You know Jim Bowie?" Houston asked Baxter, not looking at him.

He didn't wait for an answer, which he wouldn't have gotten anyway because by now Baxter's glare was enough to melt brimstone.

"Hot-tempered man." Houston shook his head, still looking at the knife. " 'Course, I admit, sometimes a man's got to have a temper."

Finally, he lowered the knife and looked across the table at Baxter. Still, for all the world, seeming to be completely oblivious to Baxter's fury.

"I should've asked your pardon for just sitting here. But I'm afraid I've got no choice. Nowadays—sad to say, but there it is—I pretty much have to take a corner table anywhere I go. It seems I've got enemies. Got to watch my back."

In point of fact, it was Baxter's seat that gave a view of the entire room. Houston's back was turned to everybody except Baxter.

Houston shook his head again. "Hard to believe, isn't it? Why, there's people say *I* caused the trouble with all the runaway slaves, even though—to any fair and judicious man— it's obvious as the nose in front of his face that the trouble was caused by that blasted Calhoun and his exclusion business."

He raised the knife a couple of inches above the table and brought the heavy pommel down. Hard.

"No, sir!" he bellowed. Baxter must have jumped the same two inches above his chair—and the glare suddenly vanished. Perhaps he'd finally remembered that that same voice had once bellowed orders across a battlefield, where British regulars had been beaten.

"No, sir," Houston repeated, forcibly if not as loudly.

"Calhoun's to blame—him and every one of those Barbary killers of his. Going around the way they have, murdering black folk for no reason."

Houston looked very, very big now, hunched like a buffalo at the table. That huge knife was held in a hand of a size to match. His left hand was clenched into a fist that looked pretty much like a small ham.

Suddenly, the buffalo vanished, replaced by Houston's earlier cheerful smile.

"But, now—why am I carrying on like this? I'm sure a reasonable-looking man like yourself has no quarrel with me."

The steak had arrived. Akins's wife shoved the plate into Ned's hands. "Get it over there quick," she hissed. "Maybe we can still get out of this without the place being torn down."

The innkeeper hurried over to the table. By now, he wasn't actually worried about the tavern itself being wrecked. Meanest man in northern Kentucky or not, it was plain as day that Jack Baxter was thoroughly cowed. That still left the problem of cleaning the floor.

Akins was proud of that floor, tarnation. Real wood. And he didn't want to think about the howls his wife would put up, having to scour blood from it. Several quarts of blood, from the looks of that knife. Not to mention maybe eight feet of intestine.

He planted the plate in front of Houston. "I'll get you a fork."

"Don't bother," Houston growled. "Can't stand forks. Never use 'em except at my wife's table. Well, and my father-in-law's, of course."

There was that, too. The buffalo who'd broken British regulars in front of the Capitol, and then again at New Orleans, also happened to be married to the president's daughter.

Jack Baxter was just about as dumb as he was mean. But it seemed his intelligence was rising in proportion to the way he was slumping in his chair.

Houston seized the whole steak with his left hand, shoved it into his mouth, and began sawing off a chunk with the knife.

"Goo teak" he mumbled. After chewing more or less the

way a lion chews—twice; swallow—he lowered the meat slightly and said: "My compliments to the good wife, Mr. Akins. Why, this steak is cooked proper, for a change!"

Akins looked at it. He'd wondered how Houston had managed to hold it bare-handed without burning himself. Now that the lion-bite had exposed the inside of the steak, the answer was obvious. His wife had been in such a hurry she'd barely cooked it at all. The meat was practically raw, once you got past the outside char.

Houston shoved it into his mouth, and sawed off another chunk. "Some whiskey, if you would," he said, after he swallowed. Again, after chewing it twice.

Akins didn't argue the matter. There was no way to stop Houston anyway—and, at least judging from his reputation and what the innkeeper had seen the night before, whiskey made him good-humored.

The innkeeper blessed good humor four times, on his way to the whiskey cabinet and back, tossing in a short prayer for good measure.

He didn't bother offering the use of a tumbler. As soon as the whiskey bottle was on the table—by then, half the steak had vanished, and what was left was back on the plate—Houston grabbed it by the neck and took a hefty slug.

He brought the bottle down with a thump. "Love whiskey with a rare steak. 'Course"—one more time, he bestowed that cheery grin on Baxter—"I dare not take more than the one good swallow, of a morning. Maybe two. As many enemies as I have."

Akins almost burst into laughter, then. He was standing by a table where a lion was beaming down on a rat. A cornered rat, at that, since there was no way for Baxter to get away from Houston, sitting where he was.

"No, *sir*," Houston stated, stabbing the steak again and bringing it back up. He reached halfway across the table and waved the piece of meat under Baxter's nose. "I got to be careful. Even though I can drink half a bottle and still shoot straight or cut slicker'n you'd believe a man could do plain sober."

The steak went back into his mouth, and the knife sawed off another chunk. By now, at least, Houston was chewing four or five times before he swallowed.

Akins heard a noise behind him. Turning, he saw that Houston's slave had come into the room. He was holding a satchel in his left hand.

"We're ready to go whenever you've a mind, Mr. Sam," he announced. "The horses are saddled, everything's packed, and—"

The same two men hissed as the slave brought a pistol out of the satchel.

"—I got your pistol here, if you've a mind for that, too."

Houston swallowed, turned his head, and frowned. "Now why in the world would I need a pistol, Chester?" He held up the steak—what little was left of it—skewered on the knife. "Cow's already dead."

The slave didn't seem in the least abashed by the apparent rebuke. Nor did anyone in the room miss the fact that he wasn't holding the pistol by the barrel, the way a man normally does when he's readying to pass it over to another. Instead, he had the handle cupped neatly in his palm. And if his forefinger wasn't precisely on the trigger, and his thumb wasn't precisely on the hammer, neither digit was more than half an inch away from turning the gun into a deadly thing.

He was holding the weapon as if he knew exactly how to use it, too. Most slaves didn't.

"You got enemies, Mr. Sam. Remember? Turrible enemies, people say."

Houston shook his head and waved the steak around the room. "Not here, surely! Chester, you ought to be ashamed of yourself. Even thinking such a thing!"

"Yes, sir, Mr. Sam. Sorry 'bout that." He didn't seem any more abashed by that rebuke than he'd been by the first one.

"As you should be! Why, I oughta have you apologize personally to every man in this room. Would, too, 'cept"—he paused for a moment while he sawed off another piece of steak and swallowed.

"Except that wouldn't be proper," he continued. "You being a black slave and them being free white men. Apology presumes equality, you know. All the philosophers say so."

He turned and scowled at his slave. "You got no excuse, neither, since you read the same philosophers. I know, 'cause I taught you how to read."

Teaching slaves to read wasn't illegal except in Virginia—
yet, anyway. Calhoun and his followers were pressing for
that, now, along with freedmen exclusion. Still, it certainly
wasn't the custom in slave states like Kentucky.

But that, too, was part of Houston legend. He might as
well have had *Custom Be Damned* for a crest on a formal
coat of arms.

"Yes, Mr. Sam. No, sir, I mean, it wouldn't be proper."

Houston chewed the last piece of steak more slowly than
he had any of the others. With a thoughtful expression on his
face, now.

When he was finished, he rose from the table. Then, suddenly and abruptly, shoved the table aside. Baxter, who'd
been frozen in place for the past few minutes, started to
jump from his chair, but Houston's big left hand jammed
him back in his seat.

The young colonel held the knife in front of his face. Baxter's eyes were round, and his complexion was ashen.

"You'll have to excuse me, sir," Houston said politely. "I
need to clean my knife, and there's nothing else handy. I
daren't soil my blanket, of course. It's a personal gift from
none other than Major Ridge himself. He'd be most offended if I showed up in the Confederacy with stains on it."

Quickly and efficiently, he wiped the blade clean on the
shoulder of Baxter's coat. Then, moved the blanket aside
and slid the knife into a scabbard.

"My thanks, sir." He bestowed the beaming smile on him.
"And now, I must be off."

He turned and strode toward the door, where Chester was
waiting. The slave raised the pistol as if to offer it to his master, but Houston shook his head.

"No, no, you keep it. I *do* have enemies, it's true enough.
Some of the rascals might be lurking outside. Since you
shoot better than I do, best you keep the pistol."

"Yes, sir, Mr. Sam. If you say so."

Houston stopped abruptly. "Of course I do! Makes sense,
doesn't it? The slave shoots them, and the master guts 'em."

He patted the knife under his blanket, turned around, and
bestowed the grin on the whole room.

"You see, gentlemen? Easiest thing in the world to figure
out, if you're not an imbecile like Calhoun. *I* never have

trouble with runaway slaves. You're not planning to flee from lawful bondage, are you, Chester?"

"No, sir. Don't need to. 'Bout another two months, and I'll have saved up enough to buy my way free."

Houston's eyes widened. "Why . . . so you will. And since you learned how to blacksmith along the way, you won't have any trouble setting yourself up."

Akins didn't know whether to laugh or cry. On the one hand, seeing Baxter get his comeuppance was worth its weight in gold. On the other . . .

Hiring out slaves as craftsmen was common, of course. Many of them were quite skilled, in fact. But Houston's practice of letting his slaves *keep* their wages was just plain . . .

"Some people say I'm a lunatic, Chester," Houston boomed. "A veritable bedlamite!"

"Yes, Mr. Sam. But maybe we ought to be going, now. Before your enemies learn where you are."

"Probably a good idea. Mr. Akins, the bill, if you please."

Less than a minute later, Akins had the money—a tavern still intact, too—and Houston was on his way.

He watched him and the slave Chester for a while. The slave rode a horse just as well as the colonel did.

"That man is pure crazy," he muttered.

His wife had come out of the tavern and was standing next to him. "I thought you said—bean't more than two months ago—that if Colonel Houston ever ran for senator from Kentucky, you'd vote for him."

"Well, yes. He got rid of the Indians for us, didn't he? And he backs Jackson against the stinking bank. The Senate's way out there on the coast, anyway. But I sure wouldn't vote for him as *governor*."

"Nobody would," his wife agreed, "outside of a bedlam house."

CHAPTER 3

"Probably shouldn't have done that," Sam admitted, a couple of hours later. They'd stopped at a creek crossing to let their horses drink.

Chester studied the creek intently, as if the small stream were vastly more fascinating than any other body of moving waters on the face of the globe. "'Probably' meaning how, Mr. Sam? 'Probably,' as in 'I probably shouldn't have baited that bear'? Or 'probably,' as in 'I probably shouldn't have stuck a pitchfork in Sam Hill'?"

Houston grinned. "Oh, surely the latter. But since I'm not a sinner—well, not much of one—what do I have to fear? Sam Hill won't have no hold on me, when the blessed day comes. Hand me the whiskey."

Chester rummaged in the saddle pack and came out with the bottle. He didn't say anything, but the expression on his face made clear his disapproval.

"And stop nattering at me," Sam said.

"Didn't say a word."

"Didn't need to." He opened the bottle, took a hefty but not heroic slug from the contents, stoppered it up, and handed it back to Chester. "See? Just needed something to take the taste out of my mouth. Blasted meat was practically raw."

As always, the warm glow in his belly steadied his nerves. Which needed it, in truth. There'd been a lot of encounters like that over the past two or three years. They'd been getting uglier, too.

The United States had been hit by a series of crises, coming in quick succession. Sam thought people would have handled the Panic of 1819 and the economic dislocation that followed.

They'd also have handled—well enough, anyway—the Missouri Compromise that Henry Clay had engineered the following year, and the political tensions that came with it. Sam was no admirer of Clay, but he'd admit the man's vaunted political skills had been fully evident in that crisis.

But together, the Panic and the Compromise had brought the nation to a heated point just short of boiling—and then John Calhoun had seized upon the Treaty of Oothcaloga and the Algiers Incident to advance his proslavery political program. His speeches and actions had met a receptive audience in much of the South and the West. Almost overnight, it seemed, Sam Houston had gone from being a man generally admired both for his heroism in the war with Britain and for his settlement of the most acute Indian land questions, to the architect of a fiendish scheme to undermine the supremacy of the European race in America in favor of its lesser races.

"Still not sure how that happened," he muttered, looking down at the back of his hand. "My own skin's still as white as ever."

"What was that, Mr. Sam?"

Houston glanced at Chester. "Just talking to myself."

He decided to change the subject. "When *are* you planning to buy your freedom, by the way? It'd be handy if you'd let me know a bit ahead of time, you rascal, so's I don't get caught in the lurch."

Chester went back to his creek-scrutiny. "Well. Wasn't actually planning on it, all that soon, Mr. Sam. Thought I'd keep saving up my money. Once we get to Arkansas, I can put it in Mr. Patrick's bank. It'll be safe there."

"Wonderful! Now you'll make me a liar, too."

Chester smiled apologetically but didn't look away from the water. "You didn't say anything about it in the tavern, Mr. Sam. I was the one said I could buy my way free in 'bout a couple of months. Wasn't lying, neither. I *could*. But 'could' and 'would' is two different things. I just don't see the point in being a freedman when I wouldn't have enough money left to do anything more than work for someone else. I'm gonna do that, might as well keep working for you. There's really not all that much difference for a poor man, when you get right down to it, between a master and a boss—and, either way, you're the best one I know."

Sam rolled his eyes. "In other words, you're agreeing with Calhoun. Slavery's just the thing to elevate the black man. While his poor downtrodden white master pays the bills."

Chester's smile widened and lost its apologetic flavor. "Begging your pardon, Mr. Sam, but I don't recall Mr. Calhoun ever saying anything about black men being free, at any time, for any amount of money."

Sam scratched his chin. "Well, no. Of course not. If Calhoun had his way, freedmen wouldn't exist at all. How'd he put it in his recent speech to the Senate?"

His accent took on a mimicry of a much thicker and more Southern one. " 'I hold that in the present state of civilization, where two races of different origin, and distinguished by color as well as intellectual differences, are brought together, the relation now existing in the slaveholding states between the two, is, instead of an evil, a good—a positive good.' "

Sam dropped the accent and shook his head. "Not much room there for freedmen. Now that they've gotten exclusion acts passed in most states, Calhoun and his people are pushing to make manumission illegal altogether. Not to mention getting laws passed that make teaching slaves how to read and write illegal."

Chester stopped smiling, then.

"He's a prize, Calhoun is." Sam leaned over and spit in the creek. Not so much as a gesture of disgust—although that was there, too—as to get rid of the taste of raw meat he still had in his mouth. The whiskey had helped some, but not enough.

For a moment, he contemplated taking another slug but decided against it. He'd already drunk almost a quarter of the bottle this morning. He wasn't worried about being able to ride a horse, of course. Sam could manage that with a full bottle under his belt. But he had an awkward interview coming up today, and he needed his wits about him.

"Come on," he said. "The horses have had enough, and I'd like to make it to the senator's house by midafternoon."

"Hi, Sam!"
"Hi, Sam!"
He grinned at the twin girls scampering around the front

yard of Blue Spring Farm, as Richard M. Johnson's house and plantation were called. "Settle down, will you? You're making the horse nervous."

The admonishment had as much effect as such admonishments usually have on twelve-year-old girls. Fortunately, Sam's horse was a placid creature.

He decided to try the tactic of parental authority. "And you know your daddy doesn't like it when his girls don't act proper. Him being a United States senator and all."

That had no effect, either, not to Sam's surprise. Richard Johnson was a genial man toward just about everybody, especially his own daughters. Threatening them with his wrath was as useful as threatening them with a snowstorm in July.

In fact, they started laughing. And they were *still* bouncing up and down.

Fortunately, the girls' mother emerged onto the front porch.

"*Settle down!* Right this minute, Imogene, or I'll smack you proper! You too, Adaline!"

That did it. In an instant, the girls were the very model of propriety and demure behavior. Their father might be easygoing, but their mother was not. Julia Chinn was so well organized and disciplined that she almost managed to keep the senator from losing his money.

Almost, but not quite. But Sam didn't think anyone else could have kept him from going broke years earlier.

Sam got off his horse and handed the reins to Chester, who began leading the horses to the barn around the side. Sam stepped up onto the porch and took off his hat. He gave a polite nod to the two disabled veterans sitting on chairs further down the porch, and then turned to the lady of the house.

"Afternoon, Julia."

Her stern look vanished. "Hello, Sam. It's so nice to see you visit again. It's been . . . what? Over a year, now. You shouldn't stay away so long."

Before he could answer, she waved a hand. "Yes, yes, I know. You're a frightfully busy man."

Richard Johnson came out onto the porch just in time to hear the last words.

"Frightfully busy troublemaker, more like," he said

gruffly. But he didn't even try to disguise the smile with which he said it.

As the two shook hands, Houston took a moment to size up the senator's appearance. It was . . .

Even more sloppy and eccentric than usual. The clothing itself simply consisted of the plain and unassuming garments that Johnson had always worn, which were part of his appeal to Kentucky's poor farmers and the workingmen of the nation's northeastern states. Nothing peculiar, in and of itself—except for the fact that the man who wore that humble apparel came from one of Kentucky's premier families and was himself one of the state's largest landowners. One of its largest slave-owners, too.

No, it was the rest of it. His hair was disheveled, his cravat was askew—only half tied, at that—and his boots had long since abandoned the status of "humble" and were pretty well past the stage of "worn down." Give them another few months, and they'd be able to proudly claim holes in the soles and heels that were nothing but memories.

The face, though, was the same. Johnson was a plain-looking man and always had been. Unassuming, in both his appearance and his manner. If you didn't know better, you'd find it hard to reconcile the man himself with his flamboyant reputation.

Flamboyant it was, too, even by the standards of the frontier. The Great Hero who'd personally shot Tecumseh at the Battle of the Thames after suffering terrible wounds himself in the battle—so the story went, anyway, and Johnson had never done anything to detract from it—was also the Great Almagamator. The disreputable fellow from Great Crossing—a United States senator, to boot!—who lived in an open state of quasi-marriage with a mulatto and who persisted in treating his quadroon daughters as if they belonged in proper society. Even took them in his own carriage to church on a Sunday!

Andrew Jackson had shown Sam some of the letters he'd gotten from outraged gentility in Kentucky and Tennessee, demanding that the general disavow his political ties to Johnson.

"They can take *that* to Sam Hill," Jackson had growled, tossing the letters back into a drawer of his desk. He even lapsed into blasphemy for a moment. "I'll be damned if I will. Johnson's as stalwart as they make 'em, even if he is a blasted race-mixer."

Fortunately for Johnson, most of his own constituents felt much the same way about the matter. Whatever they felt personally about his notorious relationship with Julia Chinn, they overlooked it in favor of the rest.

Not the gentility, of course. During the six consecutive terms Johnson had served as one of Kentucky's members in the U.S. House of Representatives, most of the state's wealthy slave-owners had been indifferent to his personal habits. He didn't represent *them,* after all, for the most part. The scandalmongering with regard to Julia and the girls hadn't really started until John J. Crittenden resigned from the Senate in 1819 and Johnson was appointed to fill out Crittenden's term of office. A congressman was one thing; a senator, another.

But most of Kentucky's citizens were neither wealthy nor slave-owners. So far as they were concerned, Johnson's family arrangements were his own business. What mattered was all the rest: the fact that he was a genuine war hero; the fact that he was politically allied with Andrew Jackson's wing of the Democratic-Republican Party; most of all, the fact that Johnson had led the fight to get debt imprisonment abolished in Kentucky and was striving to do the same thing on a national level.

And, besides, every *other* personal habit of Johnson's led poor settlers on the frontier to favor him. Both as a Kentucky legislator and now as a national one, Johnson had made great efforts to gain compensation for the recent war's disabled veterans or their widows and orphans. If Blue Spring Farm was notorious as a place where a black woman presided over the dinner table and black children sat at it, it was also famous as a place of refuge for disabled veterans and their families. The two veterans on the porch—one missing an arm, the other a leg—would have half a dozen counterparts somewhere about the house or farm. Or their widows and orphans. No one in need was ever turned away from Richard M. Johnson's estate—never mind that the aid itself was often passed over by the dark-skinned hands of his common-law wife.

Kentucky's gentility had been disgusted to see Johnson appointed to serve out Crittenden's term in 1819. They'd been positively outraged to see him handily win the election for another term in the Senate in 1822.

Sam saw that Johnson was eyeing him a bit warily. "You seen the general lately?"

Sam shook his head. "Haven't seen him in nigh-on seven months, Dick." Since there was no point in letting Johnson fret on that score, when there were so many others he did need to fret about, Sam added hurriedly, "But I can assure you that the sentiments he expressed concerning you were just as warm as ever."

That was true, after all. Even if some of those "warm sentiments" had run along the lines of *I can't believe he'd treat a nigger like she was an actual wife!*

It wasn't that Andy Jackson didn't share each and every one of the common prejudices of his day. He most certainly did—and then some, often enough. It was just that in his own rough-hewn way, the general could often look past those things to see what really mattered to him.

Poor white men mattered to Andy Jackson. Not too many other people did, but *they* did, for sure and certain. So, if one of their undoubted political champions chose to behave badly in some aspects of his personal life, Jackson would look the other way. And if the proper folk complained, they could take their complaints to Sam Hill and see what satisfaction they'd get in those very warm quarters.

"Just as warm as ever," Sam repeated forcibly. "My word on it."

Johnson's grunt combined relief with satisfaction. "Well, they ought to be," the senator stated, as if to reassure himself. "Henry Clay makes a fortune suing people on behalf of land speculators and the Second Bank of the United States, and I go broke from waiving the fees for defending them."

That was also true . . . as far as it went. Johnson was indeed famous as one of the few well-connected lawyers in Kentucky that a poor man or his widow could go to for legal assistance without being charged. Unfortunately, it was only part of the truth.

There were a lot of reasons Richard Mentor Johnson was always on the verge of being broke. His personal generosity ranked on that list, yes—and pretty high up on it. But not as high as his casual attitude toward bookkeeping, his inability to say "no" to just about every speculative scheme that came his way, and his predilection toward seeing only a blur instead of a line between his personal finances and those of the public. Not to mention his indulgence toward his brothers, who were separated by only a knife's edge from being outright thieves.

Sam liked Richard M. Johnson a very great deal. He'd never met a man who didn't, no matter what their attitudes on such subjects as race, whom he didn't think was a swine. But there was just no getting around the fact that, as often as not, both he and the general—not to mention the president of the United States—would like to take Johnson by the scruff of the neck and give him a real down-home shaking. Or thrash him outright, for that matter.

Some of his aggravation must have shown, for Julia hastily spoke up.

"Please come in, Sam. Something to drink? I've fresh-brewed some tea."

Sam was about to agree when Johnson broke in. "Tea for Sam Houston? Don't be silly, Julia. Sam'll have some whiskey. I'll join him myself."

The senator passed through the door into the house. Sam felt his resolve crumbling. A slug of whiskey *did* sound good—and it would relax him for what was coming.

As Sam made to follow Johnson, Julia placed a hand on his arm.

"How much trouble is he in, Sam?" she asked quietly.

Houston shrugged uncomfortably. "Well . . . Nobody's talking about arresting him or anything like that, Julia. But . . ."

"But nobody's going to advance him any more money, neither."

"No. Not a chance." That wasn't quite true, but close enough for the moment.

She nodded and released his arm. "Thank you. I'll join you in a while."

The restraint their mother's admonition had placed on the girls finally broke.

"Can we come in, too?" Adaline demanded.

"We want to talk with Sam!" her twin added.

"Hush, girls! Sam and your father need some private time." Julia shooed them away. "You can talk to him all you want over dinner."

CHAPTER 4

It took three slugs before Sam was finally ready. Johnson seemed to sense it, because he didn't prod Sam at all until the third slug had settled in his belly. Then, sighing, he set his own half-full tumbler on the small table next to the divan and planted his hands on his knees.

"So tell me, Sam. It's bad news, I'm sure."

"The president refuses to authorize any more funds to cover the losses from the Yellowstone expedition, on the recommendation of the secretary of the treasury."

"William H. Crawford," Johnson stated, making the simple name sound like a curse.

"I don't like him, either," Sam said. "But it doesn't matter. Even if the secretary and the president proposed it, there'd be an uproar in Congress. Financially speaking, the Yellowstone expedition was a disaster." Sam raised his hand to forestall Johnson's protest. "Dick, I know most of your constituents still think the expedition was a good idea, to keep the peace on the frontier. But most of the country considers the whole thing a boondoggle."

And probably a crooked one, to boot. Half-crooked, for sure. But he left that unsaid.

Johnson didn't pursue the matter any further, not to Sam's surprise. The Yellowstone expedition and the debts it had saddled the senator with dated back several years now. Not

quite ancient history, but ground that had now been trodden
over several times. He hadn't really had any hopes of getting
any relief there.

Instead, he moved to the subject that was much more
pressing. "And the Choctaw Academy I want to set up?"

Julia Chinn came into the room at that moment, giving
Sam a little breathing space. After she'd taken a seat on the
divan next to the senator, Sam tried to present it as positively
as possible. "Do you know Gerrit Smith?"

"That young New York fellow? Rich as Croesus, they say.
Something of a philanthropist, I also heard."

"That's the one."

Johnson's eyes widened. "He's offered to back me?"

"Ah . . ."

There was no way around it. "Not exactly, Dick. He's willing to pay the debts you've accumulated for it and take the
Academy off your hands."

"What?"

May as well give it all to him, at one swallow.

"And he won't set it up here, and he won't call it the
Choctaw Academy. He wants to establish it in New Antrim.
And he wants to turn it into a school—maybe later a college,
attached to it—that's open to children from all races. Whites,
any tribe of Indians—and negroes. He thinks that's an ex-
periment that'll work. If it's done in the Arkansas part of the
Confederacy."

Johnson was just gaping at him. Sam took a deep breath
and finished. "He's even got a schoolmaster lined up. Fellow
name of Beriah Green. Also a New Yorker."

Also an abolitionist, he could have added, but didn't.
Whatever Johnson's relationship to Julia Chinn, the man was
also a major slave-owner, with all the attitudes toward abolition that that entailed. If that seemed contradictory . . .

Well, it was. But it was a contradictory matter that Sam
knew backwards and forwards. He'd owned slaves himself
for years, despite having had reservations about slavery even
as a teenager. By now, at the age of thirty, those misgivings
had turned into a genuine detestation for the institution.

Sam had owned only a few slaves at any one time, true—
sometimes not more than one. And he didn't depend on their
labor for his sustenance the way Johnson did. Mostly, he

maintained his status as a slave-owner simply out of ambition. Sam still had hopes for a political career after Monroe left office and Sam lost—as he almost certainly would—his position as special commissioner on Indian affairs. That career would have to be in the South somewhere, probably his native state of Tennessee. Sam was already notorious enough among many influential circles in that area. Owning slaves served to keep that notoriety within limits. A southern gentleman was expected to own slaves, and so he did.

Sam didn't have the same pecuniary attachment to slave-holding that a great landowner like the Kentucky senator did. Still and all, he understood the contradiction. Better than he wished he did, even leaving aside the caustic comments that his friend Patrick Driscol made whenever he visited the Confederacy.

Johnson finally found his voice. A blasphemous one, too. "I'll be damned if I will!"

"You'll be damned if you don't," Julia hissed. She leaned over and laced her fingers together. "Exactly how much of our debts will this New York fellow assume, Sam?" she asked.

Good news, finally. "Every penny, Julia. Dick, you hear that? *And* he'll assume the financial burden of any further lawsuits arising from the—ah—"

How to put it?

Julia did it for him. "None-too-detailed nature of the books." She gave her more-or-less-husband a sharp glance. "Such as they are."

Johnson flushed. "Hey, look . . ."

"Dick, the school would have lost you money anyway," Sam said forcibly. "*Did* lose you money, even before you had a chance to open the doors. So be done with it. At least this way, you walk out free and clear. You have enough other debts to worry about."

Johnson just stared at him. Julia took advantage of the silence to speak again.

"One condition, Sam. This New York rich man has to agree to it, or we won't."

"What's that?"

She looked through the open window. Outside, the sound of girls playing in the yard carried easily. "Imogene and

Adaline get to attend the school. All expenses paid. If we decide to send them."

Sam couldn't help but laugh. "Well, *that* won't be a problem. Mr. Smith asked me to pass on to you that he'd especially like your children to attend. And he offered to pay for it himself. That's because—ah—"

To Sam's relief, that stirred up Johnson's combative instincts. "Because they're famous," he growled. Again, he blasphemed. "God damn all rich men."

The senator's curse could have been leveled on himself and his New York benefactor, of course, as much as on the southern gentry who vilified him.

We are sinners all, Sam thought to himself. It was a rueful thought, as it so often was for him these days.

The senator looked to Julia, now. "Are you sure about that, dearest? I don't like the idea of our kids being that far away."

Her face got tight. "You know any other school will take them, outside of New England—where they'd be just as far away? And even if there was one . . ."

She took a deep breath. When she spoke again, her voice started rising.

"What happens if you *die,* Dick Johnson? It don't matter what you think. By law, those two daughters you spoil so badly are your slaves."

"I freed you!" he protested.

"Not till after the girls were born," came her immediate rejoinder. "Richard Mentor Johnson, how in the world can a lawyer like you be that deaf, dumb, and blind?"

It was a good question—and the wide-open mouth of the senator made it perfectly clear that he'd never even thought about it. By Kentucky law, as well as the law in any slave state, a child born to a slave inherited the legal status of the mother, not the father. That was in complete opposition to the standard way of figuring birth status as usually applied to white people. But the South's gentry had made sure and certain that their frequent dalliances with slave women wouldn't produce any legally and financially awkward children.

As foul a breed of men as ever lived, was Patrick Driscol's assessment of southern slave-owners. Sam felt the categorization was far too harsh, as was so often true of Patrick's attitudes. But he didn't deny there was more than a grain of truth to it. Slavery corrupted the master as much as it degraded the slave. If there was any true and certain law of nature, there it was.

"Long as you're alive," Julia continued, "we don't got to worry none. But if you pass on, the girls are just part of your estate. And you got debts. Lots and lots of debts. You think your creditors will pass them over?"

"I'll free them, too, then. Tomorrow!"

She shrugged. "Good. But you trust judges way more than I do. With all those creditors circling like vultures, won't surprise me at all to find some judge will say the manumission was invalid."

The next words were spoken very coldly. "They'll be pretty, real pretty, give 'em another three or four years. But they inherited my color, too—enough of it, anyway—along with my looks. They'll fetch a nice price from some slave whorehouse somewhere. Your ghost can watch it happen."

"It's not unheard of, Dick," Sam said.

The senator was back to gaping. Again, obviously, never even having considered the matter. The man's blindness could be truly astonishing at times. The same blindness that led him into one financial disaster after another. Not so much because Richard Mentor Johnson was dishonest or rapacious as because it never seemed to occur to him that friends and relatives and acquaintances of his might be.

One of the house slave women came into the room. "Dinner's ready, Miz Julia."

One black woman addressing another as if she were a white mistress. The world had a lot more crazy angles in it than most people wanted to admit. Much less allow.

Imogene and Adaline were on their best behavior at dinner. That might have been because of Sam's presence, but he didn't think so. It was more likely because their mother had drummed it into them over the years. Dinner at a great house like Blue Spring Farm was rarely a small and private family affair. And so the girls of the family would act proper, they would, or they'd suffer the consequences.

The dinner table seemed as long as a small ship, with tall

and stately candlesticks serving for masts and sails. Johnson at one end; Julia, presiding over the meal, facing him at the other. With, in two long rows down the side, well over a dozen other people in addition to Sam and the children. Disabled war veterans or their widows, for the most part. But there was also one of nearby Lexington's prominent lawyers, and one of the local plantation owners.

Sam wasn't surprised to see them there. Not all of the South's well-to-do disliked Johnson. Many admired him. That was true, starting with the president of the United States himself, James Monroe, who came from Virginia gentry. As always, in Sam's experience—contrary to Patrick Driscol's tendency to label people in sharp and definite categories—attitudes and habits blurred at the edges. Blurred so far, often enough, that no boundary was to be seen at all.

Fine for Patrick—the "Laird of Arkansas," in truth, even if no one used the term to his face—to sit up there in the mountains and divide the world and its morals into black and white. Sam lived down here in a world of grays and browns, just about everywhere he looked. And . . . being honest, he was more comfortable in that world. He had plenty of gray in his own soul, as young as he might be, and he'd always thought brown to be the warmest color of all.

"Clay's going to make a run for it," the plantation owner predicted. "In fact, he's already started."

The lawyer sitting across from him laughed sarcastically. "What else is new? Henry Clay was dreaming about the presidency while he was still in his mother's womb. More ambitious than Sam Hill, he is."

Johnson smiled into his whiskey tumbler. So did Sam. It was the same smile, half derisive and half philosophical. The difference was simply that the senator's tumbler was half full and Sam's was . . .

Empty, now that he looked into it. How had that happened?

"Don't make light of it, Jack," cautioned the lawyer. "I'm thinking he's got a very good chance at getting what he wants. With Monroe gone after next year, who else does it leave? Beyond Quincy Adams and the general, of course— and they've both got handicaps."

"Andy Jackson's the most popular man in America!" the senator stoutly proclaimed.

The lawyer, blessed with the name of Cicero Jones, gave him a look that might have graced the face of the ancient Roman statesman after whom he'd been named—just before he fell beneath the swords of the Second Triumvirate.

"Maybe so, Dick. But . . ."

For an instant, Jones's glance flicked toward Sam. Then he looked down at his plate. "But not as much as he used to be," he concluded glumly.

That was enough to tip Sam's decision over the immediate issue at hand. He held up his tumbler toward one of the slaves waiting on the table. "Some more whiskey, if you would."

As the slave made to comply, Sam gave Johnson a level gaze. "That's my doing. The settlement I made of the Algiers business hurt the general worse than the Treaty of Oothcaloga helped him. No doubt about it, I think."

Now that Sam had said it out loud, Cicero Jones was clearly relieved. "No doubt about it at all," the lawyer echoed.

Across from him, Jack Hartfield shrugged and spread his hands. As portly as the plantation owner was, the expansive gesture did unfortunate things to his tightly buttoned vest.

Adaline managed to keep quiet, but Imogene burst into a giggle. Sam almost did, too, for that matter. The way the button flew from Hartfield and bounced off one of the candlesticks was genuinely comical.

Hartfield himself grinned. But his good cheer didn't keep the girl from her chastisement.

"Imogene!" exclaimed Julia. A hand the color of coffee-with-cream smacked her daughter, leaving a red mark on a cheek whose color wasn't much lighter. "Do that again and you'll finish dinner in your room!"

"Oh, go easy on her, Julia," chuckled the plantation owner. "It *was* pretty funny. I probably would have laughed myself, 'cept I don't want to think what my wife'll have to say when I get home. I'm afraid I bust a lot of those."

"Don't matter," insisted Julia. She wagged a finger in Imogene's face. "You behave yourself, young lady. You know better than that."

Imogene assumed a properly chastened look. Although Sam didn't miss the angry glare she gave her sister across the table, once Julia looked away. Adaline's face had that insufferably smug look that a twin has whenever her sibling is rightfully punished—and she herself gets away with it.

Again, it was all Sam could do not to laugh. Fortunately, the tumbler arrived and he was able to disguise his amusement with a hefty slug of its contents. A heftier slug than he'd actually intended. It was hard to resist, though. The whiskey served at Blue Spring Farm was the best Sam had had in months. And that was a lot of whiskey back.

Once the humor of his mishap had settled, Hartfield went on with what he'd been about to say. "I don't think it's really fair to blame young Houston. If the general had just kept quiet about the matter, instead of . . ."

He shrugged. Even more expansively than he had before, now that further damage was impossible. The button that had popped off his vest had been the last survivor.

"That unfortunate speech."

That was something of a euphemism, in Sam's opinion. As much as he admired Andy Jackson, there was no denying the man had a savage streak in his nature that was sometimes as wide as the Mississippi River. If the clash at Algiers had been between any *other* group of black men—free or slave, it mattered not—and a properly constituted white militia, Andy Jackson would have been among the first to demand loudly that the niggers be put in their place. For that matter, he'd probably have offered to lead the punitive expedition personally.

But those hadn't been just any black men. Those had been the men of the Iron Battalion, led by the same Patrick Driscol, who'd broken the British at the Battle of the Mississippi—the battle that had turned Jackson from a regional into a national figure. If Andy Jackson could be savage about race, he could be even more savage—a lot more savage—when it came to matters of honor, and courage, and cowardice.

Whatever the color of their skin—and their commander's skin was as white as Jackson's own—Old Hickory had a genuine admiration for the Iron Battalion. And, on the reverse side, despised no group of wealthy men in the United

States so much as he despised the plantation owners in and around New Orleans who had, in the main, refused to participate in the fight against the invading redcoats. And had done so—to put the icing on the cake—because they feared their own slaves more than they did a foreign enemy.

Jackson had had choice words to say about that Louisiana gentry during the New Orleans campaign in the war against the British. His words spoken in public— and reprinted in most of the newspapers of the nation—the day after the Algiers Incident had been choicer still. *Poltroons* and *criminals* applied to rich white men, and the terms *stalwart fellows* and *yeomen defending their rights* applied to poor black ones, were all true, to be sure. But they'd caused the general's popularity in the South and the West—theretofore almost unanimous except for Henry Clay and his coterie—to plummet like a stone.

Only so far, of course. Soon enough, the plunging stone had reached the secure ledge of support from the poorer class of the Southwest's voters. For the most part, they'd been no happier with the result of the clash at Algiers than any other white men of the region. On the other hand, as the saying went, it was no skin off their nose. All the more so, since the battle had been precipitated by the lascivious conduct of some of the New Orleans Creoles, whose wealth and Frenchified habits the poor Scots-Irish settlers resented— and a good percentage considered not that much better than niggers anyway.

Still, when all the dust settled, Andy Jackson's popularity in the South and West was no longer as overwhelming as it had been. Clay, of course, had immediately seized the opportunity to continue the Jackson-bashing he'd begun two years earlier over the general's conduct of the Florida campaign. The Speaker of the House had had his own choice words to say on the floor of Congress. He'd even gone to the extreme of offering to lead a punitive expedition to Louisiana himself.

The offer had been as histrionic as it was ridiculous. First, because Henry Clay had no military experience whatsoever— indeed, he routinely dismissed Jackson as a "mere military chieftain," in no way suitable for higher positions in the Republic. Second, because he knew perfectly well that there was no chance at all that President Monroe would appoint him to the position, even in the unlikely event that he authorized such a mission in the first place. Always the Virginia gentleman, James Monroe kept his private feelings to himself. But Sam was his son-in-law, and he knew perfectly well that if Monroe's dislike and distrust of Henry Clay was less savage than Jackson's, it was not an inch shallower.

Ridiculous and histrionic as it might have been, however, Clay's stance had enhanced his own popularity in the region—and the congressman from Kentucky had already been the second most popular figure there, after Jackson. Considerably more popular among the region's gentry.

"Well, it's done now," said the lawyer. No slouch himself when it came to whiskey, Cicero Jones downed his tumbler. "But don't fool yourselves, gentlemen. Henry Clay is now at the front of the pack who'll be running for president, once Monroe's term is up. Quincy Adams is respected by just about everyone—gentlemen, at least—but he's not liked all that much, either. Too cold, too harsh, too caustic—too everything. And, like Calhoun, he's almost a purely regional figure. Adams will take New England just as certainly as Calhoun will take the hard-core South. But that's not enough votes to win, no matter how you slice it."

"There's Crawford," pointed out Senator Johnson. Only a slight twist to his lips indicated his dislike for the secretary of the treasury. The tone of his comment had been neutral and matter-of-fact.

Jones shrugged. "Yes, there's William Crawford. Popular in the South also, of course, being a Georgian. And the nation's well-to-do tend to be fond of him in all regions of the country."

"As they should!" barked Sam. Most of the disgruntlement in his tone, however, came from the state of his tumbler. Once again, not even noticing, he'd managed to drain it dry. And it would be ungracious to ask for another refill so soon. Always the generous host, Johnson still had a badly frayed pocketbook—and that whiskey was expensive.

"But he's seen by too many people as too slick," the lawyer continued. "I don't think the electorate trusts him all that much. Nor should they, for that matter."

"Hah!" exclaimed Hartfield. "Why should they look cross-eyed at Crawford? He's not half the cut-any-corner and make-any-deal bastard that Clay is."

The lawyer shook his head. "Yes, I know. But Clay makes pretty speeches and knows how to pose in public. Crawford's not got half his talent for that. Not a quarter." He took a long pull on his tumbler, leaving it as dry as Sam's. "No, you watch. It'll be Clay to beat. Calhoun will throw him his support as the election nears, in exchange for Clay's backing—half-backing, at least—on the issues Calhoun holds dear. And Crawford . . . well, I think he'll settle for secretary of state, if Clay will promise it to him. That'll position Crawford to replace Clay when the time comes. He's only fifty-one years old, after all."

Sam considered Jones's assessment as he considered the lawyer's empty tumbler. He thought the assessment was about right. More to the point, he could see where it led straight to a toast.

He cleared his throat. "What you're saying, Cicero, if I'm following you, is that if Andy Jackson is to be our next president, he'll have to reach an accommodation with John Quincy Adams. Right?"

"Dead right." Jones winced a little, then. "And that'll be some trick."

"The general thinks well of Adams," pointed out Johnson.

"Who doesn't?" said Jones. "A most admirable man, versed in the classics and everything. But does the general *like* him? And, perhaps more to the point, what does Adams think of Andy Jackson?"

"He supported him during that ruckus over Florida," stated Johnson stubbornly.

The lawyer waved his hand. "Sure he did. John Quincy Adams is the best secretary of state the United States has ever had, if you ask me. Andy Jackson got us Florida, so Adams backed him. But that doesn't mean he much likes the general. Face it, gentlemen." Jones leaned forward in his seat and tapped the table with his forefinger. "First, they disagree over most issues that concern the internal affairs of the nation. Adams is still half a Federalist, when you come down to it. Half an abolitionist, too, if I'm not mistaken."

He tapped the table again, more forcibly. "Second, political affairs are determined more by matters of blood and attitude than they are by cold intellect. I don't think you could find two prominent men in the country more unlike than Andy Jackson and John Quincy Adams. They're as different as the Kentucky whiskey and French wine they each prefer to drink."

That was true enough, of course. Best of all, it was salient.

Sam rose to his feet. "A toast, then, gentlemen! To unlikely alliances!" The men at the table began to rise, all except the two veterans who were missing a leg. But their smiles were enough to indicate their full agreement with the toast.

Sam reached down for his tumbler. Then, his mouth widened as if he'd just noticed the glass was empty.

"Ah. How awkward."

"Grover!" Johnson barked at one of the slaves standing by the sideboard. "What are you daydreaming about? See to it that Sam's whiskey is refilled!"

CHAPTER 5

The next morning, at breakfast, Johnson waited until the girls were finished and had excused themselves from the table before returning to the subject of the new school.

More precisely, to where the new school might lead them.

"Tarnation, Sam—I'll make this as plain as I can—I want them to marry white men. Even if they have to move to Vermont or Massachusetts in order to do it. And how many white men are they going to run into, over there in Black Arkansas?"

"They're only twelve years old, Dick," Sam pointed out mildly. "Hardly something you've got to worry about right now."

The senator wasn't mollified. "They'll grow up fast enough. Faster than you expect. If there's any sure and certain law about kids, that's it. They *always* grow up faster than you expect."

Sam glanced at Julia. Her expression was unreadable: just a blank face that might simply be contemplating clouds in the sky. He wondered how she felt about the matter.

But since there was no point in asking, he decided bluntness was the only tactic suitable.

"They'll marry whoever they marry, Dick. If you think you can stop them—here any more than in Arkansas—you're dreaming. You heard about the ruckus with Major Ridge's son? Over in Connecticut?"

Johnson chuckled. "Who didn't? I heard the girl even went on a hunger strike."

"Yep, she did. Stuck to it, too, until her parents got so worried they caved in and let her marry John Ridge after all. Cherokee or not. But here's really the point I was making. Did you hear what happened to her family afterward?"

The senator shook his head.

"Well, after the wedding they wound up moving to New Antrim also. I guess, after visiting the town to make sure their daughter wasn't winding up in some Indian lean-to—" He grinned widely. "Which Patrick Driscol's Wolfe Tone Hotel most certainly isn't, not with Tiana running the place. Anyway, it seems they found New Antrim most congenial. Especially since it was maybe the only town in the continent, outside of Fort of 98, where their daughter wouldn't be hounded every day. Neither would they, for that matter. It got pretty rough on them, too, you know. One newspaper article even called for drowning the girl's mother along with whipping the girl herself. John Ridge himself, of course, was for hanging."

"I heard." Johnson's lip curled. "So much for that snooty New England so-called upper crust. You can say what you like about the country folks hereabouts, but at least"—he nodded toward Julia—"she doesn't have to worry none, just going down to the store to buy provisions."

"Folks are right nice to me," she agreed.

"What's your point, Sam?" asked Johnson.

"I'd think it was obvious. The one thing you can at least be sure of, if one or both of your daughters winds up marrying somebody *you* think is unsuitable, over there in Arkansas, is that nobody *else* will."

He gave Johnson a cocked-head look. "Never been there, have you? You ought to go visit sometime. Soon."

"Yes," said Julia. "Soon. But . . ."

"It can be dangerous these days," said Johnson. His hand reached out and squeezed Julia's forearm. "Traveling, I mean, for anyone with her color. Even the color of Imogene and Adaline. Those so-called slave-catchers have been running pretty wild."

Sam grinned savagely. "Less wild than they used to be, I bet. When I passed through Cincinnati, I heard about the killing."

Johnson grimaced. "Don't make light of it, Sam. Most people down here were pretty upset about that."

"Sure. So what? 'Most people' aren't running around trying to catch so-called runaway slaves. Who, most times, are just freedmen trying to make it safely to Arkansas. Which they have to, thanks to that bastard Calhoun and his Cossacks stirring up lynch mobs all over the country. So what difference does it make if they're 'upset' because some unknown abolitionist fiend gunned down a slave-catcher across the river? What matters is that the slave-catchers are a lot more than just 'upset.' " His grin grew still more savage. "Why, I do believe they're downright nervous. Seeing as how they don't know who the fiend and his fifty brothers were. Or where they might pop up next."

Sam waved a hand. "But it doesn't matter, anyway. As long as you make the trip while Monroe's in office, I can provide you with a military escort as far as the Confederacy. A small one, but that'll be enough. After that, the Cherokees will escort you the rest of the way."

Julia pursed her lips. "That gives us almost a year. How soon will this Mr. Smith have the school up and running?"

Sam shrugged. "I don't know. Not that soon, I wouldn't think. But you can put the girls up at the Wolfe Tone in the meantime. Tiana will look after them."

Johnson looked a bit dubious. As well he might. The young Cherokee princess who'd married the notorious Patrick Driscol enjoyed her own reputation in the United

States. Granted, a more favorable one than her husband's, since in her case most of it was in the form of overwrought and long-winded verses written by New England poets.

Ridiculous verses, too, for anyone who knew the realities of Indian and frontier life. Sam had shown one of the more famous poems to Tiana once—Edward Coote Pinkney's "The Cherokee Bride"—and her comment, after reading less than a third of it, had been a terse "Well, he's never gutted a deer."

But however uncertain the senator might be at the prospect, Julia was firm. "We'll do it, then. Look for us coming toward the end of the summer."

Sam nodded. "Good. I probably won't be there myself, then, but I'll let Patrick and Tiana know that you're coming."

When they found out at lunch, the girls were ecstatic.

"We get to play Indians!" squealed Imogene.

"*With* Indians," her sister corrected her.

Imogene bestowed the inimitable sneer of a twelve-year-old upon a hopelessly ignorant sibling. "In Arkansas, silly, there's no difference. Everybody knows that!"

Johnson looked to be growing more dubious by the minute. But since Julia wasn't wavering, it didn't really matter.

Johnson left shortly thereafter to attend to some business around the plantation. After he was gone, Julia asked Sam quietly: "How much of that is really true? What Imogene said, I mean."

By then—noon being a thing of the past—Sam had a tumbler of whiskey in his hand and was leaning back comfortably in one of the porch chairs. "Not much, Julia. Not the way Imogene put it, anyway."

He took a sip from his whiskey, feeling the usual contentment the liquor gave him as it warmed its way down. "You're familiar enough with the Indians down here in the South. The way they figure descent and inheritance, through the mother rather than the father, makes a lot of difference when it comes to the way they figure which race starts here and which one ends there. It's not that they don't see the difference, mind you."

He chuckled harshly. "In a lot of ways, they're worse than white men. At least, our clan feuds don't tend to spring up that sudden and last forever. But that's because what really matters to them is not which race a person belongs to, but which clan. And clans intermarry. They always have. So . . ."

Another sip, longer this time, helped him focus his thoughts. "So the country they're putting together out there in Arkansas looks strange to us. A lot stranger than their tribes used to look, I think, because they're taking so much of it from us in the first place that most of it looks pretty familiar. In Arkansas, everything's a hybrid. Race counts, sure, but it doesn't trump everything the way it does here in the U.S."

He chuckled again, but the sound this time was much softer. Amusement rather than sarcasm. "They've even got newspapers. Five of 'em, at my last count. Four in English, and one that just started up that's trying out Sequoyah's new Cherokee script. The most popular is the one that's owned by Major Ridge's son and nephew. John Ridge and Buck Watie set it up in New Antrim, you know—or 'the Little Rock,' as the Cherokees call the town."

"Why there?" she asked. "I thought most of the Cherokees lived further west."

"They do. But newspapers need big towns to prosper, and the only big towns in the Confederacy are New Antrim and Fort of 98. Even the Cherokee capital at Tahlequah doesn't have more than two thousand people."

Sam considered tracing a map for her but gave up the idea almost immediately. With Julia's stern housekeeping regimen, there wasn't enough dust on the floor of the porch to do the trick—and he wasn't about to waste this good whiskey wetting his finger in it. So, he made do with words alone.

"Patrick's chiefdom ends at Fort of 98, where the Poteau River meets the Arkansas. Most of the Cherokees and Creeks live in the lands west of there. By now, they're spread out quite a ways, each clan staking out a big chunk. Mostly along the Arkansas, Canadian, and Cimarron rivers—but Chief Bowles and his people settled south of the Red River."

Julia frowned. "I thought they weren't supposed to do that."

"They're not. According to the Treaty of Oothcaloga—I ought to know, since I drafted it—the southern border of the Confederacy of the Arkansas is marked by the Red River. But Indians don't generally pay much attention to stuff like that. People like John Ross will, even Major Ridge these days, but not someone like The Bowl and the traditionalists who follow him."

He took another sip. "Right now, nobody's saying much. But once somebody figures out how to clear the Great Raft and make the Red navigable—which is bound to happen, sooner or later—there'll be Sam Hill looking to collect the bill."

She cocked her head, gazing at him. "I'd think you'd be more upset at the prospect."

He shrugged. "That won't happen any time soon, Julia. By then, it's not likely I'll still be in charge of Indian affairs for the government. I've spoken to Henry Shreve about it. He's the steamboat genius Patrick Driscol went into partnership with, if you didn't know."

"The one who got into that big legal fight over Fulton's monopoly?"

Sam nodded. "The very man. He won that fight in court, but the Fulton-Livingston steamboat company was still able to make things miserable for him in New Orleans. Legal monopoly or not, they've got the backing of the Louisiana authorities. When Patrick made him the offer to set up his own company on the Arkansas, he jumped at it. Anyway, the point is that Shreve told me it's *possible* to clear the Great Raft out of the Red. In fact, in his spare time—which isn't much, as busy as the new companies in Arkansas are keeping him— he's starting to design a special steamboat to do the job. A 'snagboat,' he calls it. But even Henry Shreve doesn't think he could have it ready in less than five years—assuming he could find somebody to back him."

"And how likely is that?"

Sam shrugged again. "It'd almost have to be the government. A project like that would be too expensive for a private company, with no obvious quick profit to be made."

After another sip of whiskey, he added: "The U.S. government, I mean. No way the Confederacy would do it. Even if they had the money, which they don't."

Seeing her head still cocked quizzically, he explained. "John Ross and Major Ridge think the Great Raft is just dandy, Julia. Patrick probably burns incense to keep it there. Well, he would if the scoundrel had a religious bone anywhere in his body."

Her head was still cocked. Sam shook his own. "You've never met Patrick Driscol."

He finished the whiskey and set the tumbler down on the floor of the porch. "He's probably my closest friend, Julia, but there are times I swear the man scares me. Scares Sam Hill, for that matter. I don't think there's a harder man alive, anywhere in the world. He's gotten stinking rich over the past few years, but not because he paid much attention to it. That came from luck—the proverbial right place at the right time—and having Tiana for a wife." A quick grin came and went. "Not to mention Tiana's rapscallion father, who seems to be able to squeeze money out of anything. But Patrick himself never thinks like a rich man. He thinks like a poor Scots-Irish rebel, still seeing redcoats everywhere he looks. Even if the coats look to be blue, these days."

"You want more whiskey?"

"I was hoping you'd ask," he replied, smiling cheerfully. "Yes, please. One more and I'll be steady enough for that blasted horse. I felt peckish, waking up this morning."

"Well, I don't wonder. As much as you drank last night."

She said nothing more. Just got up and went into the house. One of the many things Sam liked about Julia Chinn was that she wasn't given to nattering. Not even at the senator, really.

She was back a few seconds later with a half-full bottle and refilled his tumbler. And that was another thing Sam liked about the woman. No half-full tumblers when *she* poured.

He took a hefty first sip and continued. "My point is that Patrick never stops thinking like a soldier. Doesn't matter how rich he gets. He's wound up making money hand over fist with each new company he sets up—not to mention his bank—but that's never why he does it. Each and every one of those companies, even the bank, has a military purpose."

Julia's eyes widened. "Whatever for? There's a treaty with our government, and the wild Indian tribes out there can't be that much of a threat."

"No, they're not. Dangerous, yes, but not what you'd call a real threat to the Confederacy. And, nowadays, even the Osages pretty much stay out of the Arkansas Chiefdom altogether. Patrick's soldiers are . . . rough, when they get riled. Not undisciplined, mind you." The chuckle, this time, was very harsh. "Not hardly, with Patrick's ways. But he's a firm believer that if someone picks a fight with him, he will surely give them what they asked for. And then some. Like I said, a scary man."

It was getting time to go, and Sam still had one last piece of business to take care of. So he left off the sipping and drained most of the tumbler in one slug.

"It's the U.S. he's thinking about, Julia. Not now, of course, with James Monroe in office. If John Quincy Adams succeeds him, that would be, if anything, even better. Adams is a diplomat by instinct and background. He'll always try to settle something by negotiation if he can. And I don't think Patrick even worries much, if the general gets elected instead. As ornery as they both are— and it's hard to choose between the man from County Antrim and Old Hickory—he and Andy Jackson could manage to get along. Well enough, anyway. No, it's Clay he's thinking about. You never know what Henry Clay will decide to do if he thinks it'll advance his prospects."

Julia made a face. Her common-law husband detested Henry Clay. Clearly enough, she didn't disagree with him on the subject.

Neither did Sam. He didn't share Andy Jackson's corrosive hatred for Clay, but that was simply because Sam didn't have it in him to hate anyone that much. If he did, though, Clay would be pretty much at the top of his list also. In the near vicinity, for sure. The man's personal morals stank, and his political morals were even worse.

"So, to get back to the point, there's no way Patrick would want the Red River cleared of the Great Raft. In fact, I think that's the main reason he went into business with Henry Shreve. Sure, and he's gotten rich from that partnership, too—everything Patrick touches seems to turn to gold, these days—but that's not why he did it. Now that Fulton's dead, Shreve's probably the only man in the United States today who'd have the wherewithal to figure out how to clear the Great Raft. So Patrick made sure to tie him down good and solid. As long as the Great Raft stays where it is, he doesn't have to worry about anybody using the Red River to attack him. His southern flank is pretty well protected."

Julia shook her head. "Man sounds a little crazy, to me."

Sam drained the last of the whiskey, grinning through the glass. "So people say. Lots of them."

He didn't bother to add *but not me.* The grin alone made it obvious enough.

He found Richard Johnson in one of the barns, attending to farm business of one kind or another. Something to do with a cow, apparently. Sam wasn't quite sure, because he'd decided at an early age that farming was even more boring than storekeeping. Tedium was bad enough on its own without piling study onto the affair.

He didn't need to, anyway, since as soon as the senator spotted him, Johnson broke off his discussion with the two slaves handling the barn animals and came over.

"You leaving now?"

" 'Fraid so, Dick. I want to make it to the Confederacy by the end of the month, and . . . ah . . ."

"You've got to pay a visit to the general first."

Sam half winced. "Yes, I do. Can't say I'm looking forward to it, this time."

Johnson studied him. "On account of how you figure you may have lost the general his chance to get elected president."

"You could have maybe sweetened that a little. But . . . yeah. On account of that."

Johnson looked away for a moment, then shrugged. "Well, maybe you did. Although I think Jack Hartfield's right. If Andy had just kept his mouth shut after Algiers, I don't think the affair would have hurt him much. He was not in any way directly involved, after all."

"I think Jack's probably right, too. But you know the general. Andy Jackson has a lot of virtues. Being fair-minded—especially when it involves something he did—just isn't one of them. Not usually, at least."

"True enough. Well, you have my sympathies. Give the general my best regards, will you?"

"Certainly."

Sam hesitated, then added: "But there's something else I wanted to raise with you, Dick. Tell me the truth. How bad are you hurting?"

Johnson looked away again. "In terms of money? Pretty bad, Sam." A half-whining note of resentment crept into his voice. "I was hoping the school . . ."

The one thing Sam didn't want to do was rehash that matter. "Forget the school," he said forcibly. "You would have lost money on it, anyway. *Did* lose money, and plenty of it, before you even got it set up."

He summoned up the memory of his mad charge on the Creek barricade at the Horseshoe Bend. That seemed as good a model as any.

"Look, Dick, face it. You're a man I think well of personally, and a public figure I admire even more. But when it comes to business, you're a walking disaster. You've got no head for it, at all."

The senator scowled but didn't argue the point. Given his track record, that'd be pretty much impossible, even for a man as generally insouciant as he was.

So Sam kept the charge going. "I think there's a way out of the bind you're in, but you'd have to be willing to do two things. First, go into partnership with a man who *does* know how to make businesses run profitably."

Johnson snorted. "And why would that be a problem for me? Except—good luck, finding a smart businessman who'd touch me with a ten-foot pole. Why should he? I've got nothing to bring to a partnership, Sam. No skill at it"—the scowl came back, for an instant—"as you've just been unkind enough to rub my nose in. And no capital to back someone who is. I'm broke, Sam. Worse than broke. I'm up to my waist in debts, and pretty soon the creditors are going to take me to court. The ones who haven't already, that is. Won't be surprised at all to see Henry Clay arguing the case for 'em.

My biggest creditor is the Second Bank, after all, and he's one of their top lawyers whenever he takes the time away from his political chiseling."

Sam took a deep breath, remembering that final moment when he'd scaled the barricade. Right after Major Montgomery got his brains blown out by a Creek bullet.

"I've *got* a partner for you, Dick. He'll put up the skill, and he'll put up all the money. In fact, he'll advance you enough to fend off your creditors. Far enough off to give you some breathing room, anyway, while he gets the business up and running and turning a profit."

Johnson's eyes widened, and then immediately narrowed. "*What* business? And who is this paragon? Or bedlamite, I should say. Why in the world would a sane man do something like that?"

"The business is complicated. More complicated than I can follow, to be honest. Mostly it involves setting up a big foundry—biggest west of Cincinnati—but that also requires expanding the steamboat traffic. Expanding a foundry, I should say, since it's already in operation. But the expansion would be major. The man I'm talking about is one of the silent partners in the steamboat business Henry Shreve and Patrick Driscol set up."

Another deep breath. "His name is Henry Crowell, and the reason he's silent is because he's black. He's gotten rich enough over the past few years that he'd like to expand his business into the United States, but he can't do that without a white partner as his public face."

Sam was half expecting an outraged reaction. Despite his relationship to Julia, Richard Johnson's general attitudes on matters of race weren't really all that different from those of most people in the country. Like Andy Jackson, Johnson was always willing to make personal exceptions to generalities. But the generalities themselves, he didn't really question much.

To his surprise, though, Johnson's face simply seemed pensive. "Crowell? That name's familiar."

"Well, it ought to be!" Sam exclaimed. "He was the teamster who supplied us at the Capitol during the battle with the British. He fought well himself, later, as part of a gun crew at the battle of the Mississippi."

Best to leave it at that, he thought. The same Henry Crowell had also been the cause of the Algiers Incident—as the victim who triggered it, if not the instigator—but Sam saw no reason to bring that up.

"Yes, that's it. But I think there was something . . ."

"Look, Dick," Sam said, maintaining the stout tone to keep Johnson from dwelling on the name, "Henry's as good a businessman as you can find; I don't care what color. He parlayed the supply contract I got for him for the New Orleans campaign into a small fortune—okay, real small fortune, but big enough . . ."

His voice trailed off. He'd just stumbled into the pit he'd been trying to avoid.

Alas, that was sufficient to jog Johnson's memory. "*That* Crowell? The one they castrated in New Orleans? Set off the whole blasted ruckus there?"

Sam gritted his teeth. Tarnation, he was tired of being diplomatic.

"Yes, that one," he growled. "The reason the Creoles had him castrated was because he'd gotten rich enough and prominent enough that he drew the attention of one of the girls they were grooming for one of their stinking Quadroon Balls. He almost died from the injury—castration's usually fatal, though most people don't realize it—and, yes, that's what set off the Battle of Algiers. Driscol called the Iron Battalion back into service. They marched into the French Quarter and blew the place half apart, and strung up every slave-catcher they got their hands on. Seeing as how they'd done the dirty work. Killed the Creole grandee who'd ordered it done, too. Patrick saw to that himself."

To his surprise, Johnson laughed. Quite a cheerful laugh. "And then pounded into splinters the Louisiana militia, when they got sent in to 'suppress a servile insurrection.'"

He laughed again, seeing the expression on Sam's face. "You know, Sam, you might be surprised at how a lot of people looked at that. Publicly, sure, it was a scandal and an outrage. But people have their own private thoughts—and don't ever underestimate the general. He would have done better to keep his mouth shut, but his own reaction was heartfelt. And the one thing about Andy is that he has a sure and certain knack for catching the sentiments of the common folk. That was a nasty filthy business, and there are still plenty of people in the United States for whom Patrick Driscol and the Iron Battalion are, were, and always will be the heroes who won the Battle of the Mississippi."

He gave Sam something of a sly look. "Meaning no disrespect to your own glorious part in the affair."

Sam just smiled. He'd gotten more public credit for winning that battle than Patrick had, but that was simply because he was a lot more acceptable figure than the grim and dour Irish rebel—and, most of all, because Sam's soldiers had been white. But Sam himself knew perfectly well that the valiant stand of the Iron Battalion had been the key to winning that battle. So did Andy Jackson, for that matter.

"Yes, that Crowell. After he recovered, well . . . He just got more determined than ever to be a successful man. Married the girl involved, in fact. And if he can't produce any children of his own, he makes up for it with an orphanage and the schools he set up." His tone hardened a bit. "And, yes, if you're wondering, he's Gerrit Smith's silent partner in that school of yours Smith is buying and moving to New Antrim."

Johnson shook his head. But it wasn't a gesture of refusal, more one of bewilderment.

"What in the name of Sam Hill is the world coming to?" he asked, wonderingly.

By now, Sam thought he'd come to know the answer to that question. And, for once, decided he'd say it out loud to another white man. "I'm Cherokee by adoption, Dick. What the world is coming to—if I've got anything to say about it—is that I'd like to see what happens if we use Cherokee methods for a change. At least in one part of the continent."

"Meaning?"

"Meaning I'm sick and tired of stumbling over race, everywhere I go. So I'd like to try clans, instead. I don't ask for a perfect world, just one where people deal with each other instead of categories. Imperfect as they may be."

Johnson went back to staring at the nearby wall of the barn. No reason to, really, since nothing hung on that wall but some half-rusted old tools that nobody had used in years.

"All right," he said finally. "I'm willing to give it a try. Not that I really have much choice anyway."

Sam nodded. "Good. I've already set it up at the other end. In fact, Henry told me he'd have the money ready, if you agreed. Soon as I get there, I'll have it sent. It'll be fifteen thousand dollars, to start."

That was enough to yank Johnson's eyes from the wall. "*Fifteen thousand?* What kind of darkie has—"

"The richest darkie in the world," Sam replied coldly. "Anywhere in North America, anyway. Take it or leave it, Dick."

The senator seemed more bemused than ever. "Oh, I'll take it. I surely will. But still—"

He shook his head again. "Like I said, what's the world coming to?"

Sam had already given whatever good answer he had to that, so he just shrugged. "I'll be on my way, then."

"Sam Hill, if you will!" Johnson seized Sam by the arm and half dragged him out of the barn. "This calls for a drink of whiskey!"

Sam put up something of a protest.

As they rode away from Blue Spring Farm, in midafternoon, Chester asked him, "You going to make it through the rest of the day, Mr. Sam?"

"Don't be ridiculous."

"Just wondering. You might want to put your feet in the stirrups, then."

"Oh. Forgot."

CHAPTER 6

"This is the Little Rock," announced the middle-aged Cherokee who'd escorted Sheffield Parker and his folks up the Arkansas River. There was a hint of a sly smile on his face. "Be careful. It's full of Christians."

Sheff's mother eyed the Indian skeptically but didn't say anything. His uncle just grinned, even though normally he'd have taken umbrage, as devout as he was. For whatever reason, Sheff's uncle and the Cherokee had gotten along quite well on the trip upriver.

"I thought it was called New Antrim," Sheff's sister said, half complainingly.

The Cherokee's smile widened, just a bit. "Depends who you ask. We Cherokee call it the Little Rock." He pointed to a rock formation not far from the pier the steamboat was approaching. "Got the name from that. Goes back quite a ways. When Patrick Driscol bought the area from a St. Louis speculator by the name of Russell, he named it New Antrim. Most of the white folks here use that name, too."

The smile widened still further. Sheff couldn't resist the tease. "So then, what do black folks call it?"

"Most all of them just call it Driscoltown. Though you'll also hear 'Driscolburg' and 'Driscolville.' Seeing as how you black folks make up almost three out of four people living here, but can't seem to agree on the details, I imagine it'll eventually just get known as Driscol."

By now, the smile was on the edge of being an outright

grin. " 'Course, you'll have to wait until Driscol dies. He'll skin you alive, he hears you call it that."

Sheff studied the town the steamboat was approaching. He was impressed by the size of it, even though it didn't approach the standards of his native Baltimore. But it was far grander than anything he'd expected to see way out here on the frontier, beyond the limits of the United States. When they'd reached Cincinnati, Salmon Brown had told him it had fifteen thousand residents. From what he could see, Sheff was pretty sure New Antrim was even bigger.

Quite a bit bigger, in fact, at least in terms of the number of people. The houses here were a lot more crowded together than they'd been in Cincinnati. That town had been populated mainly by prosperous white mechanics and merchants. This one, even if it didn't seem to be as beat up as the freedmens' quarter in Baltimore, was obviously a lot poorer than Cincinnati. Although it was hard to tell, really. Most of the construction was new and raw, with nothing much in the way of frills. The people living inside those mostly log-and-wattle dwellings might be in better shape than the houses themselves.

The Cherokee confirmed his guess a moment later. "They took the first census just five months ago. The Little Rock's got just over twenty-eight thousand people in it. 'Bout twenty thousand of them are black, like you. Another five thousand or so are white people. The rest—"

No question about it. That *was* a grin. "Are crazy Indians like me."

Sheff's sister had the tactlessness of most eight-year-olds. "Why are you crazy? Don't really seem like it."

"Dinah!" exclaimed their mother. She smacked her daughter on the back of her head. "Mind your manners!"

The Cherokee's grin never faded, though. "Bean't no worse than what most Cherokees call me, Missus Parker. Considerably better, in fact." To Dinah, he said: " 'Course I'm crazy, girl. Why else would a Cherokee live in a place like this? When I could be doing exciting things like chasing deer in the rain?"

He looked away from her, bestowing the grin on the town. They were almost at the pier, by now.

"Don't bother me. There's enough other Cherokees feel the same way I do, that I never lack for company. Quite a few Creeks, too. And I do declare I think we're looking to outnumber the other Indians, you give it maybe ten or twenty years."

A deafening blast from the steamboat's whistle made Sheff jump a little.

"Well, here we are." The steamboat was being tied up to the wharf while a small crew of men moved a ramp toward the side of the boat. Two other men emerged from a door in the side of a large building next to the pier.

They were both black, as were all the men moving the ramp. But the two newcomers were wearing green uniforms.

Sheff had heard rumors about those uniforms. These were men in the Arkansas Army. It was real!

Some of his excitement must have shown. The old Indian chuckled softly. "Yep, that's them, all right. The Confederate Army. Arkansas Chiefdom, anyway."

"What are they doing here?" asked Sheff's mother.

The Cherokee sucked his teeth for a moment. "I guess you could call it recruitment."

Sheff's mother immediately frowned. "I don't want my boy signing up for no army!"

The Cherokee smiled again. But said nothing.

Less than an hour later, sitting behind his mother on a stool in a large office in New Antrim's largest bank, Sheff was mightily confused about most everything. But he understood why the old man had smiled.

"It's not fair!" his mother exclaimed. The words were half a protest, half a wail.

The man sitting on the opposite side of the biggest desk Sheff had ever seen just shrugged his shoulders. "No, I suppose not. But what's 'fair' got to do with anything, Mrs. Parker? You wanted your freedom, and you got it. But what 'freedom' means, right now, is the freedom to starve."

Sheff was too fascinated with the man himself to pay much attention to his words. His name was Henry Crowell, nothing spectacular. But to Sheffield Parker he was a living, breathing dragon, testifying in person that this new fantasy world was real.

First, because he was black.

Second, because he was the biggest man Sheff had ever seen.

Third, because he was wearing fancier-looking clothes than anything Sheff had ever seen anyone wear except a few of the richest white men in Baltimore.

Finally—most glorious of all—because he was the *president* of the bank.

He *owned* it!

Well, half of it, anyway. From what Sheff had been able to understand of the man's introductory remarks, the other half was apparently owned by the same Patrick Driscol who'd become a mysterious legend to Sheff.

"It's not fair!" Sheff's mother repeated, trying, this time, for more in the way of sternness rather than simple misery.

Next to her, Sheff's uncle shrugged. "I don't really mind, Lemon."

Mrs. Parker swiveled her head to glare at her brother. "So, fine. You're a full-growed man, Jem. What about my little boy?"

The man behind the desk chuckled, causing his immense chest to ripple the fancy cloth. "Don't look so 'little' to me, ma'am. He's not too tall, but he's powerful wide in the shoulders."

Now she glared at the banker. "It isn't fair!"

Crowell sighed and sat up straighter in his chair. Then, planting two huge hands on the desk, he leaned forward and spoke softly. Softly, but very firmly.

"Mrs. Parker, there is no magic here in Arkansas. 'Less you believe in the voudou business, but not even Marie Laveau claims she can conjure up food and shelter out of spiderwebs. You came here with nothing. No money, no tools beyond a few knives and such, no capital, no livestock, not much at all beyond the clothes on your backs—and those, meaning no offense, you couldn't sell even if you wanted to. They're not far removed from rags."

Sheff's mother set her jaws. "We was poor to begin with. Then, what with havin' to leave Baltimore so sudden . . ."

"I am not *blaming* you, Mrs. Parker. Just pointing out the facts of life. How do you propose to survive while you start making a living?"

She started to say something, but Crowell cut her off.

"Never mind that. 'Survive' isn't the word I meant. I don't doubt you could 'survive,' but you'd be so dirt poor you'd be nothing but an anchor dragging behind this community. We don't need that, Mrs. Parker. The last thing Arkansas needs is deadweight. Meaning no offense, but that's what dirt-poor people are. Deadweight."

He pushed himself back from the chair a little. "Patrick established that as the very first rule, here—and all of us in the Iron Battalion agreed with him. Black people are welcome in Arkansas, but they've got to pull their weight. That's the main reason we set up this bank in the first place, back then. We'll loan people money to get started, but they've got to put up collateral. And if they've got nothing but able-bodied men in the family, then those men have to agree to serve a term of enlistment in the army."

"What if we were just women?" his mother asked, her eyes narrowing. "Did you and this fancy 'Mr. Patrick' set up a whorehouse, too? Loan us money if we put up our cunts for collateral?"

Uncle Jem winced. "Lemon!"

But all Crowell did was chuckle again. "No, Mrs. Parker. Patrick and I are running no brothels in this town. There are a couple, I'm told, but they're strictly private enterprise. To answer your question, if the borrowers are females only, we'll accept a job in one of the local workshops as collateral. But the terms aren't as good."

"What *are* the terms, Mr. Crowell?" Sheff's uncle spoke a bit hastily, probably to keep his sister from another outburst.

The big banker looked at him. "Good as you could ask for. We'll loan any family three hundred dollars for every man who enlists, two hundred for every woman or boy or girl in a workshop. The interest is five percent, compounded annually. The loan has to be paid back monthly—but we'll waive the interest for the whole family as long as at least one man is serving in the colors. And for every man who completes a term of service satisfactorily, we'll knock a percentage point off the interest."

He glanced at Sheff's mother and sister, and then at Sheff. "In your case, that means we'll loan you a thousand dollars even. No interest accumulates as long as either you or young Sheffield is still in the colors. Once both of you have finished your terms of duty—assuming you were discharged honorably—we'll start charging you three percent on whatever the balance is. The truth is, you can't find a better loan anywhere. Either here or in the United States."

Sheff had no idea if he was telling the truth or not, since what he knew about banking was that . . . well, it was a white man's business. He'd never known a black man who even went to a bank, much less owned one.

From the dubious expression on her face, it was obvious his mother was just as ignorant. But his uncle seemed satisfied. Not, probably, because he actually knew anything. But just because, as with Sheff himself, he was inclined to trust Mr. Crowell.

Crowell was famous, too, after all. And if most of that fame was due to his horrible mutilation, there wasn't actually any sign of it on the man himself. Not visibly, anyway, covered with that fancy clothing. Maybe he was a little fatter than he would have been otherwise. But it was hard to know. Men that big usually ran to fat, some, once they got a little older.

Sheff thought he was a nice man, though. Not that it really mattered. Even if Crowell had been poison mean, Sheff would have been inclined to take his word for something. The man was a *banker*. The only black banker Sheff had ever heard of.

"We'll do it," said Sheff's uncle firmly. "Be quiet, Lemon. You've had your say, and you ain't my mother, even if you are older than me."

"I'm *Sheffield's* mother."

His uncle smiled, and nodded toward Sheff. "And so what, girl? I mean, *look* at him. You tried to stop your son, he'd just run away and enlist anyhow."

Sheff tried to look innocent when his mother gave him a sharp glance. It wasn't easy. He'd spent a good part of the past half hour trying to decide between two different ways he could run away and join the army. Daytime or nighttime.

There were advantages and disadvantages, either way. Daytime would be harder to make his getaway without his mother catching him, but he could probably enlist on the spot. Wherever the spot was. Nighttime, he'd have to wander around some in the dark.

"Would you do that, Sheff?" his mother demanded.

"No, ma'am. 'Course not."

She just rolled her eyes and threw her hands up in defeat.

By midafternoon, Sheff was in a state that bordered on sheer ecstasy. It was all he could do not to bounce up and down like a little boy.

He had a *uniform!*

True, it was too big, and his mother insisted the tailoring was poor, which it probably was. The cloth was pretty stiff and rough on his skin, too.

Sheff couldn't have cared less. It was a *uniform!*

His uncle Jem seemed almost as pleased as he did.

"Oh, stop nagging, Lemon," he said to Sheff's mom. "They didn't cost us nothing. 'Sides, why don't you just do the fixing-up yourself when we get a chance? You're handy with a needle."

"Needle!" Lemon Parker gave the uniforms a look that was none too admiring. An outright glare, in fact. "Need a knife—no, a spear—to punch holes in that stuff."

Uncle Jem grinned. "Maybe they're bulletproof, then."

Before his sister could continue with her protests, Jem turned away from her and examined the room they'd gotten in the big boardinghouse. Now, his own expression took on a look of disapproval. Not deep disapproval—certainly nothing akin to the glares Sheff's mother was still giving the uniforms—just the skeptical look that an experienced carpenter bestows on the work of lesser craftsmen.

"Pretty crude," he muttered.

Even Sheff could see that that was true. The boardinghouse, from the outside, had looked more like a huge log cabin than any boardinghouse or hotel Sheff had ever seen in Baltimore. On the inside, it looked about the same.

But, again, he couldn't have cared less. He had a *uniform!* The garment was a magic shield, shedding all the minor cares of life as if they were so many raindrops.

"Never you mind, Jem!" Sheff's mother shook her head. "Me and Dinah can patch up what needs it." Shrugging: "It's solid built, whatever else. A lot more solid built than you and my little boy are, when men start shooting at you."

"There ain't no war going on, Ma," Sheff protested. But, even in his high spirits, he didn't miss the fact that his uncle had grimaced slightly.

No, there wasn't a war going on. Leaving aside clashes with wild Indians, anyway. But even at sixteen, Sheff knew enough about the world to know that a war was most likely coming.

He couldn't have begun to explain the politics that would drive that war. He was only just beginning to even think in those terms.

It didn't matter. All he had to do was look down at that wonderful green uniform he was wearing. Would the sort of men who'd murdered his father just for being a black freedman allow the father's son to wear a uniform?

He didn't think so.

But he also didn't care. What mattered was that he *did* wear the uniform of the army of Arkansas. And he made a solemn vow to himself, right then and there, that he'd learn everything a soldier needed to learn. So that when the men came to murder the mother and the daughter, the son would murder them instead.

"And why are you lookin' so fierce of a sudden, boy?" asked his uncle.

Best not to answer that directly, or his mother would start squawking again. "Ah . . . just thinking of the Bible, is all."

Uncle Jem smiled. "The Old Testament, I hope."

"Book of Judges. Book of Samuel, too."

CHAPTER 7

By evening, Sheff's elation had become leavened by caution. According to the terms of their enlistment, Sheff and his uncle had been required to report for duty before nightfall. Which they'd done—and immediately found themselves assigned to a barracks on the outskirts of the city that made the construction of the boardinghouse look like the work of fine artisans.

Just a very long empty log cabin was all it was, with a single door at either end. The building had a row of bunks down each side, in three tiers, except for a fireplace on the north wall. The bunks were crammed so close together there was barely room to squeeze between them. They'd have covered up the windows completely, except there weren't any windows to begin with. And the space between the bunk tiers was so short that it looked to Sheff as if his nose would be pressed against the mattress of the man sleeping above him. Unless he got assigned to one of the top bunks, in which case his nose would be pressed against the logs of the roof.

The air would be horrible up there, too, with this many men crammed into so little space. To make things worse, there was still enough chill in the air at night that the fireplace in the middle of the barracks was kept burning. It had a chimney, of course, but Sheff had never seen a fireplace yet that vented all the smoke it produced.

There didn't seem to be enough spittoons, either, for that many men, half of whom Sheff could see were chewing tobacco. On the other hand, he couldn't see any sign that the men crammed into the barracks had been spitting on the floor, either, so maybe they emptied them regularly.

Chewing tobacco was a habit Sheff planned to avoid, himself. It just seemed on the filthy side, even leaving aside the fact that his pious mother and uncle disapproved on religious grounds. Sheff wasn't sure exactly why they did, since he'd never found anything prohibiting tobacco in the Bible, not even in Deuteronomy and Leviticus. He ascribed it to the fact that, in his experience so far in life, he'd found that people who were really devout tended to think a lot of things weren't proper, even if they couldn't exactly put their finger on any one place in the Bible where it said so.

About fifteen seconds after he and his uncle entered the barracks, standing there uncertainly after closing the door behind them, one of the men playing cards on an upended half barrel at the center of the room looked up.

"Just joined?" he asked.

Uncle Jem nodded. Sheff added, "Yes, sir."

The man exchanged thin smiles with his two fellows at the barrel. There was something vaguely derisive about the expressions.

"Sir, no less," one of them chuckled. "Lord God, another babe in the woods."

All three of the men at the barrel were black, but this one was so black his skin looked like coal. The eyes he now turned on Sheff were just as dark.

"We ain't 'sirs,' boy. We the sergeants of this outfit. 'Sirs' are officers. You salute them and act proper when they're around. Us, you don't salute. And while's you'll learn to act proper around us, too, it's a different set of rules."

Jem cleared his throat. "And those are . . . what?"

"You'll find out. Soon enough."

The third of the trio had never looked up from his cards. He now spoke, still without looking. "Only bunks open are two in the back," he said, giving his head a very slight backward tilt. "Both top bunks, but don't bother complaining."

He flipped a card onto the barrel. "I'm Sergeant Hancock. This here"—a flip of the thumb toward the sergeant who'd spoken first—"is Sergeant Harris. The one as black as the devil's sins is Sergeant Williams. He's the friendly one."

Williams grinned. "And he's the one who tells lies all the time." When he turned the grin onto Sheff and his uncle, it seemed full of good cheer. "I'm actually mean as Sam Hill, you cross me. But I'm sure and certain you boys wouldn't even think of that. Would you?"

That didn't really seem to be a question that required an answer, so Sheff kept his mouth shut. So did his uncle.

Williams grunted. "Didn't think so. Go ahead, now. Get yourselves settled in. So to speak. The captain'll be along shortly. Maybe—if you're real unlucky—the colonel, too."

Sheff and Jem did as they were told, edging themselves and their little sacks of belongings past the three sergeants at the barrel. None of them made the slightest effort to clear any space for them as they went by. From what Sheff could tell, they'd forgotten about the new arrivals altogether and were concentrating completely on their card game.

As Sheff and his uncle made their way to the back of the barracks, Sheff was surprised to spot three white men among the soldiers. He'd had the impression that the army of Arkansas was all black, except for some of the officers.

That officers would be white was a given. The only thing surprising there was that Sheff knew some of them were black, even including the colonel who commanded the regiment. But he hadn't expected to encounter white men in the enlisted ranks.

Two of them were no older than he was, either. Including, he discovered as he came up to the bunk he'd been assigned to, the soldier who'd be sleeping below him.

The situation was . . . strange. Confusing, too.

The white boy on the middle bunk looked away from the book he was reading and gave Sheff a smile. "Got stuck on the top, did you? Poor bastard. But at least you're in a corner bunk. There's enough cracks in the wattling that you'll be able to breathe. Some, anyway. 'Course, you'll hate it come winter. But who knows? By then you might be promoted, or dead. That's for sure and certain my plan."

Sheff wondered how he'd been able to read at all. The space in the middle bunk was so tight that the boy had had to keep the book pressed practically against his nose.

Now the boy lowered the book onto his chest—which didn't require shifting it more than two inches—and gave Sheff's little sack a scrutiny. "Won't be no room for that, up there. But there's still some space under the bottom bunk."

Seeing Sheff's hesitation, his smile got more cheerful still. "Relax. Bean't no thieves in this company."

The black man on the middle bunk across from him snorted sarcastically. "You livin' in a dream world, Cal. Plenty of these curries be thieves. It's just that they terrified thieves."

He rolled over to face Sheff, his shoulder barely clearing the bunk above him. There was no smile on his face, but he seemed friendly enough.

"He's right, though, boy. You don't got to worry about nobody stealing nothin' here. Not from another soldier, anyway."

This soldier was much older than Sheff or the white boy. At a guess, somewhere in his midthirties—about the same age as Sheff's uncle. On his way down the line of bunks, Sheff had noticed that the age spread among the soldiers was considerable. None of them had seemed any younger than him, but he'd spotted one man who had to be at least fifty.

That seemed a little odd to him, also. But, then, he really knew very little about armies and soldiering.

Yet, anyway. He planned to learn, applying himself to the task.

"My, don't he look fierce all of a sudden?" chuckled the white boy. "Must be thinking of the Bible. I just hope he don't talk in his sleep, like Garner does. Not sure how much Leviticus I can take, droning in my ear when I'm trying to sleep."

The older black soldier across from him echoed the chuckle. "Say that again."

That really did seem like a friendly smile on the boy's face. Sheff felt tension he hadn't even realized was there start to fade away.

He had other memories of white people beyond those of hateful and screaming faces beating his father to death, after all. One of his closest playmates, growing up, had been a white boy from a family living nearby. Until . . .

The world pulled them away from each other. Ed Rankin, his name had been. Sheff still found himself missing him from time to time.

So, finally, he smiled himself. "I do read the Bible," he allowed. "But I don't talk in my sleep—and I bean't too fond of Leviticus anyway."

By then, his uncle had muscled his way onto the top bunk above the older black soldier. "Lord in Heaven," he muttered, edging into blasphemy. "What kind of no-account carpenter built a bunk bed that don't give you no more than two foot of space from the ceiling?"

"His name's Jeremiah McParland," said the white boy immediately. "He's not a carpenter, though. He's the member of the family in charge of the bunk bed department, and he designed them. The space is twenty inches, by the way." The boy shook his head. "I had words with him about it. Pointless though it be. He always was the greediest member of the family."

Seeing the confused look on Sheff's face, the boy's smile widened. "I'm Callender McParland. Family's rich now that we set up in Arkansas, since we own the biggest furniture company here. And the captain's a cousin of mine. Don't do *me* no good, though. The colonel's that monster Jones. General Ball's still worse—and the Laird is worse yet. Even if cousin Anthony was inclined to play favorites—which he ain't, the bastard—he wouldn't dare nohow."

There was a commotion at the far end of the barracks. Peering around the corner of the bunk, Sheff saw that two men had come in through the same door he and Jem had used.

One was white; one was black. The white one was average size; the black one was very tall and long-legged. Both of them were officers, from the fancy look of the uniforms.

The three sergeants at the barrel had come to their feet. *"TEN-shut!"* hollered Sergeant Harris.

Immediately, the white officer said loudly, "At ease, men."

From what little Sheff could tell at the distance, he seemed a friendly enough sort. Although it could just be that he'd been smart enough to realize that it would take nigh on forever for men crammed into three-tiered bunk beds to come to attention on the floor.

The black officer with him, though, didn't seem friendly at all.

The white officer came forward a few steps. "We've had

five more recruits since my last inspection. My name's Anthony McParland, for those of you who don't know, and I'm the company captain." He nodded back toward the black officer. "And this here is Colonel Jones. He's in command of the regiment."

They were both young men, Sheff suddenly realized. The uniforms had confused him, at first, automatically imparting an aura of age along with authority. But now he could see that Captain McParland was somewhere in his midtwenties and Jones not more than a few years older.

"Our complement is now full," the captain continued. "That means we start real training tomorrow. *Early* tomorrow."

Suddenly his face broke into a big smile, and Sheff could easily see the family resemblance to the young soldier in the bunk next to him. "We'll start teaching you how to kill white men. With some exceptions. Me, for starters. Anybody else in a green uniform. Civilians, of course."

The black colonel moved forward. Unlike the captain, his face was marked by a scowl.

"Don't get all eager, you dumb curries. You want to know how you kill white men? Lots of 'em, I mean, in great big heaps. Not just maybe one, here and there, while you're running like rats."

He waited, still scowling, while silence filled the barracks.

"Didn't think so," he grunted. "Well, boys, forget any fancy dreams you got about muskets and cannons and such. The way you kill lots of white men—any color of men—is by learning how to walk better than they do. Walk faster, walk farther, walk longer—and do it while carrying more than they can. Simple as that. By midmorning tomorrow—I guarantee it—you'll have learned that lesson. And you'll keep learning it, and keep learning it, and keep learning it, until even curries as ignorant as you understand it in the marrow of your bones."

He grunted again. "You'll find out." With no further ado, he turned and walked out of the barracks. The captain made to follow but paused in the open doorway and looked back. The smile seemed as wide and cheerful as ever.

"Don't eat much," he said. "I mean it. You really don't

want to eat much. Neither tonight nor—specially—
tomorrow morning. Of course, you probably won't have
time anyway."

Then he was gone.

"I do believe I'm going to forgo the big repast I was planning," McParland said. "Of salt pork and potatoes, that
being all we ever get, pretty much, so it ain't no big hard-
ship."

Sheff decided he'd do the same. Despite the smile, he
didn't think the captain had been really joking.

They were spilled out of the bunks by the sergeants somewhere around four o'clock of the morning. Felt like it, anyway. It was sure and certain still dark outside.

"This is 'morning'?" complained one of the soldiers.
Softly, though, almost under his breath. The sergeants were
definitely not in a joking mood.

Sheff shared the sentiment, but . . .

He reminded himself of the Book of Judges and—most
of all—of a mob beating his father to death, and he kept his
mouth shut.

By ten o'clock that morning, miles into the most godawful
set of hills and hollows Sheff had ever seen, he was on his
knees puking up what little food he'd had in his stomach.
Cal McParland was kneeling right next to him, doing the
same.

His feet ached, his legs felt as if they were burning from
coals within, and the heavy pack on his back seemed like the
Rock of Ages. They'd been marching since dawn, with the
captain and the sergeants setting a murderous pace. At the start
of the march, Sheff had been disgruntled that they hadn't
been provided with muskets—or, indeed, any sort of
weapon beyond the knives they all carried in scabbards at
their belts, which were really more in the way of tools than
fighting gear. Now he was deeply thankful for it.

"Funny thing is," McParland finally managed to half
whisper, "I don't actually got nothing 'gainst white men.
Being's I'm one myself."

Sheff had wondered about that. "Why'd you enlist, then?"

he asked, in the same strained half whisper. "Your family bean't poor, like mine."

Somehow, McParland managed a shrug under that huge pack. "Something of a family tradition, now. And . . . well, we like Arkansas. Got nothing against the United States, really. But if they come here, not being polite about it, we decided we'll send them back."

There was something about that answer that seemed awfully fuzzy to Sheff. But . . .

There was also something about it that would probably look real good, clarified up some. He thought he was finally coming to understand—really understand—what Abraham's people felt when God led them into the Promised Land.

"On your feet!" bellowed Sergeant Williams, trotting down the line of exhausted men. "Break's over!"

Williams didn't look any more tired than if he'd just come back from an evening stroll. Sheff envied him that ease, but mostly it just filled him with determination. If Williams could learn to do it, so could he.

He heaved himself to his feet, giving Callender McParland a helping hand as he did so. The white boy was a lot more slender than he was. That pack had to be just about killing him.

"Thanks," McParland murmured. He managed something of a chuckle, once he was erect. "And will you look at these uniforms? Good thing they made 'em out of whatever this awful cloth is. Dirty as they are, least they bean't torn."

Sheff looked down at his own uniform, which was just about as dirty and scuffed up as his companion's. There wasn't much left of the new look it had had when he got it the day before.

"I don't mind," he said softly. "It's still green, and it's still a uniform."

Williams came trotting back, whacking a few slow-movers with one of the fancy-looking sticks the officers and sergeants carried. A baton, Sheff had heard them called.

"Move it, move it, move it!" he bellowed. "March is just starting, you lazy curries!"

He pointed with the stick to some mountains whose crest could just be seen from the hollow where the captain had ordered a brief rest for the company. "Before this march is done, you gotta be up there in the Bostons! And you will be, by God—or we'll leave you dead on the road!"

Sheff took a deep breath, staring up at those mountains. Next to him, McParland did the same.

Blasphemy in the army, Sheff had already discovered, was pretty contagious. "Sweet Jesus," McParland muttered.

"Just think of it as Mount Sinai," Sheff murmured back.

"You're crazy."

"Maybe. But what I am for sure and certain is a nigger. And that looks like Sinai to me."

The march lurched into motion again. For a few minutes, neither of them said anything.

Then McParland said: "People call me Cal. Can I call you Sheff?"

As exhausted as he was, Sheff thought that might be the most triumphant moment he'd ever had in his life so far. Not that he'd had many, of course, and this one wasn't really that big. But he could already see a road of triumphs shaping ahead of him. If he just kept marching forward, no matter how tired he was.

"Yes," he replied.

CHAPTER 8

County Down, Ireland
JUNE 3, 1824

"You owe these people nothing, Robert," said Eliza Ross. "That man, in particular."

She lifted her teacup from the side table next to her divan and used it to point to his shoulder. "Except for half crippling you."

The words weren't spoken angrily, or even in a condemnatory tone. They were stated matter-of-factly, as someone might present another piece of evidence to be weighed when a conclusion is being drawn.

Her husband was standing at the window of the Ross family seat in Rostrevor that gave him the best view of the Irish countryside. The hand he'd been using to hold back the curtains belonged to the same arm his wife had indicated with the cup. For a moment, half smiling, he studied that arm. Then, took away the hand, letting the curtains swing back into place.

"Hardly that," he murmured. "A quarter crippling, at worst. I can still use the arm, after all, and the hand's fine. I just can't lift much with it."

He didn't add, as he could have, that the arm ached frequently, especially in bad weather. His wife knew that already, and besides, that wasn't really what was at issue anyway. Eliza was no more given to nursing old enmities than he was.

Still at the window, he turned to face her squarely. And, from old habit, clasped his hands behind his back, ignoring the twinge of pain the gesture brought with it.

"What did you think of the letter itself?" he asked.

She finished draining the cup, set it on the side table, and looked down at the paper in her lap. Two sheets, it was, both covered with script written in some sort of particularly heavy ink.

"His handwriting's getting better," she said, a corner of her mouth quirking a little. "Mind you, that's not saying much."

Her husband's mouth matched the quirk with one of its own. "Amazing he does as well as he does, if you ask me. There's only four misspelled words in the whole letter—and three of them can be debated. I've seen worse dispatches from English noblemen, much less an Irish emigrant with no more than a village education. Even in English, much less French."

Eliza Ross picked up the sheets and held them closer to her eyes. She was a bit nearsighted. "And there's that, too, Robert. Why does he write in French instead of English?"

It was a rhetorical question, of course. So she moved right

on to provide the answer herself. "Because Patrick Driscol, born in Ireland, learned most of his letters while serving in Napoleon's army. Because he's a man who has been England's enemy his entire adult life. For years, long before"—this time, she used the sheets to point to Robert Ross's left shoulder—"he ruined your arm."

Again, her tone was level, not accusatory. Just another fact, to be presented.

"True," he agreed. "All true."

She lowered the sheets back onto her lap. "Robert, I feel I must remind you that your standing within English society has become somewhat frayed, of late. If you accept this invitation . . ."

Firmly, her husband shook his head. "Don't mince words, love. 'Somewhat frayed' hardly captures the thing. 'Tattered as a beggar's coat' would do better."

Eliza took a slow deep breath and then let it out in a sigh. "Well, yes. Among Tory circles, at least."

She did not bother to add, as she could have, that for Anglo-Irish of their class, after the rebellion of 1798, "Tory circles" amounted to the only circles in existence. In Ireland, at least, if not always in England.

She didn't add it, partly because it was unnecessary. But mostly for the simple reason that she didn't care much. A bit, perhaps, where her husband no longer cared at all. But not much.

Abruptly, Robert Ross released the handclasp and strode—marched, almost—to the wall opposite the window. Hanging there, in a heavy and ornate frame next to the door, was an illustration.

A very odd one, to be so prominently displayed in such a house. The Ross family was an old and much-respected one among the Anglo-Irish gentry. Robert's father, Major David Ross, had served with distinction in the Seven Years' War. A still earlier ancestor, Colonel Charles Ross, had been killed at Fontenoy in 1745, during the War of the Austrian succession.

Their portraits, along with those of other distinguished ancestors, hung on many of the walls in the family seat. Along with, on another wall in the very room they occupied, all the distinctions accumulated by the current and most renowned member of the line.

Robert Ross himself, who had retired from the British army with the rank of major general. On that wall—Ross could have pointed to it with his left hand, were he willing to ignore the pain raising the arm would have caused him— were the sort of trophies that precious few officers had ever accumulated in the long history of British arms.

There was the gold medal he'd received after the Battle of Maida in 1805, the British victory in the Peninsular War that most reports ascribed to the decisive leadership of Colonel Ross, as he then was. Hanging next to it was the sword his fellow officers had presented him four years later, in 1809. Officially, it was another honor for Maida. But really, everyone knew, in appreciation for Ross's actions and leadership during the terrible retreat to Corunna. His 20th Foot had more often than not been the rear guard in that retreat, holding off Soult and the French pursuers long enough to enable Sir John Moore's army to reach the port and embarkation to England.

Next to it hung the gold medal he'd received for the Battle of Vittoria, and the Peninsular Gold Cross. And next to those, the Sword of Honor.

Other mementos were there, too, some of them personally meaningful if not as officially prestigious. Had he been so inclined, Ross could have covered the wall with his mentions in Wellington's dispatches from the war. Quite easily. From his return to Iberia in 1812 until Ross was placed in command of the British expedition to North America in 1814, he'd led troops in every major battle in the Peninsular War except Toulouse. From 1813 on, following his promotion to major general, as a brigade commander. He was largely credited with having saved the British army from disaster at Roncesvalles and with having played a key role in the British victory at Sorauren.

A brilliant career, until the expedition to America and the repulse of the British at the Capitol. But, even there, Ross's personal gallantry had excited British admiration. And since Pakenham had been in command, not Ross, when the British army was beaten again at the Battle of the Mississippi, no opprobrium attached to him for that defeat.

It might have, had he been forced to defend Pakenham from public censure upon his return to England, as he'd fully intended to do. But Pakenham's valiant death at Lille in the final campaign against Napoleon had put paid to that. Another defeat, true, but Pakenham's impetuous assault had delayed Napoleon long enough for Wellington and Blucher to trap the French army at Tournai and force the French emperor to surrender.

There were other honors on other walls, won by his predecessors, and portraits aplenty of the predecessors themselves. All of which made the illustration hanging by the door seem out of place.

Grossly so, in the opinion of many of the Anglo-Irish gentry who had, in the years since the wars, visited Ross at Rostrevor. Wellington himself had come once, some three years earlier. The moment he spotted the illustration he'd exclaimed, "Oh, dear God, Robert! Why do you have *that* hanging on the wall?"

Wellington had recognized it immediately, of course. Detested though it might be by most of England's leading figures, the illustration was probably better known to the British populace by now than the portraits of any but kings and queens. First introduced to public attention in 1789 by Thomas Clarkson and Granville Sharp, the founders of the British antislavery movement, it was a diagram of the slave-trading ship *Brookes*.

It was a horrid thing, really. Which was, of course, its whole purpose: neatly and meticulously displaying, in the form of a top-down diagram, exactly how slaves were carried across the Atlantic. Lying side by side, like so many spoons nestled in a silverware drawer—or so much meat in one of the new tin-lined cans.

Of all the methods used by the antislavery movement to advance its cause, this single diagram had always been the most effective. Against it, the claims of slave traders that their business was a reasonably humane one were simply froth against a cliff. Its copy, though not often so finely drawn, hung in taverns and workingmens' homes and lawyers' offices all over Britain. Not to mention, by now, perhaps a third of its churches. Well over half of them, if one counted only the Dissenting churches.

After staring at the diagram for perhaps a minute, Robert said softly: "I owe Patrick Driscol nothing, Eliza. True enough. But I shall never forget what I saw in America. One memory, in particular, haunts me to this day. A man—black as he might be—with a collar around his neck. Like a watchdog's collar, except the spikes faced inward, pricking the skin. The contraption is a common form of punishment for slaves, at least in Louisiana. The man cannot sleep without injuring himself—possibly even dying."

"Yes, I know, Robert. You've described it to me."

Ross smiled, a bit crookedly. "An obsession, perhaps. But I find as I age—I'm nearing sixty, you know, now much closer to my death than my birth—I find myself obsessing over the afterlife. And I wonder, almost every day now, what God will have to say about my life when my judgment comes."

He was back to that soldierly handclasping. His head swiveled, to bring the wall of honors and trophies under scrutiny. "Will he really be impressed by all that? You can find the same sort of wall, I can assure you, in the houses and mansions of many generals in many nations. For many centuries now. Each of us claiming, as we meet gallantly on the field, that the Lord favors our cause."

He looked away, back to the diagram. "Or will He present this to me? And ask me what I did in battle against *this* monstrosity? How much will the defeat of Napoleon weigh, against this?"

He heard his wife's little laugh. "That damned Irishman! He's corrupted your thinking, Robert."

The retired general's smile grew more crooked still. "Perhaps. But what do you think, dearest?"

She said nothing for a time. Then, in the same level and matter-of-fact tone: "I think that I am your wife. The same wife who rode a mule across more of Spain than I wish to remember, after you were wounded at Orthes."

"Yes," he said softly. "I remember. The weather was frightful."

"Not as frightful as the sunny day you set sail for America. I was sure I'd never see you again, Robert. And I almost didn't."

He left off his examination of the diagram to look at Eliza. Her face was tight, perhaps, but quite composed.

"I am your wife, Robert. And you shall not leave me behind this time. If you are bound and determined to return to America, in response to"—she clutched the sheets in her right hand and held them up—"the damned Irishman's request, I shall not stand in your way. But you will not leave me behind. Not again."

"Surely you don't fear—"

For the first time, some anger came into her face. Not fury, simply exasperation. "Oh, stop it, Robert! You know perfectly well why Driscol is asking you to visit him. After—what has it been, now? Nine years? Nine years of the most peculiar correspondence in the world, but none of it was accompanied by any suggestion that you might actually come to America yourself instead of simply giving him some advice from a distance."

She brought her left hand to the sheets. Looking, for a moment, as if she might crumple them altogether. But, after a slight pause, she used the hand instead to flatten the sheets back out.

Then, smiling very crookedly herself: "And spare me the pious pose. I don't doubt you mean it well enough. But I know you better than anyone. You're like an old racehorse, looking at what might be your last starting gate."

"Don't be ridiculous!"

"Ridiculous? Patrick Driscol is expecting a *war*, Robert. That's why he's asking you to come. No other reason. And . . . so are you."

He unclasped his hands and waved the left. "I say again, ridiculous. It's far too soon to predict any such thing, Eliza."

"Predict? Of course not. But generals are not in the business of predicting outcomes. You've said that to me a hundred times if you've said it once. Generals are in the business of *gauging* outcomes. And you are gauging, Robert. Don't deny it. Not to me."

He didn't. For the simple reason that he couldn't. Major General Robert Ross was indeed gauging what might be the last war of his life. And the one that might—just might—be the one that saved his soul.

After so many decades, he was tired of duty to king and country. He'd paid that duty, paid it in full—and had the wounds as well as the honors to prove it. Wounds that ached everywhere he went, whereas the wall of honor was there only on the occasions he entered this room.

"Besides, there's Ireland," he murmured.

"What was that?"

"Ah . . . never mind."

Eliza was considerably more broad-minded than most people of her class, but she still retained most of its basic outlook. Whereas at the age of fifty-seven there was very little left at all, in Robert Ross, of the young man from Anglo-Irish gentry who'd enlisted in the 25th Foot right after graduating from Trinity College in Dublin. Except courage and determination, he liked to think. The years and the wars had burned most of it away, especially that horrible war in America. And what had remained had been slowly scoured off by his years working with Clarkson and Sharp. He was no Quaker, like so many of the supporters of the antislavery movement, and never would be. But their piety was contagious, in its own way.

The general who'd been active in the British army had never wondered much about such things. No need to, really, when it was obvious that God was an Englishman. But his years since Napoleon's defeat rubbing shoulders with the men in the antislavery movement had undermined that certainty.

What was left was Ireland itself. Bleeding, tortured Ireland. Ross had never seen anything he could do, in his life, that would have benefited Ireland. But perhaps he and another Irishman, on another continent, could prevent another such endlessly suppurating wound.

It seemed worth a try, at least. There was some evidence in the New Testament, if you looked at it properly, that Jesus would favor the Irish. Quite a bit, actually. Perhaps more to the point, Ross had read the Bible front to back three times over since his return from America. Noticing, each time, that nowhere was God's color recorded.

He might even be black. Worse yet, He might have no color at all. How, then, to explain one's inaction, knowing of the *Brookes*? For Eliza, as for most Englishmen and Englishwomen—most members of the antislavery movement, for that matter—the blacks depicted as so many spoons in a drawer were miserable and suffering souls. Faceless, for all that.

But, at the age of fifty-seven, Robert Ross could now see his own wife and children on that ship. Something which, he could now understand, Patrick Driscol had been able to see since he was a boy.

"Dear God, I miss the man!" he said, as surprised as he'd ever been in his life.

Over dinner, when he told the children their plans, his oldest son raised an objection.

"I'd like to go, too."

Mrs. Ross shook her head. "David, your education—"

"Oh, Mother! I'm sick of boarding schools. Fine enough for the younger ones, but I need a change. Trinity can wait a year or two." Pouting, a bit: "Besides, it'd be good for me. Broadening of the horizons, all that. Boys my age do it all the time on the continent. The Germans even have a name for it."

"Wanderjahr," his father supplied. "Yes, I know."

He and Eliza looked at each other. After a moment, she shrugged. "As stubborn as he is, I suppose we may as well. He'd just waste a year at Trinity with sulking."

Robert nodded. "Very well, then."

Naturally, that immediately stirred up the other four children. But there, Robert held the line. Leaving aside the fact that they were too young to be interrupting their educations and forgoing the salutary discipline of boarding schools, there was the factor of disease to be considered. At nineteen, David was old enough that he'd be taking no more risk than an adult.

"No," he said. Then, swiveling his gaze as he'd once had cannons swiveled: "No. No. No."

Three days later, he set off for London. The ship he and Eliza and David would be taking to America wouldn't leave for weeks yet, and he had some final business to attend to.

Clarkson approved. No surprise there. Thomas Clarkson was the brawler of the movement. The man who, though no more a Quaker than Ross, had decided at the age of twenty-five, in June of 1785, that slavery was an abomination. And had devoted the rest of his life to ending it—throwing into that cause his fine education at Cambridge, his unflagging energy, and his extraordinary skills as a political organizer.

"When will you return, Robert?"

Ross shrugged. "Hard to say. Not for a year, certainly. Probably two. Possibly three."

Clarkson's gaze was direct, as always. Intense blue eyes looked out from under a veritable shock of hair, much of which was still the bright red of his youth.

Looked down, rather. They were standing together in Clarkson's cluttered office, and Clarkson was a very tall man.

"And maybe never," he stated.

"Oh, that's nonsense, Thomas. I can't deny I'm looking forward to seeing America again. But you may rest certain that I have no intention of *living* there."

"That's not what I meant, and you know it. You may not live there, but you could easily die there."

Ross made a little grimace, indicating skepticism. "You can't ever rule that out, of course. But the risk of disease is not as bad as people think. Our army suffered terribly, true enough; those were the worst conditions imaginable."

"That's not what I meant, Robert," Clarkson repeated. "And you know it."

Ross said nothing, for there was nothing to say. After a moment, Clarkson slouched into his chair. "Well, so be it. We'll miss you greatly, Robert. Having a military figure of your prominence allied with us has been a tremendous boon to our cause these past years."

"You think I shouldn't go, then?"

Clarkson shrugged. "I didn't say that. Nor do I even think it." He was silent for a much longer moment, his elbow perched on the armrest and his chin propped on a fist. Now, however, he bestowed that startlingly direct gaze on a stack of shelves covered with books and papers.

Finally, very quietly, he said: "Whatever we do here in England—even in our Caribbean possessions—is really a sideshow. In the end, the issue will be decided in America.

For the first time, over there in Arkansas, men are finally beginning to test all the premises upon which all sides in this dispute rest their case. If that test succeeds . . ."

He smiled then, for the first time since Robert had given him the news. "A soldier's business, that, in the end. Which I am certainly not. Whether you have God's blessing, I couldn't begin to fathom. But go with my own, Robert Ross. Go with my own."

Wilberforce disapproved. No surprise there, either. Leaving aside the issue of slavery, and despite his notoriety as the leader of the antislavery movement in Parliament, William Wilberforce was a profoundly conservative man. He was opposed to extending the suffrage to men who were not propertied, and he was opposed to tactics that relied upon mobilizing the masses instead of persuading the elite. He disapproved in particular of women who chafed against their proper place in society.

He disapproved strongly of the theater, too.

"Why, Robert? What can you possibly do in America—not even the United States, but that preposterous little nation called Arkansas—that you can't do here? Think, man! Please put our cause above your own whimsy. You are the only significant officer in the movement. I can't tell you how invaluable an asset that's been to us in Parliament."

So it went, for two hours.

Ross divided the rest of his time in London between lesser luminaries in the movement for which he had formed a personal attachment, and major luminaries in society as a whole for whom his attachments had grown very loose indeed.

Still. Protocol, as it were.

Wellington was gracious. No surprise there. He disapproved quite strongly of Robert's attachment to the antislavery movement. But, in the duke's case, that was simply due to his general conservatism. Wellington was no admirer of slavery.

Beyond that, the large and powerful Wellesley clan and its political allies had a debt to Robert Ross. The defeat of Wellington's brother-in-law Pakenham at the Mississippi might have produced a corrosive political issue in the years after the war, with Wellington's many enemies using the defeat as a stick against Wellington's own military accomplishments. True, Pakenham's valiant death in the final struggle against Napoleon had sapped most of that possibility. But the long and detailed analysis that Ross had published after the war concerning the campaign in the Gulf—which had been full of praise and admiration for Pakenham—had settled the question entirely.

Finally, there was politics, which was now Wellington's field of combat.

"I'm afraid many of my fellow Tories—Whigs, too, never mind what they claim—are too influenced by their immediate commercial ties to the slave trade and the Caribbean plantations. There is every reason in the world for England to welcome the creation of another nation in North America, south of Canada, regardless of the color or creed of its inhabitants. Especially located where the Confederacy is, in the heart of the continent. If it survives, it would serve as a useful check on American ambitions. A natural ally for England."

The duke gave Robert a skeptical glance. "Mind you, I question whether those niggers and wild Indians are up to the task."

Robert smiled thinly. "As to the first, we could visit Thornton's grave and ask his ghost. He's buried not far from here."

Wellington smiled back. Just as thinly, but it was a smile. Thornton had been one of England's best regimental commanders. He'd died on the Mississippi, and his regiment had been shattered by the black soldiers of the Iron Battalion.

"A point," the duke admitted. "Could the Americans field a force as good as Thornton's 85th? Not likely. Not even close. But numbers *do* count, Robert; never forget that. There are now some ten million Americans, and how many people in the Confederacy? Two hundred thousand, all told? Such a disparity in numbers cannot be overcome simply by valor and skill at arms."

They were standing in Wellington's garden. Now that summer was here, and with Wellington's small army of gardeners, it was a glorious place. Robert took a few seconds to admire the scenery before answering.

"Very true. But *only* true if those numbers can be mobilized. And as to that . . ."

He scrutinized a nearby hedge as if he were gauging the strength of an enemy line. "You might be surprised if you met some of the leaders of those 'wild Indians.' John Ross, in particular, is quite a diplomat. Was, even when I knew him as a very young man. And there are many Americans who would not support such a war, I think."

The duke was too familiar with foreign affairs to be put off so easily. "Not in New England, certainly. But what difference does that make? Andrew Jackson would, from everything I know of the man. And it was he and his forces—quite good ones, as you explained yourself at the time—who defeated us in the Gulf. If he went against Arkansas, could they withstand him?"

Robert didn't need to consider the question. He'd been considering it very carefully for some time now. "A full-fledged Andrew Jackson campaign, such as the one he mounted against us in the war? No, I don't think they could. They'd put up a ferocious battle, but they'd lose in the end. Jackson could organize and lead a very large army of his frontiersmen. Large, at least, by the standards of North America. And he's too capable, too determined—too relentless, most of all—for any nation with less than a quarter million inhabitants to withstand him. Not for more than a year or two, at any rate."

He looked away from the hedge to the duke. "But would he do so in the first place? He's not a savage, I assure you, despite some of the reports of him in the newspapers here. A very shrewd man, in fact, and with political ambitions of his own. So I think it would depend on how the war started, and over what issues, and based on whichever constellation of political alliances. Things which are far too complex to ascertain in advance, certainly from a distance."

"But you *are* expecting a war?"

Robert shrugged. "Say rather that Patrick Driscol is expecting a war. For myself, I wouldn't venture an opinion yet. As I said, it's too soon and I'm too far away."

The duke sniffed. "He's a sergeant."

Robert made no reply. Anything he said would simply stir up Wellington's haughty nature, always close to the surface.

In point of fact, Robert knew, Patrick's assessment was not even the crude strategic sense of a sergeant. It was something deeper and cruder still. The gut instinct of an Irish rebel that the Sassenach would someday be coming. Sassenach *always* came, until and unless they were beaten bloody, simply because they were Sassenach.

And, as he'd once told Robert, the color of their coats didn't define "Sassenach" at all. That much of wisdom the refugee from the rebellion of 1798 had learned in the years that followed.

The rest of the afternoon went very pleasantly as they reminisced over old times. Two veteran soldiers, now grown rather distant, but once very close comrades-in-arms in the most desperate war in centuries.

The Duke of Clarence refused to see him at all. No surprise there, either, although it was quite rude. But the heir to the throne was one of slavery's most public advocates.

Truth be told, Robert had requested the audience only to satisfy a mild urge to poke a stick in the crown's underbelly. Mad King George III had been succeeded by a dissolute King George IV, who was now likely to be succeeded by a younger brother who was possibly more dissolute still.

Well, a day. He'd done his social duties. Now, there was a long voyage. And, at the end of it, a man waiting for him that Robert could not precisely call a friend, nor precisely call an enemy, nor precisely call much of anything.

Except, not dissolute. Never that.

CHAPTER 9

New Antrim, Arkansas
AUGUST 6, 1824

Sam loved coming to Arkansas. Whatever open hostility or veiled antagonism he ran into these days in the United States, he encountered none of it in New Antrim. His entrance into the town—city now, really—had turned into something of a triumphal procession, once news of his arrival started to spread.

Another window filled with women, waving at him. Just the latest of many in the second and third stories of the buildings that flanked New Antrim's main street.

He waved back, grinning. True, all of them were black, and only one of them was young and pretty. But those days were behind him, anyway, and the broad smiles were enough to cheer the gloomiest curmudgeon in the world.

Chester was riding next to him, leading their remounts. "This too shall pass," he murmured. "This too shall pass."

Sam never stopped grinning, though. "I deeply regret having urged you to read the Romans. Besides, you're supposed to be whispering it into my ear, riding behind me on a chariot."

"We don't got a chariot, Mr. Sam," Chester pointed out reasonably. "Got four horses. And one of them's a nag."

"The one riding the horse next to me is the nag. Mary's just a little worn out and tired, is all."

"Shoulda left her with that tanner, back on the river."

The last jest finally caused Sam's grin to fade a little.

That tanner . . .

"What in God's name is Patrick up to?" he muttered.

Loudly enough for Chester to hear, unfortunately. His response caused Sam's grin to fade a little more.

"Stirring up trouble, what else?"

Patrick was there, along with Tiana, to greet Sam when he arrived at the hotel. Standing right on the porch of the Wolfe Tone, just like a proper laird surveying his domain.

And why not? His hotel was not only the biggest building in the city but the only one with a wraparound front porch. Almost the only one with any sort of porch at all, in fact. Sam loved the energy and vitality of New Antrim, but there was no getting around the fact that its architecture fell woefully short of the standards in any city in the United States.

Any big collection of barbarians in ancient Gaul, for that matter. He'd allow that it was probably superior to Hun encampments.

"We expected you weeks ago," were the first words out of Patrick's mouth, as soon as Sam dismounted.

"How I've missed that rasp of yours." Sam handed the reins to Chester. "Tiana, it's good to see *you*."

Tiana just smiled. It was a more serene smile, these days, than the hoyden one Sam remembered from the girl she'd been. It made her beauty more striking than ever. As he always did, encountering Tiana again after a prolonged absence, he felt a twinge somewhere in his heart.

But that was just an old reflex, grown almost comfortable with the passage of time. And not much of one, in any event. Sam's marriage to Maria Hester had eliminated most thoughts of other women.

Not all, of course. But most.

There came the rush of little feet from within the darkness of the hotel interior. A moment later, two boys emerged. One was six and a half years old; his brother, a year younger.

"Sam's here! Sam's here!" they announced to the world in unison before leaping off the porch and into his arms.

Laughing, Sam held them up. "You're getting big. Both of you."

"Sam's here! Sam's here!"

"Hush," Tiana scolded. "You'll wake your sister."

To prove her point, an infant's wail emerged from one of the windows on the second floor.

"Oh, blast," said Tiana. She gathered her skirts and vanished back into the hotel.

Sam set the boys down. "Luckily for them—and the world—they look like Tiana, not you." He gave Patrick a sly smile. "Might make a suspicious man wonder . . ."

Patrick's returning smile was a thin sort of thing. But that was just the nature of the man. He was neither offended nor made anxious by the remark. Nor, from anything Sam knew, had he any reason to be.

"Stop playing the clown, would you?"

"Oh, fine. I can remember—I think—when you had a sense of humor, Patrick. The reason I'm weeks late is because there was another Chickasaw killing. I heard about it right after leaving the Hermitage. I needed to settle things down before it all spun out of control."

"Who killed who?"

"Who killed how many, is more the question. And in what order. It started as a clan killing. Then—I never did figure out the wheres and wherebys—somehow three settlers got involved. Two of them wound up dead, along with two Chickasaws. One from each clan, to make things perfect. There were only three survivors. One white man and one each from both of the contending clans."

Patrick's blocky head made a little quiver. From another man, that might have been called a headshake. "So you had three completely different stories. How did our young Solomon settle it? And would you like some whiskey?"

"Yes. The whiskey first. The settlement was far too complicated to explain sober. It displeased everybody, of course, but since I confused them even more, it all worked out well enough."

As they entered the hotel's big lobby, Sam asked, "Why is Tiana wearing a fancy dress?"

Patrick was heading toward the saloon doors in the far wall. Over his shoulder, he said: "What do you think happens when you're this late? John Ross and Major Ridge got tired of waiting for you in Fort of 98. So they came down to New Antrim. In fact, they're already here in the hotel."

Sam made a face. "Whiskey for sure, then. What is it this time?"

By now they were in the saloon. Patrick went behind the

bar, hauled up a bottle, and started filling two small glasses. One, he filled to the top. The other, barely half. He handed the full one to Sam.

"The usual, most of it. Problems with the Osage. Problems with Cherokees who start quarrels with the Osage, as if there weren't quarrels enough. Problems with Comanches, too, now."

Sam scowled, as he picked up the glass. "Comanches? I'd hoped they'd avoid that. The Comanches are . . ." With his free hand, he gestured vaguely to the west.

"Not far enough west," Patrick stated. He took a small sip from his glass. "Not far enough, with Creek and Cherokee clans spreading up the rivers the way they've been. Not with Comanches, for sure."

He set the glass down with a little clink. "But the big problem is the runaway slave business."

Sam drained half the glass in one swallow. "Just what we needed. What happened this time? The usual?"

"No, worse. One of the chiefs decided I wasn't serious about the rules against unauthorized slave-catching. Not applied to Cherokees. So he sent three men here, looking for one of his runaway slaves."

Sam stared at him, the glass frozen on its way back to the bar top. "Patrick. You *didn't.*"

Driscol's square, harsh face looked like it was carved from stone. "Of course I did." He jerked his blocky jaw slightly, indicating a nearby window. "Hung two of them in the street, where I always hang the ones from the U.S. Hung all three, actually, but the third one was already dead. Stupid bastard tried to fight James, if you can believe a Cherokee being that dumb."

Tiana's half brother James was something of a legend among the Cherokee, true enough. But Sam's only wonder was that the other two *hadn't* tried to fight him, rather than be captured. Driscol was a legend, too.

Now more than ever.

"Are you *trying* to tear everything apart?"

"Be damned to that," Driscol rasped. "Nowhere in the Confederacy's constitution does it say that Arkansas has fewer rights than any other chiefdom. The laws regarding slavery are set in the chiefdoms, each to its own. Says so in

Article VI, Clause Three. I'm the elected chief, and those are my rules. Everybody knows it. There's no slavery in Arkansas, and the only legal slave-catching is done by the legal authorities of the chiefdom."

He said the whole thing with a straight face, too.

"You're a troll," Sam muttered. He drained the rest of the glass. "And exactly how many escaped slaves have your 'legal authorities' returned to the Cherokees over the past two years?"

"One. Which, I will point out, is one more than I've ever turned over to slave-catchers from the United States."

Sam snorted. "Why that one? Was he too feebleminded to make his way into those 'secret' settlements you maintain in the Ouachitas? And don't bother claiming you don't, Patrick. I know it, you know it, and for sure and certain every Cherokee knows it. Every Creek, too. For that matter, every slave-owner in the States."

"The truth? He wanted to go back. Once he got here and discovered freedom meant harder work than what he had with the Cherokees. Either that or a stint in the army."

Sam stared at him. Trying, for a moment, to think of any argument he hadn't already used with Patrick.

He couldn't think of a single one. On this subject, Patrick Driscol was the personal embodiment of the term *intransigent*.

So he fell back on the old staple. "This can't go on forever, Patrick."

"True enough. Either they break or I break. Guess which is more likely to happen."

Sam's temper was rising, now. "Patrick, without the Cherokees you don't have your legal fig leaf! If they declare you an outlaw chiefdom—"

"Don't be stupid. Without *me,* they don't have anything. Not when the war comes."

That stopped Sam short. Like smashing into a wall a man didn't realize was there.

"Sweet Jesus," he whispered. "*That's* why the tanner's there."

"What are you talking about?"

Sam shoved the glass in front of him. "Pour me another. And stop playing the innocent. That tanner—John Brown's his name, as if you didn't know—that you and Henry set up down on the river. I wondered why you'd financed him, that far down from New Antrim. You *want* a war, blast your dark Irish soul—and he's your trigger. Your bait, too."

Driscol finished pouring the glass—just as full as the first—and then stoppered the bottle. "I will say all your drinking hasn't scrambled your brains yet. Yes, that's why we financed him to set up there. Mind you, it's good country for a tanner. A lot of livestock down there on the plain."

"He's the man who did the killing on the Ohio, Patrick. By now, enough people figured out who it was, and the word's spreading. You *do* know how much ruckus there's been over that incident?"

He waved his hand. "Never mind. Stupid question. Of course you know. Although you might not be aware—yet— that the anti-Relief party introduced a resolution in the Kentucky legislature condemning the act and demanding that the culprit be brought to justice. Clay's behind that, of course."

Chester came into the saloon, then. Seeing that he was carrying a saddlebag, Sam waved him over. "Oh, and let me show you this, too."

He rummaged in the bag for a moment and brought forth a folded-up newspaper. Then, half slammed it on the bar top and spread it open. "Lookee here." His finger pointed to an article on the front page. "Why, I do declare. That looks like a speech by our favorite U.S. senator, the Honorable John C. Calhoun. Invoking the fugitive slave laws and demanding that the administration catch the culprit. And hang him."

"Fat chance of that."

"No chance at all, with Monroe in office. But Calhoun'll take it to the Supreme Court if he can, just to prove a point."

Sam refolded the newspaper and stuffed it back into the saddle bag. "You cold-blooded bastard. You deliberately set Brown up on the river—right smack in the territory that those adventurers down in Louisiana are hollering and whooping about 'reclaiming for the rightful owners'—just to make sure they'd attack you."

"Actually, I tried to get him to enlist in the army. He and his two brothers. Offered him a commission, even. But—"

The thin smile came and went, in a flicker. "Brown's a most pious man. He told me he'd made a solemn vow as a youngster that he'd never join any army, on account of soldiers being such a blasphemous bunch. I couldn't argue the point, of course. They are a blasphemous bunch. So I made him the second offer—but not without explaining to him the risk."

"And?"

"And John Brown's a man after my own heart. He has a right to practice his trade, doesn't he? Yes, he does. And he'd be practicing it in territory legally ceded to the Confederacy in the Treaty, wouldn't he? Yes, he would. So what does he care if some slavers damned in the eyes of the Lord claim that since it's good bottomland they ought by rights to have it, and try to take it from him? At that point, he recited some verses from the Old Testament. By heart, mind you, he didn't need to refer to the Book. Bloodcurdling stuff. Every other verb was 'smote.'"

He lifted the bottle. "Another?"

Sam realized his glass was empty. "Yes—well, no. John and Ridge ought to be here any moment. Thanks to you, I'll need a clear head. Which is the last thing I wanted, after this many days on the road."

Patrick shrugged and set the bottle back down. "A clear head's probably useless, Sam. Face it, lad. Not every dispute can be negotiated. Sometimes heads have to be broken. Yes, I set up John Brown on the Mississippi like so much bait, dangled in front of those brainless ruffians down there in Alexandria. They'll be coming sooner or later, anyway, and I'd prefer to make it sooner. For no other reason than just to remind—"

He broke off, his eyes moving to the door. "Those two, among others."

Sam swiveled his head. John Ross and Major Ridge had entered the saloon. To his considerable surprise, though, they had a third Cherokee with them. Chief Bowles, of all people.

Ross had entered in time to hear Patrick's last sentence. "Remind us of what?" he asked, mildly.

"That the only thing that stands between you and another settler land grab are those negroes you keep wanting me to hand back over to you."

"Not me," said The Bowl immediately. He was smiling

quite pleasantly. "You're talking about these Cherokees in white men's clothes." He jerked his thumb at his two companions. "No runaway slaves from my clan. That's because we don't have any slaves in the first place. Well, not hardly."

His English was fluent. That was perhaps not surprising, given that The Bowl's physical appearance showed plenty of evidence of his Scot father even if his manner of dress was completely Indian. But Sam had grown up on the frontier and understood its complexities, and he'd known The Bowl for years. Bloodlines and attitudes were just as likely to veer apart as come together, among the Cherokees or any of the southern tribes. Where a mixed-blood like John Ross might incline strongly toward adopting American ways and customs, another one like Chief Bowles—or Duwali, to use his Cherokee name—was just as strongly inclined to maintain Indian traditions.

Then, to make things more complicated still, slavery got poured into the mix. Traditionalists like Chief Bowles's people would capture black slaves, in the course of fighting with white settlers, and put them to work in captivity. But thereafter the old customs would prevail, just as they had for generations with captives from other Indian tribes. Within a few years, as a rule, a black slave had gained his or her freedom. Almost certainly, their children would. Often enough, by being adopted into the clan or marrying a Cherokee, or both. Quite unlike the status that black slaves had on plantations run by mixed-bloods who considered themselves "civilized" and had adopted white customs wholesale—which could be almost as bad as their status on white-owned plantations in Georgia or Alabama.

Major Ridge was scowling. John Ross just gave The Bowl a glance that was half amused and half exasperated.

Then he turned to Sam. "Brace yourself. It's going to be a long afternoon."

Indeed, it was. Sam didn't dare take another drink, as much as he desperately wanted to.

That night, Tiana threw a ball. She'd started doing that eight months earlier, after one of the English ladies who'd emigrated to Arkansas for reasons that defied comprehension had offered to teach everyone the latest dances. The affairs had become very popular with New Antrim's black population—at least that part of it that might be considered "upper crust."

But Sam knew that wasn't the reason she'd done it on this occasion. Like her husband, if in a more subtle manner, Tiana was also making a point.

Looking out over the crowd packed into the hotel's huge dining room, which doubled as a dance hall, Sam also realized that the point was only somewhat more subtle.

First, there were only five white people in the crowd.

Second, all five of them were wearing the uniforms of the Arkansas Chiefdom's army. Two officers and three enlisted men.

That hardly made them stand out, however, because—third—at least half of the men in the crowd were wearing uniforms.

"Out of Ireland, by way of Sparta," Sam grumbled.

"'Fraid I don't catch that, Mr. Sam," said Chester.

"Never mind. Get me a whiskey. No, two. Please."

After Chester left for the packed bar over to the side, Sam spotted John Ross and Chief Bowles and went over to them.

John Ross understood it just as well, of course. The man was as smart as any on the continent.

Fortunately, he was also even tempered. When Sam came up he just smiled. "Patrick does love to rub salt into wounds, doesn't he?"

"There's no give in the man, that's for sure. Where's the Ridge?"

Ross shrugged. "He knew what this was about, too. And he thinks dancing's silly. White men's dancing, anyway. So he's getting some sleep in his room."

"It *is* silly," chimed in The Bowl.

The worst of it was that they were all friends. Close ones, by now. Patrick also.

Eventually, John said: "And what can I say or do? Major Ridge is quietly furious, but he knows it just as well as I do. Arkansas is our shield."

"That's why you agreed to set it up," Sam pointed out.

"Yes, I know. The most obvious 'secret plan' in the history

of the world, probably. And like many such, it's backfiring on us."

The Bowl uttered a Cherokee curse word. Several, actually.

"It's your own fault. All you rich Cherokees, insisting on keeping your slaves. Set them free, why don't you? That'll solve the problem right then and there."

There was no answer to that, of course. Other than the most obvious one of all: *because they're what make us rich to begin with.* The same reason Thomas Jefferson had beaten his breast over slavery—and never freed his slaves.

"It'll wreck you," The Bowl predicted.

Finally, John Ross's mild temper frayed a little. "'Us,' don't you mean?"

The Bowl shook his head. "No, John. I mean *you.*"

And so another little mystery was solved. Sam had wondered why The Bowl had come all the way to New Antrim.

Now he knew, and, knowing, he silently cursed Patrick Driscol again. The man's unyielding determination to fight it all out was driving everything forward. Sensible or not—but there was a terrible logic to it. He'd splinter his allies and his enemies both, the way a rock on a beach divides the waves. Forcing everyone to meet him on his own field because he would not move at all.

His eyes met The Bowl's. The Cherokee chief nodded. "Way it is, Sam. No offense, but I'm not relying on any more white men." He tipped his head toward the dancers. "If there's a war, I'm with them. So are a lot of the other traditionalist chiefs. John here and the Ridge and all those other fancy folk can do whatever they want."

Chester returned, carrying two glasses. Sam took one of them and drained it immediately.

"Who do you want me to give the other glass to, Mr. Sam?"

"Don't give me any sass. You're a slave, remember?"

Almost grinning, Chester handed over the second glass. "Best not to beat me, though, Massa. Here in Arkansas, I can always run away."

Out of the corner of his eye, as he started on the second glass of whiskey, Sam could see John Ross's jaws tighten a little. But, for the first time in hours, Sam found himself amused.

"You! Up there in the Ouachitas!"

"It ain't likely," Chester agreed. "I gotten soft, these years with you. Used to the finer things in life."

So, Sam was able to end the evening relaxed as well as amused. There was always that, after all. Everything weaving in and out and around, like a ball of string too tangled to unravel any longer. Black men—Indians, too—learning how to fight and maneuver skillfully against white men, sure enough. But they couldn't do it without coming to resemble their foes. Even The Bowl and his people knew it, attached as they were to the traditional ways of the Cherokee.

It was a cheery thought. Sam didn't have any use for simplicity. The most treacherous ground in Creation, that was. Simple meant smooth, and smooth meant slick, and slick meant many a fall.

He even danced himself, at the end.

Not well, no, even though he was a very good dancer. Not after that much whiskey. But he didn't fall down, either.

The next morning, over breakfast, Patrick finally asked Sam the question.

"So. How was the general?"

Carefully, Sam laid down his spoon. Not because the spoon was fragile, or even expensive, but simply because he was doing everything rather carefully this morning. His head hurt.

"Gracious. Very gracious."

"No rancor there?"

Sam managed a careful smile. "No, not any at all. That I could detect, anyway. There is that one advantage to Andy's . . . ah, what to call it? Vigorous way of looking at things, maybe."

"Meaning Andy Jackson is more self-righteous than an eagle," said Tiana. "If women didn't exist, you'd have to invent us. Just to keep you from needing to invent a new language every ten years, the way you maim and mutilate the ones you got."

"Well. Yeah. The point being that if he wanted to get really mad at me for messing up his presidential prospects, he'd have to admit that speech he gave after Algiers was a bad mistake. Which he's no more likely to admit—not to himself, not to anybody—than the sun is to start rising in the west."

"But?" asked Patrick. "There's a 'but' somewhere in there, Sam. I can smell it."

Sam nodded. Carefully. "But, the last day—friendly-like, but also stiff and proper—he said that he felt that vow he'd made to me after the Horseshoe had been kept. So that shield is gone, Patrick."

Tiana took a deep breath. Patrick just shrugged. "It lasted ten years. That was enough. And he's right, anyway. He did keep it, as long as you could ask any honorable man to keep so vague and open-ended a promise."

Sam studied him for a moment. Then, a bit exasperated: "Patrick, if *he* ever comes at you, he'll crush you."

Andy Jackson might be more self-righteous than an eagle, but Patrick Driscol made any mule look wishy-washy. So Sam was expecting a stubborn denial. The answer he got surprised him.

"Oh, yes, I imagine so," Patrick said evenly. "But he won't."

The exasperation swelled. "Marie Laveau's been giving you lessons in fortune-telling, then? Patrick, you have no idea what Andy Jackson will do, if he takes a mind to it! He's just as riled over the runaway slave question as any slave-owner in the United States. And he's one of the biggest. Just had another one run away from the Hermitage a month before I arrived. Reported to have been heading here, naturally."

"No, I can't predict *what* he will do. But I can predict *how* he would do it."

Sam cocked his head, skeptically, then immediately regretted it. All the pain seemed to pour over to somewhere around his left ear, like water pouring off a ship's deck in a storm.

"And . . . that . . . means?" he said, through gritted teeth.

"It means he's very smart, Sam. He was a smart general, and he's a smart politician. I've done everything I could to make it plain as day to Andy Jackson that if he leads an army here, I'll bleed it and gut it. Half gut it, anyway. Yes, he'd probably win. But is it worth the cost? To his reputation, if nothing else?"

For the first time that morning, Patrick smiled. "He wants to be the next president of the United States, Sam. Failing that, the next. And he doesn't want the office simply out of ambition, the way Clay does, either. He wants it because there are things Andy Jackson believes in with a passion. You follow me so far?"

"An idiot can follow you so far." That came out more testily than it should have, being just the pain talking. Sam was actually getting intrigued. He'd half forgotten how shrewd a sergeant Driscol had been. Winfield Scott had once told him that Driscol was the best noncommissioned officer he'd ever met in his life—and when Sam passed the remark over to Robert Ross, the British major general had agreed.

They were much alike, in so many ways, Patrick Driscol and Andy Jackson. Scots-Irish to the core. Both crude and rough on the outside, and neither with much in the way of a formal education. And both with such sharp and pronounced personal characteristics that an unobservant man could easily miss the keen brains that lay beneath those thick skulls.

"Keep going," he said.

"Think it through, Sam. Yes, I know the general's furious about the runaway slaves. But was it runaway slaves who stripped thousands of poor white men of their belongings, after the Panic? Or was it the Bank of the United States, and their favored lawyer at the time, Henry Clay? Is it runaway slaves, on their way to Arkansas, who demand the retention of debt imprisonment? Or is it the men who are backing Clay and Crawford? Did any runaway slave ever accuse the general and Mrs. Jackson of being adulterers and bigamists? Or was that Henry Clay's creatures?"

Sam grimaced. Even Jackson's friends would admit—if not to his face—that there was indeed some murkiness surrounding his marriage. But who could possibly care? Rachel Jackson's first husband, Lewis Robards, had been a notorious brute and a man who copulated openly with his slave women. No one, not even Jackson's enemies, blamed Rachel for abandoning him. She and Jackson hadn't married until they'd received word from Virginia that Robards had divorced her. The fact that the divorce hadn't been finalized didn't reach them until later. For any honest man with no ax to grind, the whole issue was a legal technicality, and terms like "adultery" and "bigamy" were preposterous.

No one had ever been able to prove that Clay was behind those never-ending accusations and insinuations that kept surfacing in the press. But no one much doubted it, either—and Jackson didn't doubt it at all. It was that, more than anything, that gave Jackson's hatred of Clay such a sharp and unyielding edge.

And it was so typical of Clay. The Speaker of the House was almost the polar opposite of men like Jackson and Driscol. On the surface, as slick and smooth—and smart, no doubt about it—as any man in America. But underneath, a man whose brains were constantly corroded by naked ambition. Naked, because unlike Jackson's ambitions—which were every bit as great—there were few principles to serve ambition as a guide. So, the man couldn't distinguish clearly between small victories and big ones—and would, quite often, lose the latter because he could not resist the former.

Which, now that Sam thought about it, was also the opposite of Jackson. Even as pugnacious as he was, Andy would—Sam had seen him do it, time after time—forgo the pleasure of winning a small fight in order to win a bigger one.

"Ah," he said, finally understanding. "But . . . that's a Sam Hill gamble, Patrick."

Driscol had finished his own porridge and pushed it aside. Then, splayed out his square hand on the table. The movements weren't awkward at all, but they were just that little bit complicated. For the first time since he'd arrived in New Antrim, Sam was reminded that Patrick had lost his left arm at the Chippewa. One tended to forget, around such a man.

"Possibly. But I don't think Sam Hill would take it. Because he'd figure I'd likely win. The thing is, Sam, I'm betting that Andy Jackson is smart enough to know that when the time comes, he can negotiate a settlement with me. Not one he'd be very happy with, no, but one he could live with."

"Could he?"

Patrick shrugged. "Oh, yes. I'm not stupid. Sheltering runaways and maroons isn't any more critical to me than catching them is to Jackson. It's a dispute, that's all. A sharp one, granted. But we could work out a settlement." He smiled, the way a troll might. "Not that either one of us would call it a 'great compromise.'"

Sam chuckled. "But what if Clay wins the election? I have to tell you that he's most likely going to, Patrick. Even Andy will admit that nowadays, at least in private to his friends."

"All the better, so far as I'm concerned. Jackson would then be able to let someone else play the general, and fumble it—and then he can ride in and save the day. Four years later. What's four years, Sam? In the great scheme of things."

The boys came charging into the dining room. They got right to the verbs, as six-year-olds will. The nouns being self-evident to the world, since they were self-evident to them.

"You promised, Pa! You promised!"

Driscol pushed away from the table and rose. "So I did."

"Promised what?" Sam asked.

"That he'd take them up to the new fort today," Tiana answered. "They love forts. Do you know any little boys who don't?"

Sam was tempted to answer: *Don't know too many full-grown men who don't love 'em either. Especially if they're Scots-Irish.*

But he didn't, because as soon as the quip came to his mind he realized that Andy Jackson was one of them. The general built forts the way boys built tree houses—and, now that Sam thought about it, he realized that Andy always did prefer to fight on the defensive whenever he could.

"I'll be damned," he said.

He normally avoided blasphemy, just for the sake of appearances if nothing else. But Patrick was a freethinker, and the Lord Himself only knew what Tiana thought about such matters.

So he did it again. "I will be damned."

Patrick's rejoinder was inevitable, of course. "Most likely." But Sam paid that little attention. His headache was coming back with a vengeance.

"I need a drink," he announced.

Tiana didn't argue the point, since she never did. She just rose and went over to the cabinet.

"Hair of the dog, is it?" Patrick said. "Someday that dog'll swallow you whole, Sam."

But that was an old refrain, too, so Sam ignored it. The whiskey bottle was coming to the table, and he needed to think. Whiskey helped him think when he had a headache as bad as this one.

There might be an angle here . . . As reluctant as he was to use it, Sam's father-in-law had his own connections to the press. Very good ones, as you'd expect. Perhaps more important, so did John Quincy Adams. Who also hated Clay, because Clay's creatures had slandered him over the Treaty of Ghent. And though the issue was not as personal as the issue over which Clay and his people hounded Jackson, Adams took his reputation as a diplomat seriously.

For reasons he could never quite fathom, Sam was quite fond of Adams, and the two of them got along well. He hadn't seen him now in . . . two years? Time for a visit, perhaps.

The first slug of whiskey cleared his brain marvelously. And the sight of Patrick and Tiana embracing before he departed with his children reminded Sam that he hadn't seen Maria Hester and his son in months, either.

"I'll be going soon," he announced as Patrick headed for the door.

"Figured you would. Don't forget to toss a few bones to John Ross and Ridge before you leave."

The second slug was on its way down, now. Half of it, at least. Sam felt splendid. "You didn't leave any," he grumbled.

"Sure I did. They're just hidden. Don't ask me where, because I have no idea. But you'll find them."

And he did, before he left three days later. Little bones, and not many of them. But enough to mollify the Indian leaders for the time being, especially when they had their own problems.

Chief Bowles wasn't there for any of the discussions. He was spending all his time with Patrick and General Charles Ball and the colonels of the three regiments—and the boys, of course—inspecting the lines and discussing how The

Bowl's Cherokee irregulars could best be used in the coming war.

None of them seemed to have any doubt at all that there *would* be a war. Especially The Bowl, who shared Patrick's opinion on the subject of Sassenach and the inevitability of their coming.

CHAPTER 10

Lexington, Kentucky
AUGUST 24, 1824

"I think you've got the finest racehorses in the state, Henry," said Peter Porter. "And probably the best racetrack." Leaning on the rail fence, the former New York congressman took a few moments longer to admire the sight. It was a sunny afternoon. A bit too hot for comfort, but not intolerably so.

Henry Clay laughed. "It may not be the best, but I can assure you it's the most profitable. For me, at any rate." A bit smugly: "Indeed, my horses are superior. They earn me quite the tidy sum in prize money. But come: Crittenden's people should be arriving shortly. In fact, they may already be here by now."

Porter was hard-of-hearing, so Clay spoke more loudly than he normally would. That was one of the many gracious courtesies the Speaker of the House practiced routinely with his friends and associates, and one that was much appreciated.

The two men turned back toward the main house at Ashland. Clay had named his estate just south of Lexington for the ash trees that were native to the region. That seemed a bit odd to Porter, given that Clay was actually partial to spruces. He'd been replacing the ash trees with spruces since the day he bought the estate seventeen years earlier. Just one of the man's many personal quirks. Clay spilled over with them, but since he usually turned them to advantage or amusement, none of his friends minded.

The walk back was leisurely, taken in a companionable silence, as they followed the winding carriageway that led to the house through a grove of cypress, locust, and cedar trees. The distance to be traveled was over two hundred yards, so it took a bit of time.

There was a short interruption once they reached the path that led to a cluster of buildings not far from the house itself. That consisted of a smokehouse, a dairy, a carriage house, and the slave quarters.

"A moment, please," Clay said. "Something I must attend to." He strode down the path toward the smokehouse, leaving Porter behind.

Porter used the quarter-of-an-hour wait to admire Clay's country home, which he could see quite well from where he stood. Brick, very well built—and very large. Two and a half stories in the center, with one-story wings to either side. Clay had told him the overall dimensions were one hundred and twenty six feet by fifty-seven. One of the grandest homes in the area, it was.

When Clay returned, Porter cocked an inquiring eyebrow. A polite gesture, nothing intrusive.

"A minor matter," Clay explained, taking his friend by the elbow and leading him toward the house. "Lucretia told me that she had suspicions concerning one of the overseers, from something she overheard one of the house girls saying to another. So I just had words with the man. If I discover he's taking advantage of the slaves, I shall discharge him immediately, and I told him so."

Porter pursed his lips but said nothing. As a New Yorker born and raised in New England, the institution of slavery seemed peculiar to him. Exotic, really, more like something you'd expect to find in Araby than America. With the same aura of sexual excess, to boot. That slave-owners and their overseers had what amounted to their own harems, if they chose to exercise their power, was something understood by practically everyone, North as well as South. Though few people beyond irresponsible abolitionists chose to speak of it publicly.

Even this little incident reeked, if you insisted on sniffing at it for too long. "Discharge" a man—as a penalty for an act which, if carried out against a white woman, would result in a prison sentence. Possibly even a hanging, depending on the circumstances.

Still, it was none of Porter's business, so he said nothing. Whenever the Speaker of the House was in Washington, since his wife rarely accompanied him to the capital, Clay was an insatiable womanizer. The same, when he went on one of his many political tours. That was always a potential political liability, of course, and one that Clay's friends and associates had tried to caution him about—to little avail, unfortunately. But at least it seemed he kept his sexual exploits under control on his own estate.

The one thing they did *not* need would be for rumors of black bastards to join the other innuendos concerning Clay's personal character. Jackson might or might not get involved in that—always hard to know, with that man—but Crawford certainly would. Henry Clay had been using bare-knuckle tactics in his campaign for the presidency, just as he had in all his previous campaigns, and at least some of his opponents would gladly respond in kind.

Well, not "bare-knuckle." Never that. Clay's fists were always gloved, and in very fine gloves at that. But he never hesitated to use them, either.

As for the larger issue, slavery was simply a given. Half the nation depended on the institution economically. So there was no possibility of uprooting it now, whether or not it should ever have been created in the first place. Both Clay and Thomas Jefferson would state, quite bluntly, that if they could roll back time, they'd prefer it if slavery had never come into existence. But since they weren't the Almighty, they couldn't—and their own livelihoods depended on the institution.

There it sat, thus, and would continue to sit. For a practical politician and businessman like Porter, simply another factor to be considered in the ongoing political struggles in the Republic. An immovable one, however, like the seasons. Why waste time over it when nothing could be done anyway—and there were so many other more pressing issues that could be settled? One might as well demand legislation abolishing winter.

"Any further news on the killing?" he asked.

Clay smiled. "Indeed there is. The culprit has been identified, almost for sure. A certain tanner named John Brown, it seems, and several of his brothers."

"An Ohioan?"

"Yes. Was, rather. Apparently he belongs to an extensive family of radical malcontents. A veritable tribe of abolitionists, descended from New England Puritan stock."

Porter made a face. "Yes, I know the type. Better than I wished I did, since we have our share in New York. But, you say, he 'was' from Ohio?"

"A town called Hudson. His father's still there, according to the reports I've received. But John Brown himself, along with his wife and children and brothers, have recently moved to . . ."

The smile expanded, and became a grin. Since Henry Clay had a very wide mouth to begin with, the expression looked quite shark-like. "To Arkansas, we've learned. He's setting up a new tannery right along on the Mississippi, just north of the confluence with the Arkansas. A stretch of land, you may recall—good bottomland, quite well suited for cotton—that I argued at the time should not be included in the land ceded to the Cherokees in the Treaty of Oothcaloga."

"Yes, I remember. But Houston carried that, as well."

They were almost to the house. Porter stopped and placed a restraining hand on Clay's elbow.

"Henry, please be careful here. Don't forget that I was at the Chippewa, in command of the Third Brigade. Driscol was a sergeant then, in the Twenty-Second Regiment. One of the units that Scott sent directly up against the redcoats."

"Yes, yes," Clay said impatiently. "I recall the accounts of his exploits, after the Capitol affair. 'Lost an arm' for the nation, yack yack, 'immediately raced to the capital upon hearing news of the invasion, despite his grave injury,' yack yack; the newspapers were full of it."

"I saw it unfold, Henry. With my own eyes. They never so much as flinched. Not even in the face of volleys from British regulars, on an open battlefield. Whereas . . ." Honesty was needed here. "I couldn't keep my own men from panicking, even with woods for a cover."

"Those were white soldiers."

"They weren't white at the Mississippi," Porter replied forcibly. "Black as night, all of them—except Driscol himself. And they did the same again. Henry, you *must* take this man seriously." He waved a hand at the house. "No pack of border adventurers is going to succeed, where professional soldiers like Riall and Pakenham failed."

Clay had been frowning, as he usually did when someone raised objections to his plans. But when he heard the last, the frown vanished. In fact, he laughed aloud.

"Oh, for the love of—"

He shook his head. "This is a misunderstanding between us. Did you think I believe Crittenden's expedition would *succeed?*"

Clay glanced at the house. Gauging the distance, Porter thought, to make sure that he wouldn't be heard by anyone there. "Speaking of whom, they may have arrived already. Let me do all the talking. But, quickly: I have no intention— never did—of being attached to this except from a distance. Nor do I expect—never did—that Crittenden would win his prize. If he does, splendid. As one of the quiet backers, I shall get credit for it soon enough. Once a feat like that is accomplished, as you well know, all secrets get tossed to the wind."

Porter stared at him. "And if he fails? Which he almost certainly will."

Clay shrugged, in that incredibly graceful way he did all gestures. "Even better. Don't you see? It'll be a *cause,* Peter. 'Vengeance for . . . whatever the name of whatever wretched little town or bayou Crittenden gets hammered at.' A drumbeat in the newspapers, which will provide a rhythm for my march into the president's house."

Porter took a long, slow, deep breath. "You're gambling again, Henry. Can't you *ever* just take straight odds?"

It was the wrong thing to say, and Porter knew it immediately. Clay prided himself on his skill at cards. As well he might, true enough—but he kept thinking politics was a card game. And he could be more reckless in politics than he was at cards, because the odds were harder to gauge.

Clay grew a little stiff. "I'll want you to continue your efforts in New York, be assured. If you can make an arrangement with Van Buren, that would be splendid. I'll need either New York or Pennsylvania, and preferably both. But please do not presume to instruct me on how to win over the West. I know these people, Peter. I've lived here all my life. They're besotted with martial heroics. How else to explain Jackson's popularity when the man has no conceivable qualifications for high office beyond those of a military chieftain?"

The door opened, and Lucretia Clay emerged. "Your visitors are here, Henry. Been waiting for most of an hour."

"Yes, darling. We'll be right there." Clay took Porter by the arm this time. "Come, Peter. Just let me handle it."

SEPTEMBER 3, 1824

"It failed only this," John Quincy Adams said softly, staring out the window of his office in the State Department. He was talking to himself, since his aide had left the room as soon as he delivered the latest report from England.

Too quickly, as it turned out, although the man was simply being courteous. Adams turned from the window and went to the door. Opening it and leaning out, he called for the same aide.

"Yes, Mr. Secretary?"

"I need to see the president. See to making an appointment, if you would."

The man was back within ten minutes. "He says he can see you now, sir. Since it's that pressing."

Adams started to snap a response to the effect that he'd never said anything to the aide about the matter being "pressing." In fact, it wasn't, precisely.

But he held the reproof in check. Simply the fact that he'd felt something was important enough to ask for a special meeting with the chief executive, he realized, was enough for Monroe to label it as urgent. There was something of a compliment there, actually.

James Monroe was an imperturbable man, as a rule, so there was no expression on his face when he finished reading the relevant portion of the ambassador's report. That didn't take long, since Ambassador Rush's prose tended to run to the terse side.

The president laid the report on his desk. "I think we should ask Winfield to join us, if you don't mind."

"Of course, Mr. President." Adams rose from his chair. "I'll summon a messenger."

Since the War Department was no farther away than the State Department, General Scott arrived within ten minutes. It took him considerably less time than that to read the report.

Having done so, he sighed. "Ross, no less. And if Rush's report is accurate, he's said to have packed his uniform in the trunk." He glanced back down at the report. "His ship should be arriving in New Orleans within a fortnight. Not time enough for us to get anyone down there with a warning."

"A warning of *what,* Winfield?" demanded Adams. "That a private citizen of Great Britain—a nation with whom we are no longer at war, I remind you; indeed, are enjoying relatively good terms with these days—has decided to pay a personal visit to our shores. Even if we could get a warning down there in time, what good would it do? We could hardly have the man arrested, after all."

The general's lips quirked as he glanced around the president's office. "We *are* talking about the same 'private citizen' whose troops once burned this very residence, as I recall."

Monroe's smile was broader but just as crooked. "Indeed. But that was then—ancient history, almost—and this is now. The real question is . . ."

Scott nodded. "Yes, Mr. President, I understand. The real question is whether Robert Ross is in fact simply a private citizen, or whether he's acting on behalf of the British government. Informally, if not formally."

"We *have* been expecting such a move on their part," Monroe pointed out. "Actually, I'm surprised they haven't done it sooner. It's perfectly logical for Britain to consider an alliance with the Confederacy."

"They probably would have," Adams said, "except Canning is waiting to see what our response will be to his proposal to form a common bloc against the continental powers over the issues in South America. Keeping France from getting a toehold in the New World again is far more important to Britain than whatever gains they could make against us by forming an alliance with the Arkansas Confederacy. Besides . . ."

He pondered for a moment while the president and the general waited patiently. Like most educated men in America, they considered John Quincy Adams the nation's foremost analyst of international affairs.

"Here's what I think, Mr. President," he said at length. "Nothing I haven't told you before, of course. I believe the long era of sharp antagonism between the United States and Great Britain has come to an end. Henceforth—oh, yes, there'll be squabbles here and there—I don't foresee any major tensions. In fact, I expect we'll see the emergence of what amounts to a tacit alliance *with* Britain."

Monroe glanced at Scott. Technically, the general had no business sitting in on a discussion of the nation's foreign affairs. But, under the circumstances, Monroe apparently felt the same as Adams. Why not? Scott was astute himself, and he could be trusted to keep his mouth shut.

"Continue, John. Though I can't resist the temptation here to point out that your analysis seems a bit odd, given that you've been the member of the Cabinet who's argued most vehemently against accepting Britain's latest proposal."

"That's matching teapots against camels, Mr. President. My objection isn't to the *substance* of Canning's proposal; it's simply to its form. The foreign secretary wants Britain and the United States to issue a joint statement, and I don't. I'd far rather—as you know—see us take an independent stance against continental ambitions in Latin America than come in as—"

" 'A cockboat in the wake of the British man-of-war,' " the president concluded for him. "Yes, I know, John. And I'll agree it's a very nice turn of phrase. But, as I said, please continue."

Adams shrugged. "If I'm right—and I am—then I think the conclusion follows directly, with regard to the matter at hand. Whatever purpose Robert Ross has in coming to America, he is not acting—not in any way—on behalf of the British government."

Monroe gazed at him levelly. "Would you be willing to state as much in a private letter to Senator Jackson? I'd just as soon avoid an explosion there. Given his attitudes toward Britain—added to the tensions that already exist with Arkansas—any hint that a British officer is meddling in American affairs will be like waving a red flag in front of a bull. But he's likely to listen to you, John."

Adams caught the grimace that came briefly to Scott's face. The general, quite obviously, felt that catering to Jackson was questionable, given that the man had no real business being involved in the first place. He was a senator, now, no longer active in the military and not a part of the administration.

But however good a general he might be, Scott's grasp of politics left much to be desired. As witness the very public brawl he'd gotten into with Jackson himself, a few years back, that could have easily been avoided just by the use of some reasonable amount of tact. So Adams ignored the expression.

"Yes, certainly." He smiled crookedly himself. "Mind, it'll be a bit difficult to phrase it properly. A good part of the reason I'm certain Ross isn't acting for Canning is because he's been so closely tied to the British antislavery movement these past years. Hardly the man a Tory government would choose as a go-between—and hardly something I want to dwell on in a letter to one of Tennessee's major slaveowners."

Monroe actually laughed. "Yes, I'd say! One of Britain's most notorious abolitionists come to pay a visit to the man who is quite possibly the most notorious abolitionist in the whole world. Certainly in North America. There's as much in that to infuriate Old Hickory as in the thought of an actual British agent."

To Adams's surprise, Scott shook his head. "I wouldn't be so sure, Mr. President. They're all soldiers, don't forget, and soldiers tend to treasure two things above all: gallantry, and their own reputations."

Monroe cocked an eyebrow at him. "The gallantry I understand. I was once a soldier myself. But I'm not following you on the rest. The part about reputations, I mean."

"Have you—either one of you—read Ross's account of the Gulf campaign?"

Monroe and Adams looked at each other. Then, simultaneously, shook their heads.

"Well, I have—and you can be sure and certain that Andrew Jackson has read it also. It was published quite extensively. Very popular in Britain at the time—and any number of copies were purchased here in America."

Adams frowned. "I'm still not following you, Winfield. I've never read the thing, but I understood it was a defense of Pakenham's conduct in the—ah. I see. Yes, of course."

Monroe was frowning now, looking back and forth between the other two men in his office. "Will *someone* please explain . . . Ah. Yes, of course. No way to defend Pakenham, is there, except to speak well of Jackson?"

"Exceedingly well, Mr. President," Scott said. "I wouldn't go so far as to state that Ross used a ladle to pour praise over Jackson. But he certainly used a very large spoon. That's something Jackson will appreciate, just as he appreciates the martial accomplishments of Patrick Driscol. Meaning that you might have three men coming to a clash of arms, but all of them respect—even admire—each other. That makes quite a difference, for men who think like soldiers. Which they all do."

Monroe sat up a little straighter in his chair. "Well, that's something of a relief. The last thing we need is another eruption from Andy Jackson. So let's get down to it then. Why *is* Robert Ross coming to America?" He glanced down at the ambassador's report. "Quite clearly, in response to an invitation from Driscol."

By now, Adams thought he saw it clear. "The simplest of all reasons. Driscol expects a war—half expects it, at least—and he wants expert military counsel. More counsel, I should say. I'm remembering now that Winfield suggested in this very room, just months ago, that the fortifications in Arkansas were too sophisticated for Driscol to have developed all on his own."

Monroe looked at Scott. The general nodded. "I'd have to agree, Mr. President."

The president was now completely erect in his chair, his

fingers laced together in front of him on the desk. "Very well, then. What does either of you suggest we might do?"

"Nothing, Mr. President," came Adams's immediate response. "Other than the letter I'll write Jackson, I propose we do nothing at all, since I can't see anything we could do that wouldn't make everything worse. We've already— several years ago—put a stop to any government funding for those adventurers in Louisiana. So we have no financial leverage to bring to bear. What's left is direct military action. But against who? We have no legitimate quarrel with the Confederacy. Not one, at any rate, that would be accepted by any other nation as a casus belli. That means all we could do would be to use troops or the threat of troops in Louisiana, to prevent a freebooting expedition by the likes of Crittenden. Which would stir up a hornet's nest. Besides, you can't stop such expeditions, anyway, if they have any serious local backing. We've never been able to in the past; why should we succeed now?"

Scott hesitated for a few seconds. "I'd have to agree, Mr. President, although I feel the need to point out that if an attempt is made against Arkansas by private adventurers, it's likely to result in a catastrophe for them."

"They wouldn't be entering the fortified mountainous areas," the president pointed out. "What they'd want is simply the river plain and its broad bottomlands."

The general spread his hands. "Yes, sir, I know. But if they think Driscol won't come down to get them, they'd be badly mistaken. He will—and he'll smash them."

"You're sure of that?"

"Oh, yes. Both of the first, and of the last. And Driscol won't do it piecemeal, the way Perez drove Long's expedition out of Texas. He'll maneuver them into a battle and hammer them flat."

Monroe nodded and looked at the window. "Which political elements here would use for a rallying cry."

"Clay, to give them a name," stated Adams.

"Yes, most likely." After a moment, Monroe said: "General, if you'd be so—"

"Of course, sir," said Scott, rising from his chair and heading for the door. "If you need me any further, I'll be in the War Department."

After he was gone, Monroe's eyes came away from the window and looked at Adams. "I'll leave the decision to you, John. I've not more than a few months left in office. Whatever does or doesn't happen in Arkansas between now and then won't be something whose consequences I'll have to deal with. You, on the other hand, might. Are you so sure of this?"

"Yes, Mr. President, I'm quite sure." It was Adams's turn to hesitate. "Should it come to pass that the Republic calls on my services—I've had to consider that possibility, of late—then it's necessary for me to think in the long run. The situation with Arkansas will continue to fester, no matter what. Sooner or later, that boil will have to be lanced—but it's a mistake to lance a boil too soon, or it simply returns."

"Clay won't 'lance' it if he's elected president," Monroe said bluntly. "He'll scrape it."

"Well. He'll try. But I am not Henry Clay." Stiffly: "I refuse to adopt another man's methods—methods I consider base, sir, to speak bluntly—simply in order to put myself in his place. Where's any purpose in that?"

Monroe unlaced his hands and leaned back in the chair. "I understand. Nothing it is, then. We'll just let it keep unfolding."

CHAPTER 11

Alexandria, Louisiana
SEPTEMBER 13, 1824

"Robbed, I say again!" Robert Crittenden's voice filled the tavern, even managing to ride over the hubbub of far too many men packed into far too small a space—and with far too much whiskey packed inside them, to boot.

"Robbed, I say again!"

Raymond Thompson looked at his companion across the small table in a corner of the tavern and rolled his eyes. "How many times do you think he'll say it again?"

Scott Powers swirled the whiskey in his glass. "Ten, at least." Then, shrugging: "Better him than you or me, Ray. Somebody's got to keep the boys stirred up."

"Cheated of our rightful new state by the scoundrel Adams—that bastard Monroe, too!—and their tools in Congress! Has ever mankind seen a more infamous act of treachery than the selling of Texas and Arkansas—and for the sake of nothing more sublime than appeasing the corrupt Dons and their—"

Powers chuckled. "Sore, isn't he? Mostly he's just riled because he was sure he'd be appointed the governor of Arkansas. If the state had ever come into existence."

Thompson didn't reply. The statement was true enough, of course, but he didn't share Powers's cynical equanimity on the subject. For Powers, any expedition to seize Arkansas was just a stepping-stone to Texas. But Thompson had been counting on getting some of that fine bottomland in the Arkansas portion of the Delta. He could have sold it to speculators within a year and turned a profit on the deal. Instead, he was holed up in Alexandria, trying to evade his creditors.

"—Cherokee savages and the Quapaws, more savage still—"

But there was no point in dwelling on past misfortunes. If all went well, before long he'd be rich enough to thumb his nose at any creditors. "Any word from the Lallemand brothers?" he asked.

"Not lately. Far as I know, they should still be arriving any day."

Thompson frowned into his whiskey glass. "I still don't like the idea. You know as well as I do that they're just looking for an angle to set up French rule in Texas."

"So what?" Powers drained his own glass. "Let 'em dream. Napoleon died two years ago. Without him as the anchor—even assuming they could have freed him from St. Helena—they don't stand a chance. And in the meantime, they're willing to put two hundred and fifty trained soldiers in the field—and Charles Lallemand is a genuine general.

Fought at Waterloo, even."

"—niggers for the taking, too! Like catching fish in a pond! What say you, boys?"

Thompson and Powers both winced. An instant later, the roar of the crowd hammered their ears.

When the noise ebbed enough to allow conversation again, Thompson returned stubbornly to the subject. "French soldiers, Scott. Who's to say—"

"Not more than a third, any longer, after that comedy of errors they called Champ d'Asile. Not even Long's people scrambled out of Texas faster." Powers looked away for a moment, a considering expression on his face. "Most of the men around the Lallemands, since they settled in Alabama, are local boys. They'll listen to Charles on the field, but that's it."

He stood up, holding his empty glass. "Another?"

Thompson shook his head. "No, I've got to be able to see straight tomorrow morning. At least—"

"—problem will be catching those niggers, the way they'll run after a stout volley and the sight of level bayonets! I'm telling you, boys—"

"God, I'm sick of that man's voice," Thompson grumbled. "But, as I was saying, at least he came up with the muskets he said he would. Two thousand stand."

Powers's eyes widened. "Where did—"

"Don't ask, Scott. But you can probably figure it out."

After a moment, Powers smiled. "Benefactors in high places, indeed. But I shall be the very model of discretion."

After he left, Thompson drained his own glass.

"—envy of every Georgian and Virginian! And then! On to Texas!"

Another roar from the crowd caused Thompson to hunch his shoulders. "Enough, already," he muttered to himself.

He eyed the far-distant door, gloomily certain it would take him five minutes to work his way through the mob. More like ten, if he wanted to avoid a duel. Half the men in the tavern would fight over any offense, and they could find an offense most anywhere.

126 ERIC FLINT

Blue Spring Farm, Kentucky
SEPTEMBER 15, 1824

"I'd really feel a lot better about this if I were going along, Julia," said Richard Johnson. The Kentucky senator's face looked more homely than ever. Downright woebegone, in fact.

"Oh, stop frettin', dear. You can't possibly leave now, with the political situation the way it is." Julia Chinn nodded toward the small cavalry escort waiting patiently near the wagon. "They'll handle any little problem that might come up."

Johnson looked at the cavalrymen, trying to find some comfort in the sight.

Trying . . . and even succeeding to a considerable degree. Not so much from the sight of a dozen cavalrymen as from their commanding officer. Houston had promised a real military escort if Julia decided to take the girls to Arkansas for their schooling, and he hadn't failed on that promise.

Recognizing inevitability—Julia had remained adamant on the subject for months, never budging at all—Johnson stepped over to the side of the officer's horse and looked up at it.

"Got to say I'm downright astonished to see you here, Zack. Don't usually see a lieutenant colonel in charge of something like this."

Zachary Taylor looked down at him, smiling. A bit to Johnson's relief, the lieutenant colonel's heavy, rough-featured face seemed quite good humored.

"Hell, Dick, why not? Sam asked me to find somebody reliable when I ran into him in Wheeling. I was on my way back to my post in Baton Rouge, in any event. I figured I was more reliable than anybody I could find on short notice, and it really isn't that far out of my way. Besides, I owe you a favor."

In point of fact, coming through western Virginia and northern Kentucky to provide an escort for Julia and the children, instead of just taking a barge down the Ohio, had been considerably out of Taylor's way. But the man was an experienced Indian fighter, so terrain was no great challenge for him.

True, he did owe Johnson a favor, but it hadn't been much, really. Just the sort of minor intervention that a senator often made on behalf of a well-respected and capable military officer. And . . .

They liked each other. Taylor and Johnson had never been what you could call good friends, but that was probably just because they'd never been able to spend much time together. On those occasions when they had, they'd gotten along quite well.

They had a lot in common. Both were veterans, even though Johnson's soldiering days were over, and both came from wealthy Kentucky families—of Virginian origin, in Taylor's case, now with large plantations over near Louisville. What was more important was that while they didn't see eye to eye on some political issues, Taylor seemed to share Johnson's attitudes on slavery. An economic necessity for the nation, to be sure, but nothing to brag about and much to cause uneasiness. Certainly nothing to proclaim, as Calhoun would, as a "positive good."

Taylor was one of the few members of the slave-owning gentry in Kentucky who'd never seemed to care about Johnson's relationship to Julia. At least, the one time he'd visited Blue Spring Farm, he hadn't blinked an eye at the sight of a black woman presiding over the dinner table. Indeed, he'd been quite gracious to her and the children throughout the visit.

"Take good care of them, Zack," Johnson said quietly, in a half-pleading tone.

"Now, don't you worry yourself none, Dick. I'll see them all the way to the Confederacy myself." To Johnson's relief, Taylor voiced aloud the senator's underlying concern. "If you're worrying some slave-catchers might try to claim they was runaways, I'll set 'em straight right quick."

For a moment, Taylor's thick hand shifted to the sword at his belt. "Right quick," he repeated, almost growling the words. "And God damn John Calhoun, anyway."

There was that, too. Richard Johnson was also famous as the senator who'd fight—at the drop of a hat—any attempt to foist anything that even vaguely resembled an established church on the great American republic. In his pantheon of political virtues, separation of church and state ranked right alongside states' rights and putting an end to debt imprisonment.

Public opinion and custom be damned. Richard Mentor Johnson trusted blasphemers a lot more than he did those pious folk who could always find an excuse in the Bible to do whatever they pleased.

"That's fine, then," he said.

Julia's voice rose up from behind him. "You settle down, Imogene! You too, Adaline! Or I'll smack you both! See if I don't!"

Taylor grinned. "Besides, I won't have to worry none about keeping wayward girls in line. Way more fearsome foes than some sorry slave-catchers."

New Orleans, Louisiana
SEPTEMBER 22, 1824

"That's where the final battle was fought," Robert Ross told his wife and son, pointing off to the steamboat's left. "You can still see the remnants of the Iron Battalion's fortifications. About all that's left, any longer, of what they called the Morgan Line at the time."

David Ross gave his father an uncertain glance and said, "It doesn't really look like much."

"Some of that's the climate, son. Between the heat and the rains—the river floods, too, quite often—no construction mostly made of dirt and logs is going to wear well. Even after less than a decade's passage, much of it will be gone. And the city's poorer residents would have scavenged the iron used by the battalion to bolster the works, here and there."

The retired British general studied the distant mound for a few seconds. "But that's just part of it. Held by determined and valiant men—which they most certainly were—even a modest line of defenses can be incredibly difficult to surmount. The casualties were fearful on both sides."

"Is this where Thornton was killed?"

"No." Ross pointed further upriver, in the direction of

New Orleans. "Rennie died here. Thornton fell some hundreds of yards to the west, in the first clash with Houston's forces. Right on that road you can see pieces of, here and there."

There was silence for a time as the steamboat continued its steady progress up the immense river. David, who had been intrigued by the craft itself for most of the voyage upriver from Fort St. Philip, was now giving it no attention at all. His eyes were fixed on the terrain where, almost ten years earlier, a great contest of arms had been waged. As with most young men of his class—certainly one with his family history—martial affairs were of engrossing interest.

He already knew the terrain well, too, at least in the abstract. He'd read his father's account of the campaign as well as several other memoirs that had since been published in Britain.

"We should be approaching Chalmette field," he announced.

"Yes," Ross said, nodding. "We'll have to cross to the other side of the boat in order to see it."

Shortly afterward, the boat was passing by the location where Pakenham and Jackson's armies had faced each other—but never come to an actual battle.

"Field!" David exclaimed, half disappointed and half amused.

Ross shrugged. "It's plantation area, David. You can hardly expect people to leave such a potentially profitable area unexploited, simply for the benefit of an occasional tourist. At the time, I can assure you, that expanse of lush crops was nothing but stubble. Jackson saw to that, to give his men a clear line of fire."

David had no personal experience with battles, but as the son of a major general he had a good sense of some basic principles. He might have found it difficult to gauge the fortifications back on the Morgan Line. But, his eyes ranging back and forth across Chalmette field, he had no difficulty here.

"What a slaughter that would have been. Five hundred yards to cross."

His father nodded. "Five hundred yards—in the face of the world's best artillery. Along with thousands of riflemen and musketeers protected by an excellent rampart. And with the attacking force having no cover and no possibility of threatening the enemy's flanks. Jackson chose his position exceedingly well: his right wing anchored on the Mississippi, his left on the cypress swamps."

Ross lifted his arm and pointed into the distance. "You can see the start of the swamps quite easily. They continue on for miles. The Cherokees and Choctaws savaged our forces whenever we ventured into them."

David shook his head. There was a subtle but great satisfaction in the gesture. His father's analysis of the Gulf campaign might have been accepted by the British establishment, including its military, but there had been plenty of boys his own age who'd shared the brash certainties of youth. *One stout charge would have taken the day, I tell you!* He'd now be able to return and sneer at them with the authority of someone who'd seen the lay of the land himself.

Ross was amused. He could remember those wonderful certainties himself from forty years ago.

Eliza laid a hand on his arm where it rested on the boat's railing. "We'd best see to the packing. We'll be arriving in the city soon."

A small delegation at the foot of the ramp was waiting for them. Ross had thought Driscol would have made some arrangements, but he was surprised at the form it took.

He hadn't expected Patrick himself to be there, of course, nor Tiana. But whatever he'd expected, it certainly hadn't been four scruffy-looking men in civilian attire. Two young white men—one of whom was younger than David—and two black men. One of whom was also younger than David, and the other of whom . . .

"I didn't expect the army of Arkansas to follow *precisely* the methods used by us British," he said to that black man, after debarking onto the pier. "But I still think it's absurd for the only general in your army to be serving as the leader of a small detachment of escorts."

Charles Ball grinned at him. "Leader? Nonsense, General Ross!" He jerked his thumb at the older of the two white men standing next to him. "Here be the esteemed leader of this expedition. Captain Anthony McParland. You might be able to remember him still, just a bit. He was Patrick's lad in the war. Just a new sergeant, then, though."

Ross studied McParland. Now that he looked at him more closely, he could recognize him. But . . .

He was impressed, actually. The young man standing before him, now in his midtwenties, seemed vastly more self-assured than the very young and uncertain sergeant he could remember from nine and a half years earlier. That spoke well of the Arkansas Army, if such a quick study could be trusted. Of all the military skills praised in the literature, the one Robert had always found to be the least mentioned and most underrated was the ability of a given army to instill self-confidence in its men, especially its junior officers.

Ball's grin grew wider still. "I be the young massa's slave. So's Corporal Parker here. Sheffield Parker, that is. And he's"—the thumb now indicated the younger of the two white men—"Corporal McParland. Callender, to distinguish him from his cousin, our august commander."

Ross examined the two younger men. Boys, almost, since neither of them could be more than seventeen or eighteen years old. Callender McParland bore a definite resemblance to the captain. Average height, a bit on the slender side if quite wiry-looking, a blue-eyed open face under a thatch of sandy hair. The sort of lad one would barely notice in a crowd and never think twice about.

The black corporal, Sheffield Parker, was about the same, allowing for the racial differences. Dark-skinned, even for a negro, with very dark eyes and rather broad features. He'd never be noticed at all, except possibly for an unusual breadth of shoulders in a man who was a bit on the short side.

They both looked very fit—almost absurdly so, given their clothing. Which couldn't be depicted as "rags," certainly, but could most charitably be called nondescript. Parker was even barefoot.

Done with his quick examination, Ross cocked an eyebrow at Ball. "I assume there's an explanation for this, other than—I hope—the fact that Patrick has adopted *sans-culottes* principles for a military table of organization."

"Don' know what 'sangullot' means, General," Ball

replied cheerfully. "But, yes, there's a reason for it. I'm afraid a bit of trouble has developed lately. There's a small army of frontier adventurers been gathering themselves at Alexandria these past months. Mostly the usual Texas freebooters, but they gotten sidetracked with taking back eastern Arkansas, on account of a fellow named Robert Crittenden. He was likely to have been appointed the governor of the new state of Arkansas, except—"

That really was a murderous grin. Even this many years later, Robert could remember his impressions of Ball during the Gulf campaign. As a veteran U.S. Navy master gunner, he'd been Driscol's second in command of the Iron Battalion at New Orleans—just as he'd been in command of Houston and Driscol's artillery battery at the Capitol. The same artillery that had battered Robert's own forces when they tried to storm the seat of the U.S. government.

Color be damned. Men like Ball had been the core of every great army in history, going back at least as far as the Romans.

"—there ain't no such thing as 'Arkansas,' 'cept as the chiefdom of the Confederacy. Crittenden be righteous mad about it— and he's got plenty of backing from disgruntled local planters and land speculators who'd figured on making a killing."

"Disgruntled," no less. Ball's education seemed to have expanded a great deal. His vocabulary, at least.

"We didn't expect any real trouble from them this soon," Ball continued, "because—this be normally the case with freebooting schemes—they didn't have much in the way of arms. But just recent and sudden-like they turned up with plenty of muskets. Even got four three-pounders and a six-pounder."

Still grinning, Ball nodded toward the nearby square. Jackson Square, as it was now apparently called, not the *Place d'Armes* that Ross remembered. "The three-pounders lookin' amazingly like the ones that used to be sittin' right there, till most recently. Don't know where they got the six-pounder. New shiny-lookin' gun, by all accounts."

Ross wasn't surprised. Even in Britain and the continent, the confusing and turbulent southwestern frontier of the United States was notorious. Between the collapse of the

Spanish Empire, the shaky state of the new nation of Mexico, and what seemed like a never-ending cornucopia of Napoleonic adventurers—most of all, the territorial ambitions of Americans, official and civilian alike—every other month seemed to have a new expedition setting off to seize Texas. Sometimes for the United States, although that was usually disguised as a "revolution" to set up a new republic. Sometimes for one or another faction in Mexican politics. Sometimes as a result of Spain's continuing involvement in the region. Sometimes, even—although this had thankfully started to fade since Napoleon's death on St. Helena a couple of years earlier—as a place to magically restore a Napoleonic empire.

Often enough, any combination thereof.

Most of the adventurers—*flibustiers,* the French called them, after the old Dutch term *vrijbuiter* that had become the English "freebooter"—were poorly funded, not to mention of questionable competence. Some of them, of questionable sanity.

But, now and then, a group formed with real leadership and serious financial backing. The last such had been Dr. James Long's ill-fated Texas expedition in the summer of 1819, which might well have succeeded in carving out a big chunk of Mexican territory for an independent American-based republic. But the U.S. government, which had often tacitly supported earlier such attempts, refused to support this one. The U.S. secretary of state had finally gotten all of Florida from Spain in the Adams-Onis Treaty signed in February of that year, and he was in no mood to have the settlement upended by yet another adventure in Texas. Monroe had agreed with him, and Long's little republic had collapsed within months. Long himself had been taken prisoner by the Mexicans and then "accidentally" shot by a Mexican soldier while a captive in Mexico City.

The large and brawling community of southwestern adventurers and their backers had never forgiven Adams, of course. And now, it seemed, had found another source of support. Probably political as well as financial.

Eliza had been getting steadily more concerned. "Does this mean we'll have to suspend our journey to Arkansas? It sounds quite dangerous."

"Oh, it's not really dangerous, Mrs. Ross," Ball said. "Not for us. We should manage to pass through quite easily. But that's the reason for this odd getup we decided on."

A little wave of his hand indicated his companions. "We're just another party of Southerners, passing through the area. Nothing unusual. Got to be Southerners, seein' as how we got slaves, just like proper Southern gentlemen do."

The grin had vanished momentarily while the Arkansas general gave Ross's wife that assurance. Now it came back in full force. "Anthony been studyin' his letters right vigorously, these past years. Can't hardly believe it myself, the way he can talk now, when he's of a mind. 'Course, his accent's still Northern, but that won't stand out. Plenty of young Northerners come down here to make their fortune."

Having a much better sense of the social realities of the American South than his wife, Ross could immediately understand the logic of the scheme. Except . . .

"How about *our* accent?" he asked. "It should be a bit difficult for us to remain silent, throughout the journey."

"No problem there, either. There be plenty of Englishmen—not to mention Irishmen—comin' here to set up a plantation. In fact, Crittenden's got a whole company of Irishmen in that little army he's put together. Most of 'em just the usual adventurers left over from the wars, of course. But some of them got real money to invest."

And that, too, wasn't surprising. The wars triggered by the French Revolution and the Napoleonic era had lasted for almost a quarter of a century and had involved enormous numbers of men. Every such war epoch in history had produced, in its aftermath, a plethora of veterans who turned their military skills to this or that adventure. Some of them criminal; still more, skirting the very edges of legality.

"I see." Ross couldn't help but smile. "So my wife and I—with our son along, presumably to stay behind and manage the business—are scouting the Delta to see a likely place for a plantation. Perhaps even in newly seized—or perhaps I should say, rightfully restored—Arkansas. With our local guides and partners—that'll be you, I imagine, Captain McParland, along with your cousin Callender here—and the slaves to provide their *bona fides*."

"Yup."

Ross scrutinized Ball's face for a moment. "Which still doesn't explain the mystery of *you* being included among the 'slaves,' Charles. Surely Arkansas didn't have to use its one and only general for the purpose."

For the first time, Ball's good cheer seemed to slip a bit. "Well . . . First off, I'm *not* the only general. The Laird—ah, that's Chief Patrick, I mean—has the same rank, too, even though he ain't normally active. But he's perfectly capable of leading the army in the field, as you well know, should Crittenden and his pack take off before I get there. Don't need me for that. And the thing is . . ."

Finally, it all came into focus. "Yes, I see," said Ross. "You wanted the chance to study the terrain carefully yourself. Even be able to observe firsthand a large military force moving through it. Not because you care much about this one, but another that might follow."

"Yup." Now, Ball seemed to be scowling slightly. "Tarnation, General, you just cost me two dollars."

"How's that?"

"We had a bet. I didn't think you'd figure it out until we got halfway to Alexandria. Patrick said you'd do it before we even left the docks."

And how odd it was to see that a father's reputation with his oldest son should be cemented for all time by such a trivial thing. But, looking at David's face, Ross didn't doubt it. Books, essays, mementos, medals, swords of honor, dispatches—all abstractions, in the end. Whereas there was nothing at all abstract about seeing the conclusion of a wager between two men, one of whom stood right before the boy and looked like some sort of Moor legend, and the other of whom was an Irish troll who had almost killed his father once.

"Oh, what a splendid adventure!" David exclaimed.

Washington, D.C.
SEPTEMBER 30, 1824

Maria Hester opened the door herself. She must have seen him coming.

"I've missed you so," she said, before he swept her into his arms. Then, laughing: "Sam! Stop it! Right in public!"

He growled something incoherent, lifted her into the house, and closed the door with his boot heel, never relinquishing the embrace or leaving off with the kisses. "Missed you, too."

"Father wants to see you," she mumbled. "As soon as you arrived, he told me."

"Can wait till tomorrow."

"Daddy! Daddy! Daddy!"

Sighing, Sam set his wife down. Maria Hester was grinning up at him. "The president of the nation might have to wait a day, but your son won't."

Lurking just beneath the surface of her bright eyes was the same anticipation that was practically flooding him. The boy was only four years old, after all. Four-year-olds need a lot of naps.

A moment later, Sam had little Andrew Jackson Houston hoisted up. His son was beaming at him, too.

"Would you care for some whiskey, sir?" asked a servant, coming into the foyer.

"Of course not. It's only afternoon."

PART II

CHAPTER 12

Robert Ross and his son watched the Kentucky flatboat men carrying wood from the stacks on shore into the steamboat. They seemed to be carrying out the labor even more energetically than usual.

"Amazing, really," David commented. "The rest of the time they barely move from their accommodations on deck. And that, only to flip another card or unstopper a jug of whiskey."

Anthony McParland was standing next to them. "It's part of their contract," he explained, smiling slightly. "They bring their goods downriver on rafts, just using the current. In New Orleans, the rafts are broken up, and the wood is sold along with whatever they were carrying on them. They get this free passage back upriver—but they have to do the labor of hauling the wood into the boiler room."

"And who cuts and stacks the wood in the first place?" Robert asked, eyeing the rapidly diminishing pile of logs at the other end of the little pier reaching out into the Mississippi.

"Here? Choctaws, mostly. Elsewhere, it'd be poor white woodcutting families."

David frowned. "I thought the Choctaws had moved to the Confederacy also."

"Only maybe a third of the tribe. The rest are being stubborn, claiming—which is true enough—that they never signed the Treaty of Oothcaloga."

David was still frowning. "Is there going to be trouble over that?"

McParland's smile lost some of its amusement. "Be better to say there *is* trouble over it. Has been for years, now. And it's been getting worse. More settlers keep moving into Mississippi, and with Crittenden and his mob stirring up everybody . . .

"Chief Pushmataha is a damn fool, if you ask me," Anthony continued. "Well, not that, I guess. He's canny, by all accounts, but he's getting old. He and his Choctaws have even less chance of holding back the tide than the Cherokees and Creeks did in Georgia, Alabama, and Tennessee. And there's a big chunk of land still set aside for them in the Confederacy, between the Canadian and the Red rivers. That's where those of 'em who've moved already have settled. But if the rest of the Choctaws don't get there pretty soon, they'll start seeing the land gobbled up."

"I thought white people weren't—"

McParland shook his head. "Not by white people. Other Indians. Caddos and Quapaws, mostly. They're already moving into the area, since they're being pushed out of Louisiana."

David's frown now seemed permanently fixed in place. Like most nineteen-year-olds, he preferred the world to be a neatly organized and categorized place. "Caddos and Quapaws aren't signatories to the treaty, either," he pointed out.

The young Confederate captain shrugged. "No, they're not. Ask them if they care. Louisiana's making it more difficult for them to stay every year—and there's all that open territory over there on the other side of the Red River. Most Indian tribes are organized along clan lines. If their clan didn't make an agreement, they figure they're not bound by it—much less to anybody who is."

"There will be trouble there as well, then," David predicted sagely.

McParland chuckled. "No, there *is* trouble there, already. Just had another clash between some Choctaws and Caddos two months ago, I heard. Not to mention that neither the Osage nor the Comanches figure *any* of these tribes from across the Mississippi got any business at all in the area. Those fights are pretty much constant, now."

Robert had been listening to the exchange with only half

his mind. He'd been paying more attention to the actions of the flatboat men.

"Something's amiss, I believe," he said suddenly. He pointed to the men coming back—even more hurriedly than usual, it seemed—across the pier onto the boat.

McParland studied their movements for a moment before pushing himself away from the rail. "Do believe you're right. I'll find out."

He was back less than five minutes later, with no trace of amusement left on his face.

"They found four bodies in one of the woodpiles. Choctaws. Been scalped and skinned. Two men, a child, and a woman. The woman had also—" He glanced at David. "Well, never mind."

"Skinned?" David's eyes were wide.

"Yeah, skinned. Might have been done by settlers, but . . ." McParland's expression was grim. "Whoever did it took their time about it. That's not likely to have been settlers. Clashes between them and Indians don't generally last too long, since as a rule both sides never have all that many men, and they don't want to risk a counterattack. A quick scalping, and they leave. Besides, there were a lot of prints in the area." He pointed to the lush growth of palmettos and pawpaws that shielded the woods beyond from easy view. "That pile was back there a ways, which is why we didn't see it. Some of the flatboat men are pretty fair trackers. They think a lot of men were involved."

All three of them stared into the woods.

"I think it's Crittenden's men," McParland stated. "They must have left Alexandria sooner than we thought we would. I guess getting those guns and some cannons made them bold-like."

The steamboat was pulling away from the pier. David's eyes followed its course to the north. "But Arkansas is . . ."

"Still a long ways away," Anthony concluded for him. "Yeah, I know. But it'd be just like that crowd to figure on hounding the Choctaws along the way. They want land in northern Mississippi just as much as in Arkansas. Anywhere in the Delta, where cotton plantations can be set up. There's a lot of money in cotton, now, since Whitney made that machine of his."

Robert nodded. "It's an old pattern. The Crusaders savaged a lot of Jewish communities on their way to the Holy Land. Did more killing in the ghettos, some of them, than they did in the Levant. If they ever got there at all, which some of them didn't. The whole Fourth Crusade stopped at Constantinople after sacking it."

His own expression was grim. "War's never easy on neutrals, as a rule."

"It's an outrage," David proclaimed.

Robert's jaws were set. "Yes, it is. What concerns me more, however, is what the impact of it'll be. Up there." He used his chin to point to the north.

His son looked at him. "What do you mean, Father?"

"You've never met Patrick Driscol, David. He's a harsh man at any time. If this is indeed Crittenden's men, they'll be conducting outrages all the way upriver. Hand something like that to Patrick Driscol—the man who, as a boy, hid from the massacres in Ireland in '98—and he'll not react well. Not well at all."

"I see. You're afraid he'll be hotheaded."

Robert took a deep breath. "No, not that. Patrick is a man given to rage, but it's a very cold sort of thing. He'll not lose control, whatever else."

A subtle shift in McParland's expression made it clear that the young captain understood him. "Ah," he said. Then, a moment later: "Well, yes. Not that he'll have to stir anybody up to do it. Pretty much nobody in Arkansas is going to feel the least bit kindly to Louisiana freebooters. Even if they was behaving well, which they aren't."

"It would be a bad error," Ross stated.

McParland shrugged. "Maybe. Then again, maybe not. Sometimes the best way to set a pack of curs running is to show 'em the wolf's teeth."

"The political ramifications—"

Abruptly, Robert broke off. There was something a bit absurd, after all, about lecturing Americans on the dynamics of American politics. Even if he was almost sure he was right.

Eliza came up onto the deck. "There's been trouble, it seems. Do we continue, or go back to New Orleans?"

She wasn't pushing for a particular answer, just inquiring.

Robert glanced at McParland. "I don't believe we have

much choice, dearest. Unless we want to return on a raft. This steamboat, I'm quite sure, will be continuing north."

McParland's shoulders had become a bit stiff. "Well. Yes, I'm afraid so. The *Comet* is owned by the Arkansas River-boat Company, of which the Laird—ah, Mr. Driscol—and Mr. Crowell own half the stock. Mr. Shreve won't like it much, but that was part of the arrangement."

Eliza and David frowned at him, clearly puzzled.

"What he means, dearest, is that in the event of hostilities, the boat will be pressed into Confederate service. And, it seems, hostilities have begun."

They looked at McParland.

The young captain cleared his throat. "Well. Be better to say 'Arkansas service.' Not sure John Ross or the Ridge know anything about it."

That wasn't surprising. It had already been clear to Ross, just from his long correspondence with Patrick, that the chiefdom of Arkansas wore its theoretical subordination to the Confederacy rather lightly.

As was inevitable. Of all political quandaries faced by the human race over the millennia, this was perhaps the most in-tractable. The Romans had an expression for it: *Quis cus-todiet ipsos custodes?*

Without realizing it, he murmured the phrase aloud.

"'Who will guard the guardians?'" his son translated. "That's about the Praetorian Guard, isn't it?"

His mother smiled. "Actually, no. I believe it was a remark made by the satirist Juvenal, concerning the wisdom of hav-ing eunuchs guarding women."

Ross couldn't remember, but he suspected Eliza was cor-rect. She was very fond of the classics.

"What do eunuchs—?"

To Robert's surprise, McParland understood the point im-mediately. He realized again that there was really not much left of the shy, ill-educated, and uncertain teenaged soldier he remembered from years earlier.

"Pretty good assessment, sir. Yeah, the Cherokees and Creeks—the Choctaws soon, too, if I don't miss my guess—need Arkansas to buffer them against the United States. But you pays a price for that, always do. Just the way it is."

He seemed quite unconcerned about the matter. It was also

now clear to Robert that McParland's allegiance had shifted completely to Arkansas. There seemed to be no animosity in the young officer toward his native United States, but also no doubt where he stood in the event of a conflict. And if that was true for a white citizen of Arkansas, how much more true would it be for its black ones?

So. A war was starting, and it would unfold as wars did. Very messily.

Memphis, Tennessee
OCTOBER 1, 1824

"Perhaps you should remain here, Julia," Colonel Taylor suggested. He looked around the inn. "It seems comfortable enough, and the senator left you with plenty of money."

Julia Chinn was having none of it, as Taylor had feared. "Colonel, meaning no offense, but that's crazy. You going to leave a black woman and two black children alone—with money, which just makes it worse—in *this* town? Leavin' aside that Memphis got a reputation that's of practically biblical proportions, I remind you that Tennessee's a slave state. Give it two days, and we'd be vanished somewhere."

"I could . . ." But the sentence trailed off.

"Don't be silly. You got only twelve men to begin with. If you insist on going south into what looks like a war starting, you'll need all of them."

He couldn't argue the point. "Well. I'm sure the boat captain would agree—"

"He's going back up to St. Louis," Julia interrupted. "St. Louis is a frontier town, which means the only reason it ain't looking at Bible rank is just 'cause it ain't well enough knowed yet. And Missouri's another slave state."

"Surely there's *some* boat that'll be heading for Ohio."

She shrugged. "Prob'bly. And the captain might even be a Northerner. But most of the crew will be Southern. And as excited as they all are, since the news came . . ."

She shrugged again. The fact that the shoulders which made the gesture were still those of a fairly young and very attractive woman simply drove home her point. Being a mulatto, Julia was light-skinned compared with the average negro, but there was no chance at all she could pass for a white woman. Not even Imogene and Adaline could, for that matter. In truth, the girls' skin color wasn't really any darker than that of many white people. Italians or Spaniards or Louisiana Creoles, at any rate. But their features had a distinctly African cast.

A subtle one, perhaps—but Zachary Taylor was a Southerner himself. He knew full well that any Southerner could distinguish racial origins at a glance unless they'd been almost completely submerged. Why else the fine and precise distinctions between such terms as "mulatto," "quadroon," "octoroon"?

Silently, he leveled a curse on his native land. He understood his fellow Southerners and even liked them most of the time. But there was something ultimately savage and obsessive about his folk when it came to race.

Not all Southerners shared that obsession, of course. He didn't. Senator Johnson didn't. Sam Houston didn't. Even Andrew Jackson didn't, really, once you cut beneath the surface. At least, Old Hickory would make some personal distinctions, even if he agreed with the general attitude.

For a moment, the colonel found himself wishing desperately that Jackson were on the scene. Of course, that would mean a relentless, all-out sort of war, if it came to that. But Jackson would also keep his men in line. Whereas Crittenden's army, from all accounts they'd been getting, had been moving north like so many Huns.

True, the atrocities had been practiced on Choctaws, which meant that from the standpoint of most white Southerners in the area it was all to the good. Leaving aside their own land hunger, there had been plenty of instances in the past of Choctaw outrages against white settlers.

And vice versa, of course. It was a land that sometimes seemed to Taylor to be drenched in blood. He was an experienced and capable Indian fighter himself. But he'd never really shared the common attitude toward the natives. He'd encountered many he'd respected, even admired; and, if nothing else, he liked to think he was too fair-minded. It *was* their land, after all. And if his loyalties were to the American republic, and he didn't have any qualms about driving Indians off the land to allow that republic to swell in greatness, he wasn't going to besmirch himself by adding hypocrisy to the mix, either.

"Damnation," he muttered.

"You shouldn't blaspheme, Colonel, you know that." But Julia was almost grinning as she said it. Over the weeks of their journey, she and Taylor had gotten along quite well.

He sighed and leaned back in his chair at the table in the tavern's dining room. Remembering, as he did so, how he'd had to browbeat the innkeeper's wife into serving Julia and the girls at all.

Damnation.

A bit desperately: "Julia, I have *got* to keep going. Leaving aside the fact that I'm supposed to be reporting back for duty at my post in Baton Rouge, the War Department will want a full report on what's happening in Arkansas."

She shrugged. "So, fine. I can ride, and so can the girls. Just take us with you."

"We're going into a *war*."

The gaze she gave him was level, and rather cold. "Colonel Taylor, I been in a war zone my whole life. So's every colored person in this country. We goin' with you, and that's that."

"All right," he said, giving in to the inevitable. He could hardly refuse, after all, unless he intended to avoid Senator Johnson the rest of his life. He consoled himself with the thought that Dick Johnson served the best and most expensive whiskey in Kentucky at Blue Spring Farm—and made a silent vow, right then and there, to drink the amalgamating bastard dry the next time he visited.

"Just give me the time to write some dispatches," he added, wincing a little. Of all the duties of an officer, writing dispatches was the one he detested the most. He wasn't really that well educated.

Julia smiled. "Tell you what, Zack. I do all the paperwork at home. You tell me what you want, and I'll write 'em for you. My written English is a lot more proper than the way I talk, too."

The temptation was well-nigh irresistible. "It'll look peculiar," he half argued. "You not having what anyone would likely call a masculine hand."

"Tell 'em you sprained your wrist."
Resistance was futile. "Deal."

Natchez, Mississippi
OCTOBER 1, 1824

"Another five dollars," the man offered. He even had the
cash on hand. A half-cagle, at that, which was literally as
good as gold. Even better than the usual Spanish *reales.*

The young man's New England accent irritated the steamboat captain, who had been born and raised in Georgia and
now made his home in New Orleans. But the extra money
offered was too much to pass up.

"All right, then. We'll find you a berth somewhere's
aboard. Though I'm blasted if I understand why a poet wants
to go upriver in these times. I've half a mind not to myself.
Wouldn't, if I didn't have a contract I got to meet."

The New Englander shrugged. "I thought I'd try my hand
at some frontier extravaganzas and the like. Perhaps an epic,
if I can find a suitable topic. New York publishers love the
stuff, and a poet needs an epic to cement his reputation. I
might even be able to sell it in Europe, too."

He didn't seem inclined to explain further. He was practically talking ancient Greek anyway, as far as the captain was
concerned. Poetry. New York publishers. Europe. Epics, no
less!

"Come aboard, then."

The poet found a convenient chair toward the rear of the
deck and set himself up. There was an overhang to shelter
him in case of rain, which would likely be handy. He'd have
to sleep in that chair also, the craft being such a small one.
But the blanket in his trunk should suffice to keep him warm,
this far south and still being in early fall.

Since it would be a day, at least, before the steamboat
neared the scene of the activities he was interested in, he decided he might as well work on "Thanatopsis" further. It had
been his most famous and popular poem since he'd first gotten it published in 1817 in the *North American Review.* But
he'd actually written it in 1811, still one month short of his

seventeenth birthday, and he'd never been satisfied with the end result.

Sadly, he'd soon be forced to put aside poetry, for the most part. There was just no money in it, and now that he was almost thirty years old he needed to find an occupation that would support a family. He had one daughter already and would no doubt soon have other children to care for.

Find another occupation, rather. He'd done well enough as a lawyer but had discovered that he detested the work. Lawyers spent most of their time dealing with people they rarely liked and often loathed. Even the few whose company they might otherwise have enjoyed, they encountered under bad circumstances. So, with the support of his wife, Fanny, he'd decided on journalism, being interested in public affairs. And, now, found himself blessing the impulse that had taken him to the west to write some essays on the new Confederacy. There was quite a bit of fascination with the subject in New England, New York, and Pennsylvania.

Talk about perfect coincidence!

That evening, the captain came by for a brief visit.

"What'd you say your name was?"

"Bryant, Captain. William Cullen Bryant."

At four o'clock the next afternoon, the first corpse drifted past the steamboat. By noon, two more had done the same.

Horrid-looking things. But not as horrid—not nearly—as the corpse they passed on the riverbank. The man—apparently an Indian, although it was difficult to tell—had been spread-eagled on the wheel of an old wagon, flayed, and disemboweled. His intestines—what was left of them, after the birds and animals—trailed on the ground.

Bryant didn't vomit over the side, however, until they passed the corpses of the woman and child who'd been impaled. Both bodies were naked. The woman's breasts had been cut off and . . . something had been done to her groin. Thankfully, the details were impossible to discern in the twilight. From the blood caked in the area, the boy had had his genitals severed. He was perhaps eight years old, as near as Bryant could tell from the distance.

"Boys are bein' right rambunctious," the captain said,

shaking his head. "Don't really hold with it myself, though I understand how they feel."

Tight-lipped, trying to control his stomach, Bryant said nothing.

"Thanatopsis." A teenage boy's poem on death. It all seemed very distant, now.

Journalism, however, did not. That night, on a steamboat deck by lamplight, he began writing in earnest the first article of *An Account of the Current Situation in Arkansas*.

CHAPTER 13

The Mississippi River,
south of Hopefield, Arkansas
OCTOBER 3, 1824

Taylor never saw any bodies in the river, coming down from Memphis, since the current would have taken them away. But he didn't much doubt there had been some. The news of Crittenden's expedition had spread throughout the area. While the main body of freebooters might be coming into Arkansas from the south, there were plenty of adventurers— border ruffians, to call them by their right name—from Missouri and Tennessee and Kentucky who were eager to throw themselves into the fray. Give it a week, and they'd be coming from Mississippi; two weeks, Alabama; a month, if it kept up, from Georgia and the Carolinas; two months, from all over the country, especially the South.

From what he could see from the deck of the steamboat he'd hired—well, commandeered in all but name—some hundreds of freebooters had already passed through the area. And they were being just as rough on anybody they ran into as you'd expect from such men.

When Taylor's steamboat reached Hopefield just after dawn, he discovered the settlement had been deserted, with most of its cabins burnt. And Hopefield had been a white settlement. Taylor had seen two burned-out woodcutters' cabins in the miles they had gone since, and their owners would have also been white people. Some of them, at any rate. They might have been mixed families, whites and Indians, which was a lot more common on the frontier than many people liked to admit.

It didn't matter. By now, over four years after the treaty, it was the firm opinion of white Southerners of the type who'd be attracted to this adventure that any white man who voluntarily settled in Arkansas—anywhere in the Confederacy—was a damned nigger-lover. No better than an abolitionist or one of those detestable New England missionaries who were always prattling nonsense about the "rights of Indians."

And there was some truth to the charge, at least if you removed the loaded terms. White opinion on the subject of race, especially when it came to Indians, had never been uniform. In some ways, because contact was so much closer, even less so in the South than the North. True, there were very few white Southerners who'd admit to having any African ancestry, and none of them willingly, since the legal repercussions were so harsh. However absurd it might be, they'd try their best to use a subterfuge term like "Portuguese." But there were plenty who'd admit to having some Cherokees or Creeks or Choctaws perched in the family tree. Brag about it, in fact—even though everybody in the South knew perfectly well that the southern tribes didn't maintain the same sharp and everlasting barriers to the absorption of negroes that whites officially did. A "full-blood Cherokee" might very well be someone whom Southerners would have labeled a "quadroon" or "mulatto" if he'd been white instead of Indian.

Such white folks would be willing to move to Arkansas readily enough. There were advantages, after all. Just for starters, the treaty had among other things finally removed the legal headaches left over from settling disputed Spanish land grants and insurance claims from the great earthquakes of 1811 and 1812. The Confederacy—or the chiefdom of Arkansas—could issue legal land titles, now. For another thing, within a short time the danger of Indian attacks had receded sharply. The Cherokees were pretty well disciplined, Driscol's people even more so—and they proved soon enough that they could handle any Osage raiding parties.

The land in the Arkansas Delta was rich, once you got past the swamps along the rivers. Good land for livestock and good land for cotton. Slavery was a handy way to organize cotton agriculture, but it was by no means essential. And if Driscol's regime forbade slavery, the Bank of Arkansas was a lot easier to deal with than the Second Bank of the United States, at least if you were a poor white man. Especially since everybody knew that in a pinch, a man could always satisfy a bank debt by serving a term in the Arkansas Army—something that positively infuriated the likes of Crittenden.

Julia came out on deck, interrupting Taylor's musings. Her two daughters were following right behind her.

"How does it look, Zack?"

The question—even more so, the sight of Imogene and Adaline—made up the colonel's mind. The twins were twelve years old, nearing thirteen. Still girls, yes, but already very pretty and entering womanhood. They'd be particularly attractive to slave hunters.

"It's too chancy," he announced. "By now, from all reports I've gotten, the freebooters will have dozens of craft moving up into the Arkansas. Steamboats, keelboats, rowboats, sailboats, canoes, even flatboats—hell, you name it." He gave their own steamboat a quick survey. "No way to fend them off from this thing, not if we get trapped in the river. Not with as few men as I've got. We'll need to disembark at the nearest suitable spot and ride cross-country to Arkansas Post. That should still be safe enough."

"Whatever you say."

*The confluence of the Mississippi
and Arkansas rivers*
OCTOBER 3, 1824

"Oh, dear," said Eliza Ross. Her husband thought the comment was outstandingly low-keyed under the circumstances.

Very much "stiff upper lip," to use the expression that had started coming into vogue during the Napoleonic Wars.

He would have been amused, except there was nothing amusing about the sight of the two riverboats heading for their steamer. Longboats, the British navy would have called them, although Robert had no idea what the correct term was for them here.

True, the boats were oar driven, but with multiple oars and the advantage of the current, they would arrive long before the steamboat could turn itself around and head back to the south. They'd emerged suddenly from the mouth of the Arkansas, just as the steamboat came up. Much as if they'd been lying in ambush.

Which was probably true. Not because the freebooters were targeting their steamboat in particular, but simply because they'd been left behind to seize any steamboat that came along. The freebooters' supply train—if such a term could be used at all—was not likely to have been well planned and organized. By now, especially as scattered as his forces must have gotten from their frenzy of plundering and mayhem as they went upriver, Crittenden must be getting worried about his logistics. Having an extra steamboat would be invaluable, especially one as big as the *Comet*.

"Oh, dear," his wife repeated, as she watched the approaching craft. "What shall we—"

Her question was interrupted as well as answered by Charles Ball's emergence onto the deck.

General Ball, now. The slave disguise was gone, with a vengeance. Ball was wearing his full uniform. The hussar-style uniform had the green pants of an officer, unlike the white ones of enlisted men, with a much fancier green coatee trimmed with black, and the distinctive fur cap. It was something of an odd-looking uniform to Ross, accustomed as he was to the continental styles. But he knew Driscol had had it patterned after the uniforms worn by Canadian *voltigeurs,* and it was probably more practical in this terrain.

Anthony McParland had emerged alongside him, wearing a uniform that was very similar except for the officer's insignia. Right after them came the two corporals, both in enlisted men's uniforms and both carrying muskets. Young as they might be, Callender and Sheffield seemed to be very familiar with the firearms. Knowing Driscol, Ross was quite sure they'd been thoroughly drilled by now.

Still, while the four of them made a resplendent showing on the upper deck of the *Comet,* there were only four of them—and there were at least a dozen men in each of the approaching boats.

David came out on deck, holding a weapon in each hand. "I've brought our pistols, Father."

Six men, then—but two of them armed merely with pistols.

But Robert discovered that he'd underestimated Ball. Most of the Kentucky flatboat men had left the *Comet* the day before, not wishing any further involvement. The men who had remained behind had been the eight black ones and the three poorest-looking of the whites. The most indigent of the lot, Robert had assumed, unable to forgo the free passage no matter what the risk.

"All right, boys!" Ball shouted. "Time to show the bastards what's what, don't you think?"

The eleven "flatboat men" on the lower forward deck grinned up at him. In an instant, any trace of lackadaisical, undisciplined civilians vanished. Before Robert quite understood what they were doing, six of the men were hauling two guns from somewhere below. Four-pounders, in naval carriages.

Rummaging in his memory, Robert recalled seeing a pair of large hatches down there on one of his tours of the boat. Storage, he'd assumed.

Indeed, "storage" it had been. The other five men were bringing forth powder and balls.

Starting to, rather. Seeing what they were carrying, Ball hollered at them.

"Canister, damn you! Think we're fighting a siege? Canister—and be damn quick about it!"

Hastily, the two guilty parties scurried back out of sight. They emerged just a few seconds later carrying a tin of canister each.

"Good, boys! Good!" Ball's tone had gone from fury to praise in a heartbeat. "I want to see the bastards bleed!"

By the time the ammunition carriers got the canister tins to
the front, the rest of the men already had the guns laid and
were training them on the approaching boats. They'd also
done something to the steamboat front rail—the guard, as it
was called—that had lowered a section of it on hinges. That
allowed a clear line of fire while leaving the thick stanchions
necessary to attach the recoil slings. And there were eyebolts
already in place for that purpose. Robert had noticed them
earlier but had not thought much about their function. Tying
up the boat, he'd assumed, even though that was not normally done at the bow.

Robert understood at once that the *Comet* had been prepared for such a battle—and that Ball must have brought
with him the cream of the Iron Battalion's gun crews.

He didn't know whether he should be gratified or furious.
It was clear enough, now, that Ball had been expecting such
an encounter even before they left New Orleans. Half expecting it, at the very least.

Patrick, too, for that matter.

After a moment's hesitation, he decided on gratification.
Why not? It wasn't as if, deep down, he hadn't always
known his wife was right.

"See?" she demanded, as if to prove the point. But there
didn't seem to be any condemnation in her tone, either. Eliza
had been a soldier's wife for decades, a fair bit of which
she'd spent with her husband in the field in Iberia. She was
probably remembering Spanish and Portuguese officers
she'd cursed in the past. For not being able to do a tenth as
much in ten hours as Ball and his men had just shown themselves capable of doing in a few minutes.

And while she didn't have Robert's experience with
battles—never having actually been *at* any of them, thankfully, if not so many miles distant—the sight of those two
cannons would have cheered even the most naïve of civilians.

Robert himself was cheered immensely. True, they were
both four-pounders. It would have been foolish to bring any
larger ordnance. As big as it was, by steamboat standards,
the *Comet* lacked the sheer bulk and bracing that warships
had to have to withstand the recoil of heavier guns.

But, in the here and now, four-pounders should do very

nicely, he thought. Those two approaching longboats were even further removed from ships of the line. Cockleshells, practically, and jammed full of men.

Worried men, now. The freebooters were close enough to have spotted the cannons—which they quite obviously hadn't been expecting.

"Hey!" one of them shouted, half rising to his feet in the lead boat. "You there in the—"

"Fire!" Ball bellowed.

Belatedly remembering some of the realities of cannon fire—the wind was blowing the wrong way, too—Robert hissed: "Eliza! David! Close your eyes!"

He did the same himself. The sharp double clap of the four-pounders was followed, very quickly, by the familiar feel of unburned powder and smoke on his face. Along with, of course, that very familiar smell.

As it always did, the odor roused something deep and primitive in Robert Ross. As soon as he felt the gust passing, he opened his eyes. Only with great effort was he able to restrain himself from shouting the sort of praise and encouragement he would have shouted, in years past, to his own soldiers.

The man who'd been half standing in the bow of the lead ship was nowhere to be seen. Not surprising, that. The bow itself had been badly splintered by canister balls. Not shattered, since Ball's guns hadn't been using round shot, or even the heavy shot that naval men called grapeshot. But it hardly mattered. Canister rounds weighed three ounces each: twice the weight of a musket ball. At that range, a three-ounce ball wouldn't destroy a wooden boat, but it would do a very nice job of shredding it some. And even a four-pounder fired a lot of them at once. Like a huge shotgun, for all intents and purposes.

The men in the bow of that lead boat had all been killed or mutilated. Or both, mostly. The ones toward the rear who'd survived had done so simply because their comrades had absorbed most of the fire—and not all of them had come off it uninjured.

Three of them were just sitting in the boat, screaming, covered with blood. How much of it was theirs was impossible to determine. The rest were already throwing them-

selves overboard and starting to swim toward the west bank
of the river, over a hundred yards distant.

The second boat was desperately trying to turn around.
Clearly enough, that crew had no intention of risking all in a
fierce boarding attempt.

Wisely, Robert thought. Even if they could have reached
the steamboat before another volley was fired from the cannons, they no longer outnumbered Ball's men by any significant margin. And he didn't doubt for a moment that every
one of those so obviously experienced gunners was just
about as skilled with pistols and hand weapons.

"I want that boat down!" Ball hollered. "Don't you give
me one and not the other, you blasted curries!"

One of the white gunners flashed a grin. However much
he might have taken offense as being labeled a curry under
other circumstances, under this one he apparently simply
found it amusing.

Ball didn't see the grin. He was already turning his glare
onto Callender McParland and young Parker.

"All right, boys. Jones been braggin' you the best shots in
his regiment. That's why you here, wet behind the ears and
all." He pointed at the boat some forty yards away, which
was now halfway through its turn. A man was crouched in
the stern, yelling orders.

"Take him down," Ball hissed. "I want that bastard *down*."

Both young corporals already had their muskets leveled.
Rifled muskets, Robert now understood, from the way they
were actually aiming the weapons, not simply pointing them
in the general direction of the enemy.

For a brief moment, they seemed to hesitate. Robert recognized the moment. Just so had he seen other young soldiers, in times past, hesitate before firing their first shot
intended for real murder. Just so could he remember himself
hesitating, that first time so long ago.

Ball knew the moment also. "*Down,* I said." But he
growled the words; he didn't shout them. This was not the
time for shouting.

Sheffield Parker fired first, just a split second before Callender. Robert saw his shot take the steersman in the shoulder, lifting and turning him just in time to take Callender's

shot in the chest. A second later, his corpse—for corpse it surely was—splashed into the river.

"Good," Ball said. "Reload."

He paid no more attention to the teenage corporals, leaning instead over the guard of the upper deck and going back to hollering at his gun crews.

Hollering, now. No need for tenderness—of sorts—dealing with such veterans.

"Kill 'em, God damn you! Kill 'em all!"

Two seconds later, both cannons fired almost simultaneously. And—

Robert looked up at the target.

And it was done. For the most part, at least. There were survivors, of course. There almost always were, even with a murderous volley at such close range. Time after time, Robert had been astonished at the way the whimsy of battle would rip one man to pieces and completely spare the man next to him. That same whimsy had saved his life more than once.

Still, over half were dead or wounded. Only four of them went over the side into the river, to start swimming after their companions toward the shore.

Robert wondered if Ball would show any mercy. He didn't expect he would.

No, no chance of it.

"Reload, blast you! That boat's bloody but it's still not down! I want it *down!*"

The gun crews went through their practiced cycle. Ball turned back to the youngsters. "Don't waste shots on them while they're still in the water. But the minute they start climbing up on shore, I want to see at least two of them dead before the rest get away. You hear me? Two, at a rock-hard damn bottom!"

Callender was a bit pale-faced, perhaps. Impossible to tell about Sheffield, as dark-skinned as he was. But from the tightness of the young negro's very full lips, he seemed determined to keep whatever emotions he was feeling under control.

Splendid young soldiers. Whoever this "Jones" was, Robert had no difficulty understanding why he'd recommended them to Ball. Their marksmanship had only been part of it, as always—and not the most important part. This was probably their first real clash at arms, and they were conducting themselves with as much composure as most veterans.

The cannons went off again. That volley slew whoever might still have been alive on the second boat, and punched enough holes in the hull that it began to settle. Robert swiveled his head and saw that the first boat was still afloat. But it was drifting with the current, obviously out of control, leaking streams of blood into the water. The three men slumped in the boat might still be alive—some of them might even survive the whole experience—but they were no longer a threat to anyone.

By now, even with the difficulty of reloading rifled muskets, Callender and Sheffield had them ready. Not quite to shoulder, but close. Waiting for their targets to come out of the water. To his surprise, Robert saw that the shore was now much closer. Apparently—he'd never noticed—the steamboat pilot had been driving the craft after the men swimming toward safety.

That seemed rather dangerous, Robert thought. He was no expert on the subject, but he could remember people talking about the perils of navigating the Mississippi, much of which was still uncharted. The river was so muddy that it was impossible to see more than an inch or two beneath the surface. If they grounded on a hidden sandbar or hit a submerged snag . . .

The first of the freebooters reached the riverbank and started to clamber ashore, with two of his companions right behind. From the corner of his eye, Robert could see the two corporals aiming.

But they never fired. Instead, a volley was fired from somewhere in the thick growth next to the river. All three of the freebooters were blown right back into the river. The two remaining, who'd been with that first five, were paralyzed by the shock, crouched half in and half out of the water.

A man stalked out of the foliage, a pistol in his hand. From a distance of five feet, he leveled the pistol and shot one freebooter in the head. Then, he leaped on the other and began clubbing him senseless with the pistol butt. His opponent tried to resist, but to no avail. His attacker seemed on the slender side, but there was something utterly relentless about the way he kept slamming down the pistol butt. As if, half immersed in water like his companion, he was engaging in some sort of horrible, upside-down baptism.

Within half a minute, the freebooter slipped into the water. His body, rather. That skull had been shattered into a pulp.

The four remaining freebooters were now treading water in the middle of the river, trapped between the oncoming steamboat and whoever had fired the volley from the riverbank. Their faces looked pale. One of them was gaping like a fish.

"Did I say anything about quarter?" Robert heard Ball snarl at the two corporals.

"No, sir," replied Sheffield. "But you did say—"

"Don't sass me, boy! I said don't waste shots while they were in the water. At this range—now— that don't count. Or if it does, you not the men Jones said you were."

Parker's jaws tightened, just for an instant. Then:

"Yes, sir." He stepped up to the rail, aimed, fired. Quick as that. The freebooter with the gaping mouth went under, leaving a little patch of blood and brains on the surface.

Callender was a bit slower. Not much. Another shot, and another freebooter went down. Rolled, rather, the way a slain fish might, before slowly starting to sink.

The two survivors—the second boat's sole survivors, now—began frantically swimming downstream.

"Follow 'em!" Ball yelled to someone Robert couldn't see. The pilot, he assumed.

A voice came back. "Be damned if I will! Be damned, I say! This ain't your boat, Ball—and I ain't in the fucking army!"

A sudden moment of mercy, Robert might have assumed, except for the next exercise in profanity and blasphemy.

"God damn you, Ball, this boat is *valuable!* Henry Shreve'll have my fucking hide, I run it aground and we gotta scuttle it! Which we will, God damn your black soul, 'cause there ain't no way were gonna—"

"Oh, never mind. And shut up!" Ball hollered back. "It's all gonna be over soon, anyway, so take your blasted boat wherever you want to—as long as it's upstream and into the Arkansas!"

Soon, indeed. Robert could now see over a dozen men emerging from the foliage by the river. All of them were armed with muskets, and all of them were half running down the riverbank, keeping even with the swimmers. Like a pack of wolves trailing wounded prey.

It was over quickly. The two surviving freebooters were exhausted by now, as much from sheer fright as from physical exertion. The moment one of them slowed, a dozen muskets went off. At least one of the rounds hit. Another patch of red stain was all that was left on the surface of the river.

It took almost a minute for the repetition. Mainly because the men, whoever they were, were clearly not experienced infantrymen. They took much too long to reload. Still, another volley went off soon enough, and the last head faded from sight.

By now, a different river might have been streaked with blood. The carnage had been as horrendous as any Robert had ever seen in a small unit action. But the muddy Mississippi swept it all away within seconds.

Half an hour later, the pilot finally agreed he had a safe place to bring the steamboat alongshore. There was a pier there. Not much of one, since it had clearly been designed for a much smaller boat than the *Comet*. Still, it was enough to tie up to.

Seventeen men came out of the woods, five of them boys. Along with them came six girls and four young women, two of whom were carrying infants. All were white except for two of the adult males, one of the boys, and one of the infant-toting women. They were black.

The man who led the way across into the steamboat was the same one who'd clubbed the man in the river. Robert hadn't been able to discern his features, at a distance, but there was something distinct about his way of moving.

He was quite a young man, Robert realized, once he came aboard. He hadn't seemed so, at first, from the severity of his features.

"Name's Brown," he said to Ball. "John Brown." He turned and helped one of the young women with an infant into the boat. "My wife, Dianthe. My whole family—those as are living in Arkansas—and the people working for me."

The pistol was stuck back in his belt. Shifting his musket to his left hand, he stuck out his right to Ball. "Pleased to meet you."

"Charles Ball. General in the Arkansas Army. You the one got that new tannery set up near the river?"

"*Had* a new tannery," Brown corrected. Tight-jawed but not seeming especially angry. More like a man depicting an unfortunate turn in the weather—but such is God's will.

"They burned me out," he explained. "Not without a fight, mind you. But there was too many to make a stand, so we ran off after shooting a few."

Ball nodded. "We're heading up the Arkansas, if you want to join us. To be honest, I could use your help. Don't know what's waiting for me up there. But . . . it's likely to be another fight, and you got children and womenfolk."

"Would they be any safer anywhere else?" Brown asked, mildly. "With the land overrun by heathens? I think not. Yes, we'll join you. We'll fight, too. But—!"

He held up a stiff, admonishing finger. "I want it clearly understood that I am not enlisting in any army! I'll fight, but I won't be a soldier. Meaning no personal offense, General Ball, but you're a blaspheming lot."

CHAPTER 14

"I'm starting to get a little worried, Scott," Ray Thompson confided to his friend. The two of them were resting in a field, leaning against a tree stump, watching what remained of a small farm cabin burn to the ground. By now, it was mostly embers.

"You're just *starting* to get worried?" Powers jibed. "Gol dern, I wonder why. Could it be that it just dawned on you that Crittenden set off without having any resupply figured out? Oh, but I forget. We were gonna 'live off the richness of the land,' weren't we?"

He half leveled his musket at the smoldering cabin. "Insofar as a nigger's ain't-got-a-pot-to-piss-in shack qualifies as 'the richness of the land.' Insofar as it would have, I mean, if these crackers and yahoos weren't burning everything down the moment they come to it."

Thompson couldn't help but smile a little. He wasn't any fonder of most of their "compatriots" than Powers was. Both of them—quietly and privately, of course—had shared a laugh after four of Crittenden's men had been blown to shreds at Brown's tannery and another half dozen had been injured. It turned out that the damned abolitionist had left kegs of gunpowder behind, strategically situated. When the mob started burning down the tannery without investigating the premises first, the charges had exploded.

But the smile faded very quickly, and Thompson returned stubbornly to the subject. "Quit making jokes, Scott. Or have you got some magic sack full of food I don't know about?"

Powers sucked his teeth, idly watching a group of men raping one of the two black women they'd found in the shack. That was the young one. The older of the two— presumably her mother—was huddled over the corpse of a middle-aged black man lying in the dust some ten yards away. She was weeping softly, seemingly oblivious to everything else around her.

"No, I don't," he admitted. "But we'll find what we need at Arkansas Post." He nodded toward the corpse. "I figure he wasn't lying none. Not after his ears were cut off."

Gloomily, Thompson studied the body. Other than the skin color, it was impossible any longer to tell much about the man. His nose had been cut off also, along with his genitals and both of his hands. After the group that had been torturing him at Crittenden's command to get information were done, there hadn't been any point in keeping him alive. You'd have had to offer money to get anyone in the slave market at New Orleans to take him. So, the crackers had amused themselves for a time before he finally bled to death.

Crittenden might have told them to stop wasting time, but he'd left right after the negro had told them of the storehouses in Arkansas Post. Of course, whether they'd have listened to him or not was another question. Except for the men under the command of the Lallemand brothers, Crittenden's army was to discipline what a tornado was to decorum.

Well . . . it wasn't quite that bad. Most of the men belonged to groups of one sort or another. Even if the lines of authority were loose and informal, they existed at least on that level.

As was demonstrated, in fact, just that moment. Another man came up, wearing an outfit that bore a passing resemblance to a uniform if you squinted and were willing to make some allowances. He had a real sword, too, not one of the big knives that usually did for one on the frontier.

"Cut it out!" he shouted, grabbing the current rapist by the scruff of his neck and hauling him off the woman. There was something downright comical about the look on the rapist's face: a combination of outrage, frustration, and surprise.

"Just relax, boys. We'll be fuckin' her all the way down the Mississippi," the "officer" said, in a friendlier tone, lifting the man to his feet. "You betchum. We want that nigger pregnant by the time we put her up on the block. But we got to get going, before somebody else grabs the boat I got us."

That was standard procedure for slavers. Thompson had served for two years on the crew of a slave ship. That's where he'd first met Scott Powers, who'd been an officer of the ship. Even though the international slave trade had been illegal in the United States since 1808, it still went on despite the risk. Mostly, of course, for the profits involved; but there were also the perquisites and the side benefits. Young black women would be segregated from the rest of the cargo and raped all the way across the Atlantic. Entertainment for the crew during the voyage—and a pregnant female was worth more on the slave block when they arrived. "Two-for-one" for the buyer—and, more important, proof that the female was good breeding stock.

Grudgingly, the little crowd around the young black woman obeyed their commander. Two of them hauled her to her feet, one of them taking the time to yank her torn and dirty dress back down to her knees. The woman's eyes seemed vacant until, wandering, they fell on the corpse lying in the dirt. Then she let out a wail before one of the men holding her slapped her face.

"What do we do with this one?" another man asked, pointing with his pistol at the older woman still clutching the corpse.

The commander studied her for a moment, then shrugged. "May as well leave her. She's too old to bring much, and we ain't got enough food to begin with."

The man who'd asked the question looked back down at the woman. Then, cocked his pistol and shot her in the back of the head.

The younger woman wailed again, and got another slapping.

"Runnin' low on powder, too," the commander said sourly. But he didn't carry the chastisement any further.

Thompson didn't blame him. Killing the woman had been

pointless, but control over a crew like this was always a chancy thing. As excited and fired up as they were, Crittenden's army had been killing, burning, raping, and torturing anyone they ran across almost since they left Alexandria. Crittenden had barely been able to keep them in check until they passed beyond the borders of Louisiana—and then, only when they came across white people.

Some of those activities had had a conscious purpose—especially the ones aimed at the Choctaw—but most of them had been as mindless as a shark's feeding frenzy. Just the way it was, with expeditions like this, as a rule. Lallemands' men were under better discipline, but Crittenden wasn't so much leading this army as he was trying to half steer a raft through turbulent rapids.

Thompson and Powers watched the group as they dragged the woman into a keelboat and shoved her onto a bench alongside two other negroes they'd caught. Both young boys, in this case. Then, at a command from their leader, they pushed off from the bank and started rowing down the Arkansas toward its junction with the Mississippi.

"Damn fools," Powers said. "For the price of three slaves! You won't catch me heading off without enough men around to handle Choctaws. I don't care if I find me a pot of gold. They'll be riled right good, by now."

Thompson grunted his agreement. What concerned him, however, was that he was pretty sure a lot of the men in Crittenden's force weren't going to have the same horse sense. This was likely to be just the first of many small groups peeling away from the expedition once they'd gotten their hands on a few slaves. Not all of the men who'd come with Crittenden were looking to set up plantations in the northern part of the Delta. That took some money, no matter what else—access to loans, at any rate—and plenty of these boys didn't have any more of a pot to piss in than a negro did. A fair number of them were, quite literally, former pirates.

But there was nothing they could do about it, so he levered himself onto his feet, using the musket as a brace. "Come on, we may as well catch up with Crittenden."

"Our own veritable Napoleon," Powers sneered. But he was getting to his feet also. There wasn't really any alternative, no matter what qualms and reservations they were both

starting to have. Even leaving aside the risk of encountering
Choctaws, the land behind them had been so thoroughly rav-
aged that they wouldn't find enough food to get them back to
Louisiana.

*The confluence of the Arkansas
and the Mississippi*
OCTOBER 4, 1824

By midafternoon, Ball had made his decision.

"All right, General Ross. Much as it rubs me the wrong
way, I admit you're probably right. We oughta keep this boat
here, not be running up the Arkansas with it."

Since it had taken Robert most of a day to persuade the
black general of something so obvious, he was careful to do
nothing more than nod agreeably. Ball was far from stupid,
and a very experienced combat veteran to boot. But the problem was that, as was uniformly true of the officer corps of
the army of Arkansas from Patrick Driscol on down, his
experience was deep but narrow. It was an army led by sergeants, essentially. Granted, some of the finest noncommissioned officers Robert Ross had ever encountered, but
without enough experience at higher command levels to really grasp that war was much broader than battles.

The idea of taking such a critical piece of military equipment as a large steamboat armed with cannons—which
could completely cut off any chance of Crittenden being
resupplied—in order to use it for what amounted to nothing
more than a big water-going cavalry horse . . .

From Robert's viewpoint, the idea had been sheer insanity. But it had taken a whole night and most of a day to finally convince Ball on the matter. Again, not because the
man was stupid, but simply because he wasn't accustomed
to thinking in strategic terms.

Worse than that, really. Ball had been trained *not* to think
in such terms. In the modern era of line warfare, massed
muskets, and cannons against equal masses—and naval warfare was no different at all—the last thing an officer wanted
was sergeants who tried to think for themselves. There was
no room in such utterly brutal and up-close combat for independent initiative. What was wanted, from the men and the

noncommissioned officers who led them, was simply obedi-
ence, discipline, and courage. Don't *think.* Just face the
enemy, fire, accept the casualties, reload, step forward, fire
again. And do it and do it and do it—the very same thing, in-
variant and inflexible—until the enemy broke.

Patrick Driscol might be an exception, to a degree. To
begin with, he'd had the experience of serving as what
amounted to Winfield Scott's sergeant major in the Niagara
campaign. And with his years of service in the French army
during the Napoleonic Wars, he had a much wider range of
experience than someone like Charles Ball. Still, even
Patrick was likely to be rigid and angular in his thinking.
He'd be oriented toward war as a series of battles, rather
than seeing war as a complete campaign.

So be it. Robert was not frustrated, really, even if there'd
been moments over the past twenty-four hours when he'd
felt like hitting Ball on the head with a pistol butt. The truth
was, he was in his element.

It had been a long time. But he was finding that, near the
age of sixty, his body might be creaking a bit—leaving aside
the lingering effects of his wounds in the American war—
but there was nothing wrong with his brain. He'd been, all
false modesty aside, one of the half dozen best generals in
the British army—and that, during a time when the quality
of generalship had reached a peak because of the demands
of the great war.

His wife had commented on it, the night before. In a manner
of speaking, the memory of which left Robert feeling half
embarrassed and half smug.

"And what brought *that* on?" she'd asked, smiling from
under a sweat-soaked brow. Her hair, splayed across the little pillow in their cabin, had been almost as wet. It was a hot
and humid climate, and neither of them were what you'd
call spry any longer. He'd been covered with just as much
sweat.

How to explain?

"Never mind," she said, adding a little laugh. "Thank God
I'm too old to get pregnant, or I'd be bearing quintuplets in
nine months."

She reached over and stroked his cheek. "Robert," she

said softly, "I know you're feeling . . . useful again. But please be careful. This is not actually our war, and you are not actually a general in it."

"Yes, dearest," he'd agreed. Knowing, finally, that he was lying. Or would be, at any rate, before much longer. He would *make* it his war. Share in it, for a certainty.

All through the next day, as he argued with Ball, one part of Robert's mind had been attentive to his son. David, he understood, was making the same decision himself—and doing it with the verve and recklessness of a nineteen-year-old. By midmorning, his mother's protestations notwithstanding, he'd had a spare uniform refitted by the captain's wife and was training with one of the gun crews.

He looked to be quite good at it, too.

It couldn't be said that Ball actually sulked after agreeing to Robert's proposal. But he was noticeably gruff toward his men for a time thereafter. If Ball had been harsh and even caustic during the moments of combat the previous day, Robert had found him to be very good humored any other time.

Fortunately, the time was brief. Before the sun had reached the western horizon, Robert was vindicated.

Twice, in fact—even if, ironically, neither of the instances had anything to do with cutting lines of supply. But Ball was beginning to learn what any capable general knew in his bones: that a good strategic move always brought serendipitous results in its wake.

"Hey, we're noncombatants!" the captain of the captured steamboat protested.

"Not anymore," Ball countered cheerfully.

The captain stared at the Arkansas soldiers who were hacking away the front guard of his steamboat with axes. Then, stared at the soldiers manhandling a cannon from one steamboat to the other. It was a tricky operation, even with the two boats tied together in the middle of the river.

"This is piracy!" he squawked.

Robert cleared his throat, drawing the man's eyes. "Actually, it's not, by the laws of war. The Confederacy of the

Arkansas has been invaded by an army coming out of the territory of the United States. Until and unless the United States makes clear through diplomatic channels that there was no official involvement—and takes rigorous and public measures to put a stop to such offenses—General Ball has no choice but to conclude that a state of war exists. That being the case, he has every right—indeed, the obligation as an officer—to seize enemy property that might be turned to military advantage."

He added a smile for good measure. "Provided, of course, he follows proper military procedure and sees to it that his men remain disciplined and no outrages are committed against the persons owning the property. Which, I dare say, he has done meticulously in this case."

He turned the smile onto the American who'd been scribbling furiously in his notebook since the moment the steamboat had come into sight and been captured. "Wouldn't you agree, Mr. Bryant?"

"Oh, yes," the scribbler replied, not even looking up from his scribbling. "Been right the proper gentleman."

"Damn New Englander!"

Bryant finally looked up from his notebook. "New Englander or not, Captain, I remain a citizen of the United States. Registered to vote, I assure you. And I'm just as curious to know as General Ball is, how it came to pass that an army large enough to commit savageries that would have shamed the Huns managed to assemble, train, and launch an attack on a neighboring country from the state of Louisiana—without, so far as I can determine at the moment, any official of that state issuing so much as a peep of protest. Perhaps I shall ask you for an interview. Being as you are, I understand, a citizen of Louisiana."

The captain's jaws tightened. Bryant went on, relentlessly: "I'm curious to discover if the state of Louisiana entertains a different translation of the Constitution than my native state of Massachusetts—or any other state of the Union, so far as I'm aware. I refer you to Article I, Section 8. The right to select officers for the militia is reserved to the states, true enough, but only Congress can declare war."

"That ain't no Gol-derned militia! That's just Crittenden and his boys!"

"Ah. Pirates, in other words. Or bandits, if you prefer. May I quote you to that effect?"

"You sure as Sam Hill can *not*. Those boys find out I said any such thing, my life ain't worth a plucked chicken."

"Oh, splendid. That'll do even better." Bryant began scribbling in his notebook. "A knowledgeable local source who insisted on remaining anonymous for his own safety depicted Crittenden and his men as criminal extortionists, who would cold-bloodedly murder any man who exposed their nefarious activities to the light of day."

"I said no such thing!"

"Actually, you did," said Robert mildly. "If not in so many words."

Ball was less diplomatic. "Sure did. And fuck you. This boat now belongs to the Arkansas Army. And if you don't pilot it for me, you best stop worrying about what Crittenden's men'll do to you."

His black face could have served as the model for a bust entitled *Menace*.

"You wouldn't!" the captain protested.

Ball sneered. "No, *I* wouldn't. Don't need to. You don't do what I tell you, you be useless. Ain't no room for useless men on this boat, so I'll have to set you ashore. A ways down, though. In Choctaw territory."

The captain's face paled. Ball swiveled his head to the south. "I do believe the Choctaws be pissed, right around now. Pissed like you wouldn't believe. 'Course, they might listen to you, when you explain you just an innocent bystander. But if I was you, I surely wouldn't want to bet on it."

"All right, then," the captain muttered.

Less than half an hour later, the newly expanded flotilla made its next capture: a keelboat, filled with white men and three negroes. One young black woman and two black boys.

They didn't put up a fight. Not with two steamboats alongside and cannons trained on them. And close to thirty well-armed men with muskets leveled.

Bryant interviewed the blacks, who turned out to be captives. The boys, at least. The young woman—not much more than a girl, really—was too distraught to be coherent. Clearly enough, she'd been badly abused.

Ball's interview of the white men was extremely brief. There wasn't any mystery about their identity, after all, even without the testimony of the two boys.

"Hang 'em," he ordered, "I want to save our powder."

"You can't do that!" shrieked the man who seemed to be the leader of the group.

Ball's expression had long since gone beyond menace.

"Watch me, you pile of shit," he said. "You'll have the best view around."

After it was done, and the corpses had been pitched into the river, Ball took a few minutes to settle his anger. That was the mark of a good officer, too. Robert's hopes for the man kept rising.

Still higher, when Ball turned to him for advice.

"What do you recommend now, General? I'd dearly love to have some knowledge of what's happening upriver." He nodded to the west. "The Arkansas, I mean."

The two steamboats were now positioned right at the confluence. Controlling both rivers completely, at least until such time as an opposing force of warships could arrive. Which wasn't likely to happen any time soon, in Robert's estimation. Unless he was badly mistaken, both the state of Louisiana and the American federal authorities had been caught by surprise by Crittenden's expedition. Not the fact of it, so much as the timing. From what they'd been able to glean, Crittenden had come into a sudden and unexpected windfall in terms of arms. The expectation had been that he couldn't launch any serious attack on Arkansas until the following year, if ever.

By now, after two decades of constant freebooting activity into Mexico and—in times past—Florida and Amelia Island, the mere fact that a band of adventurers had gathered somewhere in the Gulf and was making noise didn't really mean that much. Even as large a group as Crittenden had assembled needed more in the way of arms and ammunition than personal weaponry. Following the Adams-Onis Treaty, the United States had clamped down on the former custom of providing unofficial assistance through government channels.

As he pondered the answer to Ball's question, Robert's eyes fell on Bryant. The young New England poet and journalist had left off his interview of the rescued negroes and was back to scribbling. He had the look of an energetic and curious man, as well as an intelligent and well-educated one. It would be interesting to see what his investigations turned up, once he returned to the United States. Somebody had provided those arms to Crittenden—or the money for them, at any rate. And as quickly as it had happened, it had to have been one man or a small handful. No collection taken up from a large group contributing small amounts could possibly have done it so quickly and so secretively.

A cabal, in short. The American public doted on tales of cabals and conspiracies in high places. Robert had hopes for the poet, too.

But it was time to give Ball an answer, and the answer was obvious—even if Robert didn't much like it. Still . . .

Parker and the two McParlands weren't the first young men he'd sent into harm's way in his life. Not by several decades' worth. He doubted they would be the last.

"A reconnaissance is in order, I think. Now that"—he nodded toward the captured keelboat—"you've acquired the means for it, without jeopardizing your main force. I'd recommend Captain McParland for the commanding officer. Beyond that—"

But Ball was already turning away, and Robert closed his mouth. There was really no need to give Ball advice on the rest.

"Anthony!" Ball hollered. "You and Corporals McParland and Parker. Take enough men to man the oars on the keelboat and head upriver." He pointed to the west, his finger indicating the Arkansas. "I want information, mind. Don't be gettin' in no pointless scrapes."

Robert hesitated. But before it was necessary to intervene, Ball corrected his own error.

"Ah, never mind that. I don't need the information so much as Patrick does. You do whatever you gotta to do to find him. Let him know where things stand down here."

Captain McParland nodded and began giving orders.

Robert relaxed and went back to watching Bryant at his work.

It was quite a bright day, he realized. Even now, so close to sundown.

Just after sunset, many miles downriver, another keelboat finally drifted ashore. The sole survivor of the three men in the boat clambered painfully onto the east bank of the Mississippi.

As exhausted as he was—the wound in his leg had kept him from sleeping—he was still shaking from the whole experience. Seeing most of his friends ripped to shreds by that incredible steamboat—*since when did steamboats have cannons?* he was still wondering—and then watching two of them slowly bleed to death, was never anything he'd expected when he joined up with Crittenden. He was only twenty-two years old.

He'd barely gotten ashore when he half sensed a threat. Turning his head, he got a glimpse of a war club coming at him before he lost consciousness altogether.

When he woke up, his head ached and there was dried blood caked on the side of his face. He tried to wipe it off but discovered his hands were tied.

What—?

Everything was flickering. It took him a while to realize that night had fallen and that he was seeing everything by the light of a fire in a small clearing. A while longer, to realize that he'd been tied spread-eagled between two trees in the clearing. And a bit longer still, to discover that he was naked.

Not long at all, then, to realize the rest. The dozen or so men also in the clearing were all Choctaws, from their outfits. He was pretty sure they were, anyway. Indians all looked alike to him, but since he'd moved to Mississippi from South Carolina he'd gotten to know a little of the differences in the way the various southern tribes dressed.

Knives, however—Indian, white, or Creole, it really didn't matter—all looked very much the same. And he was looking at an awful lot of them.

"Oh, shit," was all he could think to say.

CHAPTER 15

Arkansas Post
OCTOBER 5, 1824

It took a day longer to reach Arkansas Post than Zachary Taylor had expected. He'd assumed that, this being the autumn, the White River would be fairly low, and fording it would be easy enough.

And so, in fact, it had proved—once they *got* to the river. What he hadn't realized was how difficult the terrain between the Mississippi and the White rivers would be in the first place. No settlers had moved into this part of the Delta yet, and the natural landscape was essentially unmodified. Swamps, bayous, oxbow lakes, a profusion of creeks— everything that cavalrymen detested.

Crossing the White itself hadn't been a big problem, although they'd had to travel upriver a ways to find a ford. But, finally, a day late, they'd arrived at Arkansas Post.

More precisely, *would* have arrived—except by now, the fort was under siege.

"A day late and a dollar short," Taylor muttered to himself. "For want of a nail. Hell and damnation."

He didn't even have the advantage of high terrain, from which he might have been able to spot the gaps in the siege lines. There wasn't any high terrain worth talking about, in the area. The only reason he was able to observe the Post at all, from a reasonably close range, was simply because most of the area north of the river hadn't been cleared yet, and the terrain was still heavily wooded.

That there *were* gaps in the siege lines was certain, for the good and simple reason that the terms "siege" and "lines," applied to Crittenden's army, were laughable to begin with. That wasn't really an army out there; it was just a very big lynch mob. Or bandit raid—take your pick. Given the nature of Crittenden's forces, the distinction was pretty much meaningless.

Unfortunately for Crittenden—this much was also obvious, even from Taylor's limited vantage point—the lynchees who were the target of the mob's attention were hardly the sort they'd have found in a local county jail. First, because they were armed. Second, because the authorities in Arkansas had apparently taken the time since the founding of the Confederacy four years earlier to turn a ramshackle French trading post into a fort.

A frontier fort, granted, with wooden palisades instead of stone walls. But Taylor could see that they'd even dug a moat around the fortified town, on all three sides that weren't already sheltered by the Arkansas, and kept it filled with water diverted from the river. No dinky little ditch, either. This was full-scale military construction, with a twenty-foot moat, glacis, scarp, counterscarp, the whole works. There were even berms protecting the four-pounders positioned just outside the walls of the fort—with gates right behind them through which the guns could be hauled if it appeared an enemy was making a successful assault on the outer fortifications.

Not that there was much chance of that, with an enemy like Crittenden's mob. The Arkansans had kept the glacis meticulously clear of any growth and had cleared the area well beyond it. Any assaulting force would have to cross at least five hundred yards in the open, the last thirty yards while climbing up a glacis; then, have to cross the moat, whose waters were undoubtedly at least eight feet deep; and then have to clamber up a scarp before they could finally reach the fort's guns. Which, by then, would have been withdrawn into the palisade anyway. All the while, being swept by canister fired from four-pounders manned—Taylor was sure of this, too—by some of the same veterans of the Iron Battalion who had broken British elite regiments at the Mississippi in 1815 and routed the Louisiana militia at Algiers five years later.

Even the U.S. Army would suffer major casualties in any

such assault against defenders like these. Taylor himself wouldn't be willing to try it without a minimum of three regiments in the attacking force—and only if those were regular units, not state militias. In his estimate, the likelihood that Crittenden's yahoos would be able to storm the fort was about that of the proverbial snowball's chance in Hell.

Not far away, looking at Arkansas Post from the opposite side of the river, two other men reached the same conclusion.

"Well, shit," said Ray Thompson.

"We are well and truly fucked," agreed Scott Powers. Sighing, he squatted on the ground, propping himself with his musket. "God damn Robert Crittenden. God damn all Crittendens. God damn every Kentuckian who ever lived. Louisianans, too."

Thompson squatted next to him. "So what do we do now?"

Powers gave him a sideways glance. "Meaning no offense, Ray, but what's 'we' got to do with it? You got hard-nosed creditors. I don't." He inclined the musket forward, pointing toward Arkansas Post. "You want to get your head blown off trying to take that place, you go right ahead. Me, this was just supposed to be a stepping-stone to Texas. I'll take Mexican regulars over these crazy Arkansas niggers any day of the week, and twice on Sunday."

Thompson scowled but didn't make any response. He and Scott were pretty good friends, all things considered. But "friendship" in their circles had some clear and definite limits. That Powers would abandon him in an instant if he thought it necessary was a given.

The opposite was also true, of course. And now, somewhere in the back of his mind, Thompson was starting to gauge that possibility.

"Non," Charles Lallemand said forcefully to Robert Crittenden. *"Absolument pas!"* He pointed stiffly at the fort across the river and shifted to heavily accented English. "We have no more chance of storming it than we do of swimming back to Alexandria."

"Less," his brother Henri-Dominique added with a sneer. His eyes ranged over the mass of men clustered on the south bank of the Arkansas. Most of them were shouting curses and jeers at their opponents across the river, brandishing their muskets in what they apparently thought were warlike gestures. A fair number of them were even firing at Arkansas Post. At a range of perhaps four hundred yards, and getting low on powder.

It might be possible to plumb the depths of American stupidity, but Henri-Dominique suspected the line necessary would be so long that only a team of oxen could hold it up. Why had he and his brother ever agreed to this madness in the first place?

The answer, alas, was obvious. Money. Their enterprises in Alabama had turned out poorly, and they'd not been able to resist Crittenden's blandishments concerning the wealth of new plantations in the Delta. So perhaps their own stupidity was not much shallower.

Glumly, while his brother Charles and Robert Crittenden continued their argument, Henri-Dominique studied the Arkansas fortifications across the river. About the only consolation he could find was that at least they'd been designed by a man who'd also once served in the emperor's colors.

Poor consolation, though. The empire was gone, vanished, and there was today to be dealt with. Henri-Dominique and his brother had both known, of course, that Driscol was a veteran of the French army. But they'd never expected anything like *this*. And, unfortunately—he took a moment to curse himself and Charles along with Crittenden and his men—they hadn't taken seriously the few reports they'd gotten about the nature of the fortifications at Arkansas Post. In their experience, an American "moat" was a poor excuse for a ditch, a "walled fort" was a glorified log cabin, and such terms as "glacis" and "counterscarp" were quite literally foreign.

He was still surprised, though, at the quality of the design. He wouldn't have thought a sergeant, on his own, would have been able to come up with it. Especially a sergeant whose service, by all accounts, had been entirely in units on the line.

"Absolument pas!" his brother repeated.

"Merde, alors," Henri-Dominique added for good measure.

A few hundred yards to the west, and on the Post side of the river, Captain Anthony McParland had come to the same conclusions arrived at by Taylor and Lallemand.

"No chance they're going to take the Post," he told the two corporals. "Not without a siege, anyway—and the Laird'll be here long before that."

His grin was on the wicked side. "I'll add that the stupid bastards got themselves penned up, on top of everything else." He pointed backward toward the river, which was now hidden by the woods. "The Arkansas makes a loop, right there, just opposite the Post. General Ball told me that's why the Laird shifted the fort from the original French location. Any enemy who camps opposite the Post can be trapped against the river real easy, since they're in a sort of little peninsula. And I'll bet you a month's pay—mine against yours—that's exactly what the Laird's planning to do."

"What's a peninsula?" his cousin asked.

The captain glared at him. "You're supposed to know that already!"

Sheffield Parker gave his fellow corporal a quick glance. "Cal was sick that day when they covered it in the sergeants' school." To Cal, he explained: "It's what they call a piece of land stickin' out into the middle of the water. Like Florida. The whole state's basically a big peninsula."

"Oh. Yeah. I was sick that day."

"You was malingering that day, you mean," his older cousin growled. But there wasn't much heat in it. In truth, he was more surprised that Parker remembered than that Callender didn't know. The "sergeants' school" that the Laird had instituted in the army of Arkansas was a compressed sort of affair. Worse, even, than the officers' training Anthony himself had gone through—and he well remembered how many once-mentioned items he'd forgotten. Mostly thanks to being promptly dressed down by his superiors soon afterward.

"What do you want to do, sir?" Parker asked.

The young black corporal was meticulous about military

protocol in the field, unlike most of the white noncoms. So were most of the other black ones, now that Anthony thought about it. On some level, very deep, quiet, and still, he'd come to realize that the black soldiers in the army—the noncoms and officers, even more so—took the whole business more seriously than white ones usually did. All the white people of Arkansas, leaving aside the foreign missionaries, were still Americans in every sense of the term except formal citizenship. So they shared the generally casual attitude toward military matters that characterized most Americans.

The blacks didn't. For them, the army was all that stood between freedom and a return to slavery. A line so sharp, so clear, and so dark that they cleaved to military values the way a devout Christian cleaved to the cross. It was sometimes a little frightening. Anthony's education had expanded a lot over the years since the British war. He'd even studied the classics, now—some of them at least. There were ways in which the new little nation taking shape between the Ozarks and the Ouachitas reminded him of ancient accounts of Sparta, more than of anything he remembered growing up in New York. Or the Swiss of a few centuries ago, that the Laird had told him about, whose pikemen were feared by every power in Europe.

Sheff's own mother had absorbed it in the few months since the family had arrived in Arkansas. As much as she'd opposed her son joining the army in the first place, he also knew from his cousin that her last words to Sheff when he left for New Orleans were "There be a war, boy, I want you back alive. But I rather see you dead than come back and cain't tell me we won. You hear me?"

Before Anthony could make a decision, one of the soldiers from the squad he'd sent out to make a reconnaissance of the area returned.

"Sir, there's some people not far away. U.S. Army soldiers. Maybe a dozen of them. And they got three black women with them. Well, a woman and two girls." The soldier turned and pointed to the northwest. "About four hundred yards that way."

Anthony looked in the direction the man was pointing. But, of course, couldn't see more than maybe fifty yards, and that only in spots. Still mostly uncleared, the area around Arkansas Post was heavily wooded. Mostly gum and oak trees, with some cypress here and there. For all practical purposes, most of the region was still a forest.

The only cleared land, except for a few farms scattered about, was the area south of the river and right around the Post. And that had been cleared for purely military purposes. Anthony was pretty sure Crittenden's army was so mindless that they still hadn't figured out that the only reason they could all assemble easily in the peninsula opposite the Post was that it had been cleared for precisely that reason. It was a prepared killing ground—and they were the prey who'd stumbled into it.

"Are the women captives?"

"Don't think so, sir," the soldier replied, shaking his head. "The older woman's riding a horse, and the girls are sharing one. They real light-skinned, too. The girls, I mean. The woman—might be their mother—she's high yeller."

Anthony's lips quirked slightly. The soldier was black, and like most black people the captain knew, he'd parse skin shades and tones even more meticulously than a white man. It was amusing, in a way—although it could be rough at times on someone like Corporal Parker, who was very dark-skinned and had no white features at all in his face.

On the other hand, the same was true of General Charles Ball, and nobody in their right mind in Arkansas—white, black, or red—treated him lightly. Not more than once, for sure.

"All right. There's no way we can get into the Post, anyhow, except after nightfall. We may as well go see what they're up to. What's the officer's rank?"

"Don't know, sir. We didn't get close enough to be able to see the insignia. But . . . he don't look to be nothing like a lieutenant, I can tell you that. Nor even a captain, we don't think."

A small unit of U.S. cavalrymen, led by a field-grade officer. What would they be doing here?

Now, he was genuinely curious, not simply professionally interested.

"Let's go find out."

* * *

One of Taylor's men spotted the Arkansas unit, but not until they were forty yards away. Stiffly, the colonel realized that if this had been an ambush, they'd be in sore straits.

"Friend or foe?" he called out.

"Thought we might ask you the same thing!" came the response. "Seeing as how you're trespassing."

The tone didn't seem belligerent so much as amused, though. And Taylor couldn't detect any trace of real hostility on the face of the Arkansas officer who emerged from the woods. He wasn't carrying a weapon, either, although he had a pistol at his belt.

"Captain McParland, of the army of Arkansas. And you are, sir?"

"Zachary Taylor, lieutenant colonel in the United States Army." Since the next question was a foregone conclusion, he pointed a thumb at Julia Chinn, whose horse was standing next to his. "We're an escort for Miz Julia Chinn here, and her two children. She's—ah . . ."

Not even Taylor was prepared to publicly refer to Julia as Senator Johnson's wife. For a white man to marry a black woman was illegal in the state of Kentucky. Illegal in any state of the Union, so far as he knew, outside of some of the New England states. The colonel wasn't sure if that legal proscription extended so far as to banning any third-party reference to such a marriage that implied it was legitimate, but . . .

Like any career professional officer, Taylor was chary of crossing such lines. Fortunately, an alternative explanation was at hand. That a man was a husband was something a legislature could decree. That he was a father was decreed by Nature and the God who had created it—and, in this case, the father acknowledged the fact publicly and openly, and always had.

"The girls are Senator Johnson's daughters," he said. "Senator Johnson of Kentucky, that is."

Then, pointing to them: "Adaline's the one sitting in front. Imogene's behind her. The senator and Miz Julia wanted them to attend the school in New Antrim. The one that's being set up, I mean."

He could sense the relaxation in the Arkansas officer. More to the point, he could see several of the muskets in the

woods that hadn't *quite* been pointing at him, lifting away
entirely.

Still, there was never any harm in slathering the cake with
some icing. "Sam Houston asked me to provide them with
an escort."

Houston's name might be cursed as often as praised in the
United States, but it was a magic talisman in Arkansas. Now,
the captain was smiling cheerfully and waving his men forward.

"Come on out, boys. Everybody's friendly."

While Captain McParland and the U.S. colonel conferred,
Sheff Parker found himself having to fight off the urge to
ogle the three women.

Especially the girls. Lord, they were pretty. Even if they
were still too young to be entertaining any such thoughts.

"Stop staring," Cal murmured. "You bein' rude."

Corporal McParland himself, Sheff noticed, wasn't looking any other place either.

"You the one to talk."

"Prettiest girls I seen in an age. Too bad they're so young
still."

"Girls grow up."

But the moment Sheff said it, he realized how absurd he
was being. First, because Senator Johnson's family situation
was famous all over the South. Notorious, maybe, for white
people. But black folks didn't feel the same way about it.
Freedmen weren't allowed to vote in Kentucky, no more
than they were in any state of the United States that Sheff
knew of, except maybe some of the New England states. But
if they had been, every black man's vote would have gone to
Richard M. Johnson, any election he ever stood for. That
would have been true even if he wasn't also the man demanding the abolition of debt imprisonment.

These were *rich* girls. Important girls. Beyond that, they
were so light-skinned that even "high yeller" didn't apply.
Sheff might as well be entertaining fantasies about jumping
over the moon.

So, he looked away. And, an instant later, saw Cal do the
same. He realized then, not really ever having thought about

it before, that there could even be things that a white boy couldn't entertain fantasies about, either.

That thought went through his mind like a crystal, bringing many things into a clear and certain place that hadn't been so before. There was no barrier to his friendship with Cal, he suddenly realized, except things that were not decreed in any page of the Bible he knew. And he knew them all.

McParland was ordering a camp made.

"It's your turn to cook," Sheff said. "Don't argue about it. I been keepin' track and you ain't."

Life in the army did, indeed, lead to blasphemy. Even Sheff was sometimes guilty of it. "Hell of a state of affairs," Cal complained, "when a curree adds and subtracts better than a white man."

"Not my fault you miss so many days in school. And don't you be pissin' me off, or you won't have nobody to help you catch up."

"Well. That's true. I cook better'n you do anyway—even if that's upside down, too."

CHAPTER 16

Arkansas Post
OCTOBER 5, 1824

That night, Taylor and his party, along with the unit from the Arkansas Army, snuck into the fort.

"Snuck," insofar as a relaxed and almost open promenade—the U.S. party on horseback, even—could be given the term. The young black corporal with Captain Mc-Parland had led the way, advancing alone to within sight of Arkansas Post and calling out to the sentries.

Taylor had been rather impressed by his courage. Granted, there was no danger from any of Crittenden's outfit. Taylor's cavalrymen had scouted the area to make sure there were none such present. But the real risk in such a situation would come from the sentries themselves. As keyed up and tense as they were certain to be, they'd be quite likely to fire as soon as they spotted anyone moving in the area beyond the walls.

The corporal's black face had helped, of course. There'd be no one in Crittenden's army with skin anywhere near as dark. But the night was dark, too, with only a quarter moon in the sky, so sentries couldn't be certain of anyone's race at a distance. And while the green uniform of an Arkansas soldier was easily discernible in daylight, at night it simply looked like any dark garment.

Fortunately, the youngster was shrewd. As soon as he emerged from the woods he began singing "Blue Tail Fly," with its well-known refrain:

> *Jimmy crack corn, and I don't care*
> *Jimmy crack corn, and I don't care*
> *Jimmy crack corn, and I don't care*
> *My master's gone away*

Taylor found himself chuckling as he watched. Nobody in Crittenden's army was likely to be singing a song about a slave's glee at his master's death from an accident!

The boy had a very nice tenor voice, too.

"Oh, he sure sings pretty," he heard Imogene say.

He discovered that Arkansas Post was under the command of a Major Joseph Totten. A bit to his surprise, a white officer. Taylor had known, of course—Captain McParland being living proof he'd already encountered—that a number of the officers and even enlisted men in the Arkansas forces were white. But it was still a bit startling. Not so much the skin color itself as the apparent lack of concern that anyone seemed to have about it, one way or the other. Totten's second-in-command was a Captain Davies, whose dark face seemed to have a subtly Indian cast to it. Quite possibly, the son or grandson of one of the early slaves taken by the Cherokees or Creeks in the past century. Manumission was far more common in the Indian tribes than it was among white Americans, and it often took the form of a former slave or at least their children marrying into one of the clans.

That, too, was a break with American custom. Andrew Jackson had created something of a scandal by giving Driscol's sergeant Charles Ball a field promotion to lieutenant during the New Orleans campaign. That had been in clear violation of U.S. Army regulations, which did not permit black freedmen to rise to any commissioned rank.

Jackson being Jackson—with the great victory at the Mississippi to add luster to his reputation for fury—no one had dared to object officially at the time. But after Ball had resigned from the army, the authorities had quietly seen to it that there would be no repetition of the problem and that the promotion would not establish any sort of precedent.

Arkansas, clearly, had different rules. Taylor wasn't sure if he approved. On the other hand, he was no more sure that he didn't. He did not consider himself an intellectual officer, in the way that Winfield Scott was, but he thought a man had to be a plain damn fool not to understand that there was ultimately something dark and dangerous about having slavery at the foundation of a republic. Even though his own family's considerable wealth—even his own position, to a degree—rested on that same institution.

That said, he had no more use for abolitionists than he did for men like John Calhoun. Fine and dandy to denounce slavery in the abstract—but how was one to get rid of it? Two great obstacles stood in the way, the second more immovable than the first.

The first, of course, was simple economics. Slavery was profitable, and the solid basis for most of the wealth of Southern gentlemen. Easy enough for a New England merchant—whose own family's wealth might very well have derived a century earlier from the slave trade—to demand that a Virginia farmer bankrupt himself by freeing his slaves. Not so easy for the farmer.

But, even if that were done, what would happen next? How was a society to absorb two million freed negroes? That was the second rock below the surface, and the one that all schemes for abolition foundered upon.

Until now, perhaps. If the United States could not do it, what if its new neighbor *could?*

Zachary Taylor didn't know the answer to that question. What he did decide, that night, studying Major Totten and his staff of officers, was that he was glad the question was finally being asked by somebody, and in dead earnest.

Many miles away, on a steamboat at the confluence of the Mississippi and Arkansas rivers, an English lady was pondering the same issue. In her case, a rumination brought on by the experience of the past two evenings, watching John Brown leading his large family through a reading of the Bible.

A large family which had just gotten larger, and darker, since Brown had calmly assumed that the three rescued negroes—having no other family any longer—would find a home with his.

"He simply doesn't *care,* does he?" she murmured to her husband.

Sitting next to her in the sheltered rear of the *Comet*'s main deck, Robert watched Brown and his people for a moment before answering.

"No. He doesn't."

"I find him a somewhat frightening man."

Her husband smiled wryly. "I find him considerably more than 'somewhat' frightening, my dear. Still . . ."

He trailed off. Eliza suspected he had no more of a ready answer than she did.

Still . . .

The day before, in conversation with the two young corporals before they'd left with Captain McParland, the black one had told her what Brown had said the first time she met him. To a band of slave-catchers.

I believe in the Golden Rule, sir, and the Declaration of Independence. I think that both mean the same thing. And, that being so, it is better that a whole generation should pass off the face of the earth—men, women, and children—by a violent death than that one jot of either should fail in this country. I mean exactly so, sir.

Said it calmly and matter-of-factly, just as he'd calmly

and matter-of-factly slain the one slave-catcher who'd doubted him.

A frightening man, yes. A fanatic, some would say.

But Eliza had also heard the tale of the young black woman—bits of it, rather, since the poor girl was still half out of her wits. Faced with such incredible barbarity, the term "fanatic" seemed almost meaningless. She understood now, really for the first time, why her husband had found himself drawn into Clarkson's movement. Understood, finally, why he insisted on keeping that horrid illustration of the *Brookes* on the wall of their home in Ireland.

Quietly, she rose from the bench and went over to stand by the guardrail. The quarter moon glinted off the waters of the Mississippi, a shining crescent half obscured by mud and slime.

If one allowed oneself—even for a moment—to consider that those spoons shaped like people nestled in a drawer were *actually* people . . .

She could hear Brown's voice murmuring in the background. The words were indistinguishable, but she knew he was reading from Judges. A Calvinist through and through, Brown was partial to the Old Testament. His God was a wrathful deity.

Eliza being an Anglican, her God was a considerably gentler Creator. But she could no longer avoid the simple and obvious truth that if those spoons were *actually* people . . . each and every one of them a real human being . . . full and complete in every particular. . . .

Not even the sweetest cherub in Heaven would show any mercy at all. Less—much less—than any man who ever lived, be he never so fanatic.

A shudder ran through her whole body. At that moment, the Mississippi seemed like a dark torrent rushing toward a pit of eternal damnation, carrying her with it. Scream as loudly as she might, no angel would hear. Nor care, if they did.

Robert was at her side an instant later, running his hand up her arm.

"Are you ill, dearest?" His voice was full of concern. "These waters are not healthy."

A half laugh, half sob burst from her lips. "Not healthy!"

But, blessedly, the horrible vision was gone. She took a deep breath and sighed it out.

"No, I'm quite well, Robert. Just . . . a bad moment."

She leaned her head into his shoulder. "You intend to see this through to the end, don't you?"

She didn't wait for an answer. "And our blessed rambunctious son, too!"

She laughed again, very softly, but there was no half sob to go with it. "Very well, husband. I'll help. As best I can."

Near midnight, Captain McParland and the two corporals left the fort again. On horseback, having been assured by Major Totten that the few enemy units who had crossed to the north bank during the day had retreated to their own camp before nightfall. They'd have no difficulty moving up-river to find Driscol and his army—who were surely coming, the major had no doubt at all—beyond the obstacles posed by the terrain itself.

The rest of McParland's soldiers remained behind to strengthen the garrison at Arkansas Post.

After carefully asking permission, Taylor took the opportunity to inspect the fort. He was a bit surprised that Totten gave that permission. It was quite possible that a time would come, and not so far in the future, when Taylor might be investing Arkansas Post. If not he himself, some other officer in the army of the United States.

But there might lie the answer, as well. A potential foe, forewarned, might never become a foe at all. These things were always difficult to predict. For a professional soldier even more than most people, life was seen in the words of the apostle: *through a glass, darkly.*

The fort itself was quite impressive: well designed and sturdily constructed, especially by the standards of the frontier. Taylor didn't envy Crittenden at all, trying to take it.

In fact, he very much doubted that he could. Even though, by now, Crittenden's army must have swelled to something like fifteen hundred men. He'd lost some through the inevitable desertion that always plagued such jury-rigged military forces as little bands of men peeled away after finding some loot. But he'd gained more than he'd lost, since his initial force of roughly a thousand men coming up from Alexandria had been augmented by adventurers coming down the Mississippi from Missouri and the other border states.

True enough, Crittenden's army greatly outnumbered the garrison at Arkansas Post, which didn't have more than a hundred and fifty men. All other things being equal, a ten-to-one numerical superiority would normally be quite sufficient to overrun even a well-designed fort.

But all other things were very far from equal. Crittenden's force was more in the way of a mob or a gang of outright criminals than what any sane man—certainly a professional officer—would call an army. And while Taylor was sure that most of the fort's garrison were green troops, a sufficient number of them were veterans of the Iron Battalion to serve as a spine and a stiffener.

Not that much stiffening would be needed, anyway. All but perhaps a dozen of the soldiers in Arkansas Post were black. Surrender, for them, meant a life of slavery. And, if anything, the fate of the white soldiers would most likely be worse. Under these circumstances, the term "nigger-lover," for such men as filled the inchoate ranks of Crittenden's army, amounted to a death sentence. Especially after the blood they'd spill, getting into the fort.

They had women to defend, too, at least fifty of them. And children. The women would suffer worse than their menfolk if Crittenden's men made it over the wall. The youngest of the children, also, since Crittenden's men wouldn't want the burden of carrying toddlers all the way back to New Orleans. Just bash in their little skulls with a musket butt while waiting a turn to rape their mothers and sisters.

But he didn't think it would come to that. In fact, the more he wandered through the Post and studied the soldiers in their green uniforms, the more certain he became that it wouldn't. Those might be green troops, mostly, but they'd clearly had considerable training. They were tense, yes, but it was more the tension of a racehorse before the gun went off than the tension of men expecting calamity.

In fact, he was pretty sure that most of them were downright eager to see the sun come up.

He laughed, then, standing in the middle of an alien army.

So was he, when you got right down to it. Lieutenant Colonel Zachary Taylor wasn't certain of many things in life. But he surely and purely loathed the sort of men who were gathered across the river. Come morning, let the bastards bleed. And bleed and bleed and bleed, until the river ran red and the dirt was crimson mud and the stink of their emptied bowels drew every crow and beetle in Creation.

The Arkansas River,
five miles west of Arkansas Post
OCTOBER 6, 1824

Captain McParland and the two corporals found the Laird's army at half past two o'clock in the morning.

It wasn't hard. The whole river seemed covered with boats. From what Anthony could tell, by the light of the quarter moon, Driscol had commandeered every single rivercraft in or around New Antrim, from the steamboat *Hercules*—the newest of Shreve's boats, and the pride of his company's fleet—all the way down to rowboats and fishing skiffs.

By the time they arrived, it looked as if a good half of the Arkansas Army had already debarked onto the southern shore of the river. Which was, unfortunately, the opposite bank from the one they were on.

That proved to be a minor problem, however. Driscol had sent several keelboats to patrol the north bank of the Arkansas, and McParland had Corporal Parker go down to summon them.

The device having worked once, Sheff saw no reason not to do it again. He had just finished the fourth verse—

> *Well the pony jumped, he start, he pitch*
> *He threw my master in the ditch*
> *He died and the jury wondered why*
> *The verdict was the blue-tail fly*

—when the picket in the nearest boat called out: "Who's there? Name yourself!"

Parker stepped out into plain view from behind a gum tree

at the edge of the river. "It's Corporal Parker. With the Third Regiment."

"That you, Sheff? You just in time!"

Easy as that.

After Captain McParland finished his report, standing on the main deck of the *Hercules,* Patrick Driscol spent perhaps half a minute examining the steamboat. Then, cocked his head at the two men standing nearby in civilian clothing.

One was white, one was black—but their garments were both expensive, and equally so.

"It's mostly your money, gentlemen," Driscol said. "So I suppose I should ask permission. Mind you, I make no guarantees I'll accept the answer."

The white man started to glare at him but wound up just rolling his eyes. "The day I agreed to be your partner . . ." Henry Shreve sighed. "Fine, Patrick, fine. Let's go ahead and wreck *another* of my boats. Why not?"

The black man with him, who looked to be about twice his size, shrugged massive shoulders. "The captain didn't say they was wrecked, Henry. Just maybe banged up a little bit."

"Crittenden's got guns," Shreve pointed out sourly. "The three-pounders, I'm not much worried about. But a six-pounder's a different story altogether." His eyes gave the boat the same inspection Driscol's had done, except in far less time. "This boat was never designed to handle any such thing. A six-pounder'll hammer it into splinters."

"That's assumin' they fire it in time, and fire it straight," said Crowell. Again, he shrugged those shoulders. The gesture bore a fair resemblance to a small landslide encased in fine linen. "From what the captain's told us, I doubt either one of those is gonna be true."

His white partner gave him a none-too-friendly look. "And you're willing to bet money on it. Just as much of it's yours as mine, Henry."

Crowell smiled. "I'll do more than bet money. I'll bet my life." He pointed toward the bow. "We got four cannons of our own, and I still remember how to serve on a gun crew. I did it before, on the Mississippi. I plan on doin' it again."

He turned the smile onto Driscol. "Assuming, of course, our fine general will allow me to resume the colors." He stuck out a huge finger and wagged it under Driscol's nose. "Just for a day, y'understand? We ain't got no conscription in Arkansas, Patrick, even though I know your black Napoleonic soul's lusting for it, so don't be gettin' any crazy ideas!"

Driscol gave him a thin smile in return. "Leave it to a banker—black one worse than a white one—to parse the difference between conscripting a man with an honest press gang and doing it by squeezing his empty wallet. But I'll not argue the point again, tonight. Sure, Henry. Consider yourself reenlisted—very temporarily—in the Iron Battalion."

Shreve threw up his hands. "Oh, fine, then! I'll pilot the blasted thing. What I get for going into business with a curree and an Irishman. Especially the crazy Irishman."

When he brought his hands down, though, Anthony thought he might be detecting a little gleam in the shipbuilder's eyes. There had to be something of a professional interest there, he figured. Shreve really prided himself on his boats. If one of them could . . .

"But we're not doing it in daylight!" Shreve continued. "No blasted way!" He emulated his black partner's finger-wagging in the face of the general. "We do this, we're going past Crittenden before dawn—or we don't do it at all."

"Weren't you the one pissing and moaning all the way down here about the frightful risks of navigating an uncharted river by the light of a pitiful quarter moon?" Driscol asked mildly. "Let's compromise, Henry. I want the gun crews to be able to see what they're doing, even if the pilot's working by guess and memory. We'll steam past Crittenden just at sunup."

Shreve rolled his eyes again. "Don't remind me. I like to have lost five years of my life this night. I say we're still lucky the whole blasted flotilla didn't wind up stranded and snagged, instead of just two of the boats."

"Which we got off the sandbars right easily," Crowell pointed out, his tone as mild as Driscol's. "In less than five minutes each. Come on, Henry. By now you know this river about as well as you do the back of your hand."

Since that also struck to Shreve's pride, he didn't say anything. From what Anthony could tell, in the poor lighting provided by the lamps on deck, the disgruntled expression

still on his face was more a matter of stubbornness than anything really heartfelt.

"And what's this 'we' business?" Shreve asked sourly. "If
you're planning to come along, Patrick, I'm backing out
right now. No way I'm letting a mad Irishman—"

"Oh, leave off. Of course I'm not coming. I've got an
army to command." He turned toward Anthony. "Captain
McParland here will lead the expedition. He knows exactly
where Ball can be found."

To Anthony, directly: "Tell Charles I want him to stay
there. And be ready for Crittenden's men—a lot of them—
to be coming down that river sometime around late afternoon. Rowing like their lives depended on it, which they will
be."

"Yes, sir. And what—"

"Don't ask silly questions. Charles knows what to do. You
already saw him do it. Crittenden and his men are nothing
but pirates and brigands. The penalty for piracy is death by
hanging. I'm not fussy, though, so if it works better to just
shoot them down like mad dogs, have at it. I don't care. So
long as not one man from that crowd ever makes it back
alive to Alexandria."

He gave his shoulders a little shake, like a dog shedding
water. "Well . . . all right. I'll be reasonable. Some of them
are bound to escape. Might even be to the best, letting them
spread terror through their circles. But if I find out it's more
than a handful, I shall not be a happy man."

He smiled then, more thinly than ever. "Not that you need
to give Charles any such explanation. I'd not insult him."

"Yes, sir."

"Be at it, then. Get the guns ready to rake Crittenden as
you steam past. Don't linger, though—and don't aim for his
army. Wreck as many of his boats as you can. Remember
that, Anthony. Shoot up the *boats*. You can leave the killing
to me. Just make sure they've got as little to make an escape
with as possible."

"Yes, sir. Do you want me to take the corporals with me?"

Driscol frowned for a moment. "No, I don't think so.
You've no real need for them, not with gun crews from the
battalion on the *Hercules*. They're not really trained artillerymen anyway, being in Colonel Jones's regiment. From

your report, they've done very well for themselves. But with
a battle coming on the morrow, it'd be best for them to be
back in their ranks. I've got hopes for both of those youngsters, but they need real blooding on a battlefield. There's
never a substitute for that, in war."

"Yes, sir."

When he told the two corporals, they both seemed more relieved than anything else.

As Anthony watched them march off the gangplank to
join their 3rd Regiment, now mustering somewhere in the
darkness, he found himself envying the boys. Not for the
moment, but for the past memory. On the eve of Anthony's
first battle, he'd been frightened out of his wits. Of course,
it hadn't helped any that he'd been executed by Driscol not
so many days earlier.

He grinned, then. It was an odd world. Now that he was
looking toward his fourth decade of life, in just a few years,
he found that he had a more insouciant view of the world
than he'd had as a teenager. Death had been a mysterious terror, then. Today it was just a familiar enemy—and he *still*
had the world's meanest troll on his side.

CHAPTER 17

Arkansas Post
OCTOBER 6, 1824

*"Imogene! Adaline! You come down from there right this
minute! You hear me?"*

The twins standing on the gun platform above her tried for
a moment to pretend they hadn't heard their mother.

"This second! I ain't foolin'!"

Imogene stamped her foot. Watching, it was all Zack Taylor could do not to laugh.

"Mama! It's *exciting*."

"Won't be excitin' you get a bullet in your head! Or be too excitin' altogether. *Get down here.* I ain't sayin' it one more time."

Reluctantly, the two girls obeyed Julia, clambering down the ladder that led up to the platform with the peculiar combination of grace and awkwardness that seemed to be the uniform property of twelve-year-old girls. Most of all, that blithe indifference to propriety. Taylor's oldest daughters Ann and Sarah were about the same age as Julia's twins. Imogene and Adaline were just at the point in their lives when they were starting the transition from girlhood to womanhood. It simply hadn't registered on them yet that proper young ladies didn't give the world such an exposure of leg and ankle as they came down a ladder wearing dresses.

Anywhere—much like a fort full of soldiers. Especially girls as pretty as these two seemed likely to be.

Julia knew it, of course. As soon as the girls arrived on solid ground, she was looming over them, shaking a finger in their faces.

"You bein' a disgrace! If your father had seen this!"

As stern a disciplinarian as their mother was, the girls—especially Imogene, whom Taylor had already recognized as the more rambunctious of the two—weren't ready to give in yet.

"It's gonna be a *battle,* Mama!" Imogene protested. "We oughta be able to watch it!"

The shaking finger now concentrated on her alone. "And watch your language, young lady! Your daddy ain't sending you to no expensive school so's you can talk about 'gonnas' and 'oughtas'!"

Blithely indifferent, of course, to the fact that Julia's own lingo was every bit as colloquial as that of most frontier women. But the thought was simply one of amusement, not condemnation. Being the father of four girls himself, Taylor had more than once fallen back upon that most ancient and reliable staple of parenting: *Do as I say, blast it, not as I do.*

Imogene was nothing if not stubborn. "'Sides, I'm worried about that young corporal. The one who sings so pretty."

Adaline even pitched in, though she was normally the more obedient of the two. "And I'm worried about th'other one." She and her twin exchanged glances. "Me and Imogene already decided."

"Decided *what?*" Julia's expression could by now only be described as a glower. The finger shaking increased its tempo. "Don't you two be thinkin' about no boys! You too young for that! Way too young! Only thing you best be thinkin' about—I'll smack you, so help me I will!—is your lessons in school."

"School ain't started yet," Imogene said sulkily.

Smack. "Don't you sass me, girl! And don't you be usin' no 'ain'ts,' neither!"

Chuckling, Taylor turned away from the scene. The sun hadn't even come up yet, but daylight was starting to fill the sky. He foresaw a frenzied day for Julia, trying to keep her spirited daughters from finding ways to watch the battle that was about to unfold.

Zack Taylor, on the other hand, was long past the age where he had a mother to answer to. Which was fortunate, because he had every intention of watching the battle himself. Not from simple curiosity, in his case, but from professional necessity. It wouldn't surprise him at all if he found himself someday having to face the army of Arkansas. He wanted to get as good an estimate as he could of its capabilities.

Since there was no point in skulking about, however, he'd simply join Major Totten in the blockhouse, which had the best view of the cleared ground on the riverbank opposite the fort. It was possible that Totten would order him to leave, but Taylor didn't think so. As polyglot as it might be, he'd already gotten enough sense of the spirit that infused the Confederate army—its Arkansas portion, anyway—to think that Totten and his officers would consider it ungallant to refuse a fellow officer such a straightforward courtesy. Enemies they might be on the morrow, but today was today, and protocol was important for its own sake.

He hoped he was right. The battle that was about to unfold

was going to be fought by such rules as any Hun or Mongol would accept. But it was Taylor's growing belief—certainly his personal desire—that if a war did erupt between the United States and the Confederacy, such savagery could be avoided in the future. And, if so, his own behavior and conduct today might make a difference.

No skulking, then, and no spying. Just a straightforward request by an officer of one army to observe a battle being conducted by another. Who was to say, after all? The time might also come when the United States and the Confederacy were allies.

When Taylor arrived in the blockhouse, Major Totten looked away from the firing slit he was peering through and gave him a courteous nod. "You're just in time, Colonel. It appears that the Laird—ah, General Driscol—plans to start the battle by ravaging the enemy's fleet."

He turned to one of his aides. "Lieutenant Morton, be so good as to lend Colonel Taylor your cycglass. And please make room for him while you're at it, so he can get a good view."

So.

"Slow down, Henry!" shouted Captain McParland.

He was wasting his breath, of course. He'd yelled out of simple frustration. Even if Shreve could have heard him over the sound of the engines, in the pilothouse, Anthony knew perfectly well he wouldn't obey. Shreve wasn't under military discipline, and he was a lot more concerned about keeping his beloved *Hercules* intact than he was over such petty minutiae as making sure they inflicted as much damage as possible on the enemy flotilla.

"Don't worry, Anthony," said Crowell, leaning on his sponge staff. "We'll manage, well enough—and there ain't no way Henry'll pay attention nohow. He do surely love this boat."

The steamboat was almost in range. If nothing else, the speed Shreve was making had the advantage of increasing the element of surprise. And Anthony would allow that the steamboat designer was at least not trying to keep to the very middle of the river. In fact, he was skirting the southern shoreline more closely than Anthony would have himself. Of course, he was a lot more familiar with the river.

"And will you look at 'em!" came a gleeful shout from another member of the gun crew. "Scurryin' like chickens!"

It was true enough. Any commander with any brains—or one who wasn't being constantly distracted by the sort of squabbles that were bound to plague a force like Crittenden's—would have seen to it that the river was patrolled by picket boats for hundreds of yards upstream and downstream. And would have had sentries along the shore extended just as far.

But they'd seen none of that. No picket boats at all, and the one and only sentry they'd spotted had been fast asleep. Now that the *Hercules* was almost on the enemy flotilla tied up to the shore, of course, the sound of its engines was waking everybody up. But the men sleeping on those boats quite clearly had no thought at all except to either run or gape.

McParland's eyes swept the riverbank ahead, looking for the battery. It *had* to be there, somewhere. Not even an amateur like Crittenden would have been dumb enough not to move his few cannons into position during the night.

Anthony spotted it, then, and had to suppress a gleeful shout of his own. A genuine battery, sure enough. Sheltered behind an earthen berm, just like it should be. A great big one, too—bigger than Anthony would have thought Crittenden's mob could have erected in the dark.

Unfortunately, whether from inexperience or simple enthusiasm, they'd made it *too* big. Crittenden's guns could fire on Arkansas Post across the river, but they couldn't lower the elevation enough to hit anything on the river itself.

"You know what to do," Anthony said to the gun crew as he headed toward the pilothouse. "I'm going to go try and talk some sense into Henry."

He'd just reached the pilothouse when the four-pounder toward the starboard bow cut loose. He didn't turn to see what effect the shot had, though. The whooping and hollering coming from the gun crew made that plain enough.

He opened the door and stuck his head in. "Tarnation, Henry, their battery's too high to shoot at us, anyway. *Slow down.*"

Shreve was squinting through the eyeslit, peering ahead toward Crittenden's battery. Normally, of course, there'd have been a full window there. But he'd had most of the pilothouse fortified by timbers in the course of the voyage down from New Antrim. The planks wouldn't stop a cannon shot, but they'd handle musket fire pretty well.

"Sam Hill, if you aren't right." A sudden and very wicked grin came to the steamboat designer's face. "Tell you what, Anthony. I'll go you one better. Get on back there, now! You're going to be a busy man for a bit."

As he turned back toward the gun crews, Anthony heard a sudden change in the noise coming from the engine. An instant later, he felt the *Hercules* starting to shudder a bit. Shreve, he realized, was reversing the thrust on the stern paddlewheel. He was going to bring the boat to a complete *stop*—right smack in front of the whole flotilla.

"Hot damn!" shouted the gunner on the rear four-pounder. That crew had just fired its own first shot. "Boys, I want to see this gun firing till it melts! Move it!"

The bow gun fired again, jerking back against the recoil lines. The round struck the stern of one of Crittenden's keelboats and caved it in. It also slaughtered, in the process, the one man who'd been either too slow or too dumb to get off the boat in time. A big splinter flew into his back as he was trying to clamber ashore and ripped open most of his rib cage. Blood and bone bits went flying everywhere. The corpse hit the muddy bank like a sack of meal.

Crowell was at that lead gun and already had it swabbed out by the time Anthony looked back. The crew hauled the gun back into position, took cursory aim, and fired again.

The aim hadn't been as cursory as it looked, though. Or maybe they'd just been lucky. That shot hit one of Crittenden's few steamboats. A little too high, unfortunately, so it simply smashed in part of the main deck instead of holing the hull. But it was enough to send the men gawking there racing to get off the boat, even if none of them looked to have been injured any.

Good enough. There was no chance, other than by a fluke, that four-pounders would be able to destroy any of the steamboats in Crittenden's flotilla. Not badly enough to prevent them from being repaired, at least. But repairs would

take time, and time was one thing Crittenden's army now
had in short supply.

Very short supply. In the lulls between cannon fire, Anthony could hear the faint sounds of the Laird's regiments
coming. The tone of voices raised in command, if not the
words themselves; most of all, that unmistakable jingle-
jangle of their gear that masses of soldiers made, approaching at a fast march.

The four-pounder in the rear went off again, followed
closely by Crowell's gun. The same steamboat took another
hit, this one in the hull. A keelboat rocked wildly, breaking
loose its tether and starting to drift with the current. With
that hole torn in its side, though, it likely wouldn't drift more
than a few miles.

Didn't matter. A few miles would be enough, even if the
boat didn't sink at all. The sounds of the Laird coming were
starting to fill the dawn. There was no time at all, now, for
Crittenden and his men. No time at all.

"All right, Henry!" Anthony shouted. "You can get us
under way again!"

In the blockhouse, Zachary Taylor had come to the same
conclusion. And he made it a point to jot down in his unwrit-
ten mental notebook that the two oncoming regiments of the
army of Arkansas were able to march faster and for longer
than any regiment of the U.S. Army he'd ever known. It remained to be seen how well they'd been trained in battlefield
tactics. But one thing was now sure and certain. Driscol
must have had them practicing marches—relentlessly—for
months.

Taylor was not guessing. He was one of the few field-
grade officers in the U.S. Army who was adamant himself
about keeping troops well trained and in good condition.
Part of the reason his whole career had been spent on the
frontier, with none of the usual assignments to Washington
that might have advanced him more rapidly, was that he had
a reputation for being a commander who could be sent to a
poorly trained and dispirited garrison stuck in a fort out in
the middle of nowhere and rapidly bring order and discipline to what had been not much more than a half-trained

and three-quarters-drunk mob of gamblers, whoremongers, and idlers.

From what Taylor could determine thus far, on the other hand, Driscol's tactics didn't seem particularly sophisticated. Not that Taylor was fond himself of fancy tactics on a battlefield. But still, this was about as crude and blunt as it got.

Driscol had shifted his regiments from column march into lines, not more than three hundred yards from the outlying units in Crittenden's army. Risky, that. Taylor himself wouldn't have chanced getting that close to an enemy while still in column formation. Not regular troops, at any rate. It took even a well-trained army two minutes or more to shift from column to line formation, during which time it was vulnerable to a vigorous counterattack.

Against a force like Crittenden's, admittedly, there wasn't much risk. They were just as sluggish as they were brutal and undisciplined. But trained soldiers under good officers would have been able to take advantage of that recklessness on Driscol's part.

And now that he had his two regiments formed up, Driscol was just advancing them forward, side by side. No cavalry screen on the flanks—in fact, he didn't seem to have any cavalry at all—and not even any use of light infantry as a substitute. He did have a small battery of four-pounders, but those were still a considerable distance to the rear. The artillerymen were trying to bring them up on the flank, but the horses were having a rough time of it. The terrain was awfully soggy this close to the river.

Clearly enough, though, Driscol had no intention of waiting until he could bring his artillery to bear. He'd go at Crittenden with his infantry alone, relying on discipline and impact to keep his enemy off balance and prevent them from using their own artillery to good effect.

It was going to be a pure and simple slugging match. A sergeant's sort of fight. About twelve hundred men under Driscol's command, against a slightly larger force of Crittenden's.

Under the circumstances, Taylor was pretty sure this was going to be as one-sided a slugging match as he'd ever seen.

Whether between armies, pugilists, or rams in a field, for that matter. Unsophisticated Driscol's tactics might be, but those two regiments were advancing in perfect order and in perfect cadence. Trained and trained and trained. Not bloodied yet, most of them, but even green recruits, with good enough training and enough of it, could acquit themselves very well on a battlefield.

He shifted the glass to observe Crittenden's forces.

Forces. Could ever a term be so misused?

One large group of men, near the center of Crittenden's army, looked to be in something you could call a formation. Taylor had been told by Major Totten that the Lallemand brothers had joined Crittenden's expedition, along with what was left of their French troops and some Alabamans they'd recruited. That was probably them. But fewer than three hundred men were in those ranks taking shape. What was worse was that none of the other loosely knit groups of men in Crittenden's army were following their example. Not even the groups clustered around his handful of field guns. In fact, they looked more disorganized than anybody.

One man in a fancy-looking uniform, some fifty yards from the Lallemand unit, was racing back and forth and waving a sword. Taylor couldn't make out his features at the distance, but he seemed like a young man, which Crittenden was.

Probably Robert Crittenden himself, then. Taylor had met him once on one of the several visits he'd paid to John J. Crittenden when he'd still been a U.S. senator from Kentucky. Taylor liked John quite a bit but hadn't been much impressed with the younger brother. By all accounts, Robert Crittenden was something in the way of the black sheep of that very prominent family.

For all the good Crittenden was doing, he might as well have been ordering the tide to recede. Even from the distance, it was as clear as the day itself—now that the sun was well over the horizon—that none of Crittenden's men were paying him any attention at all.

That was hardly surprising. From his years serving on the frontier, Taylor was quite familiar with the sort of men who filled the ranks of Crittenden's army. Basically, they were gangs. Sometimes outright loners, with maybe a partner or two. But usually they were part of a group of perhaps half a dozen to several dozen men, loosely organized and led by one or a few dominant characters. Many of them were outright criminals, and a goodly percentage of those who weren't simply hadn't been convicted yet.

Their motives were about as rudimentary as their organization. Adventure, of course. Loot, whether in the form of money or—mostly, in this situation—slaves; evading debts; evading the authorities of one state or another. Often enough, evading other men like themselves. If the officer corps of the U.S. Army stationed in frontier garrisons was notorious for its dueling habits, men like these made them seem veritable pacifists—except that their "duels" were rarely formal affairs.

There was another sort of a man in that army, to be sure. A different layer, it might be better to say. There'd also be men like Crittenden himself, with money to invest. Looking for the cheapest land there was, at least in financial terms. Conquered land, paid for only in blood.

Someone else's blood, they'd thought. They were about to learn otherwise.

Julia finally gave up trying to keep the girls from watching at all. At least the slit they were now peering through was just a half-inch gap between two logs on the lower level of the fort. Only the most extreme bad luck would bring a musket ball to either one of them.

If any got fired at the fort at all. Julia was now peering through the same slit, and from what she could tell that was getting less likely by the minute. She couldn't see much, since almost none of Crittenden's army was visible from this angle through such a narrow aperture. But she had a decent enough view of the army of Arkansas as it marched up to the riverbank. They were spread out wide now, in clearly delineated ranks, and were starting to bring their muskets level.

Julia had no military experience of any kind. But a person facing such a completely menacing sight would have to be a lunatic to waste any shots at a fort all the way on the other side of a river. She figured the girls were safe enough.

From musket balls, anyway. Of course, there were other perils in life.

"I'm so scared," Imogene whispered.

"Me too," her sister chimed in.

Julia made the mistake of being the reassuring mother. "We're safe enough here, girls. I don't think those men are even going to be attacking us at all."

Her daughters gave her a dismissive sideways glance.

"Not worried about *us,* Mama," Adaline said.

"Our beaus might get hurt," Imogene explained. "Might even get killed."

"You don't even know those boys! And you too young to be thinking such thoughts, nohow!"

Her daughters ignored her and went back to their intent peering. Softly—though not softly enough—Julia banged her head against one of the logs. Once, twice, thrice.

"Imogene, your father finds out you eyeing that one boy! That currie be black as coal!"

"He sings pretty."

Adaline, as usual, couldn't resist the sibling rivalry. "*My* beau's white."

"So what?" came Imogene's cool response. "Bet he can't sing at all. And even if he can, who'd want to listen? That funny accent he got."

"He's from New York originally." Adaline's tone was defensive. "I axed him. Not his fault he don't talk right yet."

"'*Doesn't* talk right,'" her mother hissed. "And it's 'asked,' not 'axed.' I swear, if you two—"

The rest was buried under an explosion of gunfire coming from across the river.

"Oh!" Imogene shrieked. "They're being hurt!"

CHAPTER 18

Sheff dealt with the first fusillade fired by Crittenden's men by just gritting his teeth and marching forward. He'd been trained, and, now, clutched to that training the way he'd clutched at the Bible in other frightening moments of his life.

They'd been told—told and told and told—to expect this. It was a lesson the Laird himself insisted on imparting to the units in their training.

Let the bastards shoot first. Some of you will die. Some of you will be crippled and maimed. We all die soon enough anyway, and old age will cripple you and maim you as sure as any musket ball. Just take it. Take it and keep coming. You do that, boys—don't fire till you get the word—you'll hammer 'em. And then you'll hammer 'em again, and again, and again, and again. Until there's nothing left but victory. Those of you who survive standing tall, and the bastards lying bloody in front of you, wailing like whipped curs.

You don't matter. The regiment matters. Victory matters. That's all that matters.

"Level arms!" Colonel Jones had a good battlefield voice. Real high-pitched. Much more so than when he talked normal-like.

Sheff had to fight off an instant's urge to aim, reminding himself that he was holding a regular musket now, not a rifle. There was no point in aiming, in line formation on a battlefield. Just level the weapon at the mass of the enemy.

"Fire!"

He even remembered to yank the trigger instead of squeezing it. So he didn't embarrass himself by having his shot go off after all the others.

For a moment, the world seemed to dissolve in a thunder-clap. Everything he could see was white. Well, some gray. Gunsmoke always had impurities.

There wasn't much wind, so the clouds lingered. All he could see ahead of him was maybe twenty feet—and that, only here and there. But he was too busy reloading to be looking around much anyway, especially since he had to be sure to be the first one in his squad ready.

"Ten paces forward!"

That was Sheff's cue, since he was the corporal. A half step ahead of the others, he led them through the paces.

"Level arms!"

The next man over to his left stumbled back, falling on his rear end and dropping his musket. He'd been shot in the head by one of the many shots being fired by Crittenden's men, but Sheff paid him no more mind. He didn't matter. Only the regiment mattered. Only victory mattered. At the moment, Sheff couldn't even remember the dead man's name.'

"Fire!"

Another thunderclap, another dissolution of the world.

Victory mattered. And Sheff could start to feel it coming. The first angel he'd ever seen approaching in his life.

Taylor was genuinely shocked by that first volley fired by the Arkansans. He'd never in his life seen such a clear, crisp, perfect volley—from even a company, much less two regiments working together.

True, his whole experience had been on the frontier, almost entirely fighting Indians. Traditional battlefield tactics weren't very applicable under such conditions. Still, he'd trained his men no differently than Driscol had. But he'd never gotten results like this. Not really even close, being honest.

Winfield Scott had, probably. Jacob Brown, too. But they'd served in the Canadian theater in the war, fighting British regulars.

It took a few seconds for the huge cloud of gunsmoke produced by that first volley to roll sluggishly over Crittenden's men. So Taylor was able to see, very clearly, what effect it had.

The first thing it did was eliminate Crittenden himself. Still racing back and forth when his men began firing singly and indiscriminately, he was picked up by the volley and hurled a good five to ten yards. The sword went flying, along with the hand holding it. When his body hit the ground, his right leg came loose at the knee, held to the rest only by the cloth of his trousers and maybe some ligaments. It flopped over onto his hip like the limb of a broken rag doll.

Which was a pretty good depiction of him, Taylor knew. Those two wounds alone would probably have killed Crittenden, just from blood loss. But he had to be dead already. At least two or three other rounds must have struck him to have thrown him that far.

Except for the Lallemands' unit, Crittenden's whole army reeled back. Gunfighters and roughnecks they might be, most of them, but this was something completely outside their experience. Driscol's tactics might leave a lot to be desired, but not even Napoleon's Old Guard or one of Wellington's elite regiments could have fired a better volley.

Truth be told, it was outside of Zachary Taylor's experience also. But at least he understood the matter intellectually. He might not be the same sort of voracious reader of military manuals and accounts that Winfield Scott was, but he had studied his profession. And he'd talked to plenty of officers and men who'd fought against British regulars in the war.

On the battlefield, outside of artillery, the volley reigned supreme. That went far beyond any crude and simple arithmetic. By now, Crittenden's men might quite possibly have fired just as many shots as had come to them in that opening Arkansas volley. But first, a much higher percentage would have gone wild. And second—more important still—shots fired singly hit an enemy like a hail of rocks. A volley hit like a landslide, or an earthquake. There was simply no comparison in terms of the key factor of shock.

Taylor had always known that, abstractly. Now he could see the truth of it with his own eyes. Crittenden's men weren't simply torn and bleeding in the body; their minds were stunned.

They weren't going to get any respite, either. The Lallemands' unit managed to get off a ragged volley. Some other
individual shots were fired.

Then—*again*. The second volley shattered the Lallemands' unit, and they stumbled back in the general inchoate
retreat to the river.

Taylor cursed himself and started counting. He needed to
get a sense of the timing.

Driscol's regiments were still advancing. That same,
steady, disciplined cadence. Again, the guns came level.
Again, a volley.

He stopped the count and hissed in a breath. He knew for
a fact that not more than one or two regiments in the U.S.
Army could fire two disciplined volleys in that short a
time—and the Arkansans were going to do it yet again.

Half dazed, Charles Lallemand stared down at the corpse of
his brother.

"Henri-Dominique . . ."

There was no time for that. He turned to steady his men
and bring them ready.

But there was no time for that, either. All of them were
running away. To a river that was nothing but a trap.

He leveled a silent curse on Robert Crittenden and his own
folly. Then he turned back, thrust his sword into its scabbard,
squared his shoulders, and faced the enemy.

He had no illusions. But he was still a general in
Napoleon's army, even if the emperor himself was gone. A
condemned officer would die by firing squad. Not a hang-
man's noose.

The fourth volley came and granted him his last wish.

There was nothing left of Crittenden's army but a shrieking
mob, fighting with itself for space in one of the surviving
boats along the riverbank. You could hardly call this a battle
any longer. That first volley had broken the freebooters like
a rotten stick. Now it was going to be nothing but a massacre.

For the first time, Taylor was able to get a good look at the
banners being carried by the Arkansas color-bearers. That

wasn't the regular Confederate flag, with its simple salmon field and a blue triangle with the six stars of the chiefdoms. The triangle was still there, with the white stars, but the field was now five stripes. The outer two, salmon; the next in, white—and the fifth and center stripe, pure black.

That'd probably cause a political ruckus amongst the Confederacy's politicians. But Taylor was pretty sure Driscol was making a point to them, here, just as much if not as brutally as he was to the men who'd invaded Arkansas.

That black stripe was only one of five, true enough. But even from this distance, Taylor could sense the spirit of those oncoming Arkansas regiments and the man who commanded them. They might as well have been flying the solid black flag of no quarter.

"There ain't no more room!" Thompson shouted. But the man trying to clamber into the already overloaded flatboat wasn't paying him any attention at all.

Cursing, Scott Powers managed to pry his musket loose from the mass of men pressed against him in the boat. No way to aim, so he just jammed the butt against the ribs of the man next to him, half leveled the musket—good enough, at this range—and pulled the trigger.

The man trying to clamber into the flatboat went into the river, with the top of his skull missing. The man next to Powers, against whom he'd jammed the musket butt, screamed and grabbed his ribs. A couple of them were probably broken.

There were *still* too many men on the boat. Even as frontier flatboats went, this one was on the small side.

The man whose ribs he'd broken was at the flatboat's port rail. Powers brought the butt up against his jaw—then again, and again—and shoved him over the side. He'd probably drown, now stunned as well as having some broken ribs. But Powers didn't care in the least. He didn't care about anything except getting out of this nightmare.

No one had really noticed what he'd done anyway. Well, except Thompson—but the smile on Ray's face made it clear he approved heartily.

Things got better a moment later. Another one of those

hideous Arkansas volleys went off. The flatboat was still
close enough to the bank that some of the stray shots hit two
of the men in the bow. One went over the side on his own;
the other was helped on his way by the man next to him.
Clearly a fellow thinker.

"Let's get out of here!" Ray shouted.

The one drawback to being on the side now meant that
Powers had to man one of the poles. He didn't mind the
work itself. He'd have willingly labored like Hercules to get
them out of there. But there was no way to pole a flatboat except by standing up and making a better target.

"Damn," he hissed. Still, it was better than staying there.
Anything was better than staying there. Powers was pretty
damn sure—would have bet every penny he'd made during
his years in the slave trade—that the Arkansans weren't
going to be taking any prisoners.

So, he heaved himself up and began poling. Ray, the bastard, had managed to squirm still lower into the boat.

"There they come," Totten said. " 'Bout time."

Looking up, Taylor followed the direction of the major's
gaze. Then, brought up the eyeglass.

So Driscol did have cavalry, after all. Cherokee irregulars.
Maybe Creeks. They'd not have been of much use in the battle. Not in tight ground like this.

But they'd be of use, now. No use Taylor would have put
them to, though.

Well . . . he liked to think so, anyway. But he was fair-
minded enough to realize that his way of looking at the
world probably wasn't much the same as the way a freedman did. Especially one who'd been driven out of his home
by exclusion mobs and maybe seen some of his family die.
If not at the hands of the mob, from the rigors of the forced
journey overland to Arkansas.

He brought the glass back to his eye and swept the terrain.
Sure enough. Around three hundred Cherokees or Creeks.
Maybe four hundred. It was hard to be certain, between the
distance and the fact they were scattering out.

Inevitably, some of Crittenden's men were escaping the
ever-closing trap on the little peninsula on the south bank of

the Arkansas. Some, leaving by boat; others, by swimming downstream; still others, simply by scrambling and running. Driscol was still keeping the regiments in formation and probably would until almost the very end. So, like a piston driving into a very loose and sloppy cylinder, a lot of steam was escaping from the sides.

Most of them wouldn't get far. Not across that terrain, with hundreds of Indian light cavalry hunting them down.

Another volley came. By now, that was like hammering porridge. But if nothing else was clear to Zachary Taylor about the man they called the Laird of Arkansas, one thing was. All of war, for that man, would be a hammer or an anvil. Beat or be beaten against, he'd not yield at all. Taylor had always wondered a bit how such a peculiar unit as the Iron Battalion had managed to break British regiments on the Mississippi. He didn't wonder any longer.

He brought the glass down to examine the situation at the river. What was left of Crittenden's army—still a good half of it, in sheer numbers—was now crammed along the bank, many of the men spilling into the water. The Arkansas regiments were still coming, ten paces at a time.

The volleys were finally ending, though. Now, lifting the glass again, Taylor could see that Driscol had given the order "Charge bayonets." The two regiments had their muskets in the proper position, the right hand holding the stock at hip level, the left keeping the barrel and the bayonet about chest high. The bayonet assault would begin momentarily.

The charge itself was well executed, overall. A bit ragged, finally, but bayonet charges usually were. The emotion involved was intense, and much more difficult to control than ranked volley fire.

The resistance put up by Crittenden's men with whatever musket butts, pistols, knives, and sabers they had—and could bring to bear, so tightly were they crowded against the river—killed or injured some of the Arkansans.

Not many, though, and almost none at all once the butchery began.

Taylor stepped away from the firing slit and handed the eyeglass back to the aide.

"Thank you, Lieutenant Morton."

"You're done with it?" Totten asked. "You're welcome to keep it through to the end."

"No need, thank you." He could have added *and certainly no desire,* but didn't. The officers and men in the blockhouse might have taken that as a veiled insult, which it actually wasn't. Taylor had no difficulty at all understanding why those men, most of whom were black, were watching the scene across the river with an intensity that bordered on fervor. Had they lost this battle, they would have been butchered or enslaved, their babes murdered, their women-folk ravaged.

No, he didn't blame them. But he wanted no part of watching it, either.

He decided to go below and find Julia Chinn and her daughters. The sight of those two fresh-faced girls would be good for him. He liked daughters, fortunately, since he had several of his own.

Sheff would never be able to explain to anyone, afterward, the sensation that swept over him when he plunged his bayonet into the chest of his first victim. As strong as he was, despite his relatively short stature, the narrow triangular blade slid all the way through with no difficulty at all. Prying it out had actually been much harder.

He'd had the time, doing so, to watch his opponent die. The face, its mouth contorted, eyes wide, had resembled nothing so much as the faces he remembered beating his father to death. Except the froth coming out of this white's man mouth was bright red, and the eyes were filled with terror instead of glee.

Welcome to your afterlife, white boy. The direction you're headed is down.

The sheer savage exultation of that moment was like nothing he'd ever experienced in his life. So grand, so glorious . . .

And he never wanted to again. Some saner part of him recognized the abyss and dragged him away from it lest he follow his enemy.

He slew two more, and probably a third with a strike of the musket butt to the skull. But that was done much as he'd fired the volleys. Effectively and well, according to his training. But what mattered was no longer him, simply the regiment and the victory.

At the very end, he found himself using the bayonet—the threat of it, at least—to drive off some of the men in his squad. The killing was done, but they kept on.

"Stop it, boys!" He shifted the musket to his left hand and dragged off one of his privates. "He's dead, Adams. You just mutilatin' yourself now. Obey me, damn you!"

Fortunately, the Laird arrived then, and the pointless business ended immediately.

Sheff took a few deep breaths and looked around. Now that it was over, he was feeling exhausted. Only the superb conditioning of the Arkansas Army's training regimen was keeping him on his feet.

Some killing was still going on, but that was being done by squads under the direction of officers or sergeants. No bayonet work—there was nobody left alive on the bank— simply shooting at enemies in the water trying to swim downriver.

There was no room on the bank for Sheff's squad, anyway. He was more relieved than anything else.

To his surprise, he saw the Laird was watching. Then, summoned him over with a wave of the hand.

"Yes, sir?"

"You're Parker, aren't you?"

"Yes, sir. Sheffield Parker."

"One of Crowell's so-called volunteers?"

There seemed to be a twist in that craggy mouth, which might be humor. Hard to tell, though, as it always was with the Laird. He really was something of a troll.

"Yes, sir."

The Laird nodded. "If you're willing to go career, I'll give you a field commission. Right now."

Sheff's eyes widened. "Sergeant, sir?"

The Laird chuckled. "I said *commission,* lad. Second lieutenant."

Sheff couldn't think of anything to say. Except . . .

"I'm just turned seventeen, sir."

"I figured. That's why I'm making the offer. Any lad your age who can . . . Never mind. Let's just say I couldn't have done it at the age of seventeen. Find it hard enough at the age of forty-two. Which is why I'll always be a sergeant and you've got the makings of an officer. So what do you say, Corporal Parker?"

Now Sheff couldn't think of anything to say at all. His mind seemed to be a complete blank.

The Laird waved his hand. "All right, think it over. The offer will stand for a week."

He left then. Attending to whatever business a general attended to after a victorious battle.

Once Sheff was sure his squad was settled down, he decided he had a bit of time for personal matters. He went looking for Callender.

But Callender was gone. Struck down almost at the very beginning. Still alive, apparently, when two of his squadmates carried him off to be loaded into a boat and taken across to the Post. But nobody knew what had become of him since.

"Oh, blast it," Sheff muttered. He stared at the carnage all around him. The cleared south bank of the Arkansas River, across from Arkansas Post, was a slaughterhouse. Corpses or pieces of them everywhere he looked, mashed in with enough blood to make them seem like bits of meat in a stew cooked by the Devil.

There were a few black corpses, here and there, that hadn't been carried away yet. One white one, also in a green uniform. But nine out of ten—more like nineteen out of twenty—were white men. The same sort of white men who had terrified Sheff all his life until a short time ago.

They'd never terrify him again, he knew. And realized also, with genuine surprise, that the main reason wasn't really that he'd been able to kill them. It was because, now that he'd proved he could, he found himself a lot more concerned over the fate of a white boy who might be dead than he was over all the ones who most certainly were.

His uncle Jem was still alive. Alive and uninjured, except for a small powder burn.

Sheff found him on his knees, praying.

Probably for deliverance, although he couldn't make out the murmured words. And probably words from one of the

Gospels, this time. The day had started as an Old Testament
day, sure enough, but Uncle Jem was plenty smart enough
to know that it was much wiser for a man to end it in the
New. Probably for a black man, even more than for a white
one.

And, thankfully, Cal had survived, too, although Sheff
didn't find out until late in the afternoon, when his squad
was rotated for a rest period in the Post.

He found Callender in the mess hall, which had been
transformed into an infirmary. He was lying on a blanket on
the floor, there being no more cots available and—
thankfully again—him not being one of the really bad cases.

He'd suffered a flesh wound, which had torn through the
muscles of his right arm but hadn't broken the bone. That
was something of a minor miracle right there. Sheff knew
full well from the accounts of veterans that the .69- and .75-
caliber bullets used by most of the muskets on either side of
the battle usually pulverized the bone so badly that the only
treatment was immediate amputation. Cal wouldn't even
lose the use of the arm, he'd been told by the surgeon who'd
given him a quick examination.

On the other hand, he'd need to spend weeks in
recuperation—and the Laird had a rigid policy that soldiers
recovering from wounds would be billeted in private resi-
dences. He had some sort of peculiar detestation of army
hospitals. Called them guaranteed death houses, from what
the veterans had told Sheff.

That posed a bit of a problem, though, since the whole
McParland clan lived way up in Fort of 98. Too far for Cal
to travel, for at least a week or two.

The problem was solved almost immediately, once the
surgeon came back through and pronounced Callender fit to
be removed to a billet. For, as it happened, Senator Johnson's folks had been gathered around him when Sheff arrived.

He didn't understand why. Couldn't even really think
about it, since he was too nervous about the one girl—that
was Imogene, he thought—who kept her eyes on him the
whole time. Real pretty eyes, hazel colored.

When the surgeon left, the other twin immediately piped up. A peculiar sort of imperious wail.

"Mama!"

Julia Chinn took a deep breath through tight jaws. Then, glared at Callender for no reason Sheff could figure out. Then, glared at *him*.

"Oh, Hell and damnation!" she muttered. "Fine. It ain't worth listening to it for the next God knows how long." She looked back at Callender and gave him what someone as dumb as a carrot might call a smile. It was really just a baring of naked teeth.

"Mr. McParland. I believe the lodgings Senator Johnson has reserved for us at the Wolfe Tone Hotel are reasonably spacious." She was talking a lot more formal-like than she had been earlier, too. That was even scarier than the "smile."

"I therefore extend the offer to provide you with billeting in our rooms." The smile vanished like dew under Sam Hill's breath. So did the formal speech. "Only till you be strong enough to go to y'own folks, y'hear? Mind me, now!"

She was even shaking her finger under Cal's nose as if he'd done something wrong. Sheff was starting to wonder if the woman wasn't a little off in her head, or something.

"Sheff can come sing for him, too!" Imogene said brightly. "Pick up his spirits. That's important, Mama, for someone's been hurt so bad."

Julia glared at her. Then, swiveled her head and glared at Sheff again. That was about the most unfriendly look Sheff had ever gotten from anyone, except a white man in a killing mood. And he hadn't done nothing!

"Is there anything you can do besides sing, boy?" she demanded.

Sheff thought about it. Well, tried to. Those hazel eyes made it hard to think. Blast it, the girl was only twelve!

But it made a decision easy. Real easy.

"Pretty soon I will, ma'am. I've been offered a commission in the army. So I'll be an officer come next week."

For some reason—the woman really had to be a little crazy—that just made her glare even more.

Imogene, on the other hand, was smiling so wide it looked

like her face might split in two. Sheff had to remind himself—again—that she was way too young for him to be having any such thoughts like the ones his brain was skittering around like spit on a hot griddle.

"Well, it's all settled then," Adaline pronounced. She was giving Cal a smile just about as wide. And, weak though he might be from blood loss, Sheff could tell that his friend's brain was skittering around on the same griddle.

"Oh, Hell and damnation," Julia repeated.

CHAPTER 19

*The confluence of the Arkansas
and the Mississippi*
OCTOBER 6, 1824

By the time their flatboat reached the confluence with the Mississippi, Scott Powers and Ray Thompson knew they were facing the most desperate situation either of them had ever encountered, in lives that had both been full of perils aplenty.

To make things worse, the flatboat was under the control of a gang of seven men under the leadership of a fellow named Robert Lowrey. His lieutenant—using the term loosely—went by the charming monicker of Alfred "Two Bear" Decker. The nickname came from Decker's immense size, but it could just as easily have been a reference to his intelligence.

Or his disposition, which rivaled that of a grizzly with a sore paw. Before they'd gotten more than three miles downriver from Arkansas Post, Decker had killed one man in the boat by clubbing him to death. Why? Who knew? Apparently the man had made an offensive remark of some sort.

Offensive, at least, once filtered through Decker's mudflat of a brain.

The second man he killed—a stabbing, this time—was at the command of Lowrey.

Why? Who knew? Apparently the man had made an offensive remark of some sort. Offensive, at least, to Lowrey—who, if he was smarter than his sidekick, also seemed to have an even more tenuous grasp of reality.

As he proved again, the moment the flatboat came into sight of the flotilla of Arkansas steamboats that commanded the confluence.

They'd known of the flotilla already. Half an hour earlier, a small steamboat had come chugging back upriver, calling out a warning to the stream of crafts that were trying to make their escape into the Mississippi.

"You cain't get past 'em, boys!" shouted one of the men on the steamboat. "They got's cannons and everything! Fuckin' niggers are killing anybody they get their hands on!"

Lowrey had ignored the warning and kept going. Being honest, neither Powers nor Thompson had blamed him at the time. What was the point of going back upriver? They were butchering everybody up there also. Besides, the Mississippi was a big damn river. Surely—at least with some luck— they'd be able to get past a couple of steamboats being run by illiterate negroes who thought a wrench was a funny-looking hoe.

But now that they could actually see the Arkansans' flotilla, Thompson and Powers immediately recognized the mistake.

Just for starters, there were *five* steamboats, not the two or three they'd expected. The Arkansans must have captured prizes and turned them into jury-rigged warships. Five steamboats were more than enough to cover a river even the breadth of the Mississippi. For a second thing, sure enough, they had cannons.

Quite a few of them, too. Peering past the monstrous figure of Two Bear in the prow, Thompson and Powers watched as two of the enemy vessels converged on a keelboat and pounded it into a wreck in less than two minutes.

And, sure enough, men at the guardrails of the steamboats

were shooting anybody who went into the water. A goodly number of the men doing the shooting were white themselves. Where in Creation had they come from?

Finally, if those boats—not to mention the cannons—were being crewed by illiterates who had no idea what they were doing, there sure wasn't any sign of it.

"We're fucked," hissed Powers, slumping back into the bench they'd taken at the very stern of the boat, to get as far away from Lowrey and Decker as possible.

"What do you want to do?" asked Ray. He kept his voice as low as Scott's, not wanting the maniacs running the boat to get it into their heads they had mutineers to deal with.

Thompson's eyes scanned the riverbank. At least Lowrey had had enough sense to stay closer to the northern than the southern shore. By now, the south shore of the Arkansas was practically crawling with Cherokees and Creeks, coming down from the massacre at the Post and looking to add to it as best they could.

"We could slip over the side and make it to shore," he whispered. "Can't be more than fifty yards."

"And then what?" Scott demanded. "What's the point of being stuck in Arkansas, with no food and no horses, the clothes on our backs, and—" He checked his pouch. "Hardly any shot or powder left. Unless you got some I don't know about."

In point of fact, Thompson's pistol—he'd dropped his musket in the panicky flight to the boats—had the one shot loaded, and that was it. He was out of ball and powder altogether.

"And *then* what?" Scott repeated.

Ray had no answer. True, the Arkansans might not extend the pursuit to the north bank of the river. Given the maniacal way they'd conducted themselves thus far, though, he rated the chances of that somewhere a long ways south of winning a horse race with a cow. But even if they didn't, that still left the prospect of trying to get through rough country to St. Louis, or at least the nearest settlements in Missouri. With no food, no mounts, and hardly any ammunition.

The smartest thing left to do, of course, would be to wait until nightfall to try to run past the blockade at the confluence. But sundown was still a good two hours off, and Thompson was glumly certain that a man like Lowrey didn't have the patience.

Sure enough. "Let's go, boys! Throw it into those poles! Them niggers cain't shoot straight nohow!"

Thompson wondered, given the day just past—not to mention the sight of another keelboat being ripped to pieces by the cannons up ahead—if he'd ever heard a more idiotic statement in his entire life.

They were dead meat. Especially once they got into the Mississippi where the steamboats were cruising. Poling down the Arkansas was possible, most places. Poling down the Mississippi was chancy. They'd have to unship the oars.

All one of them. Two Bear had shattered the second one during the first killing. Nobody knew what had happened to the other four that should have been on board.

Dead fucking meat.

"Pole, boys, pole!"

Any second, Lowrey was going to look around and see that neither Thompson nor Powers had joined in the poling.

There was only one chance, slim as it was. Thompson had half considered it earlier, on the assumption it was each man for himself, and too bad for Scott. But now, seeing the relentless way the Arkansans were continuing the slaughter, he realized the only chance at all would depend on including Powers.

"You lie pretty damn good, Scott," he whispered. "And you met Henry Clay once, didn't you?"

"Yeah—and so what? Met him in his office in Washington that time—"

"Never mind the details. Ever been to his place in Kentucky?"

"No."

Damnation. Thompson would just have to hope the description of the Clay estate he'd gotten from Crittenden would do the trick.

"Okay. You just stick to the personal details about Clay. I'll do the rest of the talking."

"What are you—I—"

"Shut up." He jabbed a finger toward the bow. "Shoot

Two Bear. Now. I don't dare try it with this pistol, not as big and crazy as he is. I'll handle Lowrey."

"What in the—"

One of the steamboats was coming. Coming fast. It looked as big as a mountain.

"Just shut up and do it!" he half shrieked.

Lowrey heard, and started to turn around. Two Bear was still leaning into his pole, as were some of the other men on the boat.

"Well, shit," Powers muttered. He rose to a crouch, leveled the musket, and shot Two Bear in the back.

Nice clean shot. Even a man as big as Two Bear Decker couldn't survive a .69-caliber round fired at close range that cut his spine and probably jellied half his guts in the process. He threw his hands wide, the pole went sailing, and over he went with a big splash.

"You fucking—!" Lowrey was drawing his pistol, but Ray already had his leveled. He damn near missed altogether, with the unsteady footing, but he managed to hit Lowrey in the arm. Not much of a wound, but enough to make his own shot go wild.

Scott was frantically reloading. Not seeing anything else to do, Ray drew back the pistol and prepared to throw it at Lowrey.

And then a hail of canister from the steamboat's forward gun made it all a moot point. Lowrey took maybe half the rounds himself. By the time he hit the river he was in pieces.

The same blast killed three other men toward the bow and wounded a couple more. The steamboat started to swerve, bringing the rear gun in line.

Ray stood up as straight as he could, balancing precariously on the bench, threw his pistol in the river, and spread his hands wide.

"We give up! We give up! I know something you want to know! I *know something!*"

Scott was no dummy. He'd already pitched his musket in the river and was emulating Thompson's stance.

"Yeah! Yeah! We know everything! You don't want to kill us! You'll never find out how it happened!"

The surviving men in the middle of the flatboat were gaping at them. The steamboat's rear gun went off and took care of that.

The steamboat was almost alongside, now. Five men—two of them white—were leaning over the guardrail with their muskets leveled.

"We know something!" Thompson shrieked. Desperate, now. Those men didn't look the least bit interested in expanding their education.

"It was Henry Clay!" Scott screeched. "Henry Clay hisself! I talked to him! Right there as near as you and me!"

There seemed to be a slight hesitation in the way the guns were coming to bear. Well, not that. They were *already* to bear. Still—

Belatedly, Thompson remembered. It was risky, but . . .

He lowered his hand—left hand—and pointed to his haversack under the bench. "It's all in there! All of it! I got the records! I was Crittenden's moneyman!"

No use. Ray could tell, just from the way the guns weren't wavering.

But then—

"Hold up!" A young man in a fancy Eastern-style frock coat came to the rail. "Hold up!"

He leaned over the rail. "Did you say 'Henry Clay'?"

"Yes!"

"Yeah! Henry Clay hisself!"

The meanest-looking negro Thompson had ever seen was at the guardrail. Wearing a fancy uniform that Ray would have laughed at seeing on any black man anywhere else, even a doorman in Philadelphia or New York. But there wasn't anything funny about this one.

"You lyin' through your teeth," he proclaimed.

Scott started to protest their innocence, but Ray could tell that was no use at all with this black bastard.

"Try us, then!" he shouted. "What you got to lose?"

The negro hesitated, then glanced at the Easterner. The young man in the frock coat came to his side and whispered something.

The uniformed negro looked back down at them.

"Fine. Swim on over. You tellin' the truth, I'll let you live." A grin colder than Canadian winter came to his face.

"Best dive in quick, though. You 'bout to have no boat under you."

Thompson and Powers just barely made it off the side when another cannon blast shredded the flatboat's stern.

So, the worst day in Ray Thompson's checkered life ended in a miracle.

Two, actually. They didn't even get beaten after they were hauled aboard the steamboat.

Well. Nothing unreasonable, anyway.

CHAPTER 20

Arkansas Post
OCTOBER 7, 1824

The closer the *Comet* got to Arkansas Post, the worse it got. Even Robert Ross, with his years of experience in the bloody and often savage Peninsular War, had never seen anything quite like it. The pursuit Driscol had launched after the battle had been utterly pitiless. Of course, a few of the boats fleeing from the disaster had managed to get through Ball's blockade at the confluence. Days from now—assuming they weren't ambushed by the Choctaws they'd ravaged on the way upriver—a relative handful of the free-booters would make their escape to Alexandria or New Orleans.

But not many. Not many at all. Perhaps one or two hundred, all told, of the roughly fifteen hundred men Robert Crittenden had led to disaster in front of Arkansas Post.

Bodies were scattered all along the banks of the Arkansas, most of them on the south bank, for miles downstream. A few were perched on snags in the river itself. There would have been still more the day before, Robert knew. Some of the predators in the river were large enough to pull entire corpses into the water, and almost all predators would scavenge if given the chance.

Alligators he'd expected to see, but he'd also seen at least two types of fish large enough to do the work. One of them resembled the catfish he'd seen in New Orleans, except grown to enormous dimensions; the other had been similar in appearance—from a distance, anyway—to a sturgeon of some sort.

"Yup, giant catfish," one of the gunners confirmed. "They'll eat anything if it ain't movin'. T'other fish was what they call an alligator gar in these parts, General. Big damn things. Can get to ten foot, maybe even more. They not too dangerous, though, long's a man's still kicking. It's the gators you gotta watch out for."

Naturally, birds were everywhere. By now, a day after the slaughter, they'd already stripped much of the flesh from the corpses. What was left would be finished by small scavengers, insects. Worms, eventually. By next year, there'd be nothing but skeletons left, and most of those bones would be scattered.

From the middle of the Arkansas where the *Comet* was steaming upriver, it was usually impossible to determine the cause of death. Those might have been simply victims of some sort of fast-spreading plague rather than violence. But two corpses had quite obviously been slain by human hands. One of them had been hung upside down from the fork in a dead tree leaning over the river. His facial features had been removed, along with his scalp, and his arms severed at the elbows. He might have blessed that last indignity, under the circumstances, since at least he'd have bled to death quickly.

The other such corpse . . . Eliza had retreated from the open deck then, back into the blessed gloom of the boat's interior. She'd been quite pale. Robert's son had given the men on his gun crew a look that was half reproach and half sheer horror.

"Hey, look, David, wasn't us," the black soldier said, uncomfortably. "That was Cherokee work, or maybe Creek. They be settlin' a lot of old grudges. Cain't say I blame 'em much."

"I was told the Cherokee were *civilized,*" David hissed.

Charles Ball happened to be standing nearby, close enough to hear the remark. He chuckled, very harshly. "*Which* Cherokees, boy? You talkin' about John Ross, his sort? Oh, he be very civilized. I visited him at his house in Tahlequah. Twice, now. Could almost call it a mansion. Books everywhere, and nice linen on the table."

The black general's smile had little humor in it, and his black dialect seemed to deepen with every sentence. "Oh, very civilized. That's 'cause he got upwards of fifteen slaves to keep him in proper comfort, so's he can study them books. But them out there—"

Ball jerked his head toward the bank. "Those be what they call the traditionalists out there, doin' the killing. Cherokees who stick to chiefs like Duwali—The Bowl, he's also called—and Tahchee. They be right savage, sometimes."

His smile thinned and lost any humor whatsoever. "'Course, on t'other hand, they don't got no slaves. Hardly none, anyways. And they right friendly to us niggers, 'cause they ain't tryin' to bleed us dry and they smart 'nough to know we their best chance at keepin' their old ways." He jerked his head again, this time upward, indicating the banner flying from a mast above. "They got no problem with that red-white-and-black-striped flag of Arkansas. It be the civilized Cherokees who gonna squawk and scream about it, and make threats. Not that we goin' pay no attention to them. Sure as Creation not after yesterday."

"Be quiet, David," his father said softly. "I can assure you that was not the first man I've ever seen impaled. It was a common enough sight in Spain. White men everywhere you looked—perpetrators and victims both—and the only sign of civilization was that they'd generally use a prepared stake of some sort rather than the sharpened end of a severed sapling."

His son fell silent then, a bit abashed. Only a bit, of course, which was fine with Robert.

"No, I don't approve," he continued, more softly still. "But if you plan to be a soldier, be prepared to see such sights. The rules and laws of war are just a veneer that we insist on so strongly because the veneer can crack so very, very easily. Never think otherwise."

*   *   *

Arkansas Post was worse. Much worse.

Only a day after the battle, the corpses of the men who'd been trapped and butchered on the peninsula were piled up in heaps. Fairly tidy heaps, now, since they'd been moved there to clear ground for the shallow mass graves that were starting to be dug by Arkansas soldiers. But the tidiness simply served to underscore the sheer scale of the slaughter. Hundreds of corpses scattered on a level are bad enough; the same hundreds stacked like so much firewood are considerably worse.

But the worst of all was the fort itself.

Seeing the decorations hanging from the walls, like so many ornaments, Robert sighed.

"As I feared. Oh, Patrick, will you *never* put that damned road to rest?"

At least sixty corpses were hanging from the walls. The only reason there weren't more was simply that there was no more room. Another three dozen or so were hanging from three long A-frame gallows that had been erected on the flat ground by the river.

No sign of torture, thankfully, though Robert wasn't surprised at that. Torture wasn't Driscol's way.

It hardly mattered. Close to a hundred men, hands tied behind their backs and hung from the neck, was plenty bad enough. Even the absence of torture was a relative thing. The men pitched off the walls might have had their necks mercifully broken—most of them, at least—but all the men hanging from those low A-frames had simply strangled to death. Garroted, for all intents and purposes.

It remained to be seen, but Robert was now fairly certain that the only prisoners the army of Arkansas had taken after the battle were the two men who'd been seized by the *Comet.* And he wouldn't be at all surprised to see them hung on the morrow, once they were turned over to the man called the Laird of Arkansas.

Not a bad cognomen, actually. For all of Patrick's devotion to the most radical modern political philosophies, there had always been that streak in him that was purely medieval. Savage Scot clan medieval, at that. No Camelot, here.

* * *

Patrick was waiting for him at the pier.

Alone. No aides or soldiers anywhere within thirty yards.

Robert understood. "Please wait here, Eliza. David. General Ball, I'd appreciate a private moment with General Driscol."

Ball inclined his head. Two soldiers extended a gangplank, and Robert marched onto the shore.

"I'll have no part of this, Patrick," were his first words. "Either you agree—I'll want your word on this—that we abide by the rules of war, henceforth, or I shall simply return to Ireland immediately."

In a gesture familiar from so many years ago, Driscol lowered his head slightly. Like a bull, preparing a charge.

But instead of the harsh proclamations Robert expected, concerning the hypocrisies and perfidies of gentlemen, Patrick simply smiled.

It was not much of a smile, granted. But Robert remembered that also. A face so square and craggy that it led many to compare the man to a troll did not, after all, lend itself well to cheery and insouciant expressions.

"Oh, leave off, Robert." Patrick twitched his arm slightly, as if he had started to point back at the fort with its grisly decorations. "You think I'm still exorcising the ghosts of '98?"

Before Robert could answer—and the answer would have been yes—Patrick shook his head.

"Leave off, I say." This time he twitched the other arm, the left arm that ended above the elbow. "I buried that bloody road in County Antrim at the Chippewa, along with my arm."

Patrick took a slow breath. "Well, most of it, anyway. But what was left . . ." He shrugged. "I figure that went with your own arm, that I ruined at the Capitol."

"Then why—"

The familiar glower was back. "*Gentlemen.* Robert, I have no doubt at all you have much to teach me concerning the science of war. But what you know about the training of soldiers—the *real* training I'm talking about, not that petty business with drill and the manual of arms—is what any gentleman knows. Which is absolutely nothing, because you do not know the men."

This time, when he moved his remaining arm, the gesture was as full and complete as the arm itself. A stiff finger pointed to the corpses hanging from the walls and moved slowly across.

"I didn't do this—or that killing across the river—for my own sake. Robert, did you ever—once—ask yourself how you teach a man to be a soldier who has no memory of any victories at all? Not in his life, not in his father's, not in his grandfather's—not in any generation so far back as he can trace them. Which, in the case of my soldiers, is usually not more than two, and those on the distaff side."

Ross straightened. "Well. Ah . . ."

He cleared his throat. "Well. No, actually. I haven't."

The glower faded, replaced by that crack of a smile. "Didn't think so. You take it for granted, no reason not to, that even the lowliest recruit to British colors—be he never so drunken, never so indigent, never so stupid, and never so shiftless—has endless memories to hold him up. He goes into his first battle knowing that his forefathers, perhaps as lowly as he, still managed to triumph. Over and over again. If he didn't know the names before he enlisted, he learns them soon enough. Start with Crecy, almost five hundred years ago, and now you can end with Waterloo. In between, there are how many dozens?"

Robert thought about it. "I'd have to sit down and write them up, actually. Couldn't really do it proper justice, off the top of my head."

"Yes, you would. So would a French general. So would a German. And their soldiers."

Driscol paused for a moment. "Yesterday—he accepted this morning—I issued my first field commission. To a black boy named Sheffield Parker. Splendid lad, I'm thinking. I have considerable hopes for him. How many victories does he have, d'ye think? A lad who watched a mob of white men beat his father to death—with impunity—on a street in Baltimore, in broad daylight. I happen to know in his case, because I investigated his history. Such as it is. I couldn't do the same for most of the black men in my army—and they constitute over nine out of ten—but you'd find the story was much the same. Add into the bargain as many generations as they can remember, which are precious few, of men who had to watch their women debauched—again, with complete impunity—by slave-masters."

Ross was silent.

"How many victories, Robert?"

"One. Yesterday's. Fine—but there was still no reason—"

"Yes, there was. I can't train men to control their violence until they learn—learn down to their toenails and fingernails—that they can unleash it as furiously as any men alive. Never letting them run wild, mind you. This was no barbarian frenzy. But they know—*now*—that they can do it. And if they can do it once, they can do it again. As many times as it takes."

He took a deep slow breath and let it out just as slowly. "That said, once is enough. I'm glad you're here, Robert. So very glad, to be honest. And I accept your condition. Was planning on it, anyway."

Whatever else, Patrick Driscol had never been a liar. And if he was far more likely to sneer at the phrase "word of honor" than use it, Robert Ross had met precious few men in his life who took the heart of the thing more seriously and earnestly.

"Well. Fine."

And then it was time for the smiles and the handshake— even the embrace.

"Eliza! David! Come down! I'd like to introduce an old and very dear friend!"

Arkansas Post
OCTOBER 9, 1824

"I'll thank you again, General Driscol, for the use of the *Comet*."

The Arkansas commander nodded. "My pleasure, Colonel Taylor. I'd not wish it on any man, unless he were my bitterest enemy, to make that journey downriver overland. At any time, much less now, with the Choctaws on the warpath. That country's malarial, as often as not."

Taylor hesitated. That raised a perhaps delicate issue, and not one that was really under Taylor's authority. Not at all, in fact. At least, at the moment.

Understanding, Driscol continued. "As soon as the *Comet* leaves you off at Baton Rouge, she's got orders to return and help with ferrying the Choctaws across the Mississippi. Chickasaws, too, if they make the request."

"Ah. Have you by chance—"

Driscol shook his head. "I haven't been able to establish contact with Chief Pushmataha yet, no. But I got a letter from John Ross yesterday. He and Major Ridge should arrive on the morrow, and the *Hercules* will be taking them down to parlay with the Choctaws. I don't imagine Pushmataha will continue being stubborn. His people will have wreaked whatever vengeance they could, by now, and they're simply in no shape to deal with the state militias that are surely being mustered. Neither are the Chickasaws, certainly, as few in number as they are. You know how it works as well as I do. It doesn't matter who started the killing; it'll be the Indians who get blamed for it."

He stiffened a body that was already a bit stiff. "Everywhere except in the Confederacy, that is. And no militia— perhaps no army—can get to the Confederacy without coming through Arkansas. Which is not so easily done as all that."

He didn't bother to point out the window of the blockhouse. There was no need. The prisoners he'd hung had been taken down after a day, their bodies lowered into the same shallow graves that had been the burial site for Crittenden and the rest of his men.

Very shallow graves, which meant that Taylor could see the mounds easily, even from across the river.

Had he bothered to look, which he didn't. He had the memories of the actual battle, which did better for the purpose.

As Driscol well knew, of course.

That left the final matter. Again, though, Taylor hesitated. This, too, was really beyond his authority.

Fortunately, however brutal-looking the man's face was, Driscol had quite the shrewd brain beneath that blocky skull.

"Please be assured, Colonel Taylor, that in the unfortunate event a state of war should exist between the United States and the Confederacy—Arkansas, at any rate—I shall conduct my own operations giving respect to the established rules and customs of war. Provided, that is"—there was just the slightest emphasis on *provided*—"my opponent does the same."

Taylor nodded. "For my part, I can assure you that in that same unfortunate event, should it come to pass, I will see to it that my own officers and men conduct themselves accordingly." Honesty required him to add, "That's assuming I'm in a position of command, of course, which will not be my decision."

"Yes, I understand." There came a smile, then. Not much of one, perhaps, but a smile nonetheless. "At the same time, the army of the United States is not so large as all that. So I imagine you'll have various conversations with your fellow officers. Here and there."

Taylor couldn't help but laugh. "Oh, yes—you can be sure of that! Bunch of old women gossiping, I sometimes think."

There was nothing more to say, really. And he'd already made his farewells to Julia and the girls, since they'd left for New Antrim the day before.

"I'll be going, then. Again, my thanks for your courtesies."

There was a last courtesy still to come. Driscol even had an honor guard waiting by the steamboat to see Colonel Taylor and his men off.

For his part, Taylor mustered his small unit on the deck to exchange the honors as the *Comet* pulled away from the pier.

Very punctilious, it was. That seemed wise to Taylor.

Apparently it seemed wise to his men, too. Toward sundown, as they neared the confluence with the Mississippi, Taylor happened to pass by two of his cavalrymen on the deck. They were leaning on the guardrail, looking at the riverbank with its grim mementos.

"Hope we don't find ourselves comin' back up this river, any time soon," one of them commented.

"Not wearin' a uniform, for sure," his mate agreed.

*   *   *

After Colonel Taylor and his cavalrymen left, Driscol went to the blockhouse in the fort that had been turned into an impromptu jail.

"Well?"

Smiling a little ruefully and scratching his head, William Cullen Bryant looked down at his notepad. "Can't say for sure, Patrick. I'm almost certain that at least some of what they've told me is a lie. But . . ."

"A lie, how?"

"Well, that's the thing. Mostly, I think they're just exaggerating how much they were personally involved. A good part of this"—he tapped the notepad—"could well be hearsay. On the other hand, Thompson certainly has the financial figures. He's got the records to verify it, too, unless we want to suppose that he somehow managed to fake such a thing on the off chance he might get captured and be able to use it to parlay leniency for himself."

Patrick shook his head. "No, that's preposterous."

"Exactly. And the financial figures *are* the heart of it. What's left is simply proving that Clay was personally involved, to the extent they claim he was. Which would amount, in effect, to the Speaker of the House having been the linchpin in a conspiracy to divert funds from the Second Bank—some of its directors and officers, at any rate—into Crittenden's coffers. Which is all that allowed him to provide his army with that sudden influx of weapons and ammunition they needed."

"Where's the weakness in their testimony, then?"

Bryant shrugged. "Basically, it'll be their word against Clay's. Powers's depiction of Clay's estate in Kentucky, I couldn't vouch for one way or the other. I've never been there myself—although you can be sure I'll make it a point to visit on my way back to New York. But I can tell you that his description of Henry Clay himself is dead on the money, all the way down to that peculiar habit he has of using a snuffbox to emphasize points while he's speaking. I've observed the Speaker giving speeches."

Driscol scratched his jaw. "In short, they claim to have met with Clay in private at his estate, but they can't prove that part of it. I don't care about that. This is not something that will ever be put to a test in a court of law, anyway. It's the public's opinion that'll matter."

"Ah, Patrick. . . ." Bryant seemed uncomfortable. "You do understand . . ."

"I'm not a babe, William. I know perfectly well that such a report would—for a time—boost Clay's popularity in a lot of the states. Send it soaring in the South, and elevate it in the border states and probably some of the middle Atlantic states."

Bryant nodded. "New England will be outraged, in the main. New York also, leaving aside the wealthiest circles. No way to know, yet, how Van Buren and his crowd will swing. Pennsylvania, probably; Philadelphia, certainly—again, leaving aside the bank circles. But I'm glad to see you're not fooling yourself."

He hefted the notebook. "If I publish this—well, *when* I publish it—the impact will be mostly to Clay's advantage, not disadvantage."

"In the short run. Yes. But what about the long run, William?"

The poet-turned-reporter mused on that for a bit, then shrugged again. "There's no way to know, Patrick. There simply isn't. Yes, it will also establish that he's an unscrupulous and unprincipled maneuverer. Even a Machiavellian one. But at least half the country knows that already. That's why so many people think John Randolph was referring to Clay, when he described a man—"

Patrick chuckled. "Yes, I read it. I will say Randolph has a fine way with words, insane as he might often seem. 'He shines and stinks like a rotten mackerel in moonlight,' wasn't it?"

Bryant nodded. "Yes. He was actually talking about Livingston, but if you recite that phrase to most Americans and ask them to guess, two out of three are likely to name Clay."

He lifted the notebook a few more inches. "But so what, Patrick? History is littered with cases of successful schemers and demagogues. It may well be the case that Henry Clay is America's Alcibiades—but I remind you that Alcibiades had a long and successful career."

Driscol stared at him. After a moment, Bryant smiled ruefully. "Well, yes, also a career that ended quite badly."

Patrick grinned. "'Quite badly.' A bit of a euphemism, wouldn't you say? A career that ended with him just as dead as Randolph's mackerel. And why, William?" He moved right on to the answer. "Because it's one thing to maneuver a country into a war for the sake of personal aggrandizement. Another thing entirely to maneuver that same country through the bloodshed—when the heady first moments pass, and the butcher's bill comes due, and the same men who hailed you once are now wondering what it was really all for and about in the first place."

He looked toward the east. "I think I'll bet on the American republic. Publish it with my blessing, William. Publish all of it. If Jackson came against us, I doubt we could stand. Not for more than three years, at least. But I don't think Jackson will come. I think it'll be Clay. Whatever else, Jackson has principles. Clay has none at all. That fish is foul. No more capable of forcing through a great victory than any rotted meat. He'll come to pieces if he tries. Watch and see."

Bryant left the next morning on a keelboat. Arrangements had been made for him to wait at Brown's camp, where the tanner was rebuilding his works, until either the *Comet* or the *Hercules* came by to take him to Memphis.

To his surprise, Thompson and Powers were frog-marched on board to join him.

"Do as you will with them," Driscol told him.

"I imagine I'll just set them free, once we reach Memphis." Bryant spread his hands. "I'm hardly equipped to be a jail-keeper."

"Fine with me. They'll have no choice but to flee the country altogether—or keep telling whatever lies might be in that report of yours."

He swiveled his head to bring the two prisoners under his cold gaze. They were obviously trying their best not to look like the most relieved men in North America, but not succeeding too well.

"Excellent liars, I'm thinking," Driscol mused. "We'll know soon enough, of course. Before they get to Memphis, they'll have to survive a few days in John Brown's company."

The looks of relief on the faces of the two adventurers vanished instantly. Driscol and Bryant shared a laugh.

"I recommend an immediate immersion in Judges," the poet advised them. The reporter added a caveat: "But don't try to claim any particular expertise. Arguing biblical text with John Brown—the mood he's in, and given your history would be about as insane as any act I can imagine. Short of invading Arkansas again."

PART III

CHAPTER 21

When Peter Porter entered the dining room of the lodging house on Ninth Street near Pennsylvania Avenue where Henry Clay was residing in the capital, he found that the Speaker of the House and his close political associates had taken it over, for all intents and purposes, and turned the chamber into what amounted to a staff headquarters. Fortunately, the landlady was an amenable woman. Easily intimidated, at least.

"Peter!" called out Josiah Johnston, cheerfully. He waved a hand at an empty chair at the large table in the center of the room. "Take a look at the latest reports. The situation gets brighter day by day."

Porter came up to the table and gave the newspapers spread across it no more than a glance. He'd already seen them, and they were much of a piece. The headline on one newspaper that had been vigorously backing the Crawford campaign was typical:

HORRID DETAILS CONCERNING THE MASSACRE
IN ARKANSAS
A river awash in blood
The banks covered with corpses
Driscol the Robespierre of the West

He pulled out the newspapers he had tucked under his arm and handed one of them to Henry Clay, who was sitting at the head of the table. The other three he tossed onto the table.

"You'd better look at this before you start celebrating. It's the latest issue of the *National Intelligencer*. I commend to you in particular the article by William Cullen Bryant. You can't miss it. The *Intelligencer* gave it half the front page."

He pulled out a chair and sat in it heavily.

Clay had already put on his eyeglasses and was scanning rapidly through the article. After a minute he exclaimed: "This is a tissue of lies! I've never met these two men in my life. Never even heard of one of them. This Powers fellow, whoever he is."

Johnston, who'd been scowling as he read the same article, looked up. "It's simple, then. You issue a straightforward denial and point out that the *Intelligencer,* being well known for its Federalist sympathies, has a long history—"

"Won't work, Josiah," Porter said bluntly. He gave Clay a look that was not entirely friendly. As much as Porter generally admired the Speaker and thought he would make by far the best new president of the United States, the man was not without his faults. "I'm afraid that Henry was using hyperbole when he referred to a 'tissue' of lies. That there are some lies in the story, scattered here and there, I don't doubt. In fact, I know one of them to be a lie, because Thompson and Powers were most certainly not at the meeting reported in this article."

He gave Clay another look. The Speaker avoided his eyes, choosing to look out the window.

"Yes. I know that for a fact, because I *was* at the meeting—and so was Henry. And while Thompson was not at the meeting, it is indeed true that he was the man we were instructed to have the money sent to. That's why, you might notice, Henry can say he never heard of *Powers.*"

The landlady was entering with another pot of tea and an extra cup. Porter shoved the pile of newspapers aside to make room for the service, gave her a polite nod, and waited until she'd left the room.

"I never heard of Powers, either," he continued. "But I don't doubt that most of this report is accurate enough."

Across from him, the Kentucky legislator Adam Beatty

had been reading the same article. Now he laid down the newspaper and shrugged his shoulders.

"What difference does it make? This report is coming in too late to have any effect on the election. But even if it had come in sooner, I doubt it would have made a difference." He chuckled. "I can assure you all, gentlemen, that my constituents are outraged by the events in Arkansas and demanding action. So are people all over the South. In fact, I was told just yesterday by one of Crawford's people that new recruits are flocking to the Georgia militia, lest their wives and children—"

"—be subjected to depravities at the hands of rampaging African savages," Porter concluded for him. "Leave off, Adam. You're not giving a campaign speech here. And you know just as well as I do that there is no chance whatsoever that the virtuous damsels of Georgia—or Tennessee, or Mississippi, or Missouri, or Louisiana, for that matter, which are considerably closer to Arkansas—are at any risk at all. From Arkansas negroes, at any rate. Choctaws might be a different matter. But all reports—including Bryant's—are agreed that the Choctaws are migrating to the Confederacy in the aftermath of the Crittenden incident. So are the Chickasaws."

He peered down at the offending article. "If this is accurate—and I'm quite sure it is, in these particulars—the total forces that met in front of Arkansas Post amounted to no more than two or three regiments on each side. Hardly enough, even without subtracting the half, to launch an invasion of the United States."

Beatty was quite unabashed. "Sure," he said, grinning. "So what? There wasn't any real chance the Creeks could overrun Kentucky, Tennessee, and Georgia, either. That didn't stop the massacre at Fort Mims from being a rallying cry eleven years ago—and I will point out to you that the slaughter at Arkansas Post was far worse."

Porter restrained his temper. Truth be told, he didn't much care for the Westerners and Southerners who had come to represent an ever-growing percentage of Henry Clay's coterie. They had a blithe disregard for simple logic that offended his New England upbringing, and an instant readiness to resort to naked emotionalism in the conduct of public affairs. Almost as bad as Jackson and his people, in that regard.

Almost . . . but not quite. Firmly, Porter reminded himself that his support of Clay derived from far more cogent and profound sources. Without Clay's American System, the manufacture and commerce of the nation would be stunted. The United States would remain a bucolic, agrarian backwater in the world, always at the financial mercy of England and other European powers.

"I say again, leave off," he growled. "The comparison is absurd. At Fort Mims, white people were massacred by Indians breaking *into* a fort. At Arkansas Post, they were massacred by negroes trying to keep them out."

Beatty shrugged again. "All true—and again, so what? If you think the average Westerner or Southerner is going to care—especially Southerners—I can assure you that you are quite mistaken. All that matters here is that white men—lots of them—were butchered by niggers. A wave of patriotism is sweeping the country in response." He pointed a finger at Henry Clay. "And it will sweep our man into the president's house."

Patriotism, no less. Porter found Beatty to be perhaps the most offensive of the lot.

"All very well and good," he replied, forcing himself to keep his tone civil. "*If* Henry wins a straightforward majority in the electoral college. But none of us have ever thought he could. Our campaign strategy was always to get him enough electoral votes to force the election into the House of Representatives. Where . . ."

He left off the rest. Henry Clay's control of the House of Representatives was doubted by no one in the United States, least of all his closest advisers. The Constitution provided that, in the event there was no clear winner of a presidential election in the electoral college, the House would choose between the three candidates who won the most votes. For the past year, therefore, their strategy had been predicated on that simple arithmetic.

There had been five major candidates for president at the start of the election campaign: Clay, Jackson, Adams, Crawford, and Calhoun.

At one point, fearing that his popularity in the Deep South

was being too badly eroded by Jackson, Calhoun had almost retired from the race to run for vice president instead. But he'd eventually concluded that the continuing repercussions from the Algiers Incident and Jackson's response to it had steadied his own supporters.

In truth, Calhoun had no chance of winning the presidency nor even of being one of the three top contenders in the event no one won a majority. His support was completely regional, restricted entirely to the Deep South. Essentially, he was running now as a power broker. If someone won an outright majority of the electoral college, of course, that would be that. But in the far more likely event that the decision was thrown into the House, Calhoun would have considerable political leverage in the negotiations that followed.

Still, since at least the beginning of the summer, it had been clear that the election was narrowing down to the other four candidates. Three out of four, now, who'd wind up in the House in the event no one won a majority in the electoral college. All they had to do was just make sure that Henry Clay ended up among the top three. The rest, the Speaker would take care of himself.

"What's your point, Peter?" asked Josiah Johnston. He, too, had been reading the *Intelligencer.* Now he lifted it up. "And although you're right with regard to the past, I'm not at all sure this latest development *won't* give him a clear majority."

Clay finally stopped looking out the window. "Not much chance of that, Josiah, I'm afraid." He gave all the men at the table his winning smile. "I wish it were true—mind, it *should* be true—but we need to keep our feet on solid ground."

He squared his chair around, propped his elbows on the table, and began counting off on long, slender fingers.

The forefinger went up. "First, New England won't budge from Adams's camp, no matter what."

Then, the middle finger. "Neither, I'm afraid—not even after Arkansas Post—will Tennessee desert Jackson."

The ring finger came to join them. "I had hopes for Pennsylvania, as you know, but those seem to have been dashed. Pennsylvania—for reasons that still defy comprehension, given that it's the foremost manufacturing state in the nation—is going for Jackson. Don't ask me why."

Porter knew the answer and was a bit amazed that Clay didn't. For all his many marvelous qualities, not least of which was sheer intelligence, the Speaker could sometimes blind himself to unpleasant realities.

It was hardly complicated. Pennsylvania had the most populistic constitution of any of the states, where South Carolina had perhaps the least. As far back as 1776, at the outset of the revolution, Pennsylvania had granted suffrage to all adult white males, with no property qualification whatsoever.

Yes, Pennsylvania was now the largest manufacturing state in the nation, and thus—by right and reason—should incline toward Clay's American System. And indeed it did. Pennsylvania's delegation in Congress had led the fight for the tariff that had finally been enacted this year over strong Southern objections—the first truly protectionist tariff in American history.

But there were a lot more men working in those factories and workshops in Pennsylvania than men who owned them, and everything else about Jackson appealed to them. Nor, despite being a Southerner, was the Tennessee senator seen by America's northeastern and mid-Atlantic workingmen as being alien or hostile. Jackson had spoken in favor of the tariff and voted for it himself. In something like thirty separate votes in the Senate, he'd sided every time with Pennsylvania. In fact, Jackson was so favorable toward tariffs that John Calhoun routinely accused him of being a traitor to Southern interests.

Which was true, leaving aside Calhoun's histrionic way of putting it. Whatever else Andrew Jackson was—this was the man's one quality that Porter respected—he was a nationalist. Jackson had made clear many times, both as a general and as a senator, that he'd always place the interests of the United States above the narrow interests of any of its geographical sections. In that respect, you couldn't honestly say that Clay was any better.

The real problem, of course, came thereafter. Jackson's policies, should he become president, would favor the nation as a whole, true enough. But the nation he would favor was not the nation Porter wanted favored. Although he did not share the extreme views of the old Federalists, and never had, Porter didn't doubt for a moment that a republic needed to be led and dominated by its propertied classes. To do otherwise would surely begin the descent into chaos and civil strife that had brought down the ancient Roman and Greek republics.

Clay had been droning on about the details—complex to the point of madness—of the negotiations with Adams's and Van Buren's people in New York. Now that he was coming to the point, Porter concentrated on his words.

"—that seems to be the best we can do, after this latest arrangement. We'll get no more than seven electoral votes from New York."

Beatty had been jotting down figures. "So. We can still count on Kentucky, Indiana, Ohio, Illinois, Missouri, and Louisiana, as we have from the beginning." He jabbed his pen toward the newspapers piled on the table. "There's certainly nothing in there that'll change that equation. The reports are that militia recruitment is up in all the northwestern states, too."

It would be better to call those rumors than reports, Porter thought, although he tended to believe them accurate himself. Still, it didn't necessarily mean much. The militias were a political powerhouse in most of the states, especially the western ones. They usually had a surge in recruitment during election campaigns.

"—figure we can win in New Jersey also," Beatty continued, "although we can't be sure of it. Jackson's got quite a following in the mob of that state, almost as much as Pennsylvania. And we've got a good chance in Delaware and Maryland. Still, even if none of the three come over to us, we've got enough to push Crawford aside for one of the three slots in the electoral college. All the more so since the knowledge of the stroke he suffered last year is now widespread, despite all the efforts of his advisers to conceal his medical condition."

He laid down the pen carefully. "New England, of course, won't desert Adams. What that leaves, therefore, is the South. If we can reach a suitable accommodation with Crawford's people and Calhoun, we might even be able to win a straight majority. Although I agree with Henry that that's most unlikely. Still, we can certainly get enough votes to be included in the House's selection. In fact . . ."

His bright eyes swept the men gathered at the table. "I think we've got a very good chance of coming in with a plurality. Which we'd never thought we had before."

"That'd be a blessing," Johnston grunted. He had his chair tipped back, with his hands folded across his stomach. "Without a plurality, Henry can win the presidency if the election gets tossed into the House. But he'll never hear the end of it for the next four years. There'll be endless accusations about 'rotten deals' and 'corrupt bargains.' Watch and see."

"The next *eight* years," Clay said stiffly. "I have every intention of serving two terms in office. That said, I agree with Josiah. Let's remember, gentlemen, that the whole purpose of this exercise is not to assuage my own ambition but to advance the interests of the nation. To do that, I need eight years in the president's house—"

He rose and pointed dramatically out the window. "*And* the support of Congress. Enough of it, at least, to get my American System so firmly rooted in the country that no one can tear it back out."

The window he was pointing to faced west, as it happened, which was the opposite direction from the Capitol. But Henry Clay was never given to fussing over minutiae, Porter thought wryly.

He also had some wry thoughts about the Speaker's insistence that his own aggrandizement was not involved. Many of the insinuations against Henry Clay were false, in Porter's opinion. His reputation for sexual debauchery, for instance, was grossly exaggerated. But the accusation that he was as ambitious as Lucifer was . . .

Close to the mark, at least.

Still, Porter knew that Clay meant what he said. It wasn't mere flippery for the sake of cloaking personal goals. The frequent charge that the Speaker had no political principles at all was just wrong. He was quite committed to his project of strengthening the United States through his American System. If for no other reason, out of pride in having forged it in the first place. And that, in the end, was what mattered to Porter and men like him.

Clay sat down. "So, yes, let's hope for a plurality. It won't matter either way in terms of the election. But it will matter for the next eight years."

"The election's in three days, Henry," Josiah pointed out. "It takes weeks for news to spread across a country as big as ours. How—"

Impatiently, Clay waved his hand. "That's news to the mob. Fortunately, in their wisdom, the founders of this nation saw fit to create a true republic. That means that what matters in the long run is not the opinion of the populace as such—which is often uninformed and always prone to emotionalism—but the opinion of its elected political leaders. They—not the mob—will be the ones who make the decisions. And while senators and congressmen are naturally influenced by popular opinion in their states, they are not bound by it. Not legally, not morally—certainly not politically."

His famous broad smile appeared. "And many of the congressmen have now arrived in the city. *They'll* get the news, in plenty of time."

"*What* 'news'?" Porter asked, half dreading the answer.

Dramatically, as he did most things, Clay held up the *Intelligencer*.

"This!" he replied, shaking the offending newspaper. "Not only shall I not attempt to deny any of these charges—so-called charges—I shall take them for my own. Brandish them like a spear before battle, if you will."

Porter had to fight not to roll his eyes. "Henry, you're gambling again. I strongly urge you to say nothing at all. Simply ignore the reports. It's only one newspaper, as influential as it might be in some circles."

Clay's sneer was every bit as broad as his smile—and just as famous. "Play it safe, you mean? I think not!"

He rose again and pointed out the window. "No, gentlemen! To lead this great nation, boldness is always required!"

At least he was pointing in the right direction, this time. The president's house was that way, indeed.

Washington, D.C.
NOVEMBER 6, 1824

" '—has it come to this? Are we so humbled, so low, so despicable, that we dare not express our sympathy for suffering Louisiana, lest, peradventure, we might offend some one or more of their imperial and royal majesties?' "

Standing at the window to his office listening to the attorney general quoting from Clay's speech of the day before, James Monroe barked a laugh. "Isn't that the same language he used a few months ago to excoriate us for refusing to intervene in the Greek rebellion?"

"It's almost identical," said John Quincy Adams, sitting in a chair nearby. "Oh, but it gets better. Please continue, Bill."

William Wirt scanned farther down the newspaper in his lap. "I'll skip a bit, Mr. President. There's some pure verbiage here, mixed in with the merely histrionic."

The attorney general cleared his throat and continued quoting from the speech. "Here's where he gets—finally—to the point. 'I would rather adjure the nation to remember that it contains a million freemen capable of bearing arms, and ready to exhaust their last drop of blood and their last cent, in defending their country, its institutions, and its liberty.' "

Wirt fell silent and lowered the newspaper.

President Monroe continued to look out the window, gazing at the country's capital city. After a few seconds, he said softly: "This is the same Henry Clay who praised us for our stance of forbidding any further European intervention in the New World. Albeit, to be sure, criticizing us for taking so long to do so. Am I not correct?"

Adams laughed sarcastically. "And adding into the bargain that he was prepared to wage a war against the whole world for it, even England. Somehow, a man of his undoubted intelligence failed to grasp what was clear to anyone with an ounce of sense with regard to foreign affairs: that our policy had the full if tacit support of that very same England he proposed to war against. Bah! He knew perfectly well, then, that his bombast with regard to England was as safe as a man threatening to wage war against the tide—when it is receding."

Adams pointed to the newspaper on Wirt's lap. "Just as he knows perfectly well, now, that threatening to wage war against the European powers should they dare to interfere in the Arkansas situation is every bit as safe. If an attack on the Confederacy is launched by the United States, it will be condemned the world over. But no one will send any ships or troops to support Arkansas. How could they get there, anyway?"

Monroe still hadn't turned around. "You have to admit it's a fascinating chain of logic," he mused, "even for Henry Clay. I'm still not quite sure how he managed to segue from the need to defend the bleeding Greek heroes against the Turk oppressor who rules Greece, to the need to defend the states of our nation from which a band of criminals sallied forth to conquer a neighboring country of ours, which hasn't threatened them at all. If you didn't know better, you'd think Louisiana and Mississippi were groaning under Arkansas occupation."

Finally the president turned around. "Has Jackson said anything?"

Wirt shook his head. "Not a word, sir. Not in public, anyway, and even his private thoughts seem a mystery to everyone. Possibly even his closest confidants."

"Any guesses?"

"With Jackson, Mr. President, it's always hard to know. Most people are assuming he'll side with Clay, if for no other reason than to keep Clay from undercutting his support in the West and the South. But . . ."

Monroe cocked an eyebrow. "But you're not so sure."

"No, sir, I'm not."

Adams had been listening intently. "Why, Bill? It's the obvious move to make, for a presidential candidate in his position."

Wirt shifted uncomfortably in his chair. "Yes, it would be. But I'll remind you that it would have been politically shrewd for Jackson to have opposed the tariff bill, too. But he didn't. In fact, he was one of the administration's strongest supporters in the Senate. That cost him in the Southern states, probably as much as he gained in the manufacturing ones."

Monroe shook his head. "Not the same thing. No one's

ever doubted—not anyone who's politically educated, anyway—that Jackson is a firm supporter of the principle that the United States is a *nation,* not simply an aggregate of states. In that respect, he's quite unlike John Randolph or Crawford's Radicals. It still doesn't follow that in this instance he wouldn't take the same stance as Clay."

"You could even say that the very same nationalist principles called for it," Adams added. "If I might play devil's advocate for a moment, one could argue that the massacre at Arkansas Post was a humiliation of the United States that needed to be set right. As a matter of national pride, if nothing else."

Wirt gave him a level stare. Adams looked aside. "Well, you *could.*"

"Finish the sentence, John," the attorney general said. It sounded a bit like a command, oddly enough.

Adams smiled crookedly. "If you weren't me. Or Andrew Jackson."

Wirt nodded. "Yes." He turned to Monroe. "And that's really my only point, Mr. President. There's simply no way to know what Jackson will do. His origins, his history, his background—certainly his temperament, which can be quite savage—will all be pulling him in one direction. But he's also the same man who outraged Louisiana's plantation owners by arming black freedmen in the war against Britain, don't forget."

Monroe's smile was almost as crooked as the one that had been on Quincy Adams's face a moment before. "Not to mention outraging the War Department when he gave that black gunner a field commission. Yes. I remember."

The president now looked at the secretary of state. John Quincy Adams had risen and was standing at the same window the president had been gazing through earlier.

"There's always that about Jackson," Monroe said softly. "One never quite knows, until the moment, exactly where his principles might fall. But he is a man of principle."

Adams made no response. He seemed completely preoccupied by the sight of the city beyond. Which was actually not that prepossessing, outside of the Capitol in the distance.

CHAPTER 22

"We can take a carriage, if you prefer," Houston said. "It's chilly out."

Maria Hester shook her head. "Oh, stop being so pestiferously male, Sam. I swear! I'm not even sure I'm pregnant in the first place. If I am, it's not more than a few weeks."

She looked up, giving him a sly smile. Then, leaned into him a bit, squeezing his arm more tightly. "I will say you didn't waste any time, once you got back."

Sam didn't know whether to look smug or embarrassed. He tried for dignity instead.

And failed completely, judging from his wife's giggle.

"Come on," she said. "If you want to talk to Andy before he says anything public, you'd best do it now. It's already noon." She nodded toward the distant Capitol. "Besides, we only have to walk a mile. This time of year, Pennsylvania Avenue won't even be that muddy."

After a hundred feet, she qualified the statement. "Well. Compared to summer, anyway."

"I've seen pigsties that were cleaner than this city," Sam muttered.

"Stop it!" Maria Hester scolded. "You promised. No politics until we get to the senator's chambers."

When John Coffee entered Andrew Jackson's office, the senator was looking out of a window. In his case, positioned as it was on the second floor of the Capitol, one that gave him a very nice view of the president's house he hoped to occupy soon. The White House, some people were starting to call it, now that the house had been repaired and repainted after the British vandalism of the past war.

All of the key men in Jackson's entourage were already present in the chamber, seated here and there about the room. Judge John Overton; Tennessee state senator Hugh Lawson White; John Henry Eaton, Tennessee's other U.S. senator; and Eaton's brother-in-law, William H. Lewis.

Lewis seemed gloomy, but Coffee discounted that. The man's heavy face always gave him a solemn demeanor except when he was talking. But both Overton and Eaton seemed out of sorts as well.

Jackson, on the other hand, seemed in something of an impish mood. Hearing Coffee enter, he gave him a peculiar smile and waved him toward one of the empty chairs. "Have a seat, John."

"Yes, do," said Overton. "Maybe you can talk some sense into him."

Sitting down, Coffee cocked his head. "Sense about what?"

"This," said Eaton. He picked up some sheets of paper and handed them over.

Coffee immediately recognized Jackson's handwriting, which was quite unmistakable. Even if it hadn't been, the senator's sometimes eccentric spelling and syntax would have identified the author.

It was a speech, evidently the one Jackson proposed to give to the Senate later that afternoon. Coffee took the time to read it slowly and carefully. Being one of Andy's closest friends, he wasn't surprised at all by the quality of the speech. Its intellectual content, at least, if not the specific thrust. Even after all these years, many people still kept thinking of Jackson as if he were some sort of semiliterate frontier roughneck. In point of fact, although the senator's rudimentary formal education still left traces in his prose, Jackson was as astute and well-read a politician as most any in the United States. John Quincy Adams excepted, of course.

When he was finished, Coffee laid the speech down on the low table in front of him.

"If you just keep your mouth shut, Andy, I'm pretty sure this will all blow over."

"That's just what I told him," Eaton complained. "The votes were in all over the country before the news from Arkansas had time to spread. Much, anyway. And those people out West and in the South—most of the Southern states wouldn't have gotten the news at all, before the election—who did hear about it would just assume . . ."

"That Andy Jackson was another God-damned Henry Clay," the senator interrupted. But the words weren't snarled. Actually, they'd been said quite good-humoredly.

Eaton flushed. "Andy, that's not the point and you know it."

"Actually, it is the point," Overton said mildly. "And you know it as well as anyone here does."

The judge raised his hand, forestalling Eaton's further protest. "Not the part about another Henry Clay—and, Andy, don't let Rachel hear you blaspheming like that. Nobody thinks Andy and Henry Clay are any more alike than bulls and roosters. What they *do* think is that the general who won the Horseshoe Bend and the Mississippi ain't likely to stand by twiddling his thumbs while a bunch of niggers butcher white folks."

"He's right, Andy," said Coffee. "Just keep your mouth shut, and everybody will assume that Old Hickory will be Old Hickory. Plenty of time after you settle in the White House to set them straight."

Jackson had been pulling out the chair to his desk, preparatory to sitting down. But now he stopped and stood up straight. "Steal the election, you mean."

Ramrod-straight. Coffee heaved a sigh. "You and your damn pride—and don't give *me* lectures on blaspheming, Judge Overton. You, of all people."

"I'll be blasted if I will," said Jackson. "All that happened here is that Henry Clay—as foul a man as ever besmirched the halls of Congress; I hate that bastard with a passion, and you all know it—financed a pack of bandits, using his connections with the stinking Bank to raise the money, in order to weasel his way into the presidency. Give me one good reason I should support that."

The earlier good humor was gone, now. He gave his advisers the same blue-eyed glare that was famous across much of the country. "No, sirs, I shall not."

But none of those men had remained Andy Jackson's friends and advisers by being easily intimidated. "That ain't the point, Andy," said Overton. "It all comes down to the race issue. You know it just as well as we do. Yes, sure, Crittenden's men were bandits. But they were *white* bandits—and the men who massacred them were all niggers."

"The commander who gave the order wasn't," Jackson fired back. "There's no dispute over that, not in any of the reports. His name is Patrick Driscol. As Scots-Irish as I am, and with a skin paler than mine. Formerly of the United States Army. A major, when he resigned. I know. He served under me in New Orleans and was one of the best officers I've ever had."

Silence filled the room for a time. Jackson shoved the chair back under the table and went to stand at the window again.

By the time they were halfway down Pennsylvania Avenue, Sam wished he'd been firm about calling for a carriage. Maria Hester might have a fortitude to shame most frontier women, but—dammit—his boots were filthy. His favorite boots, too.

Of course, his wife's shoes were a hopeless wreck. But those were the old ones she didn't care about anyway, that she only kept for just such promenades. Like any experienced lady of Washington, she had a nice set in her purse, ready to change into when they reached their destination.

"Are you sure—"

"Sam Houston, Injun fighter and war hero," his wife jibed. "Defeated by a little mud. Just soldier on, soldier."

"I retired from the army, remember?"

"Then why does everyone keep calling you Colonel?"

Jackson let out a sigh, his stiff shoulders easing a little. "There's something wrong with John Calhoun," he said, so softly the men in the room had to strain to hear him. "Him, and all the men like him."

Overton frowned. "We were talking about Henry Clay."

Jackson turned around. "No, we weren't. Clay doesn't give a damn about Crittenden's men, even less than I do. This isn't about Henry Clay. Not really. This is about John Calhoun. Might be better to say, the South that Calhoun is doing his level best to bring into existence. Like some sort of Araby heathen, trying to summon a demon out of a sealed lamp."

Jackson now had his hands clasped behind his back. His jaws seemed more gaunt than ever. "I got no use for Sam Houston's fancies about black folk. Indians, maybe a little, but not niggers. Never did, never will. It's just a fact that the black race is inferior to the white race. Taken as a whole, at any rate. I'll allow for the exceptional individual, here and there."

He paused, scanning the room. "Anybody here disagree with me?"

After a moment, they all shook their heads.

"Didn't think so. That's why slavery doesn't bother me any. Never did. If that fraud Thomas Jefferson wants to beat his breast over it—though I notice he has yet to free a single one of his slaves—let him do it. I won't." His jaws grew tighter still. "But that doesn't mean I agree with Calhoun, either. That man . . ."

He took a deep breath. "That man is just plain mean. He's like all that type of slave-owner. The same ones who played the traitor at New Orleans. The fact that I don't think black men are the equal of white men doesn't mean I think they aren't still men. They're not dumb animals, tarnation, with no rights at all. And that's exactly what John Calhoun thinks—and that's exactly where he wants to lead the nation. With Henry Clay playing his tune, because he's the fanciest piper in town."

He went over to his desk and picked up one of the news-papers lying there. "Never thought I'd see the day when I thought the *Intelligencer* was the best paper around," he said wryly. "But today, at least, on this issue, the fact is they are."

He held up the paper. "Got another article in here by that Bryant fellow. Gives you all the details you want to know—or don't want to know—about how Crittenden's men con-ducted themselves. You've read it, I assume?"

Again, they all nodded.

"So, fine," Jackson continued. "Let me ask you this, then. Suppose a gang of white criminals broke into a black freedman's house right here in Washington—and don't bother yapping to me about the exclusion laws, because you know as well as I do they aren't enforced half the time. There's too many black servants their masters want to keep around, free or not, including me. Why? Because some of them are good servants, that's why. Not to mention they don't want to listen to the kids hollering when their nanny gets sent away. Or the cook who gives them treats when their parents aren't looking."

Still holding the paper in his left hand, he ran the fingers of the other through his stiff gray hair. "Truth is, I'm sorry now I ever voted for those blasted laws. They're just a violation of human nature, is all. Inferior or not, black people are still people, and most people—any color, leaving aside the Calhouns of the world—form attachments to each other. Free or slave, it don't matter. It just don't."

He stopped the hair-ruffling and slapped the paper back on the desk. "So let me ask you. A gang of white criminals breaks into a black man's home, starts stealing everything he owns—which ain't much—and sets to raping his womenfolk in the bargain. So he shoots them dead, like any man would do who was worth his salt. Am I supposed to demand that *he* gets arrested and punished? Just because he's black?"

He was back to glaring. "Well? Answer me. Am I?"

After a moment, everyone looked away.

"What I figured. Be damned if I will. They want Old Hickory, I aim to give 'em Old Hickory. Right between the eyes."

Thankfully, the Capitol was only a hundred yards away. For all her determination and teasing, Sam could tell that his wife was tiring. Plowing through mud was hard enough for a big man like Sam. He could just imagine how a mile of it would exhaust a small woman like Maria Hester.

Coffee had been watching Jackson closely through his little peroration. When it was done, he chuckled.

"What's so funny?" the senator demanded.

"You are, if you want to know the truth. Sam Houston's still sticking in your throat, isn't he?"

Jackson glared at him. "I kept that promise, and it's done. Told him so myself."

"Yes, I know. So what?" Coffee didn't flinch at all from that blue-eyed fury. Worst thing you could do around Andy Jackson.

After a few seconds, the glare started to fade. After a few more, Jackson even started chuckling himself.

"Blast that youngster," he muttered. "Still worse, once he named his firstborn after me. Now that the kid's old enough to talk, he calls me Grandpa. Damn little conniving clever politician like his daddy."

He yanked out the chair and folded himself into his seat. "Yes, fine. I suppose so." He stuck out his bony finger, like a gun. "Not that I didn't mean it when I said I had no use for Houston's fancies. Still."

Coffee understood. "You said he'd turn down the rose of fortune when you offered it to him. And you were right. He did. Proud as a peacock you were, afterward."

"I sure was. Proud of both of us. Him for turning it down, and me for knowing he would and knowing why."

He swiveled his gaze toward the other men in the room. "Do you understand, now? We've talked it over, like we always do. But the decision's mine, and I've made it."

He'd never lowered the finger. Now, the bony weapon pointed to the newspaper. "There's my rose of fortune, gentlemen, that you're waving under my nose. The answer's no. We'll go into the president's house through the front door, or we won't go in at all. Let Henry Clay sneak himself in through the servant's entrance if he wants it that bad."

The steps of the Capitol were a blessed relief from the mud. As soon as they reached the top of the steps, Maria Hester crouched and began opening her bag.

"No way I'm going in there in these filthy things."

Sam smiled.

"Colonel Houston!"

He turned, still smiling, but the smile faded almost immediately. The man coming up the steps toward him had no friendly look on his face. As much of it as Sam could see, at any rate. The fellow had a broad-brimmed hat to go with a long cloak. He looked positively conspiratorial, like something out of a cheap stage performance.

"May I help you, sir?"

"You were born in Virginia, am I not correct?"

Coffee nodded. Whether because he agreed with Jackson or not, he didn't even know himself. But that wasn't the point, in the end. You could always trust Andy Jackson. Not to be right, necessarily, but to be Andy Jackson. For Coffee, that was good enough.

Judging from the nods that went around the room, the other men had come to the same conclusion.

"All right, then," said Eaton. "We'll almost surely lose this election. But there's 1828 to look to."

"Clay's sure to go for two terms," cautioned White.

Overton started to say something, but Jackson cut him off. "He'll *try*. Whether he can do it or not—"

A loud clap coming from outside interrupted him. Jackson's head twisted around to the window. "That was a gunshot."

Sam never went armed in the streets of Washington. Now he was half regretting it. He was fully regretting not having accepted Chester's offer to come along. This man—

"I asked you a question, sir!"

"And did so most uncivilly," Sam snapped back. "But the answer is no secret. Yes, I was—"

"You are a traitor, then!"

"Sam!" Maria Hester shrieked.

A pistol was coming out from under the cloak. Sam started to lunge for him.

Maria Hester came up from her crouch, wildly swinging her bag. The fancy shoes she'd gotten half out went flying, one of them into the man's face.

He flinched. The pistol went off but missed. Sam smashed his face with a fist. It was a big fist, and Sam was in a fury. His assailant's lips were shredded against his teeth, and some teeth went skittering down the steps. So did the man himself, his hat coming loose and his cloak swirling like a blanket.

Sam started to follow. He was going to beat this bastard into—

"Sam . . ."

Overton was the first one at the window. "Oh, dear God," he said.

By the time Coffee and Jackson and the others came out of the Capitol onto the steps, Maria Hester had bled to death. The shot that Sam thought to have missed had struck her instead, severing the big artery under her arm. Coffee couldn't remember the name of it. But he'd seen men die on a battlefield from just such a wound.

Of the assailant there was no trace, beyond spots of blood and broken teeth. Houston had, understandably, paid the man no further attention once he realized his wife had been shot.

"Put a five-thousand-dollar reward out, in my name," Jackson ordered. His face was pale as a sheet, and he was trembling with rage. "Dead or alive."

Coffee nodded. Medical orderlies had arrived by now and were tending to Maria Hester. To her corpse, rather. Or trying to. Houston was still holding her body, his face blank. His own clothes were soaked with her blood, but he didn't seem to notice.

"Anything else, immediately?"

"Yes." Jackson swallowed. Just a reflex, to control his fury. This was no feigned Andy Jackson tantrum, either. Coffee knew the signs. This was the real thing, the rage of a man famous all over the frontier for his capacity for violence.

"Yes," he repeated. "Just remember that I'd already made my decision."

Coffee hissed. "Andy, you *can't* give that speech this afternoon. In your state—"

"Watch me."

*   *   *

The speech was as bad as Coffee feared. Not the words themselves, so much. It was the tone and, worst of all, the coda that Jackson added that had never been part of his written text.

". . . the basest, meanest scoundrel, that ever disgraced the image of his God—nothing too mean or low for Henry Clay to condescend to, secretly to carry his cowardly and base purpose . . .

". . . he is personally void of good morals, and politically a reckless demagogue, ambitious and regardless of truth when it comes in the way of his ambition . . ."

That the words he spoke were all true, in Coffee's opinion, made no difference. All the assiduous work that Andy had done in Washington since he'd been elected senator two years earlier—and done exceedingly well—were washed away. The suave and sophisticated political leader that the capital's elite had come to know and even admire was gone; the frontier half savage that they feared, risen to the surface.

It didn't help that he'd ended his speech by referring the Speaker of the House to "all the laws which govern and regulate the conduct of men of honor." Which amounted, under the circumstances, to a challenge to a duel, should Clay choose to take exception to his remarks.

To be sure, Clay himself had been known to make similar noises in the course of public controversies. But "noises" were all they were: just typical Clay theatrics that nobody took in earnest.

Coming from Jackson, the words were taken dead seriously. The senator from Tennessee was one of the most notorious duelists in America.

Clay made no public response, of course. Since he hadn't been present in the Senate when Jackson gave the speech, he could ignore it. To do otherwise would be politically foolish, and personally . . .

Quite possibly fatal.

Besides, he was too relieved by the latest news to give much thought to Jackson.

CHAPTER 23

"Well, breathe easy, gentlemen," said Adam Beatty, as soon as he entered the dining room of the boardinghouse. "They found him."

Henry Clay, who had been slumped in a chair gazing out the window, came erect immediately. "They caught the bastard?"

Beatty shook his head. "Well, no, they didn't *catch* him. It looks like he made his escape from the city. But they know for sure who did it. No question, apparently."

He smiled so widely it was almost a grin. "What's important is . . . He wasn't one of ours. A Radical, it seems. One of Crawford's people. Well, not directly. From what I was told, there's no evidence he was active in Crawford's campaign. But those were definitely his sympathies."

Most of the other men in the room were starting to smile, too. Porter wasn't, though—and he was glad to see that Clay wasn't, either. In fact, Clay's expression was darkening fast.

"No, Mr. Beatty!" the Speaker snapped. "What's important here is that an innocent young woman was foully murdered on the very steps of our nation's Capitol. What in Sam Hill is wrong with you?"

That wiped the smiles off. Clay glared around the table. "For the sake of all that's holy, gentlemen. Yes, I want to be in the White House, and you want me there. But if I ever see you gloating again because a young woman's murder can't hurt us politically, I shall ask you to leave my company at once. And don't return. Is that understood?"

The nods came as fast as the smiles had vanished. Clay could be as gracious and charming as anyone in the world when he wanted to be—which he usually did. But there was a very sharp edge to him, also, as any number of rambunctious young congressmen had learned when they thought heedlessly to cross lances with the Speaker of the House. Clay had not dominated that very unsubmissive chamber of legislators for years by being unable or unwilling to crack the whip, when need be.

Beatty had taken a seat, now, doing everything in his power to look as inconspicuous as possible.

There was perhaps half a minute of strained silence. Then, sighing, Clay slumped back in his chair again.

"Henry, I'm sorry—" Beatty began.

Clay waved off the apology. "Never mind, Adam. Didn't mean to bite your head off. It's just . . . Dear God, what a horrible thing to have happen. I think Maria Hester was the president's favorite child, too, even if he'd never admit it. I don't want to think what he's going through, right now."

Josiah Johnston made a face. "She was certainly my favorite of his daughters. The other, Eliza . . ."

He left off the rest. Eliza Hay, Monroe's oldest daughter, was rather notorious in Washington. A very attractive and intelligent woman, to be sure. Also very vain, and given to being haughty and sarcastic. Maria Hester had been much the more charming of the two.

Silence, again, for a minute or so. Then Clay sat up straighter in his chair.

"Very well. The needs of the nation continue, after all. So what's the news, Adam?"

This time, very wisely, Beatty gave his report with neither smiles nor commentary. "It's been clearly established that the culprit was a certain Andrew Clark. From a family—rather prominent, it seems—in Savannah, Georgia. His father owns a large plantation in the area."

"Clearly established—how?" Porter asked.

Beatty shook his head. "I don't know the details, Peter. I got the news from a reliable source in the War Department. But there are definitely eyewitnesses to the man's making threats about Houston. Had been since he arrived in the city a fortnight ago, it seems. Nobody took much notice of it, because . . ."

He shrugged. There were plenty of taverns in some quarters of the capital, patronized by Southern gentlemen, where damning the traitor Sam Houston and wishing all manner of ill upon him went with practically every round of whiskey. Nobody took much notice of it, not even the ones doing the damning and cursing. That type of Southern gentleman issued bloodcurdling threats routinely on every controversial subject imaginable, as casually as other men commented on the weather.

"The description fits, too," Beatty continued, "all the way down to that bizarre hat and cloak. And when the hat was shown to the man's landlady, she identified it as being his."

"What's the connection to Crawford?" asked Johnston.

"Nothing direct, as I said. He doesn't seem to have been active in the campaign. It's more a matter of being an extreme Radical."

Porter grunted. "Why call him a Crawford man, then? More likely to be an admirer of John Randolph."

Obviously still smarting from Clay's rebuke, Beatty opened his mouth and closed it. His expression was a bit like that of a stubborn child, wisely silent after a parent's chastisement but not having changed his mind any.

Clay's broad mouth quirked into something that bordered on a smile. "Oh, fine, Adam. Say it."

Beatty's words came out in something of a rush. "Look, Henry, I apologize if my earlier remark was unseemly. But, blast it, it's *true*. It would have been a disaster if this bastard had been associated with us. As it is . . ."

Johnston picked up the cue. "Just being a known extreme Radical is enough. Who cares what he thought of Crawford himself, Peter? Much less Randolph. Randolph's not the Radical candidate for president. Crawford is. That's what counts. Everybody's furious about this, regardless of what they thought about Sam Houston. But it won't come down on our heads."

"In fact," Beatty added, "it makes Jackson's grotesque performance yesterday look worse than ever."

Clay gave him a sharp look. Not a hostile one, though, more in the way of cold calculation. "You think so?"

Beatty's detestable hearty bluffness was returning, alas. "For sure and certain, Henry! Why, the man practically threatened to kill you, and you had nothing to do with it at all. So why'd he attack you instead of Crawford?"

Porter tightened his jaws. That had to be one of the stupidest comments he'd ever heard. The reason Jackson had gone after Clay instead of Crawford—could even a dimwit not grasp this?—was that Clay had helped fund the Crittenden expedition, and Crawford had had nothing to do with it. That had been the subject of Jackson's speech. He'd said nothing about Mrs. Houston's murder.

On the other hand . . .

Grudgingly, Porter allowed that Beatty might be right, if not for the reasons he advanced. Whatever else, the murder had horrified everyone in Washington. The reasons behind it meant less than the sheer brutality of the deed itself. Which meant that the emotional reaction was likely to spill against . . .

Ironically enough, Andrew Jackson, the man the dead woman and her husband had named their firstborn son after. Not because anyone thought Jackson had any connection to the murderer but simply because he, more than any other candidate, exemplified that capacity for violence in the first place. Did a nation that had just witnessed the daughter of its president shot down on the steps of the Capitol want that president's successor to be a man who'd killed another in a duel? A man who'd once held a gunfight in a hotel with the Benton brothers?

"It's over," Beatty predicted. "It's all over but the shouting."

Clay's expression was darkening again. Hastily, Johnston interjected: "Well, no, Adam. There's a funeral first, remember? Tomorrow."

"Oh. Yes, of course."

Later that afternoon, Clay spoke in private to Porter.

"Jackson put up five thousand dollars for that reward; am I right?"

Porter nodded.

"Fine. Then I'll put up ten."

Porter started to shake his head, but Henry had already seen the problem.

"No, no, that won't do. It would make it seem as if I were engaged in a petty contest with Jackson. But I can put up an equal amount, I think. See to it, would you, Peter?"

John Quincy Adams worked later than usual that day, well into the evening. Not because there was anything particularly pressing to be done, but simply because he couldn't think of anything better to do.

By eight o'clock, he decided it was time to go home. On his way out, however, a sudden impulse led him to the president's office. Monroe was not in, having spent the entire day in the private quarters of the house with his wife and surviving daughter and his grandchildren. And Houston.

The same impulse—half sensed, not understood—led Adams into the office itself, and to the window behind the president's desk that Monroe liked to look through.

Perhaps a minute later, Adams discovered himself sitting in the president's chair. He'd been so lost in his thoughts that he hadn't even realized he'd done so.

He began to rise immediately, but froze halfway through. That half-felt, not-understood impulse had come into sudden focus. So, sighing softly, he sat back down again.

There was still a duty to be performed this day. Not one that John Quincy Adams wanted to perform, nor one that suited him well at all. But, whatever else, he was not a man who had ever shirked duty.

He spent perhaps an hour lost in his thoughts again. Only a small sound at the doorway brought him out of them.

Turning his head, he saw that James Monroe was standing there. Instantly flushing, Adams rose from the chair.

"Mr. President. Ah . . . my apologies. I don't know what I was thinking. Please excuse my impertinence—"

"It's fine, John," Monroe said softly. He came into the room, waving his hand a bit. "Sit back down again. Why not? You may very well be sitting in that chair for four years, come March. Possibly eight. No reason not to see if it suits you."

Monroe's face seemed more drawn than usual, but it was hard to tell. The president was a man with such self-control that he would have been the envy of any Roman stoic.

Adams didn't know quite what to say. He'd already visited the family earlier that day to extend his condolences. Repeating them again would seem . . .

Not like John Quincy Adams. For the same reason, the impulse to ask Monroe how he was managing died stillborn. For all the mutual respect between them, there had never been much in the way of personal intimacy between Adams and the president. Monroe was rarely given to such; and Adams, still less.

Monroe was at the window now, looking out over the darkened city. Not that he could actually see it. With the lamp in the corner shining against the windowpane, he could see only his own reflection.

Fortunately, it was always possible to ask about women. "How is Mrs. Monroe doing, sir?"

"Not well, as you might imagine," the president replied softly. "Her health has not been good for some time, as you know. This . . ."

He drew in a long deep breath. "This was as bad as anything that could have happened. Fortunately, Eliza is with her, and bearing up well."

Adams nodded. As was true of most people, he didn't much care for the president's oldest daughter—only daughter, now—but she was certainly a woman of strong character.

"And Mr. Houston?"

Monroe took another long deep breath. "I'm more concerned about Sam, immediately."

"Is he . . ."

Monroe shook his head. "No, John. He isn't drunk. I don't believe he's done so much as glance at a bottle of whiskey. He's spent most of the past day with his son, trying to explain to a four-year-old that he'll never see his mother again."

There might have been a slight catch to Monroe's voice, right there at the end. A very subtle thing, though, if it had been there at all.

Adams frowned. "Then . . . What's the nature of your concern, if I might ask?"

Monroe's head turned, half facing Adams. "Never forget that Sam Houston is Scots-Irish, John. Perhaps the most warmhearted and good-natured Scots-Irishman who ever lived, true. But he's still of that stock. Which is one that is given to rage, and dark furies, and forgives very little—and that slowly if at all."

"Ah. You think he'll take out after the murderer?" A worse possibility occurred to Adams. Andrew Jackson wouldn't be the only man who'd think to lash out at a political opponent as detested as Henry Clay.

Monroe might have smiled slightly, then. If so, the smile came and went almost instantly.

"No, John. Don't underestimate my son-in-law. I've come to know him quite well, these past years. He's a man who thinks . . . very large thoughts. No, he'll not seek his revenge on the man who murdered his wife. Should he happen to encounter him, of course, he'd certainly kill him. But he'll let the law handle it, otherwise."

He was silent for a moment: "But I'm much afraid, in the mood he's in, he will seek revenge on the *nation* he holds responsible for Maria Hester's death in the first place."

Adams's eyes widened. "But how . . . Ah."

That, too, suddenly brought many things into focus. "He's right, actually, Mr. President. In a way, at least."

Monroe took yet another one of those long slow breaths. "Yes, I know he is." For the first time, a genuine sadness entered his voice. "He most certainly is. Only a nation—a republic, to make it worse—that was mad enough to place slavery at its foundation could produce such a monster as Andrew Clark. And the madness is growing, John, year by year. Fueled by greed: the greed glowing hotter as more and more cant and hypocrisy is piled upon it, the flames then fanned by men like John Calhoun. With, now, even men like Henry Clay aiding and abetting the madness, for no purpose more sublime than personal ambition."

Another long slow breath. Then, quietly, sadly: "I have often wondered if my mentor and friend Thomas Jefferson was right when he foresaw a terrible vengeance by a just God. Now I know he was. I saw the proof of it yesterday, in my daughter's bloody corpse."

There might have been a slight tremor in the last few

words. Perhaps not. Monroe's stoicism was truly exceptional.

"And yet . . ." The president shrugged. "And yet it continues, since very few men—and I am not included among them—have the courage to stand squarely against it. And, again, for no better reason than greed." His lips twisted a bit. "Well, perhaps that's too harsh. Economic and financial strain, more often—but is that really any better than naked greed?"

He'd had his hands clasped behind his back. Now he brought them to the fore and looked down upon them. "I can see my daughter's blood on my own hands if I look closely enough. I am in debt, as I'm sure you know. Most Southern gentlemen are, especially if they've spent as many years in public service as I have."

Adams had known that of Monroe's personal situation, although he didn't know any of the details. Public office was not very remunerative in the American republic, even in high posts, and many of the expenses had to be borne by the officeholder out of his own purse. Unless a man was an outright thief—which Monroe himself was certainly not, though some of the men who'd risen to prominence with him might be so accused—he'd soon enough find his personal finances badly strained.

Adams himself suffered from the problem, despite the frugality of his Puritan New England upbringing. Almost no Southern slave-owning gentleman ever managed to get out from under a small mountain of debt, even if he devoted himself entirely to his plantation. The manner of the Southerners' lives, their habits, their customs—not to mention the vagaries of any agriculture, and their dependence on English financiers and brokers—made it effectively impossible.

A few managed. George Washington had gotten completely out of debt and had turned away from plantation agriculture as the source of his sustenance, to make sure that he'd remain debtless. So, he was one of the very few slaveowners who'd freed all his slaves in his will. A few others had done so, here and there. At least one of them had freed all his slaves and then moved to Ohio so he could get away from slavery altogether.

But such were a rarity. Most Southern gentlemen were in

debt from the time they reached their maturity to the day they were lowered into their graves—and the debts were then inherited by their offspring. Which meant that the same profligate, wasteful, slave-based plantation economy that had placed them in lifelong debt to begin with would continue, generation after generation. So long as a man retained his plantation and his slaves, he could, at the very least, find a creditor willing to lend him more money.

"So," Monroe continued, "I shall no more be able to free my own slaves upon retiring from this office than Thomas was before me. Once you set Mammon upon your shoulders, ridding yourself of the demon becomes impossible. Unless you're prepared to become a pauper, at least, which few men are. Certainly I am not one of them."

There was more of fatalism in Monroe's tone than Adams had ever detected before. Not surprisingly, perhaps, given that the man was coming to the end of many decades of a life given over to the service of the republic. In four months, James Monroe would become a private citizen and, now at the age of sixty-five, would almost certainly remain one for the rest of his life. Whatever he could do, he had done. Whatever he had failed to do, he could not do now. Whatever he had harmed, he could no longer repair.

None of which was true of John Quincy Adams himself.

And so, now, it was time. As difficult as the task might be for a man like Adams. But he would not shirk his duty.

"Do you think I would make a good president?" he asked abruptly. Then, raising his hand sharply: "Please, James. I know it's an uncivil question. But I really need your opinion. I can't think of any man who'd know better. Certainly not one who no longer has any personal stake in the issue."

Monroe turned from the window to face Adams squarely. His hands, as if by automatic reflex, clasped behind his back again.

"Yes, I understand." He thought for a moment. Not, obviously, to ponder the question, but simply pondering the right words for an answer.

"You'd not be a bad one, John. In some respects—foreign affairs, for a certainty—an excellent one. But, overall . . . Let me put it this way. I do not think you'd make the president that the republic needs in this time, this place in our history. You're too much the intellectual, too much the executive, too much the manager."

Adams grimaced ruefully. "I'm certainly not much of a politician."

"No, you're not. Although—" Monroe smiled for the first time since entering the room. "I do recommend you spare yourself your usual Puritanical self-condemnation, John. Consider, rather, that your many other fine qualities— superb ones, to speak frankly—have allowed you to reach a position of influence in our nation that precious few politicians have ever achieved, regardless of their skill. That is hardly something to sneer at."

Adams issued a soft grunt. As it happened, he'd been thinking much the same thoughts this past hour. The sole consolation for what was coming.

"But that's not even the point," Monroe continued. "What the republic needs now is not another politician, either. Henry Clay is the most accomplished and talented politician in the nation. But—being as frank and open as I can—I'd far rather see you sitting in that chair for the next four or eight years than see Clay sitting there."

Monroe looked aside for a moment, now studying the whale-oil lamp sitting on a small table in the corner of the office. There was nothing remarkable about the lamp itself except for being finer than most, with a decorative glass base and an attractive pear-shaped font. It seemed more as if he were simply trying to extract the light from it.

"You would make a fine president, John, if we lived in a time when the nation simply needed to be steered a course through the inevitable fog of public affairs. So would Henry Clay, being fair to the man. He's not a brute, after all. A very fine man, in a number of ways, and many of his views are ones I share myself. The problem is simply that he can't— never could—control his naked ambition. But if we lived in different times, his talents would probably make up for it, once that ambition was satisfied. But we don't live in such a time. I had hopes—delusions, perhaps—that we did, when I came into this office. But I know now, eight years later, that we are entering turbulent waters, not simply foggy ones. And the turbulence will get worse before it is all over. Much worse, I fear."

Adams nodded. Being a rather accomplished poet, he'd have used less pedestrian metaphors himself. But perhaps that lay at the heart of the matter. Monroe was an excellent politician, and Adams was not. If the president's imagery was mundane, so was the nature of politics, in the end. Prosaic as it might be, the language was apt.

"Jackson, then," he stated.

Monroe turned back to look at him. "You've read Jackson's speech of yesterday by now, I'm sure."

It was not a question. The chance that John Quincy Adams wouldn't have, within a day, read—no, studied—a major speech by a major political figure was so small as to be laughable.

In fact, Adams did laugh. Once, softly. "Oh, yes. Of course."

"And your opinion?" The president jerked his head. "Leaving aside that perhaps grotesque coda."

Adams scowled. "Grotesque, indeed."

But he forced himself away from that comfort. It was time for the heart of the truth, and that alone.

"It was a magnificent speech, Mr. President. In the main. But what else really matters now?"

"Nothing," Monroe stated flatly.

"Yes. Truly magnificent. In fact . . ." It was Adams's turn to take a slow, deep breath. "I shall not be surprised—not that I'll live long enough to know—if posterity records it as the most important speech given in the United States in this entire decade."

Monroe looked away again, pursing his lips. "I hadn't thought of it, in those terms. But you could well be right."

He turned his head back, his expression suddenly very stern. "Enough, John. It's time for you to give me your opinion. Simply to say it out loud, if nothing else."

Adams nodded and levered himself out of the chair. There was no reason to stay in it any longer.

"What I believe, Mr. President, is that we are entering Jackson's time. For good or ill—or both, most likely. Truth be told, I've had that sense for some years now. Resenting it deeply, to be honest, but still sensing that it was probably true. Now I see it cannot be avoided at all. The difference the speech makes is very simple. On the eve of that time, the man who is best suited to lead the nation through has revealed himself to be, in every important particular, a man of deep and abiding principle. Even when those principles bring him to a distasteful conclusion, and one that requires him to stand against many—perhaps most—of his own followers."

He took one of those slow deep breaths that seemed, that night, to be a requirement for occupying the office. "That being the case, for me to continue to oppose his entry into this very chamber, would be—in the end, when all is said and done—no more sublime a deed than whatever Henry Clay is plotting tonight." Harshly: "Ambition, nothing more."

Monroe cocked his head a little. "That's very well said, John. And let me take this moment to tell you that you are a man I much respect and admire."

Adams jerked a little nod of the head. "Thank you, sir."

"Will you allow me to put it in my own terms?" Monroe issued his second smile of the evening. Like the first, it was a thin and fleeting thing, with more than a trace of sadness in it.

"Yes, of course."

"I've had years—decades—to ponder the matter. The last eight of them, as the nation's chief executive. In the end, just as our Roman forebears knew, republics stand or fall on virtue. Simply that, nothing else. Policies might be wrong, but policies can be corrected. Let virtue fail, the republic fails. Yes, it's Jackson time, for good or ill—so let Jackson take his rightful place. Help him or oppose him on any particular issue or question, as you will. But I can foresee no worse disaster than if, by clashing, the two principal men of virtue in today's American republic allow another man to slide by them and take this office. I disagree with many of Jackson's opinions and views, as you know. But I can live with Jackson. The republic can live with Jackson. Right, wrong, indifferent, or just plain mad, Jackson always has virtue. Henry Clay has none at all."

Adams jerked another little nod. Then, smiled. "You understand, Mr. President, that after Senator Jackson's speech yesterday, it is very likely that Henry Clay will slide by us anyway."

Monroe shook his head firmly. "No, John. He won't *slide* by you. He'll win enough votes, and thus, by the rules established by our Constitution, come to occupy this office. But the Constitution does not embody the nation's virtue, simply its political principles. So long as you and Jackson stand against him—clearly, sharply—then the nation will not be confused, except momentarily."

The president shrugged. "It's impossible, for any republic that lasts for more than a few decades, to avoid the occasional Alcibiades winning the favor of the populace for a time. That matters little, so long as the republic does not come to see Alcibiades as a man of principle."

He waved his hand at the window, through which nothing could be seen except the reflection of the chamber's own light. "Let Clay enjoy—if that's the term—his four years of triumph. I think he'll find it turns sour on him, soon enough. Even faster—if men of principle stand their ground—will he find the nation's favor turning sour also. It's one thing to gain office by pandering to prejudice, unreason, and blind fury. Quite another, to guide a nation based on them. The first can be done, yes. The second, not at all."

CHAPTER 24

Washington, D.C.
NOVEMBER 8, 1824

Fortunately, Jackson was still awake. Adams had hesitated disturbing the senator so late at night. But he'd feared the consequences of waiting till the morrow. Far too easy, even for a Puritan, to find that morning's glow sapped resolve. Some things were best done in the middle of the night, not for the sake of its secrecy but simply because darkness had no false auras. Mornings were always treacherous times, with their ever-returning promise.

"My apologies for the hour, Senator," he began, as soon as a black servant ushered him into the salon where Jackson was waiting for him. "It's just—"

"Not at all, Mr. Secretary." Jackson was standing in the middle of the room, his posture that familiar ramrod one. But it was simply erect, not stiff at all. He was smiling broadly and seemed inclined to be as gracious as he could often manage, sometimes to everyone's surprise.

"Some cordials, perhaps?"

"No, thank you, I . . ." Adams peered at the row of bottled spirits on a cabinet against the wall. He waged a regular battle with himself to maintain temperate habits, and when he did drink he preferred wine, not whiskey.

Then again, new times.

"Well, perhaps a small whiskey."

"Of course." The servant headed for the cabinet, but Jackson waved him off. "I'll manage it, Pompey, thank you. You may retire for the evening."

After the servant was gone and the whiskey poured, Jackson waved Adams to the divan. "Please, have a seat." As Adams did so, Jackson perched himself on a nearby chair.

There was no point delaying it. If a man was to fall on his sword, it was best to do it quickly and firmly.

"Senator Jackson, I have come to inform you that I shall be urging those who are supporting me for the presidency to vote for you instead."

There. It was done. No way to retract anything now. Not even the meanest scoundrel in America could do that. And Adams had always allowed, whatever else, that he was very far from that. A sinner, yes; a scoundrel, no. Certainly not a mean one.

Jackson's eyes widened. Slowly, he set his untouched whiskey down on a low table next to the chair.

"Well. I will be dam—ah. Well. Tarnation, sir!"

At least he hadn't completed the blasphemy. Adams's gloom lightened a bit.

"Tarnation," Jackson repeated. "That comes as quite a surprise. I wouldn't have thought . . ."

He paused, his bright blue eyes peering at Adams intently. "It was the speech, wasn't it?"

"To a degree, yes. The murder that came before it, perhaps as much."

The famous blue glare entered Jackson's eyes. "Yes, that too. I'll see that man hanged if I do nothing else in my life. Be sure of it, sir. If the laws allowed, I'd have him drawn and quartered first."

Adams wouldn't flinch from that, either. "I must, however, tell you that while I admired the speech itself—greatly, in fact—I took considerable exception to the ending. I felt that was most unfortunate. Uncalled for."

For an instant, the fury fell on Adams. But only for an instant. The blue eyes simply became blue, a color like any other. Jackson even smiled a bit. Even ruefully.

"Well, I'm not sure I'd agree that it was uncalled for. But, ah, perhaps unfortunate."

The smile returned, now with more humor in it. "For sure and certain, all my friends have been berating me for it since, I can tell you that! Still . . ."

He shrugged and took a first sip of the whiskey. "What's done is done, and I'm not a man given to fretting over the past."

No, that he wasn't, for good or ill. And Adams would also allow that, in these times, that was probably to the good. For the most part, at least.

Suddenly Jackson chuckled. "You do understand, I trust, that you just made a promise you might not be able to keep."

Adams frowned. "Excuse me, sir." Stiffly: "I can assure you—"

"It doesn't matter what *you* assure me, Mr. Secretary. The people of the republic decide who'll be the president, not you or me. What if you win an outright majority in the electoral college? How could you possibly, then, hand the office to me as if it belonged to you? When, in fact, it belongs to no man in the country, not even the one who currently occupies the office. It is the sole and exclusive property of the nation itself. Its electorate, at any rate."

Adams stared at him. He'd . . .

Simply not considered the possibility.

"That's quite unlikely," he protested, knowing full well that wasn't Jackson's point.

Jackson just stared at him. Adams cleared his throat.

"Well. I suppose I couldn't. Given that eventuality."

"No, of course you couldn't. Nor could I accept."

Now, Jackson was smiling very broadly. "I'm not needling you, Mr. Secretary. And I agree it's unlikely that any of us will win an outright majority, given the political divisions in the party. I simply wanted to make sure that we understood each other."

Adams finally took a sip of his own drink. It was very good whiskey. The liquor was not to Adams's particular liking, true. But . . .

Very good whiskey, indeed.

"Agreed," he said abruptly. "But I will do so if the election is thrown into the House. That I *can* assure you, Senator Jackson."

"Call me Andy, if you would. All my friends do."

Trying not to be stiff—well, stiffer than necessary—Adams shook his head. "We're not actually friends, Senator Jackson. And being honest, I rather doubt we ever will be."

Jackson's cordial smile didn't fade in the least. "Probably not, though much stranger things have happened. But I'd still prefer it if you'd call me Andy. Consider it a matter of personal preference, if it pleases you."

Adams thought about it. Reciprocation would be necessary, of course.

It really was very good whiskey. He took another sip.

"Very well. Andy. And please call me John."

"Right!" Jackson set his whiskey glass down. Then, actually slapped his hands together. "Oh, Lor—ah, whatever. Am I going to enjoy gutting that bastard Clay!"

"I have to tell you, Sen—ah, Andy—that I actually doubt we can now stop the Speaker from being elected to the presidency."

Now Jackson was *rubbing* his hands together.

"Oh, sure. My estimate is we've got almost no chance if it gets thrown into the House. Not after that speech I gave yesterday. Coffee and Eaton tell me I'll do well if I can hang on to the Tennessee delegation. Pennsylvania, they think remains certain. I probably had a chance to win over some of

Crawford's and Calhoun's support, but not now. On the other hand—here's an interesting thing—I might still be able to take Kentucky from the bastard."

That *was* interesting. Assuming the assessment of Jackson's advisers was accurate. But Adams knew they were a very shrewd lot, Westerners or not.

"Yeah, it seems Kentucky's not all that pleased with Henry Clay, be it his home state or not. Kentucky's a border state, still more Western than Southern. Like Tennessee, really. Nobody's at all happy at the idea of black men killing a lot of white men, sure, no matter who the white men were or what they were up to. But they haven't forgotten that it was Henry Clay—not Patrick Driscol, not Sam Houston, and sure as Sam Hill not some negro in Arkansas—who spent his two-year retirement from the House getting rich by serving as the Bank's main lawyer, suing people going bankrupt, and stripping every last thing from them."

Jackson picked up his glass and took a big swallow from it. "No, that was done by good old 'man-of-the-people' Henry Clay. Who now proposes to start a war using poor white men to kill poor black men so he can spend four years swindling the nation on behalf of the rich and mighty."

Adams couldn't help but wince. That was exactly the sort of plebeianistic, class-against-class rhetoric that made Jackson and his followers so disliked in his own New England.

Well. Not disliked by New England *laborers,* to be sure. Actually, Jackson was quite popular among such folk.

Seeing the wince, Jackson grinned. "Relax, John. I promise you I won't be calling for storming the Bastille. Which we don't have in America, anyway, being a republic." He pointed a stiff finger at him. "But I'm not whitewashing anything, either. That's exactly what the bastard is planning on."

Adams cocked his head a little, considering the matter. "Yes . . . and no. I agree that his rhetoric all implies that Clay, if elected president, will launch a war against Arkansas. But the truth is, Andy, I don't think he will. Don't forget that the core of his support—certainly his financial support—comes at least as much from Northern . . . ah . . ."

He couldn't help but laugh, softly. "What I believe you would call the moneyed interests."

Jackson laughed with him. "Oh, tarnation, no. That's *way*

too namby-pamby. Bloodsucking leeches comes closer. But to keep peace in the room, I'll settle for 'Northern upper crust.' How's that?"

Adams nodded. "That's why he's got a fair amount of backing even in New England. None of those people— certainly not the ones close to the Bank—are going to be interested in a war with Arkansas. If anything, they'll be inclined to oppose it."

Jackson finished the rest of his whiskey in a quick gulp. After setting down the glass, he shook his head. "You're right, John, as far it goes. But that doesn't go far enough. This is *still* a republic, despite all the efforts of Nicholas Biddle and the rest of that pack of Bank scoundrels to undermine it. Money counts, sure, but it's not the trump card. Not yet, anyway—and not ever, if I get into the White House."

Adams tightened his lips. He himself wasn't fond of Nicholas Biddle, the head of the Second Bank, but he agreed with President Madison—and Henry Clay—that a national bank of some sort was important for the nation's economic well-being. However, that was a battle with Jackson that could be postponed for the moment. The Bank's charter ran until 1836, after all. Even if Jackson got elected to the presidency, he couldn't do much about it.

"The point being," Jackson continued, "that if Clay's to win the presidency now, he doesn't have any choice but to throw in his lot with Crawford and Calhoun. Not with you throwing your support to me, in the House."

That . . . was true. Adams realized that he'd been so preoccupied with the personal aspect of his decision to withdraw from the race that he hadn't considered what tactical results would follow in the political arena. If the election was thrown into the House, with his supporters giving their votes to Jackson . . .

He drew in a breath so sharply it was almost a hiss. "Oh, good heavens."

Jackson nodded. " 'Good heavens,' is right, John—except I wouldn't put the word 'heaven' in there at all. There's only one way Clay could win. He'd have to get Calhoun's full support and almost all of Crawford's."

"I don't think he can get all," Adams mused. "Van Buren

and his people are supporting Crawford because of his extreme states' rights views. They're New Yorkers, not Southerners. They'll have no liking for a war with Arkansas."

"No, they won't. But the problem is that Van Buren—they don't call him the Little Magician for nothing—is sometimes too smart for his own good. Might be better to say, he's so good at political tactics that he tends to lose sight of their purpose. He's likely to figure that Clay's war talk is just hot air. Campaign blather, that'll vanish like the dew after the inaugural address."

The senator rose, went over to the cabinet, and unstoppered the whiskey bottle. "Would you care for another?" he asked as he began refilling his own glass.

Adams looked down at his whiskey. There wasn't much left.

It really was very good whiskey. On the other hand, he reminded himself, he was prone to intemperance if he didn't maintain good self-control.

What decided him was an oddity. He was starting to *enjoy* this conversation.

"Yes, please."

The glasses refilled and Jackson back in his chair, the senator resumed. "What it all comes down to is that Clay is going to have to throw his lot in with Calhoun and Crawford. Lock, stock, and barrel. And you can be damn sure that Calhoun is going to insist on a war. In fact—watch and see if I'm not right—he'll insist on the post of secretary of war for himself, so he can make sure it gets done."

Adams sipped his whiskey thoughtfully. "Yes, I can see that. Clay will offer the position of secretary of state to Crawford, of course. That would position Crawford to succeed him in the White House, four or eight years from now."

"In Crawford's medical condition," Jackson said mildly, "he couldn't handle the work. No one knows that better than you."

Adams sniffed. "No, he couldn't. Frankly, I don't think he could even on his best days. But it doesn't matter, Andy. All the better from Clay's point of view, since the Speaker—"

Oh, blast it. He'd thrown in his lot with frontier roughnecks, after all, so why not at least enjoy the benefits?

"Since the rotten bastard fancies himself a great diplomat,

he'll just figure on managing the State Department personally."

Jackson grinned. "Still sore over the Russell letter, huh?"

Adams couldn't resist returning the grin. It was quite in-
fectious, really.

"Certainly. The man committed a forgery to try to smear
my reputation during the negotiations with Britain—and I
know perfectly well Clay was the one put him up to it. If
only I could prove it."

He took another drink. No sip, this time. "I genuinely detest Henry Clay."

"Well, so do I, partner. So, like I said, let's gut the bastard.
Forget this election. We'll have four years to do it—and
we'll know exactly where to find him." He waved the glass
in the direction of the White House. "Just down the street a
ways."

Monroe came upon Houston just as his son-in-law was gen-
tly closing the door to his grandson's room.

"Is he asleep, finally?" he asked.

Houston glanced over his shoulder. "Yes. He'll have
nightmares again, though. So, with your permission—"

"Of course. I've already told the servant to vacate the
room next door so you can occupy it for the night."

Houston looked genuinely haggard. He'd gotten no sleep
himself since the murder. "Thank you. I wouldn't want to
sleep in our—that—bedroom anyway. I don't think I could
bear it."

"Yes, I understand. If you'd like, I can manage other
arrangements. More permanent ones, I mean."

Houston shook his head. "No, thank you, sir. Any arrangements you made would be invalid come March, anyway.
But, as it happens, I've already decided to seek residence
elsewhere."

"You're going to Arkansas." It was a statement, not a
question.

"Yes, sir, I am. As soon as I think the boy is up to the trip."

"Sam . . ."

"No, sir." The dark fury Monroe had sensed was rising to
the surface now, filling Houston's face. "No, sir. You
forget—most people forget—that I belong to two nations,

not one. My name is also Colonneh. 'The Raven,' in English."

"Sam—"

"No, sir. I didn't get much of a look at the man who murdered my wife. But I saw enough to know one thing, for sure. That man was not a Cherokee. That man was one of those stinking, filthy Georgians who drove the Cherokee off their land. To call 'relocation'—yes, I know I engineered the treaty, and I used it, too—by its right name."

A little shudder passed through his big body. Then, softly: "So I'm going home, and taking my boy with me. Meaning no offense to you, sir, but I want him to meet his Cherokee grandfather. While John Jolly's still alive."

Monroe sighed. "Please don't forget that you shared five years of Maria Hester's life, Sam. And I shared all of them."

Houston's eyes teared. "I know that, James," he said softly. "I don't mean to belittle your grief, or her mother's, or her sister's. But you do what you feel necessary, and I will do the same. I'm not bringing up my boy in a country that murdered his mother, because it was a country full of spite and meanness. No way in Hell. We're for Arkansas."

Monroe recognized the impossibility of altering his son-in-law's course. Still . . .

Forty years of political life produced unshakable habits. "Don't burn any bridges you don't need to, Sam. Lafayette's visiting the country, as you know."

Sam frowned, thrown off by the remark. "Well, sure. His tour's taking the whole country by storm. In fact, I met him—well, shook his hand and exchanged pleasantries—at a festival in his honor just two weeks ago. But what's that got to do . . ."

His voice trailed off, and the color of his eyes seemed to lighten a bit. "Oh."

Monroe was careful not to show any visible relief. If Sam Houston didn't have much of the Scots-Irish capacity for rage, except in his worst moments, he had all of that breed's aptitude for political maneuver. Considerably more than his rightful share, in fact.

"Oh," he repeated. Then, shook his head slightly. "I doubt he'd receive me, James. He's deluged with well-wishers, and he doesn't know me at all."

"Don't be foolish. He knows who you are. Just because the Marquis is now sixty-six years old, don't think for a moment he's become less acute when it comes to political affairs. The hero of the Capitol, and then New Orleans?"

Monroe cleared his throat. "Not that it matters. He certainly knows who I am, since I'm not only the president of the nation but the one who extended the invitation for him to visit. He'll see *me*, Sam. In fact . . ."

Monroe had to swallow for a moment. "He's coming here tomorrow, as it happens. He asked if he could accompany us in person to the funeral."

Sam nodded. "In that case, I'll be able to see him. At least briefly."

"Briefly, yes. Tomorrow. But . . ."

Monroe paused, for a moment, thinking. "Can you postpone your departure for a week or two?"

"Well . . . Yes, I suppose. Andy won't be up for traveling immediately, anyway."

"Good. In that case, I think I can manage something quite a bit better than 'briefly.' "

Houston was looking at him very intently now, his fury almost completely gone. "What are you thinking, James?"

"What I am thinking, my dear son-in-law—which you are and will remain, whatever else—is that the last sight of you I want the United States to have, before you depart for Arkansas, is receiving the blessing of the Marquis de Lafayette. Who fought with George Washington and shed his blood on American soil at Brandywine, that republicanism might triumph in the world."

Washington, D.C.
NOVEMBER 19, 1824

Eleven days later, at the state dinner hosted by President Monroe at Williamson's Hotel and attended by practically every member of Congress, the Marquis sat beside Sam Houston.

That caused pained looks among some of the congressmen present, but not many. Word was already spreading that John Quincy Adams would throw his support to Jackson in the event the election was thrown into the House. Which, with the first election results beginning to come in, now seemed certain to happen. State dinners of this sort were such enormous affairs that there was plenty of time and space for quiet dickering. Most of the congressmen were too busy with their whispered consultations to pay much attention to the formalities of the affair.

Peter Porter was one of the exceptions. He'd gotten an invitation through the offices of the Speaker, so he was there also. But since he was not a congressman, he paid little attention to the small maneuvers taking place at the multitudes of tables in the huge dining room. Instead, he spent the time carefully studying the men at the central table.

James Monroe. Sam Houston. The Marquis de Lafayette.

Porter had had enough military experience to understand—he was pretty sure, anyway—what he was seeing. Strategists at work, not tacticians. He tried, at one point in the evening, to get Clay's attention. But the Speaker was preoccupied with his negotiations with several of the congressmen from North Carolina.

"Tomorrow, Peter. I couldn't possibly find the time to speak to you tonight."

Toward the end of the evening, the Marquis rose and offered three toasts.

The first, in solemn remembrance of the president's daughter.

The second, in honor of his heroic son-in-law, who had so valiantly defended the Capitol of the United States from enemy attack—and then repeated the deed, a few months later, at New Orleans.

The third—

Smiling broadly, the Marquis prefaced his toast by announcing that Sam Houston was moving to Arkansas and taking his young son with him. They would depart two days hence.

So, another toast: "To the New World, so clearly blessed by the Almighty! To the New World! Which has produced yet another great republic on its soil!"

Andrew Jackson was the first to rise to the toast. Had he not been a bit too portly, John Quincy Adams might have beaten him to it.

* * *

Outside the hotel, later, Clay brushed Porter off again. "Not now, Peter, sorry. Yes, I know it's a bit awkward. A minor setback. But I think we're on the verge of taking all of North Carolina from Jackson. South Carolina, Calhoun can promise us for sure."

Off he went. Porter was left alone in the night, watching the crowd spilling out of Williamson's Hotel.

Setback.

"Jesus Christ," Porter muttered to no one at all. "Who cares about that? This thing is careening out of control."

CHAPTER 25

Natchez, Mississippi
DECEMBER 15, 1824

The bullet missed, but it did manage to shatter a bottle of whiskey sitting on the bar top that was close enough to shower Ray Thompson with its contents. Crouching behind the bar next to Powers, he cursed bitterly. It was rotgut, naturally. He'd be stinking for hours. Assuming he survived the next few minutes.

"Can't you *ever* just keep your mouth shut?" he hissed.

Powers finished reloading his pistol. "Damnation, this tavern was my old watering hole." He peered up at the bar top above them. "How many were there?"

"Four, till you shot one and I shot another."

"The tavern keeper?"

"He ran off. I don't think he was one of them. But they'll have friends coming, you watch. And meantime they've got us pinned here, and"—Ray rapped a knuckle against one of the planks that formed the base of the bar—"sooner or later it's going to occur to those stupid yahoos to try to shoot through these planks to see how thick they are. I'm not looking forward to the results."

Powers winced. "Neither am I." He gave Thompson a calculating look. "We got no choice, I'm thinking. Right at 'em is the only way."

Ray shook his head. "Yeah, we got no choice. But I'm only joining you if you *swear* you'll stop using your own name."

"Yeah. Fine. I swear. Mother's grave, whatever you want."

Thompson didn't bother to answer. He was too busy gauging the distance to the only unshattered bottle still on the bar top.

"I'll go first, right over the top. You come around the side."

Powers nodded. Since there was no point in dallying, Ray rose up enough to tap the bottle over with the barrel of the pistol.

Almost instantly, a shot was fired, smashing into the wood behind the bar.

"Thank God for yahoos." But he was erect before he finished the statement, where he could see the room, his pistol tracking the man who'd fired.

Dumber'n sheep. The idiot was standing up, reloading. Ray shot him in the chest. Then, lunged to his left, just in time to evade the shot fired by the man's partner. He kept lunging leftward, half running and half scrambling, but never dropping out of sight. That would keep the man's eyes on him while Scott—

Powers's shot came from the other side of the bar. Ray stopped and looked over. Good enough. He didn't think Scott had killed him outright, but it was good enough.

"Fucking yahoos," Powers snarled on their way out of the tavern. "Why the hell do they care if we hurt Clay's chances? The bastards never bother to vote, anyway. Too stupid to read the ballot."

Ten minutes later they were ready to head for the Natchez Trace.

"Now we're horse thieves, too," Ray complained as he led his mount out of the barn they'd broken into.

Powers was in a cheerier mood. "Lookit this. Found it tacked on the wall in there."

He handed over a printed notice.

Thompson didn't look at it, though, until they were out of the town's limits. Killing three or four men might be forgiven in Natchez, depending on who their friends and relatives were, but stealing a horse was a hanging offense.

When he did look at it, reading slowly because of the horse's gait, he whistled.

"Ten thousand dollars. *Whoo-eee.*"

Then he shrugged and handed it back to Powers. "Lot of good it does us."

But Powers was still smiling. "O ye of little faith. I *know* him, Ray. Andrew Clark's the first cousin of an old friend of mine."

Thompson looked over at him skeptically. "And what of it? He did the killing in Washington, Scott. If your geography's gotten hazy since our seafaring days, that's about a thousand miles from here as the crow flies—and we ain't crows. By now he could be anywhere."

" 'Could be,' sure. But he won't be. Where's he going to go? That's a snooty family he comes from, real Georgia gentlemen. If he'd killed *Houston,* he'd have been all right. They'd hide him as long as it took. But killing Houston's wife, won't nobody in those circles touch him. In fact, they'd turn him in faster'n anybody. Even the yahoos in Louisiana would. Well, half of 'em, anyway."

Ray thought about it. That was true enough, actually. Killing a woman, unless she was a whore or a cheating wife, was one of the few ways a man could cross the line with Southern and Western roughnecks. Almost as bad as horse stealing.

The last thought reminded him of their own predicament. "What're we going to do with these horses, Scott?"

"Let 'em go; what else? As soon as we reach Port Gibson. That's stretching it a little, but I figure we can probably get away with it. Being as there was four of them, and us not knowing how many friends they might have."

Again, Ray thought about it. That was . . .

Also true enough. There was a certain protocol involved. Actually *stealing* a man's horse was a hanging offense, sure enough. But if a man let the horse go while it was still close enough to find its way home—or be returned by someone else who knew the brand—most people were inclined to let it go as more-or-less borrowing the horse just to get out of a bad spot. Which theirs had certainly been. Often enough, it became a laughing matter.

It wasn't surefire, of course. But at least it gave you an arguing point if you got caught.

"Okay, then what?"

"Port Gibson's where we want, anyway." Powers flashed Thompson a grin. "Being as how you and me is for a Mississippi steamboat and St. Louis. I figure we can get hired on, easy enough. This soon after the massacre, a lot of the regular men'll still be nervous about steaming past the Arkansas."

Thompson grimaced. "Scott, *I'm* nervous about steaming past it. Unless they're even dumber than yahoos, they'll still have that flotilla there. One or two boats anyway—and they're likely to be none too fussy about diplomatic protocol. What if they stop our boat and search it? They find us, we're for the rope."

"Yeah, sure. But it's been two and a half months since Arkansas Post. I figure by now the U.S. State Department has made plenty of protests to the Confederacy on the subject of interfering with American commerce on the Mississippi. Say whatever else you will about the bastard, Quincy Adams ain't no slouch. As long as we stay out of sight when our boat gets to the Arkansas, we should be safe enough." His cheery expression was disfigured for a moment by a scowl. "Which won't be hard, since we'll probably be working in the boiler room."

Ray matched the grimace. Boiler room work was just as hard as it was dangerous.

Not, however, as dangerous as staying in yahoo country, with their names black as mud because of that damned Bryant. And even if they always used aliases, there were just too many men in the area who knew them personally.

Nor could they return to more civilized parts of the United States. Leaving aside what difficulties they might encounter because of Bryant's articles—which could be serious, given that Clay might well be the next president—they had several other awkward issues to deal with. Scott had arrest warrants out for him, and Ray had creditors. Not the sort of creditors who demanded imprisonment for debt, either, as a last resort. The sort who started with broken knees.

"All right, then."

"Oh, stop being gloomy," Scott said. "We need to get to St. Louis anyway, on account of this." He patted the pocket into which he'd stuffed the reward notice.

"Why?"

"Don't you pay any attention? I *told* you. Well, maybe not all of it. Andrew Clark's cousin is the black sheep of the family. He's the one person Clark could find shelter with, and he's in Missouri."

"In St. Louis?"

"Well. No." Powers seemed to be avoiding his gaze. "Further west. Missouri Territory."

Ray rolled his eyes. "Wonderful. He's a bandit, isn't he?"

"Some might call him that, I suppose."

"'Some,'" Ray mimicked sarcastically. "Let me guess. Ninety-nine out of a hundred citizens of Missouri."

Scott grinned. "Nah, not that many. Maybe ninety-five out of a hundred."

He gave Ray a sideways look. "What? You worried about our good names?"

Thompson said nothing. What was there to say?

"What I thought. Face it, Ray. We ain't exactly upstanding citizens, our own selves. Not even around bandits. Southern ones, for sure."

New Antrim, Arkansas
DECEMBER 16, 1824

"I don't care if we go bankrupt, Henry." Patrick Driscol's rasp seemed more pronounced than ever. "What difference does it make if Arkansas goes under? I'll be dead on a battlefield, you'll be a slave picking cotton in the Delta, and even the engineer fellow here"—a thumb indicated Henry Shreve, who was scowling at him from the doorway—"is likely to be standing trial for treason. Never gave up his U.S. citizenship, you know."

"That's not funny, Patrick!" Shreve's scowl grew darker still.

"No, I suppose not. It's still true." Driscol smiled thinly. "Of course, you could always have a sudden conversion on the road to Damascus. 'Reconversion,' I guess I should say. Hurry on down to Memphis, confess the error of your wicked ways, and offer your services to the Fulton-Livingston Company. Word has it they've already got the contract for supplying the U.S. Army, in the event war comes. I'm sure they'd hire you on."

Now Shreve's scowl could have terrified an ogre. "Stop playing the fool! 'Hurry on down to Memphis.' In *what?* A rowboat?—seeing as how you've already seized everything I own, you damn tyrant. Worse than any Federalist who ever lived, you are."

Henry Crowell's grunt combined amusement and exasperation. "Don't forget the years he spent with Napoleon, Henry. Conscription—seizure of personal property—all out for the war effort. Nothing's too low for the Laird. By next Tuesday, I figure he'll start debasing the currency."

"Don't call me that, damnation. I hate that term."

"Why? It's true, Patrick. And before you start prattling about your republican principles—about which Henry's right; you've shredded every one these past two months—you might keep in mind that the term is prob'bly worth another regiment, as far as the army's morale goes."

Shreve's scowl lightened a bit. "He's right about that. Black heathen savages. Bad as Frenchmen. *Vive l'empereur! Allons enfants de la patrie!*"

His French accent was quite good. Better than Driscol's, in fact, although Driscol was more fluent in the language. So Crowell had been told, anyway. His own knowledge of French was limited to the Creole he'd picked up in New Orleans.

"They're hardly heathens," grumbled Patrick. "Most of 'em are downright Calvinists, by now, since Brown started his preaching."

Shreve gave him a skeptical look. Driscol shrugged. "Well, fine. Some of Marie Laveau's voudou in there, too, I suppose."

"John Brown doesn't actually preach," Crowell said mildly. "It's more just that black folks admire the man so much. And why shouldn't they? The Catholics are doing pretty well, too, actually. Especially since all that money started coming in from Pierre Toussaint to fund them."

Shreve rolled his eyes. "You had to bring that up, didn't you?" Sourly, he crossed his arms and slouched in the doorway. "I can remember a time—O blessed days of innocent youth—when my world was a lot simpler. Sure as hell didn't include rich black bankers in Arkansas and still richer darkies in New York. And a crazy Scots-Irishman to fan the flames of their insane ambitions."

Crowell's grunt this time was simply amused. For all of Shreve's more-or-less constant carping and complaining, the fact was that the Pennsylvania steamboat wizard had thrown in his lot with Arkansas as unreservedly as the poorest freedman. Henry wasn't sure why, exactly, since it certainly wasn't due to any commitment on Shreve's part to abolition or even any deep faith in human equality. Shreve didn't really care that much about such things, one way or the other. He had the mind and soul of an engineer, first, last, and always.

In the end, Henry thought, that was the key. As much and as often as Shreve protested Driscol's ways—which did, indeed, sometimes border on Napoleonic high-handedness if not outright tyranny—the fact remained that the Laird of Arkansas had supported and funded Shreve's plans and schemes far more extensively than any person or institution in the United States had ever done. Or ever would, so long as the Fulton-Livingston Company could throw its money and influence around.

But it was time to settle the current dispute. "Fine, Patrick. Seeing as how you're being stubborn—"

"When is he *not?*" demanded Shreve.

"—we'll sink every dime we can into buying iron plate from the foundries in Cincinnati and Pittsburgh. The ones who'll still do business with us, anyway."

Seeing Driscol's sarcastic expression, he chucked. "Which, I admit, is all of them. Amazing, in a way, since Ohio's supposed to be solid for Henry Clay."

Shreve snorted. "'Solid' refers to politics. Money has no country."

He glared at Driscol. "Besides which, the United States is a republic. A nation of freemen, where the idea that the government could tell a man what he could and couldn't do with his own property is anathema."

"Especially when the property talks and has a black skin," Driscol fired back. "So don't preach to me about 'freedom,' Mister Shreve. I find myself quite willing to abrogate the lesser freedoms to maintain the great ones. We're *still* going to buy all the iron plate we can, since we can't make it in our own little foundries, so that when the bastards come up the river it'll be our boats—yours, when I give them back after the war—who steam out of the encounter. And theirs which go under. Or would you rather we did it the other way around?"

Put that way . . .

Shreve threw up his hands. "Fine! I'm going back to work. Otherwise your lunatic scheme will sink the boats right there at the piers, all the iron you'll try to bolt onto them."

"I wouldna dream of telling an engineer his business," said Driscol, his Belfast accent thicker than usual. "Mind, I'd appreciate the occasional reciprocation."

But Shreve had already left.

Washington, D.C.
DECEMBER 18, 1824

"Well, that's it," said Adam Beatty. "We'll have a merry Christmas, gentlemen. With Louisiana's vote having come in, everything's been reported."

At the head of the table in the boardinghouse, Henry Clay rubbed his face wearily. "Summarize it, please."

"Nationwide, Jackson has the plurality of votes, though not by as large a margin as it appeared he would in midsummer. That's the 'Arkansas effect,' most likely, coming in at the last minute. Still, he's got eighty-five electoral votes, just a little under one-third of the total. Adams comes a pretty close second, with seventy-six."

"In short," Peter Porter said bluntly, "our two principal

enemies—who've now formed an alliance, with Adams willing to throw his support to Jackson—have a total of one hundred and sixty-one votes. Which is a clear majority in the electoral college. And the same percentage, roughly speaking, in the popular vote."

"A little over sixty percent," Beatty agreed. "But it really doesn't matter, because the electoral college is not where the issue gets settled, according to the Constitution. Since no *single* candidate won a majority, the three top candidates are the ones chosen from by the House. And there—"

He smiled widely. "Henry's the third man. Clear-cut, no question about it. He got forty-two votes to Crawford's thirty-four and Calhoun's twenty-five. All we've got to do, gentlemen, is turn that forty percent in the electoral college into fifty-one percent in the House."

Put that way, Porter mused, it didn't sound so bad. But the sense he'd had of a situation steadily unraveling was getting stronger all the while. Because the *other* way to look at it was that the man who could only muster . . .

Porter was good at arithmetic. Silently, in his head, he did the calculations.

And was appalled. Henry Clay had gotten barely *sixteen percent* of the popular and electoral votes. Which Beatty was cheerily projecting he could triple—more than triple— in order to get elected, purely and solely based on political maneuvering in the House of Representatives.

That it *could* be done, Porter didn't much doubt. Clay's ability to manipulate the House was practically legendary by now. But could a president elected in such a manner actually carry out the tasks and duties of the nation's chief executive in the years to follow? That was another matter entirely.

His musings were interrupted by Clay's voice. "Peter, are the rumors we've been hearing about Van Buren true, in your estimate?"

A bit startled, Porter looked up. "Well . . . It's hard to know. Van Buren plays the game very close to the chest. But I think it's likely, yes. Jackson, unlike Adams, has always had a clear stance on states' rights, which is what matters to the New York Radicals. They simply don't have the same concerns regarding Arkansas and the issues surrounding it that Calhoun's people do, and some of Crawford's." He cleared his throat. "Some *others* of Crawford's, I should say, since they were in that camp themselves."

Clay nodded, his expression weary but still alert. "In other words, Crawford's camp is breaking up."

"Pretty much, yes. His Northern supporters shifting toward Jackson, his Southern ones in our direction. More toward Calhoun than us, though, and keeping in mind that it's certainly not a split down the middle. Most of his support was in the South, to begin with. New York was really his only major Northern stronghold."

"The key's the South, then," stated Josiah Johnston. "It's that simple. We haven't got enough, even getting all of Calhoun's and Crawford's votes. And we can't possibly hope to crack anything away in New England, that matters. Or Pennsylvania and New Jersey. Or Tennessee."

He stopped there, a bit awkwardly. Porter didn't blame him. He could have added *or Kentucky, probably*. The two most populous border states had gone for Jackson, even Clay's home state.

Clay sat up straight. "All right. I agree with Josiah. It's simple enough. We've got to keep Calhoun solid—that, whatever else—and win over Crawford's Southern supporters. Then—"

He took a deep breath. "Ignore New England altogether. Ignore Pennsylvania and New Jersey. Go straight at the Southern congressional delegations, and a few of the softer Western ones, like Indiana and Illinois. We can assume that Ohio and Missouri will remain solid for us. Persuade them that the allegiance many of their states showed for Jackson was an error, produced by the fact that news of Arkansas— and Jackson's disturbing reaction to it—hadn't had time to reach the populace before they voted. Surely they would have voted otherwise, had they known."

"Remember Arkansas Post!" Beatty exclaimed. "That's the drum we beat."

Clay looked around the room. Everyone nodded. Even Porter, in the end. What else was there to do?

CHAPTER 26

"Please, Colonel Taylor, have a seat." General Brown half rose from the seat behind his desk when Zachary entered his office, motioning toward a chair next to the one occupied by General Winfield Scott. A bit to the side sat Thomas Jesup, the army's quartermaster general.

Taylor would have felt awkward under any circumstances in such august company. Since the reorganization and drastic reduction in the size of the army ordered by Congress in 1821, Jacob Brown was the only remaining major general, and thus the commanding general of the entire U.S. Army. Winfield Scott was one of its two remaining brigadier generals of the line and commanded the eastern department of the military. For the moment, at least. Rumors were that he and Brigadier General Edmund Gaines, who commanded the western department, would soon be exchanging posts.

In short, he was sitting in an office with three of the army's four generals. Nor were they "political generals," although Brown had begun his career as a political appointee. All three of them were considered by the entire U.S. military—except for a few rivals in the officer corps like Gaines—to be the army's best fighting generals. Brown had been in overall command of the Army of the Niagara, which had won the first major American land victory in the war with Britain; Scott, the general in command of the forces that triumphed at the Chippewa; Jesup, then a colonel, had commanded the 25th Infantry regiment that Scott had used in the battle to drive back the British right flank.

The presence of Jesup was a bit reassuring, since Jesup had been Taylor's principal supporter in the army's high command since the days they'd worked together in the northwest frontier. Still, the situation was nerve-wracking. Zachary had been half expecting to receive a summons for a court-martial since he arrived in the capital.

He decided to deal with that immediately. "General, I'm quite aware that I had no specific orders to report to Washington. Still, as soon as I was assured that my post in Baton Rouge was in good order, I felt it incumbent—"

Jesup chuckled. Brown waved his hand. "Oh, relax, Zack. You're not in any trouble."

"Not from us, anyway," Scott murmured.

Taylor glanced at him. Then, looked back at Brown.

"The reason I asked you here," the major general said, "is because of these." He leaned over and picked some papers from his desk. The movement was stiff and ungainly, as his earlier rise from the chair had been. Brown had suffered a bad stroke three years earlier and was still recovering from the effects.

· Even from the distance, Taylor recognized the handwriting on the sheets. Which was hardly surprising, since it was his. Well . . .

Brown's stiff face broke into a smile. "First, by the way, let me congratulate you on the sudden and marked improvement in your penmanship."

Taylor felt himself flushing a bit. "Not mine, actually. I'd suffered, ah, something of a sprain in my wrist. Miss Julia Chinn wrote the dispatches for me, at my dictation."

Jesup frowned slightly. "Chinn. Isn't she Senator Johnson's woman?"

"Wife, I believe, in reality if not in law," corrected Scott. He gave both Jesup and Brown a quick, hard glance. "Shall we get to the point, gentlemen? We wouldn't have invited Colonel Taylor here if we didn't think he was trustworthy."

Trustworthy of what? Zack wondered. But from the look Scott was now giving him, he realized he was about to find out.

"Here's how it is, Colonel," Scott continued. "I'm from Virginia, as you are. So's Thomas Jesup. Our august commander"—a thumb indicated Brown—"on the other hand, is a Pennsylvania Quaker."

"More of a New Yorker, really," Brown said mildly, "although I was born in Pennsylvania. And I abandoned pacifism quite some time ago."

Scott ignored him, his eyes still intent on Taylor. "Not a single New England abolitionist in the lot, you'll notice. That said, all three of us think John Quincy Adams would make the best next president of the United States. Failing him, Andrew Jackson—yes, even me, despite my well-known feud with the man. But what's most important is that all three of us think the election of Henry Clay, which now seems almost certain, is going to be a disaster. Not simply for the nation, but for the army in particular."

Brown winced. Jesup was scowling openly.

For his part, Taylor was simply trying to keep from gaping open-mouthed. Even by the standards of the U.S. Army, whose top officers politicked aggressively, this sort of blunt and open statement concerning current politics was almost unheard of. From any officer, at least, who didn't expect to be relieved from duty.

Which—

Scott smiled crookedly. "Oh, I shan't give the bastard the satisfaction of discharging me. The day it's officially announced that Henry Clay will be the sixth president of the United States, I shall tender my resignation from the army."

"So will I," said Brown. "My health is poor, as it happens, so that gives me a graceful way to do it." He gave Scott something of a sly glance. "Unlike what I suspect will be Winfield's more flamboyant language."

"The tactics Henry Clay is using to win the presidency are a stench in the nation's nostrils," stated Scott, "and I will not hesitate to say so publicly when the time comes. Leaving aside everything else, he's recklessly using the army as if we were simply a card in his game. He knows perfectly well that the army is far too grossly understrength to be talking as if a victory over Arkansas is simply a matter of will and purpose."

Jesup cleared his throat. "I'll stay. They'd find me hard to replace, and they won't care that much anyway."

That was probably true, Taylor thought. Jesup had brought professional order and system into what had in earlier times been a disgracefully slapdash manner of keeping the military supplied. And since the quartermaster corps was outside the normal chain of command for line units, an ambitious officer like Gaines wouldn't consider him a rival.

Not knowing what to say, Taylor kept his mouth shut. He looked back at Brown.

"You'll be staying in service, yes?" asked the major general.

Zack nodded. "Yes, sir."

"Good," said Brown. He lifted the sheets. "These reports were excellent. What's your assessment of our chances in a war with the Confederacy?"

"It depends, sir. If it were done right, there's no question we would win. Despite the Confederacy's considerable geographic advantage in a defensive war —which is what they'd be fighting, of course—the overall disparity in numbers is simply overwhelming. The United States has a population of about ten million people; the Confederacy, less than two hundred thousand. But it won't be easy, it won't be quick, and . . ."

He relaxed a bit. The rest of what he had to say would certainly bring no censure from the men in *this* room. "And, finally, it's just absurd to think it can be done with an army the size ours has been since the demobilization after the war with England. We've got—what? Not much more than six thousand regular soldiers in the whole country?"

"About that," agreed Brown. "Officially—the real numbers vary a bit—the bill passed by Congress in 1821 allows us five hundred and forty commissioned officers and slightly over five thousand, five hundred enlisted men. Divided into seven infantry and four artillery regiments."

"Clay will call for an immediate expansion of the armed forces," Jesup predicted.

Scott's answering grimace was just short of a sneer. "Oh, splendid. Even in the war with Britain, it took a year and a half to build up to fifteen thousand men. By the end of the war, we had not more than thirty-five thousand regulars. Half of whom, throughout, did purely garrison duty. And that war was generally popular outside New England. This new war, if it begins, will be anathema in New England and popular nowhere except in some—not all—of the Southern states."

Now the expression on his face was an outright sneer. "The same states of the Deep South, I remind you, whose contributions to the war against England were pitiful."

Jesup grunted. "They didn't even do much against the Creeks except plunder helpless villages. The real fighting, outside of regulars, was done by border state militias."

It was a harsh indictment, but Taylor couldn't find any real fault with it. Throughout the recent war, Jackson's Tennessee militia had borne the brunt of the fighting in the southern theater; first against the Creeks and later the British. The Kentuckians had contributed a large number of soldiers also, although they'd generally produced mediocre officers. The rest of the South, outside of the many officers produced by Virginia, hadn't done much. The Georgia militia, in particular, had been as notorious for its incapacity in the field against a real enemy as for its penchant for committing atrocities against noncombatants. Jackson had despised them and made no bones about it.

"And Clay won't have the Tennessee militia as a southern anchor, this time around," Jesup continued. "Not a chance. Not with the stance Jackson's taken. He's already starting to call it Henry Clay's War. Usually with a string of adjectives attached, the mildest of which is 'benighted.' "

Winfield Scott raised an eyebrow. "William Carroll's the governor of Tennessee, though, Tom. Not Andrew Jackson—and they're political enemies."

Jesup waggled his hand. "Yes and no. There's no personal animosity between them, and not really all that much in the way of real political issues in dispute. Their 'enmity' is mostly just a matter of old factional quarrels in Tennessee politics. Go back a few years, and they were close friends and allies. Who's to say they can't be again?"

"Yes, I agree," said Brown. "Despite his reputation, Jackson's perfectly capable of ending a feud if there's no personal injury involved."

"Even then!" snorted Scott. "He's burying the hatchet with Thomas Hart Benton right now."

Moving stiffly, Brown sat up straight in his chair and placed his left hand on the desk. His other hand remained in his lap, since he'd lost most of the use of his right arm after his stroke.

"There's no chance at all that Governor Carroll will agree to let the Tennessee militia be used in any war against the Confederacy," he said firmly. "Not this war, at any rate. And there's no better chance, in my judgment, that the Kentucky militia will be available to Clay, either. The current governor, John Adair, served under Jackson at New Orleans. And both he and his successor, Joseph Desha, are members of the Relief Party. They're Clay's political enemies, not his friends."

Taylor didn't have the familiarity of the three generals in the room with the politics of the nation as a whole, but he did know Kentucky politics. So, finally, he ventured an opinion.

"I agree. And for sure and certain, Senator Johnson's going to be against any such war. Leaving aside his political allegiance to Jackson, his two daughters are going to school in Arkansas, and his—ah—Julia Chinn is still residing there also. At least for the moment."

Brown cocked his head. "She didn't return to Kentucky?"

"No. That was her original plan, but . . . well . . . The girls are only twelve."

He had to fight a little to keep a straight face. It'd have been more accurate to add *going on thirteen, with their eyes already on two boys not all that much older.*

"So, there it is," stated Jesup. "A war fought with a regular army stripped to the bone, and without the Tennessee and Kentucky militias to provide the additional men we relied on in the southern theater against the Creeks and the British."

Brown picked it up immediately. "Yes, there it is. So what's your assessment, Colonel Taylor? And please add, if you would, your own recommendations."

"Assume for the moment that you were in overall command," chimed in Scott.

Taylor didn't hesitate. He'd now spent months considering the problem. "Whatever else, avoid the obvious route.

The Arkansas River valley is a trap that could easily turn into a death trap."

He saw Scott and Brown exchange glances. Triumphant, in the case of Scott's; acknowledging, in the case of Brown's. Apparently he wasn't the only one who'd been pondering the matter.

"Well fortified?" That came from Jesup.

"Arkansas Post is as well built a fort as any in North America, outside the coastal regions," Taylor stated. "I wasn't able to personally inspect the fortifications farther up the river, but from what I was able to determine, they're possibly even more formidable."

"I *did* inspect them, not long ago," said Scott. "Your assessment is quite accurate, Colonel."

Taylor nodded. "I'd simply establish a stronghold at the confluence to block the Confederacy's access to the Mississippi. Then, launch a diversionary attack up the Red River—"

"How would you deal with the Great Raft?" Brown interrupted.

Taylor smiled. "With great difficulty, sir."

A little laugh filled the room. "Still, with some patience and good logistics," Taylor continued, "it's not impossible. But I stress that this would be merely a diversion. Its main purpose would be to force the Confederates to maintain a considerable military force on their southern border. The Confederacy's great advantage is geography; its great disadvantage, a small population from which to draw soldiers. We'd need to use the former, as best we could—however hard it might be—to place as great a strain as possible on the latter."

The three generals looked at one another. "Makes sense to me," said Jesup. Scott nodded.

Brown looked back at Taylor. "Please continue."

"But the main attack would come from the north. A big army—very big, with lots of cavalry and a well-organized supply train—marching up the Missouri from St. Louis and then down onto the Indian lands of the Confederacy, following the Arkansas. The emphasis would be on using our potentially much superior cavalry in relatively open terrain, and placing pressure on the Cherokees and Creeks to sever their relations with the blacks in Arkansas. If we can succeed in doing so, we'll then have Arkansas in a vise. Over time, by methods of siege and economic strangulation if nothing else, they'd have to surrender."

"You'd not go directly against Driscol's chiefdom?"

Taylor shook his head. "No, sir. The Indian nations in the trans-Arkansas region of the Confederacy are still not that well organized, not even the Cherokee, and there are already strains among them over the issue of slavery. Moreover, while they're certainly brave enough, none of them can field a disciplined and well-trained professional army that could face U.S. regulars in the field. I cannot stress enough the need to stay away from major direct clashes with the Arkansans on their own terrain. That'll be a bloodbath, sir. Even if we win—and I am not frankly sure we could at all, on their terrain, without a minimum of fifteen thousand men in the field—the casualties would produce an uproar in the country."

"Explain," Brown commanded.

Taylor shifted uncomfortably in his seat. "Sir, if you'll allow me to say so, the great danger is that the army will underestimate the Arkansas forces because of their color."

"Jackson wouldn't," Scott said immediately. "The core of that army is the Iron Battalion. If he's ever had anything to say about them other than praise, I've never heard it."

"No, he probably wouldn't," Taylor agreed. He smiled then, for the first time since he'd entered the office. "But I think if there is one single thing we can be sure and certain of, it's that Old Hickory is the very last man Henry Clay would ask to command an expedition against the Confederacy."

Another laugh filled the room. Not a little one, this time.

Brown nodded. "Harrison's likely to be put in command. By all accounts I've heard, he's champing at the bit."

Taylor thought about it for a moment. William Henry Harrison had resigned from the army in a huff in 1814, after a dispute with Secretary of War Armstrong, and had since then been engaged in a middling-successful career as a politician. He'd lost as many elections as he'd won, but he had just managed to get elected as one of the U.S. senators from Ohio. He was known to be a Clay supporter. What was more important was that, second only to Andrew Jackson, he was widely considered the nation's greatest "Injun fighter" because of his victories over Tecumseh's alliance at Tippecanoe and the Thames. If Clay offered to return him to the army as a major general and placed him in command of a war against the Confederacy, Harrison would most likely accept. He was an ambitious man, and he must by now have realized that his principal strength as a politician was his military reputation. Resigning from a Senate seat he'd not even warmed yet in order to answer a patriotic call to duty in a war against the Confederacy would position him nicely to succeed Clay in the White House.

Assuming he won the war, of course.

"What about General Gaines?" he asked. Zack raised the question diffidently, since he'd been very careful to keep a distance from the feud between Winfield Scott and Edmund Gaines that had, for years now, divided a good portion of the officer corps into two hostile camps. Still, it needed to be asked.

Brown shrugged. "With me and Winfield both resigning, Edmund will automatically become the next commander in chief. Unless Clay decides to supersede seniority altogether, which I think unlikely."

"Not a chance," stated Scott confidently. "Harrison wants the glory of a successful campaign, so he'll not be interested. And with you and me both resigning—and I'll make my reasons blunt and explicit, Jacob, even if you won't—Clay will have enough problems with the remaining officers. If he alienates Gaines, he'll have nothing."

Again, Scott sneered. "Of course, Clay can rely on Gaines to wag his tail obligingly, no matter what nonsensical military results he demands."

There was always that to be said for Winfield Scott. As vain and arrogant as the man could be, there was a genuine streak of integrity in him. More than a streak, actually. Jacob Brown had come into the army as a politician, and although he'd gained the respect of the military for his demonstrated courage and prowess as a soldier, he remained a politician. Scott wasn't, and never had been. He was quite capable of resigning from the army on grounds of political principle, and stating them publicly.

Gaines, on the other hand . . .

Mentally, Zachary shook his head. He'd never taken sides in the long-running Scott–Gaines feud, since there'd been no practical reason to do so personally, and the causes of the feud were petty in any event. But if he had to choose between the two men, either as generals or simply as men—especially the latter—he had no doubt which way he'd go.

Yes, Gaines would wag his tail and do what his master bade him if the food bowl was filled.

"So let's sum it, Colonel Taylor," Scott said. "We're looking at a war with John Calhoun as the secretary of war, Edmund Gaines sitting where I am now, Winfield out of the army entirely, and William Henry Harrison placed in command of the campaign against the Confederacy. Into this, you propose to recommend a campaign that ignores seizing Arkansas and humbling the negroes—which is the main purpose of the war from Calhoun's viewpoint—in order to fight a long and protracted campaign against Indian tribes with which, were it not for their ties to Arkansas, the United States no longer has any real quarrel."

Taylor took a deep breath. "Yes, sir. That's what I recommend."

The three generals in the room grinned.

Jesup spoke first. "Jacob, I told you so. By all means, promote this splendid officer."

Brown chuckled. "Indeed I will. Zack, it's within my power to promote you to full colonel. Beyond that, of course, I can't go without authorization from Congress. If I could make you a brigadier, I would. What I can do also, however—which is more important than anything, if you'll accept—is place you in command of all U.S. Army forces in Missouri. That'll require you and your family to relocate to St. Louis, of course."

While his mind worked on the matter as a whole, Taylor dealt with the latter issue. "That's not a problem, sir. To be honest, I'd prefer moving the girls out of Louisiana. That's not been good for their health. For the rest . . ."

He hesitated. Normally, of course, any officer would be delighted by such a promotion. But, although he was no expert on the workings of political infighting in Washington, Zachary Taylor was not stupid. For all intents and purposes—even if nothing was said directly—by accepting the promotion and the assignment he would be joining what amounted to a conspiracy against the man now almost certain to become the next president of the United States.

A most far-ranging and vast conspiracy, at that. One which, soon if not already, would have Andrew Jackson and John Quincy Adams involved in the cabal.

He looked at Scott. "If you'll permit me the liberty, General, what do you plan to do upon your retirement?"

Scott smiled. "First, of course, I shall pay a visit to Senator Jackson. It's time, I think, for he and I to end that old feud between us stemming from the Florida campaign. Second, I shall pay a visit upon John Quincy Adams to tender my respects. He's a man I both like and admire. Thereafter . . ."

The smiled widened considerably. "I believe I shall try my hand at journalism. That William Cullen Bryant fellow has expressed an interest in continuing his reportage on the situation in the Confederacy. But he told me—I happened to run into him just the other day—that he could benefit from the advice of a military expert. And apparently several editors at several of the nation's major journals have indicated a willingness to pay for it. Quite well, in fact."

Taylor looked at Brown. The army's commanding general shrugged. Most of the motion was in the left shoulder. The right barely moved at all. "My health really is very poor, Colonel. My doctors have been urging me for some time to relinquish the strains of military command. So I'll simply return to private life in Brownville and resume my business affairs. Which I need to do, in any event, since I have some major debts I need to retire."

He cleared his throat. "Of course, I retain certain connections in New York politics."

Now Taylor looked at Jesup.

"I shall give you whatever support I can, Zack," the quartermaster general stated firmly. "Rest assured of it."

Much as it went against his cautious temperament, Zachary felt he had to say the heart of the thing out loud. "If I understand you correctly, General Brown, you fear that the coming war is likely to damage the U.S. Army."

"Half wreck it, say better," hissed Winfield Scott. "God damn Henry Clay."

"And you want me to do what I can to salvage something from the disaster."

"It really is too bad you can't promote him to brigadier, Jacob," mused Jesup.

"In essence, yes," said Brown. "I realize it won't be easy, Zachary. But if you can give us a good campaign in the north, I think"—he glanced around the room—"and we all think, that the damage can be repaired when the time comes."

"Ah, General . . . Generals." Zack shook his head. "There is no way—not if I were Napoleon or Alexander the Great—that I could defeat the Confederacy with a northern campaign unless it were properly mounted, equipped, and supplied, with enough men. None of which is going to be true." He gave Jesup a quick apologetic glance. "Well, perhaps the supplies and equipment will be adequate."

"They won't even be that," Jesup growled. "But I'll give you whatever I can."

Brown started to say something, but Scott waved him down. "It's time for you to keep quiet, Jacob. Private citizen and behind-the-scenes politician, remember? Let me state what needs to be stated openly."

Brown nodded and slumped back in his seat, rubbing his right arm. The general seemed very fatigued now.

"Here's the truth, Colonel Zachary Taylor," said Winfield Scott, looking at him directly. "Who cares if you beat the Confederacy? We have no legitimate quarrel with them in the first place. Jackson's right. This war, if it comes—which now seems well-nigh certain—will be nothing but 'Henry Clay's War.' A war launched by an unprincipled schemer and demagogue to satisfy his own personal ambitions; a war which, in terms of its goal and purpose, is nothing more sublime than John Calhoun's rabid determination to prove to the country that a nigger is a nigger and fit only to be a slave."

For a moment he looked as if he might spit on the floor. "Just fight us a good, clean, hard, and honest fight, Zack. That's all. Best you can. So at least the real army will have something else to point to when Clay's expedition comes to its catastrophe at Syracuse."

Taylor frowned. There was no "Syracuse" in Arkansas.

Brown snorted. "Winfield, *will* you please stop showing

off your classical education?" To Taylor, he said, "It's a reference to the disaster the Athenians suffered in the Peloponnesian War when they followed the advice of Alcibiades and invaded Sicily."

"Oh."

Later that day, after he returned from the War Department, a message was delivered to Zack at his lodgings. From Thomas Hart Benton, inviting him to dinner at the Washington home of the senator from Missouri.

Taylor had never had more than the most casual encounters with Benton, but the senator greeted him as if they were old friends. Which was perhaps not that surprising, since, just before dinner began . . .

Andrew Jackson arrived. Ushered in through the rear entrance—to avoid being spotted, Zack assumed—but otherwise treated by Benton as if he were a long-lost brother.

The only term Zack could think of was "bizarre." To the best of his knowledge, the last time Andrew Jackson and Thomas Hart Benton had met in person was on the front porch—later spilling into the lobby—of the City Hotel in Nashville. Being as it was one of the more legendary affrays of the frontier, Zack even knew the details. That encounter had begun with Jackson threatening Benton with a pistol, then being shot in the shoulder by Benton's brother Jesse, then exchanging shots—all of which missed—with Benton himself, who, for his part, was then assailed by Jackson's friend John Coffee, whose first shot missed and whose subsequent attempt at pistol whipping Benton was thwarted by the now-senator's fall down a flight of stairs in the hotel.

Meanwhile, Jackson's nephew Stockley Hays had wrestled Jesse Benton to the floor of the hotel, stabbing him repeatedly in the arm with a knife. Fortunately for Hays, when Jesse shot him at point-blank range with his second pistol, the gun misfired.

Half raw violence, half comic opera. And here they were, twelve years later, the two principals in the brawl—acting as if nothing untoward had ever happened between them!

Zack would have ascribed the weird situation to the old saw about politics making strange bedfellows, but . . .

Politically speaking, they weren't strange bedfellows at

all. The feud between Andrew Jackson and Thomas Hart
Benton had always been purely personal, stemming from
Benton's anger at Jackson's behavior when the general—as
he then was—had served as William Carroll's second in Carroll's previous duel with Jesse Benton. There had never actually been any serious political quarrels among any of the
men involved. Twelve years later, Jackson was a Tennessee
senator, Carroll was the governor of the state, Benton was a
Missouri senator—and all three of them detested Henry
Clay.

So, Zack wasn't surprised when, after dinner, the whiskey
bottle was opened and talk immediately turned to his forthcoming assignment.

Which Jackson and Benton both knew about—in considerable detail—not more than eight hours after Taylor himself had first been informed.

Wide-ranging conspiracy, indeed. He almost felt sorry for
Henry Clay.

"I'll see to it you get the Missouri militia put under your
command, Zack," said Benton.

Taylor tried to stifle a wince but, obviously, was not entirely successful.

Jackson laughed. "The colonel's got no use for any blasted
volunteers, Tom! Can't say I blame him much. Until they'd
been tested and horsewhipped, no militia I ever seen—not
even Tennessee's—was worth the contents of a spittoon."

"I've not had any great success with militia units in the
field," Taylor admitted cautiously.

But Benton just grinned. "Who does? Yeah, sure, it's
proper Republican doctrine, and we all swear by it." He
waved his half-empty whiskey glass at Jackson. "Him, too,
you betchum. But nobody with any sense wants to fight a
real war with anything except regulars. Still and all—"

He slurped some more whiskey. "The main thing is that I
figure if you're in charge of the militia, you can at least keep
them out of mischief. Use 'em to garrison your supply de-
pots, whatever. Otherwise—sure as sunrise if Harrison's in
charge—they'll be sent down to Arkansas."

When he set down the whiskey glass, his good cheer
seemed to have vanished. "Here's the thing, Zack," the Missouri senator said quietly. "When all the dust settles, I figure

Missouri will still have Arkansas to deal with on our southern border. And I'd just as soon the war didn't leave the kind
of memories behind that winds up with ten or twenty years
of border raids, ambushes, and massacres of isolated settlements afterward. You understand what I mean?"

Taylor eyed him a bit warily. "Missouri's a slave state,
Senator."

"I told you. Call me Tom."

"Tom. No matter what I do, there'll still be the problem of
runaway slaves."

Benton sneered. Jackson was more pungent.

"Fuck that," he said forcibly. "That's just a problem—and
it ain't that big a problem anyway. Problems can be negotiated. Put me and Patrick Driscol across from each other at a
table, and within a day we'll have a solution for it that won't
please anybody much but everybody can live with."

Zack shifted his skeptical gaze to Jackson. "I feel obliged
to remind you, Sena—ah, Andy—that John Calhoun
wouldn't agree with you. Neither would most big plantation
owners in the South."

"That's because John Calhoun is a stinking liar and a man
with a cesspool for a soul, and most slave-owners have the
brains of rabbits." The Tennessee senator half slammed his
glass back onto the table next to him. Fortunately, it was
empty by now.

"I'm one of the biggest slave-owners in Tennessee, Zack.
So is Dick Johnson. You want to know why neither one of us
is hollering and yelling about it? Because the plain and simple truth—any slave-owner knows this, if he's willing to be
honest about it—is that the only slaves that run away from a
master who treats his slaves properly are the ones who are
troublemakers anyway. Good riddance, frankly. If I catch
one of my slaves running away—sure, it happens, from time
to time—the first thing I do is have him whipped. On general
principles. But the second thing I do—always—is sell him,
because I don't want him around. And if he makes his escape to Arkansas, I just shrug it off. Let Driscol deal with the
shiftless bastard if he can."

Taylor's family were major slave-owners in Kentucky.
And . . .

Well, Jackson was right. If a plantation was managed

properly, with the slaves decently housed and fed and the overseers kept on a short leash, most slaves didn't run away. And the ones who did, sure enough, were usually a problem in any case.

Still . . .

"Calhoun's not likely to agree with that, Andy, no matter what the evidence."

Jackson's glare was a genuine marvel to behold. Given that it wasn't aimed at Zack, at least. He'd hate to be on the receiving end of the thing.

"I told you," Jackson snarled. "Calhoun's a heathen; I don't care how many times he goes to church and invokes the name of the Almighty. Calhoun doesn't care about runaway slaves any more than I do. What he *does* care about is his pagan notion that slavery is a positive good. Which it ain't, as any man with any sense can plainly see. It's an economic necessity for the republic, that's all it is. So we keep it."

He held out his glass to Benton for a refill. "Who knows?" Jackson continued, after taking a sip. "Maybe Sam Houston's right, and maybe someday we'll give it up finally. But in the meantime we've got it— and Calhoun is bound and determined to lock slavery in forever. And *that's* why he's demanding a war. If a bunch of niggers out there in Arkansas can build a country of their own—whipping white men in the bargain, in a fair fight—then what happens to his heathen idolatry?"

Taylor hesitated. Jackson was being very friendly, but . . .

Mentally, he shrugged. This was another thing that just had to be said out loud. "I feel a need to point out to you, Andy, that if negroes can build a reasonable country of their own—and defend it—then. . . ."

But Jackson simply grinned. "Yeah, sure. Then what happens to *my* point of view?" He waved the glass about. "Or Tom's. Or yours, for that matter."

Cheerful as could be, the Tennessee senator took another sip from his whiskey. "I'm not worried about it, though, because I think you got a better chance—lot better chance—of filling an inside straight than seeing negroes build a country that's worth anything. Doesn't mean they can't defend it, mind you. Give 'em good leadership, and they make plenty

good soldiers. They proved that in New Orleans, and they're
proving it again now. But all the rest? A stable republic,
prosperity, learning, and education? No, I don't think so."

He gave Zack a disconcertingly direct stare. "From the
way you're fidgeting a little, I take it you don't agree?"

Zachary had been nursing his own whiskey, too nervous in
such company to be relaxed enough to match Jackson's and
Benton's pace. Now he shrugged, and downed his glass in
one gulp.

"To be honest, Andy, I don't know. A few months ago, I'd
have agreed with you without even thinking about it. But
I've been to Arkansas myself recently. And . . . I just don't
know anymore. Some of those black people are right impressive. And that's just the way it is."

Jackson didn't argue the matter. Instead, he maintained
that calm, level, blue-eyed stare while he finished his
whiskey. Not by downing it, just with a steady even sip.

When he was done, he set down the glass and grinned
again.

"Well, maybe that's true. If it is, though, we're in trouble.
First, because we'll have to listen to Sam Houston crowing
'I told you so' till we're ready to strangle him. What's worse
is that all three of us—me for sure—are likely to have some
fast talking to do in the afterlife."

So, what had been perhaps the most peculiar day in
Zachary Taylor's life ended with a laugh. And he was able to
tell himself, as he half staggered his way back to his lodgings, that at least he'd joined a cabal that drank whiskey instead of wine. Even John Quincy Adams, apparently, these
days. And wasn't that another marvel?

CHAPTER 27

It took Sam and his little party a month to reach Pennsylvania. That was at least a week later than he'd planned on when they'd left the nation's capital. The delay had been partly due to a stretch of rough weather in early December that caused him to stay over in Hagerstown for a few days. Little Andy had been handling the rigors of the journey quite well, but they were now into winter, and Sam didn't want to expose him to severe conditions.

Much of the delay, however, had been due to something quite unexpected.

Crowds. Small ones, true, in the smaller towns, and smaller still in the hamlets. But in every city or town or hamlet that Sam and his party passed through, crowds came out to greet them.

Crowds, not mobs. There might have been someone in those masses of people who disliked Sam Houston, but if so they were quite wisely keeping their mouths shut. The mood and temper of the crowds was adulatory toward Houston—and Andrew Jackson—and just about as hostile toward Henry Clay as people could get short of loading firearms.

Sam had begun his journey by taking the National Road, which started in Baltimore and had now been completed through most of Ohio. So, he'd traveled through most of Maryland on his way. At the last moment, Lafayette had decided to accompany him for the Maryland stretch. The presence of the Marquis meant that the crowds were especially large, and it had been difficult to gauge their sentiment. Obviously, Lafayette himself was the focus of much of the interest, more than Houston, although the two were now so closely tied in the popular mind that it was hard to separate one from the other.

Very closely tied, indeed. Henry Clay's political camp had a lot of influence and connections with moneyed interests, but it was weak when it came to controlling or influencing the newspapers. Most of the nation's press had been either pro-Jackson or pro-Adams. Now that the two men had made a political alliance, a veritable torrent of anti-Clay material was pouring out of the printing presses everywhere in the country except the Deep South. And most of them had made sure to quote Lafayette's toast to Sam and the New World.

But if the presence of the Marquis accounted for most of the crowds in Maryland, once Sam entered Pennsylvania at Uniontown, that factor vanished. Everything now became very clear.

The former governor of Pennsylvania, Joseph Hiester, was there to greet him, as was his successor, John Shulze, who'd just been elected. They were quite a pair. Both of them spoke English with a heavy German accent, being members of the state's large German community—which was often called Pennsylvania Dutch but mostly consisted of immigrants from the Palatinate in southwest Germany.

The former governor, Hiester, was a generation older than his successor and had retired after one term of office. Like Andy Jackson and Lafayette, he'd fought in the Revolution. The new governor, Shulze, was part of the extended Muhlenberg clan that was a long-standing powerhouse in Pennsylvania politics, partly because of their close ties to the Hiester family. Governor Shulze's grandfather, the Reverend Muhlenberg, had been the founder of the Lutheran Church in America.

In short, official Pennsylvania—and, in particular, the central political figures of the state's large German immigrant population—had turned out to greet Sam Houston. Who was himself emigrating to Arkansas on the eve of a likely war with the United States.

Pennsylvania was now solid Jackson country, and the state's heretofore muted hostility to slavery had risen to the surface. In one of those ironies of history that Sam had become acutely aware of in his years as the country's Indian commissioner, Henry Clay's cynical and opportunist pandering to John Calhoun's political attitudes had given the South Carolina senator's extremist slavery program far more weight in the nation's political life than it would have had otherwise. It had also, willy-nilly, transformed Andrew Jackson—a man who was himself a major slave-owner—into the nation's principal spokesman against any deepening extension of the institution.

Less than a year ago, only a small number of hard-core New England abolitionists had referred to the "slave power" as a menace to American freedom and liberty. Today, the phrase spilled trippingly off the tongues of Pennsylvania's current and former governors—and if the phrase was spoken with an accent, so what? German immigrants were rarely slave-owners, and they had their own long and bitter memories of the oppressions of the high and mighty. There was nothing these two governors were saying, in their fulsome speeches to the crowd at Uniontown, that Pennsylvanians weren't saying in the privacy of their own homes.

The massacre at Arkansas Post wasn't the issue any longer. Not to anybody, really, not even in the Deep South. In the way these things can happen in a nation's political life, Arkansas Post had become the catalyst for crystallizing antagonisms within the United States that had been lying under the surface for a long time. Dormant, for the most part—until Henry Clay forced the issue. Ironically, the man who liked to be thought of as a great compromiser.

Which, indeed, he was. The problem was that this time, Clay was greatly compromising the nation's political stability in order to further his own personal ambition. He made Sam think of a captain at sea who, not knowing how to navigate, simply ran before the wind. Hoping, presumably, that the sheer swell of the waves would carry him over any unseen reefs ahead.

The icing on the cake came the following morning as Sam was leaving Uniontown. A small group of young men came up to him and very solemnly presented him with a handmade banner.

"A pledge," said the youngster who seemed to be the leader of the group. He had not a trace of a German accent, which wasn't surprising. The German immigrant communities were concentrated in the eastern and central parts of Pennsylvania. This far west, the population was more likely to be of Anglo-Saxon or Scots-Irish stock.

Sam spread out the banner as best he could while sitting on a horse. It was the familiar Pennsylvania state flag, more square than rectangular, with the state coat of arms flanked by two rearing horses on a blue field. But the usual slogan under the coat of arms—*Virtue, Liberty, and Independence*—had been removed. In its place, someone had laboriously stitched a writhing serpent beneath the horses' hooves, which bore the label "the slave power."

At least, Sam was pretty sure the effect being aimed for was "writhing." An uncharitable soul might have used other terms, such as "lumpy" or "misshapen" or even "looks more like a worm than any snake I ever seen."

"Splendid," he pronounced. He started to hand it back, but the youngster shook his head.

"No, sir. That one's for you. We're having more made up, in case."

Sam hesitated. He wasn't entirely sure he wanted to know . . .

"In case of what?" he asked.

The youngster—he couldn't have been more than eighteen, like all of them in the group—gave Sam a puzzled expression. "Well, in case the traitor Henry Clay gets to start his war. What else?"

Eagerly, he pointed to the space just below the serpent. "There's still room there, we made sure. So we can add 'Pennsylvania Lafayette Battalion.'"

"'Battalion Number One,'" another of the little group proclaimed. "No way we're gonna let those upstarts in Harrisburg claim it. They can be Number Two."

Sam had a weird sense of dizziness for a moment. Not a physical one, simply . . .

More like a man might feel who contemplates what a barrel might feel if the men handling it lost their grip and it began to career out of control.

Which was altogether a crazy notion, in the first place.

"Ah, fellows . . . The only way Henry Clay can start a war is if he's president of the United States. In which case—"

He cleared his throat. "You might want to reconsider taking up arms against it."

Now all of them were giving him that puzzled expression.

"That's what you're doing, isn't it?" asked the same youngster who'd laid such proud claim to Battalion Number One.

"Well . . . yeah. But."

But what? he had to ask himself. He realized now, for the first time, that the rage and grief he'd been consumed with for the past nine weeks had half blinded him. His own motivations—conscious ones, anyway—had been so emotionally rooted that he simply hadn't considered how other people might react to the same events.

The traitor Henry Clay.

This wasn't the first time he'd heard people use that expression. Often mixed in with "the slave power"—and almost always with "woman killers."

Nobody, including Sam himself, thought that Clay had any direct connection to Maria Hester's death. For that matter, nobody thought she'd even been the assassin's intended victim in the first place. He'd murdered her quite by accident while trying to kill her husband.

But that simply didn't make any difference to a lot of people. Henry Clay had stirred up the lurking reptile, hadn't he? The fact that the murdered woman had been the daughter of the nation's president was, in many ways, more important than the fact that she'd also been Sam's wife. These were people—traitors—who would stop at nothing, who would commit any crime to force their slavery onto the nation.

None of this might have been entirely rational. But there was an inexorable logic to it once you went deeper into the nation's soul. There were, and always had been, two different conceptions of the "United States" abroad in the land. Often enough, residing within the same person—Andrew Jackson himself being a case in point, as was James Monroe. As had been, before them, George Washington and Thomas Jefferson.

Now, perhaps long before it might have been otherwise, Henry Clay was driving that underlying contradiction right to the surface. Arkansas Post had been the catalyst. Not because it had to have been, but because Clay and Calhoun had made it so.

The facts themselves were obvious to everyone, and not in dispute. Arkansas had been attacked and had defended itself. Perhaps with much greater harshness than was warranted—although not many people in the North and the border states would even agree with that any longer, since William Cullen Bryant's gruesome depictions of the atrocities committed by Crittenden's army had become widely spread.

Still, there was no real dispute over the legalities involved. All the more, since Arkansas was an independent sovereign nation to begin with, established by treaty with the United States.

So, what was the problem? The only answer Clay could give—pandering to Calhoun to get the votes he needed in the House of Representatives—was that the law be damned. The real issue was slavery itself. More precisely, Calhoun's dissatisfaction with the institution's current state of semi-disrepute and his determination to foist his extremist version of it upon the whole United States. From John Calhoun's point of view, and that of the people who followed him, what was really at stake was the intolerable notion that black people could have *any* rights at all, even if they were not slaves.

Most of the nation was simply choking on that. Black people might be inferior to white people—most definitely were, in the opinion of all but a handful—but that didn't make them animals. Women were inferior to men, also, when you got right down to it. Certainly children were. Like freedmen, they weren't allowed to vote. Like freedmen, their ability to exercise control over their finances was tightly circumscribed, as was their control over property in general. Like freedmen, their status in life was and would always remain—in the case of women, at least, if not male children—lesser than that of men.

Did that mean they had no rights *at all?* Could a man choose to murder his wife with impunity? If he couldn't—which he certainly couldn't, not even in South Carolina or Georgia—then why could the same be done to black people?

The nation's single most popular political figure, Andrew Jackson, had done more than choke on the notion. He'd spat it right out and ground it under his heel, calling it a vile abomination to the principles of the republic. Whereupon the political figure who was the nation's most respected—if not much liked outside of New England—had done the same.

Andrew Jackson owned more slaves than all but a tiny number of Southerners, and John Quincy Adams had probably read more books than anyone in the whole country. Could *both* of them be wrong on the subject?

Outside of the seven slave states of the Deep South, and with Virginia and the border states teetering back and forth, a national consensus was beginning to emerge.

No.

And if Henry Clay thought he could shove it down the nation's throat simply by maneuvering in the House of Representatives to get himself made president . . .

Made, not elected. By now the results of the national election were known to everyone in the country. Clay hadn't gotten but one vote in six.

Then to Sam Hill with Henry Clay. Was a whole nation—the majority of its population and its constituent states—to be labeled traitor by an American Alcibiades? Or was the term properly laid at his own feet?

That's what Sam thought, anyway, sitting on a horse in Uniontown at the onset of winter and looking down at a blue banner. And it occurred to him that this was the first thing he could probably call *thought* at all since he'd seen the life fading out of his wife's eyes.

"Sam," she'd kept whispering until the end, looking up at him more in confusion than in pain. What made the agony complete—still did—was the trust that had also never left her eyes. Maria Hester had been just as certain that her husband would make it right as he'd been certain, from several battlefields, that there was no way in God's earth he could possibly keep her from bleeding to death from that wound.

There'd been nothing in him but guilt, rage, and grief since that moment. Until now.

"I'll keep it then," he said abruptly, folding up the banner. Rolling it, more like. Folding, properly speaking, was an awkward business while one was sitting in a saddle.

But soon enough it was done, and the banner stuffed into his saddlebag. He leaned over, extended his hand, and shook those of all eight of the youngsters.

"I'll look for you in the summer," he said firmly. "If the
traitor starts his war."

"We won't fail you, sir!" exclaimed one of them.

Sam shook his head. "Got nothing to do with me. Just
make sure you don't fail your state and your country."

He rode out of Uniontown to the same chant he'd ridden
out of every town before it since Baltimore. *To the New
World!*

Louisville, Kentucky
JANUARY 14, 1825

He'd spent the time he could, after Uniontown, chewing on
his thoughts. He couldn't do more than that, between the rigors of the winter journey and the need to care for his young
son. Chester was a help, of course; even more, Andy's
nursemaid Dinah and her teenaged daughter Sukey. But
there was still plenty to keep Sam occupied.

In Louisville, though, they'd have at least a week's lay-
over. It would be best to forgo overland travel and take a
steamboat the rest of the way to Arkansas, since it would be
much safer for Andy. The Ohio and the Mississippi were
navigable in winter by a captain who knew his business, but
the same captain would wait for the best possible weather,
also.

Louisville was hospitable, fortunately. Sam hadn't been
entirely sure it would be. Kentucky was a border state—and
the same state that had produced Richard Mentor Johnson as
a senator and Henry Clay as the Speaker of the House.

But, in the end, the state seemed to be swinging the same
way as its newly elected governor, Joseph Desha, and the
Relief Party for which he was a champion. Whatever private
thoughts they might have about the issue of slavery, or the
ins and outs of Arkansas Post, their overriding concern was
the still deep distress of the state's poorer citizens since the
Panic of 1819. Much of the nation might be coming to the
conclusion that Henry Clay was a minion of Sam Hill, but
Kentucky's Relief Party had come to the conclusion several
years earlier that the principal lawyer for the Second Bank
of the United States was no "minion" at all. At the very least,
he was one of Sam Hill's chief demons. If not the creature

himself, which some of the Relief Party's more vocal partisans thought quite likely.

Desha hadn't been sworn into office yet. But it hardly mattered, since the man he was replacing in the governor's office, John Adair, was also a leader of the Relief Party. Like Pennsylvania's former governor Hiester, he'd fought in the Revolution and, years later, had been in command of the Kentuckian forces under Andy Jackson in the New Orleans campaign.

The state capital of Frankfort being nearby, both men came up to visit Sam after learning of his arrival. Theirs was more in the way of a private visit to pay their respects than the sort of public spectacle staged by Hiester and Shulze in Uniontown. Kentucky was a slave state, after all. But they made no attempt to disguise their arrival, either, and the visit itself was most cordial.

Sam remembered Adair, of course, since both of them had fought the British at New Orleans.

Well, Sam had fought them, at any rate. Adair had never had to, beyond the clashes of the first days. The reason he'd never had to was that Sam—along with Patrick Driscol's Iron Battalion, made up almost entirely of black freedmen—had met the British regiments who launched the opening assault on the west bank of the Mississippi. Opening and only assault, because their defeat had been so crushing and complete that General Pakenham had wisely chosen to withdraw from the field at Chalmette rather than launch the assault Adair and his men had been braced for.

So, there was that, too. Now that his brain was starting to work naturally again, Sam was gauging the fact—quite significant, he thought—that most of the men in the United States with real command experience in combat did not share the blithe assumption of Clay and Calhoun that any war with Arkansas would be a trifle. The only outstanding exception that Sam knew about, in fact, was William Henry Harrison—and for that, there was the usual culprit to blame.

Ambition. It didn't matter what Harrison really thought. Like Clay himself, that would be subordinated to his personal goals. Which might make sense, looked at from a narrow and immediate perspective, but which, in the longer run, struck Sam as nothing less than a form of insanity.

"Nice to see you again, General," he said, exchanging a handshake with Adair. "Some whiskey?"

"And you as well, Colonel. Yes, please."

Chester had the drinks poured within seconds. Once the glasses were in everyone's hands, the serious dickering began. That was mostly with Desha, naturally. Adair was essentially there as a wise old man giving advice to his successor.

"—not like to see Kentuckians on the wrong side of the Iron Battalion's bayonets, Joseph; even more, their six-pounders—"

Being the gist of it. Wise old man, indeed.

By the time they left, Sam had the private agreement he wanted. There'd be no Kentucky militia forces sent against Arkansas in the event *that man*—they might as well have said "traitor" and be done with it—chose to start a war.

He was pleased. Granted, the Kentucky militia wasn't as good as Tennessee's. But it was probably the second best state militia in the country.

"You want the rest of your drink, Mr. Sam?" Chester asked after the two governors had gone. He held up the glass, which was still mostly full.

"No. Just pour it out. No, that'd be a silly waste. Finish it yourself, Chester."

"I don't drink, Mr. Sam. You know that."

A bit surprised—he'd been half lost in thought—Sam stared at him for a moment.

"Oh, that's right. Sorry, I forgot. Give it to Dinah, then."

"She don't—"

Sam threw up his hands. "I'm surrounded by temperance fanatics! Fine. Give it to the dog. Any dog you can find. Tarnation, it's good whiskey."

Chester looked dubious. Sam snorted.

"They're *Kentucky* dogs hereabouts, Chester. Of course they'll drink whiskey."

"Well. That's true."

After he was gone, Sam checked the time. It'd still be hours before Dinah and Sukey would want his help with little Andy.

Time enough to start. He went over to the writing desk in

the hotel room—he'd made sure it had one, when he arrived—and took a seat. Then, settling down with paper and pen, he began working on his first letters to Andrew Jackson and John Quincy Adams.

He'd get his revenge for Maria Hester, sure enough. But it had also finally dawned on him that his father-in-law's advice, unheeded at the time, was undoubtedly correct. It was just as much a form of insanity for a man like himself to seek a different man's form of vengeance as it was for Henry Clay to think he could lead a nation into a war by posturing like Achilles.

Sam knew how to use a gun—cannons, too, and quite well—and would again if he needed to. But there were other weapons he'd learned how to use in the years since New Orleans. If the pen was not mightier than the sword on a battle-field, it was much the mightier weapon on other fronts.

A different man might be satisfied by inflicting as much harm as he possibly could on the likes of Henry Clay and John Calhoun. For which purpose, guns would do nicely.

What a trifling ambition.

Sam scrawled the date at the top of the sheet: January 14, 1825.

Ten years, almost to the day, since he and Patrick Driscol had won the Battle of the Mississippi. He'd been twenty-one years old, then. Now he was thirty-one, and already a widower.

Still, he was a young man. With most of a lifetime left to devote to the conscious and deadly purpose of utterly destroying Henry Clay, John C. Calhoun, all other men like them, and everything they stood for.

He wasn't at all sure that he could, of course. But he was positive and certain he could give it a mighty run. Mighty enough that when the time came, in the afterlife, that he saw two trusting eyes again, he wouldn't have to look away with a husband's shame.

CHAPTER 28

Henry Clay was elected president of the United States on the first ballot in the House of Representatives. By the rules established in the Constitution, each state got one vote, determined by the majority of its delegation. Thirteen votes were thus needed for Clay to be elected president, since the nation had twenty-four states.

That's exactly what he got. Thirteen votes.

The solid core came from the seven states of the Deep South, delivered by Calhoun's people and those of Crawford's who were not breaking away with Van Buren and the New Yorkers:

Alabama
Florida
Georgia
Louisiana
Mississippi
North Carolina
South Carolina

He also picked up Virginia, although it was a much closer call than he and his associates had expected.

On the one hand, the state was politically dominated by the same class of slave-owners who ruled the roost in the Deep South. In fact, Virginia had historically led the South in the direction of ever harsher laws regarding slavery as an

institution and black people as a race. In 1785, it had been
the first state to officially declare any person with "black
blood" to be a mulatto and to legally define mulattos as Negroes. In 1799, it had banished white mothers of mulattos
with their children. In 1806, it had required slaves to leave
the state within a year of manumission. And, finally, in
1819, Virginia had been the first—and was still the only—
state in the union that outlawed blacks and mulattos, whether
free or slave, from meeting for the purposes of education. It
also forbade anyone, including whites, from teaching black
people to read and write.

On the other hand . . .

The Old Dominion's elite took great pride in its political
history and saw Virginia as the nation's preeminent state.
And why should they not? Four of five presidents of the
United States had been Virginians—and all of them had
served two terms, unlike the one-term tenure of the sole out-
sider, John Adams. The Old Dominion had produced a sim-
ilarly disproportionate number of the country's political
leaders in Congress and the judicial branch.

So, even with their class interests inclining them toward
following Clay, their well-honed political instincts were
shrieking alarm bells. The manner in which Clay was taking
the office—and no other term than "taking" could really be
used—was far outside the parameters of what many of Virginia's congressmen could easily swallow.

But eventually, enough of them did. The quirky and un-
predictable John Randolph perhaps swung the matter when
he abruptly decided—following a train of logic that was
semi-incomprehensible but, as usual, brilliantly expounded
on the floor of Congress—that electing Henry Clay was essential to the preservation of slavery, an institution that he
personally viewed with dubiety but whose stalwart defense
was necessary to prevent the ever-growing encroachment of
federal dictatorship upon the liberties of the states.

"In a phrase," John Quincy Adams caustically remarked
afterward, "John Randolph felt it necessary to install a tyrant
in order to forestall tyranny."

What made Randolph's actions particularly bizarre was
that he detested Clay personally. When they met in a corri-

dor of the Capitol shortly after the vote, Randolph stood his
ground and hissed at the newly elected president, "I never
sidestep skunks."

Clay smiled. "I always do," he replied, and deftly skirted
him.

The border states split. Tennessee and Kentucky voted for
Jackson; Missouri and Maryland, for Clay. No surprise
there.

Granted, a different sort of politician might have been embarrassed by the fact that his own home state had voted for
another candidate. But Clay was above such picayune concerns. As well he might be, having managed the notable feat
of getting elected as the nation's chief executive with five
out of six voters opposed to him.

He did lose New York, which caused a momentary panic
among his advisers. At the last minute, Martin Van Buren
broke publicly with Crawford and Clay and threw his support to Jackson. Van Buren himself was a senator, not a congressman, so his own vote was irrelevant. But they didn't
call him the Little Magician for nothing. Van Buren had created the nation's first really well-oiled political machine in
New York, and the machine delivered.

The decision came from the West. Ohio, Illinois, and Indiana
all voted for Clay.

Ohio's vote was expected by everyone and really had little
to do with the ruckus over Arkansas Post. Ohio had long
been "Clay country" because it was the state that felt it had
the most to gain from the newly elected president's American System.

So, in the end, Illinois and Indiana were the key—and
their votes were purely the product of panic over Arkansas
Post. Both states were new—Indiana had been admitted to
the union in 1816; Illinois in 1818—and both bordered on
"wild Injun country."

Most of all, both were sparsely settled, which made them
feel vulnerable to the nebulous danger of being suddenly
overrun by hordes of murdering Negroes surging out of
Arkansas. The fact that Arkansas was hundreds of miles

away and no sane man could think of any conceivable way the Confederacy would or could attack Illinois or Indiana without stumbling over Tennessee and Kentucky—with their large populations and the nation's two most powerful and best-organized militias—was neither here nor there. By that point, Clay's partisans had pulled out all the stops and were fanning every spark of fear they could find into a blaze of terror.

So, there it was. In the nation as a whole, in the presidential election of 1824, about 360,000 popular votes were cast. Of that total, the decision was made by the delegations representing 16,000 voters in Indiana and fewer than 5,000 in Illinois—and, in both states, by narrow margins.

"In the history of the world," Andrew Jackson would thunder the next day, "was ever a greater mockery made of the phrase 'decision of the people'?"

Needless to say, the question was not rhetorical. Old Hickory proceeded to answer it at length many times thereafter. To the end of their days, the mildest term anyone could remember him using to refer to Clay and his minions was "the rascals."

John Quincy Adams was more restrained. But the capital's political observers noted that he immediately announced his intention to run for Congress from Massachusetts.

The House, not the Senate, interestingly enough. Given that a Senate seat would also be available in 1826, and that the Senate was generally considered a more prestigious body, Adams's choice seemed odd.

But perhaps not so odd, in the opinion of the more astute of those observers. True enough, a "senator" was a more august personage than a mere "congressman." But those terms were abstractions. The concrete reality remained that no senator—indeed, no person in the country save the president himself—potentially wielded more power and influence than the Speaker of the House of Representatives.

True, the thought of John Quincy Adams serving in the same post that Henry Clay had transformed into such a political powerhouse was extraordinarily peculiar. Clay was the nation's most adroit and adept politician, as everyone including his bitterest enemies would agree; Adams, its most awkward and inept.

But perhaps that was what Adams was basing his calculations upon. After two years of Henry Clay in the White House, perhaps by 1826 the nation would welcome a Speaker—freshman though he might be—who was everything Henry Clay was not. Stubborn on matters of principle where Clay was lizard-quick, thoughtful and deeply read where Clay was clever and facile, and if not as gracious in his manners, more than his equal in intelligence.

A week after the election, the announcement was made that William Crawford would be Clay's nominee for the nation's next secretary of state; John Calhoun, for its next secretary of war.

That drew another round of thunder from Jackson. "So you see, the Judas of the South has closed the contract and will receive the thirty pieces of silver. His end will be the same. Was there ever witnessed such a bare-faced corruption in any country before?"

To no one's surprise, Crawford said nothing. The Georgia politician's physical ailment was now so widely known that everyone understood the appointment was a mere fig leaf. Crawford's partisans would be allowed to use the State Department to pass around perks, privileges, posts, and the like, but Clay himself would direct the nation's foreign affairs.

Calhoun, still only forty-two years old, was in his prime. But he also made no public response to Jackson's denunciations. Instead, he limited his riposte to an indirect one.

He immediately announced that he would be urging Congress to approve a rapid and major expansion of the nation's armed forces "to deal with the barbaric threat arisen on our western border." Then, with an implied sneer, wondered how such an expansion could possibly be opposed by prominent figures—he did not mention Jackson by name—who had long advocated the same measure.

That was a pointless tactic, given Old Hickory. Jackson's response came the next day:

"In times past, I advocated strengthening the nation's armed forces to fend off foreign murderers, arsonists, and robbers. Calhoun calls for its expansion for the sole purpose of murdering, burning, and robbing neighbors who have never attacked us at all. Judas, did I name him? If so, I insulted Judas."

The most astute of the capital's observers, however, ignored this predictable byplay. They were quite fascinated by something else.

John Quincy Adams was starting to profess—in public—a liking for whiskey. So long as it was the corn-based whiskey distilled out West, not the Eastern rye-based stuff. What some people were starting to call "bourbon."

Arkansas Post
FEBRUARY 9, 1825

Patrick Driscol and Robert Ross were at Arkansas Post when Sam's steamboat arrived. Not because they'd been awaiting him there, but because they'd been engaged in negotiations with Pushmataha and other major chiefs of the Choctaws.

The Choctaws, Sam discovered, had almost all crossed the Mississippi by now and had taken up residence in the Confederacy. They'd not had much choice in the matter. Whether they were signatories to the Treaty of Oothcaloga or not, in the aftermath of Arkansas Post—not to mention the retaliations the Choctaws had taken on local settlers for Crittenden's outrages—the states of Louisiana and Mississippi had mobilized their militias to drive them out. Alabama had eagerly sent its own militia in support. Not so much because they cared about the Choctaws but because it gave them an excuse to drive the last remaining Chickasaws out of northwestern Alabama.

The Chickasaws, in the end, had crossed the Mississippi also. Whether or not they were the most warlike tribe in the Southeast, as both they and several other tribes contended, they were simply too small to stand against that sort of concerted attack. There weren't more than five thousand Chickasaws in the whole world.

So, by the time Sam arrived, Arkansas Post appeared to be under siege again—only, this time, not by fifteen hundred freebooters but by more than ten times that number of Indians. Fortunately, it was a relatively peaceful sort of siege, being waged by wheedles, threats, demands, proposals, and offers of compromise rather than by guns and bayonets.

"Glad you're here," Patrick gruffed to him as he escorted Sam and his party off the boat. "Maybe you can talk sense into them."

"What's the problem? There should still be plenty of land left for them in the trans-Poteau area. Blast it, that's awkward. Have they settled on a name for it yet?"

Driscol grinned humorlessly. "Indians, remember? Contentious bastards are worse than the Irish when it comes to finding a point of dispute over any subject under the sun. The Cherokees—the ones following Ross and Ridge, anyway—had pretty well settled on 'New Kituhwa' and seemed to have bullied and sweet-talked most of the Creeks into it. But no sooner did Pushmataha and most of the Choctaws arrive than they denounced the name as an instrument of Cherokee oppression. They're arguing for 'Oklahoma,' on the grounds that since it means 'red people' it's fair to all the tribes, which 'Kituhwa' isn't. Ross seems inclined to concede the point to them, but Ridge is holding stubborn. His argument is that it may mean 'red people' in Choctaw, but it means no such thing in Cherokee."

His grin widened and even gained a bit of real humor. "The most delicious part of it—well, to a Scots-Irishman, anyway—is that I think they're all going to finally agree to adopt English as the official language of the whole Confederacy. Seeing as how there's no way any one of them will accept the language of any other instead. Ha! Damned Sassenach. Same dirty rotten trick they pulled on us."

A bit apprehensively, Sam looked up at the fort they were nearing. "They're *all* in there?"

"Every last chief of any note at all, from all four of the tribes. There's even somebody claiming to speak for the Seminoles, although nobody's paying much attention to him. Seeing as how most of the Seminoles—talk about stubborn—are still holed out somewhere in the Florida Everglades."

He gave Sam a sly glance. "Now that you're here, though, I figure you can exercise that famous silver tongue of yours and persuade all of them to move the whole ruckus upriver to New Antrim. At least we'd be able to reside in the Wolfe Tone Hotel instead of this place, which"—his blocky, ugly face got blockier and uglier than ever—"is *supposed* to be a fort, damnation."

Sam shook his head. "Patrick, big as it is, the Wolfe Tone's smaller than Arkansas Post."

An odd expression came to Driscol's face. Half embarrassment; half . . .

Pride?

"Not any longer. Been a lot of new construction since you were here. Tiana persuaded me to add another extension. A wing I'd call it, except, well, it's actually bigger than the rest of the hotel. We had to tear down two whole city blocks to make room for it."

Hurriedly: "The people living there got compensated, of course. Including the right to rooms in the new wing of the hotel, which—comes down to it—is in a lot better shape than the log cabins they'd been living in."

Sam peered down at him. "Laird of Arkansas, indeed. What's next, mighty one? Do you figure on claiming all land in the Delta as your personal domain? Yes, I know, you'll graciously allow the serfs to run their sheep on the land. The one or two you'll leave them with."

"That's not—!"

"Oh, I think it's quite funny. No sense of humor, Patrick; that's always been your problem. But that aside, why *did* you expand the hotel? I'll admit you're not actually greedy."

Driscol grunted. "Didn't have much choice. The new wing isn't really what you'd properly call a hotel. It's more like a giant dormitory." Defensively: "And I'm not charging anybody more than maintenance costs to stay there. Tiana agreed to that. Even browbeat her father when the plundering algerine tried to talk us into raising the rates."

Sam listed an eyebrow. "Something I don't know?"

"Guess so. Though you must have been blind as a bat not to have noticed, coming as you did all the way from Washington. Started in the summer, once everybody figured Clay would most likely win the election. The biggest wave of freedmen migrations since the very first days of Arkansas. I think we've gotten another fifteen thousand of them in the last three months. Another five thousand or so in the way of runaway slaves and maroons."

Now that he thought about it, Sam *had* noticed an unusual number of black people working their way down the Ohio and the Mississippi on flatboats. But he'd been so engrossed in his own ruminations—grief, too, still—that he hadn't paid it much attention.

Which he should have, he chided himself. Black people tended to shy away from traveling on flatboats down the rivers. Yes, it was an easier form of travel, but a much harder one from the standpoint of evading slave-catchers. There was also the danger of lynch mobs, passing by some towns.

Something must have showed on his face. Driscol's grin returned—but this was the troll's grin. The savage, pitiless one that fit Patrick's face to perfection when the mood took him. Sam's best friend or not, he really was a frightening sort of man.

"Oh, there's been no trouble. John Brown's doing, that is. Odd fellow, the tanner, no doubt about it. A man after my own heart, though. As a matter of religious principle, he refuses to join any army. But it seems his reading of the Bible allows him to raise what amounts to his *own* army. So, he did."

Sam's eyes widened.

"Oh, aye, lad! And not such a small one, neither. By now I figure he's got something like four hundred men—at least half of them white, mind you—serving under his . . . well, can't call them colors, really, since they don't have a banner. But they're his army, never doubt it. He doesn't call them anything but stalwart lads, but they've taken to calling themselves Brown's Raiders. For the past three months, they've been patrolling the rivers—in U.S. territory also. Everybody knows they're there—especially would-be slave-catchers—but since they don't wear uniforms . . ."

"Who in the name of—" Sam shook his head. "Who *are* they? I mean, I know the Brown clan breeds like rabbits, but there aren't *that* many of them."

"His own family's the core of it, still. But most of them are just boys from Ohio and, mostly, Pennsylvania. Some other Northern states. Abolitionists, I'd call them, except this new breed has little of the Quaker in them. Nothing at all, actually. Bloody-minded fellows."

"I didn't think there were that many abolitionists—outright ones, anyway—in the whole United States."

Driscol snorted. "Probably weren't, a year ago. But—"

He stopped abruptly. They were now not more than twenty feet from the bridge leading across the moat that surrounded the Post.

"It started changing rapidly after the battle here, Sam. Which has been my whole life's experience—and the reason I was utterly merciless in this place, be damned to what you or any other politician tells me. The old-style abolitionists were a handful, feeling sorry for the miserable negroes. Middle-aged, most of them, fat and prosperous. There are a lot more of the new-style ones—young men, overwhelmingly, and most of them from modest circumstances like John Brown himself—and they don't feel sorry for negroes at all. Why should they? The negroes showed—in battle, where it counts—that they could take care of themselves, thank you. So now it's just a matter of principle. People will petition to redress an injustice, Sam, but they'll *fight* for a principle. That's because injustice is a property of the weak and powerless, but principles belong to the strong."

Sam stared at him. He had a tendency to forget—and chided himself for it, once again—that beneath Driscol's craggy forehead lay a brain that, whatever it lacked in the way of formal education and wide reading, was as acute as any Sam had ever known.

Granted, it was a sergeant's brain, with a sergeant's harshly practical and ruthless way of gauging the world. But was that really such a handicap under these circumstances?

Driscol cleared his throat. "And then . . . Ah, lad, I am sorry for it. I truly am, and so's Tiana. But for whatever it might be worth, your wife's death may have saved a nation's life. We'll never know, but that's what I'm thinking."

He looked away, down the Arkansas. Not avoiding Sam's gaze so much as simply giving him some personal space. "It all changed again," he said quietly, "after Maria Hester's killing. There'll be no going back now, Sam. Not for the boys John Brown is gathering around him. No going back, no give, no surrender—and damn little in the way of mercy, unless Brown himself calls for it. I swear to you, I think they'd even frighten the old Hebrews. They can't possibly be any more Old Testament." He grinned again, very crookedly. "Even the Tennessee and Kentucky state militiamen are giving them a wide berth on the rivers, as long as they leave the settlements alone and only go after slave-catchers."

Sam didn't know what to say. As always—it hadn't lessened a bit, not even after almost three months—the thought of his wife dying just took his breath away. A man with a silver tongue, struck speechless.

When he was able to talk, he grasped at it. "You think so? About Maria Hester, I mean."

"Oh, aye." Driscol seemed to swallow. Hard to tell, of course, with a neck like his. "I—ah—should perhaps give fair warning. You know—ah—that rich black fellow in New York? The one from Haiti who's been sending so much money here."

"Pierre Toussaint."

"Yes, him. He's a devout Catholic, so most of the money he sends goes to support the Church here." For just a moment, the Scots-Irish Presbyterian surfaced. Patrick had been raised in that creed, even if he himself had long since become a freethinking deist. "Heathen lot, even if—well, I'll grant they do a lot of good work. Charitable stuff. But the point is, they're given to saints and icons and graven images and such."

Sam coughed. "Oh, come on, Patrick! Not even the Catholics—"

"Not on their own, probably. But Marie Laveau decided she was a Catholic two years ago, and she's been busy ever since importing as much of her voudou as she can into the Church." Again, the Presbyterian surfaced: "Which isn't hard, of course, being as the papists half-think like voudou anyway."

Sam couldn't help but chuckle. Which, thankfully, leached away some of the grief-surge.

Driscol chuckled with him. "Marie's got quite the following, too. Except for Tiana, she's probably the most influential woman in Arkansas. So . . . Well, look, here's the point. Don't get all worked up if you come to find out Maria Hester's . . . well, actually, they've already declared her a martyr of the Church."

"She wasn't Catholic!"

"Don't argue with *me* about it. Marie Laveau can explain it to you, if you can manage to follow the logic. Which I couldn't, after she got to the part about consulting—ah, never mind. The point is, they'll probably be making her a saint by next spring. They already have an image of her—a veritable icon—up on the wall of the big church in New Antrim. The priest squawked, but they made it stick."

"I thought only the pope—"

"Marie Laveau can explain that to you, also. It seems— this is *her* version, mind you, I doubt the pope in Rome would agree with her—that since it's obvious the Virgin Mary is equal to the Christ, it follows as night from day that saints can also be declared by the Women's Council."

"*What* 'Women's Council'?"

Patrick cleared his throat again. "Well, the one that she and Tiana set up. Tiana being a Cherokee, of course, the notion came naturally to her. Especially since Nancy Ward urged it on her, just before the ancient *ghighua* finally died last year. Marie Laveau thought it made perfect sense, too. Which isn't really that surprising, when you think about it. Slavery being what it is, black people mostly have a matrilineal society, too, in practice if not in theory."

That was true enough. But—

"The chiefdom of Arkansas now has a *Women's Council*? Run by Tiana and Marie Laveau? Good God in Heaven!"

"Yes, that's exactly what Major General Robert Ross said. When his wife Eliza got invited to join. Then he repeated the exclamation—twice; I heard him; I was there—when she accepted."

"Good God in Heaven!"

Driscol shrugged. "It's the nature of the soil in Arkansas. Very contagious terrain."

CHAPTER 29

"Thank God you're here!" John Ross said when he spotted Sam entering the fort's big mess hall, which had been set aside as an impromptu conference room.

The Cherokee leader pointed an accusing finger at Pushmataha. The principal chief of the Choctaws was ensconced on a chair in a corner, for all the world as if he were seated on a throne. "Explain to this madman that if he doesn't get his people moved across the Poteau into New Kitu—ah, blast it, Oklahoma—that they'll starve. As it is, it's going to be touch and go."

Sam studied Pushmataha. The old chief was famous all over the frontier for his canny ways, but all it took was one glance to know that he wasn't going to budge.

"They murdered and raped and robbed—Crittenden and his devils—all up and down the great river," the chief growled. His English was fluent, if heavily accented. "Then their militias did it again when they came at us afterward. We will not move from this place until we have our revenge. We will certainly not go to hide across the Poteau, leaving—"

Pushmataha choked off a term that was the Choctaw equivalent of "nigger." He took a slow, shaky, old man's breath. "Leaving the blacks to do all the fighting."

Sam decided to shift the matter into Choctaw—in which he was by now just as fluent, and had considerably less of an accent. "Well, of course not. But your women and children can't fight, Pushmataha. Not many of the old men, either. So it only makes sense . . ."

* * *

By evening, he'd managed to work out a compromise. Most of the Choctaws would winter over in New Antrim. That would require hastily erecting enough shelter for an additional fifteen thousand people, in a city that was already bursting with more than thirty thousand. But Driscol announced he'd exercise his full powers as principal chief of Arkansas and institute the measure he'd been considering for some time now.

Conscription. Pure and simple—no blasted inefficient, haphazard Sassenach press gangs, either. Arkansas would do it the proper way. The Napoleonic way.

However, exemptions would be given to able-bodied men engaged in necessary labor.

Building housing on short notice for the newly arrived Choctaws was decreed necessary labor.

The principal chief of Arkansas foresaw no great problem.

"Can Patrick actually manage it?" Sam whispered to John Ridge, with whom he'd been quietly consulting on the side while Driscol and John Ross and Major Ridge and Pushmataha continued their wrangling over the details. "Conscription, I mean."

Major Ridge's son was extremely astute, had been residing in New Antrim for some time now, and, along with his cousin, Buck Watie, who was standing alongside him, owned New Antrim's biggest and most influential newspaper. Sam figured his assessment would be as good as any. And whatever he missed, Buck wouldn't.

"There'll be a ruckus, of course. But . . . yes, he can."

"Of course he can," Buck chimed in, speaking as softly as his cousin even if the words came out like a snort. "Don't let all the similarities fool you, Sam. There are some ways— and not just obvious ones involving race—that Arkansas is about as different from the United States as both of them are from, I don't know, someplace in Mongolia. One of them is the attitude people have toward the army here. Even a lot of the whites and Indians. The truth is, the way things are now, if Chief Driscol called for a massive number of volunteers, he'd get them. There'll be a ruckus over conscription, like John says, but it'll be mostly for show."

Sam looked back and forth from one to the other. Neither of the young Cherokees looked at all happy.

"And the problem is?"

John, as usual, took some time to think about his answer. Buck, as usual, gave it right away.

"Isn't it obvious, Sam? What happens if we *win* the war? And come out of it at the end—"

John finished the thought: "—with what amounts to an all-black army, in a confederacy that's supposed to be mostly for Indians? That's a recipe for another war. A civil war, this time. In fact, we're already getting closer to it than I like. If you go out and talk to some of the Cherokees in New Kit—ah, Oklahoma—you'll hear some nasty predictions and even calls for action. Especially from some of the richer mixed-bloods who own a lot of slaves. Some Creeks are talking the same way, too."

Sam studied the leaders in the corner of the mess hall. In deference to Pushmataha's age and infirmities, all of them had gathered around the Choctaw chief's chair.

All the races of the continent were represented there. Mostly Indians, with two white men in the form of Patrick Driscol and Robert Ross. Only one black man. That was Charles Ball, the general in the chiefdom of Arkansas' little army.

But it didn't matter. All Sam had to do was step outside and walk about the fort for a few minutes. Everywhere he went—manning the twelve-pounders, not just holding muskets—he'd see almost nothing but black men. With a sprinkling of whites, constituting less than ten percent of the whole. One or two Indians, at most—if there were any at all.

"The solution's obvious," he said harshly, not caring now if his voice carried. "Pick up the load yourselves, damnation."

Both young Cherokees flushed. "We'll fight, Sam, and you know—"

"That's not what I meant, and *you* know it. Sure, you'll fight. Nobody ever accused Cherokees—or Creeks, or Choctaws, and sure as Sam Hill not Chickasaws and Seminoles—of being cowards. And so fucking *what*?"

He jerked his head in the direction of Major Ridge. "You'll fight the way your father—and your uncle, Buck—

fights. A great warrior; nobody denies it. Not me, that's for sure, having fought next to him at the Horseshoe Bend and the Mississippi. And it doesn't matter, because the only role he and his men could play at the Horseshoe and the Mississippi was that of auxiliary troops. There's no way—not on their own—they can stand against what's coming."

Now he jerked his head in the direction of Driscol and Ball. "They *can*, on the other hand. Because whether you like it or not—whether it rubs your Cherokee customs and traditions the wrong way or not—they'll fight the white man's sort of war. And that's what kind of war this is going to be. And you know it. So cut out the tomfoolery. I ask you again. You know the solution. Are you willing to accept it?"

John and Buck looked at each other. "Yeah, all right," said Buck almost immediately.

"My wife can handle the newspaper," John chimed in. "Truth is, she manages it pretty much already, on the business end."

"Well, good."

The Chickasaws wouldn't budge at all. So, finally, Patrick cut the Gordian knot.

"Fine, then. I'll be pulling out of Arkansas Post come spring. Because there's no way to hold it, against the size army the United States will send. So you can winter over in this area, and you can have the Post thereafter, if you think you can hold it. I give it to you. You'd still be smarter to send your women and children—them, at least—over into Oklahoma."

Sam translated. The Chickasaw chiefs swelled.

"We'll hold it! Watch and see if Chickasaws can't!"

Ten minutes later, most of the mess hall was cleared of people. The only ones who remained behind were Driscol, Robert Ross, Sam himself, and the four Cherokee leaders: John Ross and Major Ridge, and Ridge's son and nephew.

"Idiots," Robert Ross stated. "The American army will overrun the Post, and they'll all die. Most of them, anyway. A few might escape at the end."

Driscol shrugged. Every ounce of him the ice-blooded troll, now. "So let 'em die. They're Chickasaws; they won't die easily. They'll bleed the bastards, be sure of that. And once it's over"—the troll's grin, as pure as you could ask for—"it'll be us instead of Henry Clay hollering 'vengeance for Arkansas Post!'"

Driscol turned to Sam, glowering at him. "I've half a mind to forbid you from enlisting in the army altogether. I've got the legal authority to do it, too, at least here in Arkansas."

"Damn you, Patrick, I didn't come all the way—"

"Damn *you,* Sam Houston! Look, sooner or later wars have to be *ended,* too. And . . ." For a moment, the troll almost looked embarrassed. Impossible, of course. "Well, the truth is, I'm a poor one to try to make a settlement. You, on the other hand, are a natural diplomat and could probably manage the trick—*provided* you weren't actually involved in the fighting and killing."

Before Sam could continue the argument, Robert Ross intervened.

"Patrick, you're being foolish. First, you have to win the war in the first place. Which, as it stands now, you mostly likely won't."

Driscol glared at him. The British major general didn't seem to care in the least.

"Be as stubborn as you want. Here's the truth, Patrick. You've got probably the best army anywhere in the world that could have been created by sergeants. The world's best sergeants, I'll add that into the bargain. But sergeants can't win wars. They can rarely even win battles. What you need is what you don't have. A real officer corps. You don't have real cavalry, either, but you can probably survive that lack. You won't survive without officers. Real ones, and enough of them."

Ross nodded toward Ball. "There are some exceptions, I grant you. Charles here is one of them. I'm not really sure yet about Jones. A very fine soldier, and I'd trust him on any battlefield. But . . ." He shrugged. "He's still more of a sergeant wearing a colonel's uniform, really, than an actual colonel."

"We've got some youngsters coming up," Driscol grumbled.

"Yes, you do. Some very fine ones, I'm thinking. Young Parker is especially promising. So is McParland—the younger cousin, I mean, not Anthony, who already thinks like an officer. But his injury may keep him out of line command."

He shook his head. "It's not enough, Patrick. Not with only a few months to prepare."

Ross jabbed a finger at Sam. "So, now, here arrives—at your service—one of the most capable and experienced commanding officers on the North American continent, and you propose to refuse him the colors. Are you mad?"

Patrick sighed and looked away. "It's not really that, Robert. Sam is also my best friend."

"Death's always a risk in war," Sam stated. "It doesn't bother me."

He hesitated then. But the rest was a given—he'd known it since the moment he decided to come to Arkansas—so it might as well be said aloud. "My son wouldn't even be an orphan. Not with you and Tiana for his parents. Or even just Tiana, should you fall also in the war."

Patrick shook his head. "That's not what I'm talking about, Sam. What happens when the war is over—and you *survive*?"

Sam stared at him, groping at the question.

"Sam, face it. You're an American at heart. I'm not, since I was an immigrant here to begin with. But you'll never really be comfortable as an Arkansan. Even as a Confederate. If your wife hadn't been murdered, you'd never once have considered changing your citizenship. You'd have stayed in the United States and done what the man you named your son after will be doing. Opposing the war, surely—but never once crossing the line marked 'allegiance.'"

Sam continued to stare at him. Groping at the answer.

"Tell me I'm wrong."

Sam . . . couldn't.

"What I thought. That's why, at bottom, I'd much prefer to keep you out of uniform. Whatever else, when the war's over, no one will be able to claim there is any American blood on your own hands. You were just a diplomat."

Robert Ross sighed, now. "Patrick, you *can't*. Neither can Sam, being honest, unless he simply wants to return. The army of Arkansas desperately needs experienced officers. And Houston—my opinion, at least—is possibly the best field-grade officer in North America."

That was enough to break Sam's paralysis. "Be damned to the future, Patrick. Yes, I suppose in a perfect world, someday I'd return to the United States." Harshly: "But in a perfect world my wife wouldn't have been murdered. And I made a vow and I intend to keep it. And that's all there is to the matter."

Driscol said nothing. But Sam could tell from his stance alone that he was conceding the argument.

Time for diplomacy, therefore, and a silver tongue.

"As for the rest," Sam said cheerily, "I am pleased to announce that both John Ridge and Buck Watie are volunteering for the colors. The *Arkansas* colors, mind you."

The two young Cherokees stepped forward. Without hesitation, either—although both of them avoided the gaze of the two Cherokee chiefs.

Especially that of Major Ridge, who was now glaring at his son and nephew.

"Of course, you'll offer them commissions," Sam continued smoothly. "I've no doubt of it at all."

"Of course he will!" exclaimed Major General Robert Ross. "Splendid young men! From a fine family, and well educated. Perfect officer material."

"Well, sure," said Patrick.

The glare faded from Major Ridge's eyes. Five minutes later, he was even embracing his young kin.

New Antrim, Arkansas
FEBRUARY 14, 1825

The thing was there, all right. Just as grotesque as Sam feared it would be.

Shivering a bit—even with his Cherokee blanket, the great stone church was bitterly cold, in mid-February—he stared up at the icon. The newly proclaimed *martyr of the Church.*

"She didn't look in the least bit like that—that—"

"Don't be rude, Sam," said Tiana. She gave Marie Laveau a look that Sam couldn't really interpret. Something so profoundly female that it was just beyond his comprehension.

"So we make up another one," Marie said, shrugging. The tall, gorgeous quadroon gave the icon a dismissive glance and an equally dismissive wave of the hand. "It's just some painted wood, you know. Has no holy power in itself. Might have, if they'd let me sprinkle—well, never mind. Father James is a good priest, even if he is just as superstitious as men always are."

She half turned and imperiously summoned forward a short, very dark-skinned black woman who'd been hanging back in the shadows of the cavernous church. "Antoinette here is a magnificent carver. Almost as good with the paints, too. With your guidance"—she waved again at the icon perched on the wall—"she can soon have that replaced with an image that captures the martyred wife to perfection."

Sam opened his mouth, about to proclaim that under no circumstances would he be a party to any such half-papist, half-voudou heathenist nonsense. He was something of a freethinker himself, to be sure, not a dyed-in-the-wool Protestant. Still and all!

But the words never came. They were choked off by the worst of the grief. That he had lost his beloved wife, Sam could eventually accept. What he couldn't accept was the knowledge that his son—only four years old when Maria Hester died—would never really remember his mother.

It was worse than that. Sam knew—had known from the day he made the decision—that he was looking at another of the world's terrible ironics. No matter what happened, little Andy *would* have a mother, here in Arkansas. It would be Tiana Rogers—Tiana Driscol, now—the woman whom Sam had once thought, from time to time, might be the mother of his own children. And so, in a way, she would be. But only at the price of obliterating any real memory of his son's natural mother, Maria Hester, née Monroe and died Houston.

Now . . .

If the boy could come, any day, any time, to a revered place, and look up and see . . .

"All right," he said.

"Good!" proclaimed Marie. "And once Antoinette has made the proper icon, and you pronounce yourself satisfied, I will do the rest. Properly, this time. *Pfah!*"—that was a very rude gesture—"to what the priest says."

"Just stay out of it, Sam," Tiana quietly counseled.

He decided the counsel was good.

PART IV

CHAPTER 30

The first thing Winfield Scott said to Patrick and Sam, after they'd taken seats in a quiet corner of the Wolfe Tone Hotel's huge foyer, was this:

"You understand, gentlemen, I cannot pass on to you any information that might be detrimental to the United States or its armed forces. At the same time, you have my pledge that I will not pass on to General Harrison—or any of his subordinates—any information that is not contained already in the reports Mr. Bryant and I will be sending to the newspapers back home."

It was said a bit stiffly, but pleasantly enough. Understanding and accepting the protocol, Patrick and Sam simply nodded. Then both of them turned their eyes to William Cullen Bryant.

The poet-turned-reporter looked a bit uncomfortable. "Ah . . . I must insist upon the same conditions. My personal sympathies—well, never mind that. If nothing else, the reports General Scott and I will be filing must be viewed by everyone as uncompromised."

Sam kept a placid expression. Patrick's face twisted into something close to a sneer. Winfield Scott sneered outright.

"Oh, that's ridiculous, Cullen!" he exclaimed. "No matter what we do, Clay and his supporters will accuse us of spouting a pack of lies. So will every newspaper in the administration's camp. They're *already* saying so, before we've even filed a single report. What's involved here isn't practical; it's simply a matter of our personal honor."

Bryant looked stubborn. "Yes, I know they'll accuse us of lying. But it doesn't matter, Winfield, nor do I agree with you that it's simply a matter of honor. At least half—more like two-thirds, I suspect—of the population of the United States is reserving their judgment. What we report *will* have an influence—provided it's not tainted with charges of bias, that aren't coming from people who have an obvious bias of their own."

"Gentlemen, please," Sam said smoothly. "It's really not a problem. We have full confidence in your integrity, and you can rest assured we will respect it, on our part."

Winfield Scott's eyes ranged up and down Sam's figure. The gaze was curious and perhaps a bit cold.

"It's an attractive uniform," he said abruptly. "Though I think that fur hat will get very uncomfortable now that we're in midsummer."

Patrick smiled. "Oh, we've got summer headgear, General Scott. But we'll wear the fur hats except when it's unbearable. It's a small thing, but it helps remind the troops that we're expecting a winter campaign."

Scott turned the same curious perhaps-a-bit-cold gaze onto Driscol.

"You don't think it'll all be over within a few months, then."

"Not hardly," Sam stated. "By the first snowfall it'll just be starting."

Scott looked back at him. "Are you . . . *uncomfortable* in that uniform, Colonel?" He glanced at the insignia. "Excuse me. Brigadier, I should say."

Sam didn't hesitate. He'd now had almost half a year to think about it, since he'd taken Arkansas citizenship as soon as he'd arrived back in February.

"No, not in the least. That's because I don't really think of it as a change in uniform to begin with. As far as I'm concerned, the uniform I used to wear has been stolen by a swindler and his accomplices. The political principles for which I'm fighting today are no different than they were on the day I stood"—he gestured at Patrick—"when then-Lieutenant Driscol and I stood side by side facing the redcoats in front of the Capitol."

"May I quote you to that effect, General Houston?" Bryant asked. His pad and pen were already in hand.

"Oh, yes," Sam said brightly. "Please do."

An hour later, Patrick offered to give Scott and Bryant a tour of New Antrim's military installations. They accepted, of course, leaving Sam alone in the foyer's corner.

Not more than fifteen seconds after Driscol and the two reporters left the hotel, Salmon Brown took the seat formerly occupied by Winfield Scott.

He began without preliminaries. "We figure they've landed close to six thousand troops at the confluence, almost half of them regulars. The only artillery they've got—so far, anyway—is the First Regiment. Colonel Abram Eustis is in command. They were stationed—"

"In Charleston, South Carolina. Yes, I know." Sam scratched his chin. "Interesting. It would have been a lot easier to bring in the Fourth Artillery under Armistead. What's the infantry?"

"They've got four infantry regiments. The First, the Fifth—which used to be the Fourth, it seems—"

"That's Harrison's old unit," Sam interrupted, "from the Thames campaign. They renamed it after the war, when they consolidated the regiments during the reduction. The Fourth did pretty well in the war with Britain, except for when Hull surrendered his whole army at Detroit. But nobody's ever blamed the regiment for that. Harrison'll be leaning on them heavily, I'm pretty sure. If it was me, I'd be more inclined to rely on the First Regiment. The Battle of the Thames was a long time ago, and who knows what shape the Fourth's in today? The First, on the other hand, has been in Baton Rouge under Colonel Taylor, who's an excellent troop trainer."

Salmon Brown shook his head. "Taylor's no longer in command of the First. Colonel John McNeil is."

Sam's eyebrows rose. "Then where's Taylor?"

"Don't know for sure, Sam." Like John Brown himself, his brother was not given to military formalities. "Word is, though, that he was sent up north. To St. Louis."

Sam's eyes moved to the northern wall of the foyer as if he were trying to look through it. "*St. Louis?* What . . . Ah, never mind. Let's deal with what's at hand, for the moment. Which are the other two infantry regiments Harrison's got down there on the confluence? The Seventh is probably one of them. They were stationed not far away."

"That's right. Colonel Matthew Arbuckle's in command. The other one is the Third, with Lieutenant Colonel Enos Cutler in command."

Sam chewed on it for a moment. "So. One regular regiment of artillery; four of infantry. The United States sent four out of their seven regular infantry regiments and a fourth of their artillery. Against which, we've got at the moment—all told—three infantry regiments and an artillery regiment."

He laughed, once, very sarcastically. "They're overconfident. They should have sent six infantry and two artillery regiments. Six infantry, anyway. It's always hard to pry artillery units out of their garrisons, because the local politicians put up such a fuss. Need 'em there to defend the town against—whoever. Barbary pirates, maybe, come all the way across the Atlantic."

"John and me figure they got you outnumbered three to two," Salmon pointed out dispassionately. "That's just in regular troops. Unless you decide to use the three new regiments."

"No, that'd be a mistake. Those recruits aren't ready for a pitched battle on the open field in the Delta, yet. Send them into one, they'd just shatter—and it would take a year to rebuild their self-confidence." He went back to scratching his chin. "And your arithmetic's just about right, although it wouldn't be if we could send all of our regiments down there. But we can't. We need to keep the First in reserve as well as using it to train the new regiments. And we can't risk the whole artillery regiment on the open Delta. We'll need it intact when the war moves up the river valley, which it will. We always knew we couldn't stop the United States from taking the Delta."

Sam shrugged. "On the other hand, our regiments will be stronger than theirs. We can muster at least six hundred men to a regiment, maybe seven. They'll be lucky if they're even half strength. I'm willing to bet not one of those infantry regiments down there has more than five hundred men actually present. At least one of them won't have more than maybe four hundred. Desertion and absence without leave is rampant in the U.S. Army; always has been. Not much of a problem for us. Give it a few months, down there in the Delta—disease will make it worse."

He took a moment, doing the math. "Figure . . . they'll have two thousand infantry, actually on the field, when we meet. We'll have about one thousand, three hundred. They'll have an advantage in artillery, but that terrain isn't very good even for field artillery. Not anywhere near the river, anyway. If we maneuver properly, they won't be able to move their ordnance up quickly enough. And the one thing I'm sure and certain about is that Arkansas infantry can out-march any infantry the U.S. Army's got. Like I said, they're overconfident."

"They got lots of militia troops, Sam. At least three thousand. About half of them are the Georgia militia. The rest are mostly Louisianans. A few units from Alabama. Nothing yet but a handful from Mississippi."

Sam's sneer was magnificent. At least, he hoped so.

"The Georgia militia." He uttered the phrase the same way he might refer to offal or animal refuse. "Ah, yes. The same heroes who retreated precipitously from the Red Sticks during the Horseshoe campaign—I can remember Old Hickory's choice words at the time—and then ravaged defenseless towns of friendly Creeks and our Cherokee allies. Jackson had choice words about that, too."

The situation seemed worth the effort of a gesture. So, although he didn't chew tobacco, Sam rose, stalked over to a nearby spittoon, and used the device loudly. He didn't miss, either.

After returning to his seat, he pulled the cap off his head and plopped it into his lap. Winfield Scott was right. The blasted thing might look splendid, but it was going to be a pure nuisance in the months ahead.

"One thing we'll do," he continued, "—I've already discussed it with Patrick and Charles, and General Ross agrees—is break those Georgia bastards. If we get any kind of a chance, anyway. Have they started their usual atrocities?"

Salmon Brown disapproved of tobacco entirely. But for a

moment he looked as if he wanted to use the spittoon himself. "They fell upon two families of Indians who'd somehow remained near the river. Quapaws, probably, or Caddos, not paying attention to anything except their immediate business. They wouldn't have been Choctaws or Chickasaws."

He didn't volunteer any details, nor was Sam about to ask. Georgia militiamen were notorious for their brutality and had been for decades. Disemboweling pregnant Indian women, after they'd been gang-raped, was pretty typical behavior. Sometimes the fetus would be mutilated also.

They could do so with impunity, because the state of Georgia adamantly refused to discipline them. During the war with Britain, Andrew Jackson had become so furious with the depredations of the Georgia militia that he'd had an entire unit placed under arrest by regular troops. Unfortunately, he'd had no legal choice but to turn them over to the Georgia authorities—whereupon a Georgia jury had promptly declared them innocent of all charges.

"Break them," he muttered. Then, shaking off the moment's anger: "Harrison'll try to use the militia's numbers, but they won't be much use to him. Not against our regulars, at least. Against the Cherokees, Creeks, and Choctaws . . . It's always hard to tell. Militias are prone to panic. Leadership's always the key. With strong enough leaders, they can usually beat an equal number of Indians. Although . . ."

Again he shrugged. "We'll just have to see. Part of the reason they can is simply because the Indians don't ever have much in the way of guns—and especially ammunition."

Salmon smiled. In that moment, he looked very much like John Brown's brother. "That won't be no problem here."

Sam smiled back. In addition to terrorizing slave-catchers and serving as a genuinely excellent spy network, over the past months Brown's Raiders had also proved to be superb gunrunners.

It had taken Henry Clay weeks after his inauguration to cajole and bully Congress into declaring war on the Confederacy of the Arkansas. But the very day after his inauguration, he'd made several sweeping decrees prohibiting the sale of weapons or other warmaking goods to the Confederacy.

And what a laugh that had been! All the Northern and border states had immediately raised an outcry over federal tyranny, the trampling of states' rights—Jackson leading the charge in the Senate—and even some of the Southern states had choked on the measures. Virginia's John Randolph, contrarian as always, had immediately turned from being Clay's loudest supporter in the House to his loudest critic.

The only immediate effect had been to double the transfer of arms that Brown's Raiders carried down the rivers. It wasn't until the federal government was finally able to get enough armed steamboats patrolling the Ohio and the Mississippi that the flood was stymied at all. Even then, it was never stopped altogether.

By which time, the proverbial barn door had been locked after the horse escaped. Arkansas was still a bit short of heavy iron plate for armoring the steamboats. But it already had enough cannons and muskets and powder and shot to fight for years.

It hadn't even had to pay for most of it. Clay's campaign and election had stirred the sparks of Northern abolitionism into glowing coals, and Clay's War was fanning them now into roaring flames. A political sentiment that might have taken decades to develop was now growing explosively. There were still not more than a few hundred abolitionists in the United States willing to take up arms themselves, on behalf of "bleeding Arkansas," either as part of Brown's Raiders or the small Lafayette Battalions that were springing up here and there. But thousands of people were willing to donate arms of some sort—and tens of thousands willing to donate money, most of them asking no questions about what the money was spent on.

Salmon was long gone by the time Scott and Bryant returned with Patrick, late in the afternoon. Sam made sure of it. Brown's Raiders were a double-edged sword, and they had to be handled carefully. Mostly unseen, a mysterious presence lurking in the heavily forested rivers and the mountains and the woods, they were something of a terror to the enemy's soldiers. But if Arkansas let them get too visible, the political repercussions were likely to outweigh the military gains. As it was, Clay's partisans—not to mention the entire press of the Deep South—were doing their level best to portray the Mississippi valley as being overrun by murderous fanatic abolitionists.

"Overrun" was absurd, of course. "Fanatics" could be argued. But "murderous" was the plain and simple truth. Patrick had put it quite well. Brown and his men were reminiscent—perhaps frighteningly so—of the Hebrews of the Old Testament. Doing God's will to defend the Promised Land, and not at all concerned as to how many Philistines got chopped to pieces in the process. Those of them who weren't John Brown's brand of Calvinist when they joined the Raiders soon became so.

It was a peculiar variety of that harsh strain of Protestantism, admittedly. John Brown was actually quite tolerant of religious differences and didn't care about theology at all. He'd even accept Catholics in the Raiders, if they were black, and make no attempt to persuade them to abandon popery. But they'd still join every night in the Bible readings. And if Brown's interpretation of the Old Testament was perhaps a little eccentric, it had the great advantage for irregular soldiers of being very clear and straightforward. As Patrick Driscol liked to put it, every other verb was "smite."

Winfield Scott was—had been—undoubtedly the best trainer of troops in the United States Army. He'd proved that during the war with Britain, and after it he'd been placed in charge of developing the army's new manual of drill and field regulations.

So it wasn't surprising that the first thing he said after resuming his seat in the hotel's foyer was "I commend your decision not to send those three new regiments into combat quickly. But . . ."

He glanced at Patrick and then shook his head. "Dear God, are you really *that* confident? Patrick—Sam—you *have* to meet Harrison in the Delta. At least once, even if it's a draw. Even if it's a *defeat,* when it comes down to it, as long as your forces can be extracted afterward and you bloody him

badly. Whereas if you allow him unchallenged posses-
sion—"

Abruptly, he closed his mouth. Then swallowed.

"Excuse me, gentlemen. It occurs to me that if I insist you
respect my personal integrity, I must place the same condition upon myself. Not my business, after all, to be counsel-
ing officers of what is, in fact, and leaving sentiment aside,
a nation that is at war with my own."

Patrick nodded solemnly. Every bit as solemnly, Sam said,
"Yes, of course."

But he was finding it hard not to laugh, and he was quite
sure Patrick was waging the same struggle. They'd come to
the same conclusion themselves, four months ago. Robert
Ross had been particularly adamant about it. Sam remembered the conversation as if it'd happened yesterday.

"We've *got* to fight them as soon as they cross the river.
Not a month later, not a week later—well, perhaps a week,
but no longer than it takes to march our forces down there.
Speaking of which—"

"Relax, Robert," grunted Driscol. "We've been using a
good half of the forced labor—sorry, the shiftless bastards
who're shirking the colors—to finish the road to Arkansas
Post."

"It'll be ready by the end of May," Charles Ball added,
"and there's no way they're coming any sooner than that."

"No chance at all," agreed Houston. Of the four generals
and four colonels sitting around the table in the Arkansas
Army headquarters, Sam had by far the best sense of American politics. Ross was British, Driscol was a Scots-Irish immigrant, and the other six officers were all black men whose
color had made it effectively impossible for them to engage
in politics until they settled in Arkansas. "It's now mid-
March, so Clay will have just gotten inaugurated. Figure it'll
take him till the end of April before he can get Congress to
declare war."

"Can he do it in the first place, Sam?" Ross asked. The
British general seemed simultaneously curious and bewil-
dered. "I confess I find the inner workings of your American
political system well-nigh unfathomable, at times. You've
just explained—it was only yesterday—that Clay's election
does not reflect any real sentiment for war on the part of most

of the United States. So why would Clay be able to get Congress to agree to a declaration of war?"

"Because Congress—*that* Congress—doesn't have any choice. Most of them are going to be in hot water when the session's over and they return to their home districts, Robert, and they know it. The truth is, if Clay didn't have to get the Senate to go along also, he could probably get a declaration of war in a week. Every one of those congressmen who voted him into the president's house has to stand for reelection in two years. Less than two years, now. What they'll all be hoping is that a short, glorious, and victorious war will wash away the memory of their sins."

"Ah." Robert leaned back in his chair. Then, as his gaze moved across the officers at the table, a smile came to his face. "Well, then. As your more-or-less official military adviser—and one who has often been critical these past months—let me be the first to state that the prospects that the United States will enjoy a short and glorious war in Arkansas are slim to none. They might still achieve victory, of course. But they won't win quickly, and they certainly won't win easily."

Most of the officers returned the cool smile. Charles Ball's was openly sarcastic. "Glorious, is it? They'll find out all 'bout glory, come winter in the Ozarks and Ouachitas."

"But I interrupted you, Sam," said Ross. "Continue, please."

"Figure he'll get his declaration of war by the end of April. Then, it'll take him—the army, I should say—another six weeks to get their units ready to be moved to the confluence."

"Clay could order the preparations to be made prior to a declaration of war, couldn't he?"

Sam waggled his hand back and forth. "Yes . . . but it won't be as easy as all that. Especially if he leaves Jesup as the quartermaster general. Which he almost has to do, now that Brown and Scott have resigned from the army. He's too short of experienced officers to let Jesup go also."

"You told us—again, just yesterday—that Jesup was a superb quartermaster."

It was Sam's turn to smile coolly. "Indeed he is. But I'll remind you that great skill at doing a job efficiently can just as easily be turned to doing it incredibly *in*-efficiently—but in such a way that Jesup's bosses can't figure out what he's doing. Somehow, in all the smoke and dust and confusion, everything just seems to take forever."

"Why would—"

Ross broke off and leaned back. "Ah. I see. The war is no more popular in the army than it is in the country at large."

"Well . . . it's not that simple. Harrison—you can bet on it—will practically jump for joy when he receives Clay's summons to return to the army as a major general. So will Gaines, when he finally realizes his ambition to replace Brown as the head of the army and gets rid of his archenemy Winfield Scott. There'll be some other officers, too, especially the ones around Gaines, who'll see the war as a route for quick promotion. But most of the officers . . . Well, a lot of them are Southern, true enough, but those are mostly from Virginia and the border states. They'll certainly do their duty, but they won't be making any great exertions until Congress declares war and it's a settled issue."

Sam half rose, reached into the middle of the table, and placed his finger on a spot in the big map that covered much of it. Then, shifted it to two others. "I figure they'll muster at Louisville, St. Louis, and Baton Rouge. There's another few weeks. It'll take time to assemble enough riverboats, if nothing else. There's no way Harrison's going to try to move that many troops without using the rivers and water transport. Then Harrison will want to move all his units at once—as best as he can coordinate it—so he doesn't get caught on the Arkansas side of the river with only part of his forces available. That can be done, but it'll also take time."

He leaned back from the table into his chair. "Mid-June, at the very earliest. Personally, I think it'll take him a month longer than that."

Ross nodded. "So. Mid-July. Enough time for one big battle in the Delta—perhaps two, if the engagement is close— before both armies will have to take time to regroup and recuperate. And by the time that's done, we're well into fall. Most likely, Harrison will wait until next spring to start his march on New Antrim."

He started to say something but broke off. Sam wasn't sure, but he suspected Ross wanted to reopen the issue of how—or whether—to defend New Antrim. But since that was a contentious issue, and one that didn't need to be settled immediately, the British general returned to the Delta.

"Where in the Delta? I remind you, gentlemen, that I don't much care for the terrain around Arkansas Post. It's not terrible, but the terrain farther upriver would be more in our favor. Their artillery is considerably superior—in weight, at least. The soggier the terrain, the better for us."

"We don't have any choice, Robert," Driscol said. "Yes, we all agree, the Chickasaw chiefs are bedlamites to think they can hold Arkansas Post. But—they're Chickasaws. Just as fierce—and just as dumb—as any Scot highlanders. They'll insist on standing their ground, and . . ."

He shrugged. "As much as it might please my more cold-blooded instincts, we can't very well just stand by while they get massacred."

Patrick started to say something further, but Sam cut him off. In the few weeks since he'd arrived in Arkansas, he'd inevitably become the principal liaison between the Arkansas Army and the Indian chiefdoms in Oklahoma. And the Choctaws in New Antrim, for that matter.

"It's more complicated than that. The mixed-bloods politically dominate the Chickasaws nowadays, just like they do the Cherokees and the Creeks. With the Chickasaws, that's centered on the Colbert clan. But it's a touchy business, and they can't afford to aggravate the full-bloods too much. Those are still, by a large margin, the majority of the tribe, and their blood is up. If it was just up to the Colberts, I'm sure they'd already be halfway to Oklahoma."

"With their slaves," Patrick growled. "Of which they have a good thousand, for four thousand Chickasaws. A higher percentage than your average white Southern state has, South Carolina aside."

He leaned forward in his own chair and pointed a finger at Sam. "So don't you even think of arguing the matter when the time comes. If we have to save those Chickasaw bastards from their own pigheadedness, they'll pay the price, Sam. Pay it in full. We will strip them of every single one of their slaves. Every—single—one."

A grunt of agreement went up from the six black officers at the table. Well, five of them. Charles Ball just grinned.

But Sam wasn't fooled by the grin. The top-ranked black officer of the army of Arkansas wasn't much given to denouncing the injustices of the world. Or even worrying about them in private, for that matter. But he was, if anything, the most ruthless of the lot.

Sam hesitated for a moment. He didn't care at all about the Chickasaws losing their slaves. The smallest of the Southern tribes, they'd been the one that had adopted slavery more extensively than any of the others. Between that and their own current stupidity, he figured they had it coming. The problem was that any such peremptory action would certainly stir up a lot of antagonism with the other tribes, especially the Cherokees. And relations between Arkansas and the Oklahoma chiefdoms were already tense.

But—

The ancient Romans knew it, and so did Sam. *Quis custodiet ipsos custodes?* If the Indian tribes in the Oklahoma portion of the Confederacy depended on the black soldiers of Arkansas to protect them from the United States . . .

They might as well just sign slavery's death warrant and be done with it. Sooner or later, it was bound to happen, and Sam found himself not caring much any longer how it came to pass. He hoped it could be done peacefully. But if it couldn't, he was no more forgiving of slavery in his new country than he'd become of it in his old one. The day he'd crossed the Mississippi and set foot on Arkansas soil was the day he'd left slavery behind forever.

The first thing he'd done had been to free Chester, Dinah, and Sukey. When Chester had then offered to pay back the cost of his purchase—Dinah's and Sukey's, too—Sam had refused the money.

"It's blood money," he said curtly. "My wife's blood. You keep it, Chester, and make a life for yourself."

Dinah and Sukey had started wailing immediately—and it hadn't taken little Andy more than ten seconds to start wailing also, when the boy figured out he might be losing his nursemaids.

"Tarnation, I didn't say you had to leave!" Sam exclaimed, throwing up his hands with exasperation. "I'll hire you.

But—I'm warning you!—I haven't got much money left. So the pay's as bad as you could ask for."

"Better'n it was, which was nothing, Mr. Sam," Chester pointed out placidly. "In that case, I believe I'll hire on, too. May as well keep saving up my money."

CHAPTER 31

New Antrim, Arkansas
JULY 18, 1825

That night, the Women's Council threw a ball for the soldiers of Arkansas. It was specifically intended for the 2nd and 3rd Infantry Regiments and the 3rd Artillery Battalion, who would be marching out of New Antrim on the morrow to meet the invading U.S. Army coming up the Arkansas. But the women weren't being particularly finicky about the matter. As long as a man was wearing a uniform of the Arkansas Army—or that of one of the other chiefdoms, of which there were a handful present—he'd be allowed into the festivities.

Winfield Scott and William Cullen Bryant were granted an exception, being distinguished visitors vouched for by the Laird himself. But the three old black women guarding the entrance to the Wolfe Tone Hotel gave them no friendly looks as they were passed through. Nothing personal, just a matter of principle.

Once they got past the fearsome trio, Scott chuckled. "Amazing to see such devotion to the classics, wouldn't you say, William? Given that—I'd wager a year's income—not one of them can read."

Bryant gave him a quizzical look.

Scott waved his hand expansively. They were now halfway into the great foyer, heading for the still larger central dining area that doubled as the ballroom. The foyer was packed with people, and from the sounds coming through the double doors, the ballroom was more crowded still.

"The three-headed Cerberus at the door—and *Lysistrata* here, right before your eyes. Upsidedown, of course, the way most things are in Arkansas. I predict a wave of births nine months from now."

Bryant examined a group nearby. Five young soldiers—four of them black, one white—were exchanging repartee with six young black women. The uniforms of the young men were matched by what came very close to uniforms on the part of the girls. "Ballroom gowns," technically, but in addition to being very simply and plainly made, they were all the same color. White, with a bit of blue trim here and there. Bryant was pretty sure they'd been mass-produced for the occasion by one of the same clothing companies that made the uniforms.

Those were private enterprises, technically. But Bryant had already come to realize that for Arkansans—especially black Arkansans—the distinction between private enterprise and government was much fuzzier than it was in the United States. Chief Driscol and his political subordinates did not meddle with the ownership of enterprises, to be sure. But they did expect the businesses to be cooperative with the chiefdom's policies—and they had the Bank of Arkansas to enforce their desires, if nothing else.

True, Driscol and Crowell's bank was also supposed to be private. But in practice it served Arkansas in the capacity of a state bank—even more so, really, than the Second Bank of the United States.

There was a certain irony there. Patrick Driscol, in terms of his political ideology, was as ferocious a democrat as any in the Republican Party in the United States. But the American Party was and had been from its inception heavily influenced by the aristocratic attitudes of men like its founder, Thomas Jefferson—not to mention its current most extreme partisan, John Randolph. For such men, government was always the great threat to their personal liberties, so they emphasized its iniquities. For a man like Driscol, and for those who followed him, the government—so long as it was their own—served as both a shield and a support.

The merits of either view could be argued in the abstract. But in the end, Bryant had concluded it was simply the different perspectives of wealthy slave-owners versus poor freedmen. The methods used by Driscol and his people worked in Arkansas—worked quite well, in fact—because the mostly black businessmen of the chiefdom saw nothing peculiar or unreasonable about them.

Nor, for that matter, did the Cherokees or Creeks. Nor would the newly arrived Choctaws. The southern Indian nations had their own customs and traditions, which harmonized far more closely with Arkansan practice than they ever had with that of Americans. The whole of the Confederacy, as it had emerged since its foundation in 1819, was a hybrid society—and nowhere more so than in Arkansas.

While ruminating, Bryant had continued to observe the group of young people standing by the entrance to the ballroom, waiting for enough space to be cleared to allow them to enter.

Two of the girls were obviously mulattos, or perhaps a quadroon in the case of one. The lighter-skinned of the two was very pretty, as was one of the negresses. All six of the girls, however, shared the general attractiveness of lively young women, regardless of appearance. And all of them had very bright eyes.

So did the young men. Boys, almost. Not one of them—or one of the girls—looked to be older than twenty.

Bryant found it all somewhat unsettling. His upbringing led him to disapprove of Arkansan customs when it came to sex. He wouldn't go so far as to use the term "licentious," himself, but he wouldn't strenuously object to it, either, if used by someone else. When it came to relations between the sexes, Arkansan youth behaved in a manner that was quite scandalous by American standards, especially those of New England. Still worse were the lax and tolerant attitudes of their elders.

But . . .

Another hybrid, he supposed. The black people who had poured into Arkansas over the past few years had come from shattered communities that had never, even in the best of times, enjoyed much in the way of social cohesion. So, already predisposed toward it anyway, they'd come to adopt and modify many of the cultural traditions of their Cherokee neighbors, if not some of the extreme customs of the Creeks. Just the year before, for instance, the chiefdom had passed a law allowing for matrilineal descent if a family chose to exercise that alternative. Whether they did or not, women were under no restrictions concerning property, and in the event of divorce they were entitled to keep whatever they'd brought into the marriage as well as half of whatever had been acquired since.

Bryant did not really approve, especially since he knew of several New England women who were already expressing an unhealthy interest in Arkansan custom. Giving such unnatural latitude to women, he thought, led to a casual attitude toward fornication. Bastardy, which was a major scandal and disgrace in the United States, was treated in Arkansas as a purely civil matter. The man involved—or boy, often enough—was expected to recognize his paternity and, if nothing else, provide support for the child. If he didn't, in fact, the penalties visited upon him by the woman's male relatives could be extremely harsh.

But that was as far as it went. He could marry her or not as he chose. For the girl, the matter was purely one of personal preference. She had no worries of being cast out by her family or of being unable to care for the child. As with the Cherokees, the bastard would simply be brought up by the clan—extended and interconnected families, in the case of the negroes—which were developing some of the features of outright clans, as if it were perfectly legitimate.

"And will you look at that white fellow!" Scott chuckled softly. "Every bit as lustful as any plantation owner's scion, except he won't bother hiding the matter."

It was true enough. The young white soldier's eyes were just as bright as those of any of his comrades in uniform, and he was paying very close attention to the prettiest of the negresses. She, for her part, seemed to reciprocate his interest. The New England poet and reporter wouldn't be at all surprised to discover that, some nine months hence, the world's population had been increased by another mulatto.

Again, Bryant's lips tightened disapprovingly. But Scott's quip also brought out that other side of his upbringing. The white Arkansas soldier's lust might be as reprehensible as that of any young plantation owner's son in Virginia or South Carolina, but there remained one critical difference.

"I'm afraid I can't see the analogy, General. Where I come from, rape is not considered to be a form of seduction."

Scott's back stiffened. Bryant realized he'd offended him. His general disapproval of the situation had made his comment emerge more harshly than he'd intended. Winfield Scott was a Virginian himself, after all.

Fortunately, after a moment, Scott seemed to relax. Indeed, he smiled sardonically.

"True enough, William. True enough." Scott gave the young white soldier another glance, then shrugged slightly. "And I'm also a soldier," he murmured, "and a few days from now that boy might very well be torn in half by a cannonball. So I can't say I'll fret over the possibility he might leave something of himself behind."

He took Bryant by the elbow. The crush at the door was easing. The group they'd been observing was already passing through the double doors. "Finally. Our chance! Come on, William. I confess to being rather fascinated by the chance to see how Arkansans will manage a formal ball. Mind you, I expect the worst."

So it proved. By the end of the evening, Bryant felt like a lemon on two legs, so sour had he become.

In truth, it was worse than he'd expected. He'd thought to see a primitive, awkward version of what he might have observed in New York, Boston, or Philadelphia. He'd completely forgotten—or hadn't taken into account—that a high percentage of the population of Arkansas had come here from New Orleans.

That sinful city, with its Creole ways—all the worse, for its black Creoles. *La Place des Nègres,* the semirecognized open market for negroes in northern New Orleans, was notorious for its nightly revels. Its wild dancing to the sound of *bamboulas* and *banzas* was now being replicated in New Antrim.

Finally the band started playing more familiar music, and

the young revelers assumed the more dignified stances that Bryant associated with American-style dancing. He heaved a small sigh of relief.

Alas.

Not five minutes into the new music, Bryant realized his error. For all the heedless abandon of the previous dances, they'd actually had not much in the way of unsuitable intimate contact. They'd been group dances, basically: congeries and lines of people weaving in and out. Now, however, the theoretically more sedate music allowed young couples to interact quite personally. Which, indeed, they were doing—to a degree that would never have been tolerated in good society in the United States. Not even in Philadelphia or New York, much less Boston.

It was all rather confusing. Part of him was certain he was observing a modern equivalent of Sodom and Gomorrah. In the making, at least, if not quite yet to the biblical standard. Another part, however, was just as certain that the anger of a wrathful deity was centered on other men—the ones even now advancing upon the sinful city from the southeast.

They'd know soon enough, he supposed.

"No."

"Mama!" The wails were simultaneous. Imogene's might have lasted a split second longer.

"No way I letting you two out there. No. Not a chance. End of discussion. And Adaline, too much of your shoulder is showing."

"It's not fair!"

CHAPTER 32

Callender was inclined to give up. "There's no chance she's going to let them out on the floor, Sheff. May as well look for some other partners."

Sheff was made of sterner stuff. Or maybe it was simply that his interest wasn't exactly the same. For Cal McParland, the twin sisters were very attractive even if much too young. He'd enjoy spending an hour or two with Adaline, sure enough. He didn't even have to guess at that. The weeks he'd spent in the care of Senator Johnson's women before he finally recuperated from his wound had been quite pleasant, in that regard.

But he'd enjoy the company of other girls at the ball, also—with the added incentive that, just possibly, an older girl might have a more concentrated purpose in coming here this evening. They'd be in a battle very soon. Callender was feeling all of his mortality and the ancient urges that went with it.

Yes, Adaline was a very pretty girl, and quite vivacious. She was also only thirteen. Even leaving aside that dragon mother, Cal's interest in her could only go so far. Three or four years from now . . .

Was three or four years from now. Cal might very well be dead in three or four days.

Sheff understood all that. He felt some of it, himself. But, for him, Imogene Johnson also represented something else.

He didn't care about her age. Well, not much. A pity she wasn't older, of course, but time would pass. That assumed he survived the war, but Sheff didn't see any point in brooding on that. He would or he wouldn't. If he didn't, it was all a moot point.

But what if he *did*?

In the months since he'd accepted the Laird's offer of a commission, Lieutenant Sheffield Parker had come to be consumed by an emotion so exotic that it had taken him some time even to recognize it for what it was.

Ambition.

Not the cramped, stunted, freedman's version of it, either. This was the great, vaulting, white man's variety. The one that saw no limits between a man and what he might achieve, except the capabilities and determination of the man himself.

Sheff had spent weeks thinking about it, in the methodical way he did such things. He was not impulsive, the way his friend Callender often was. Perhaps that was the result of their different upbringing, perhaps simply a difference in personality, most likely both.

So far, he'd come to three conclusions. Two of them firm, the third . . . firming up quickly.

First, and most obviously, he needed to get an education. A real one, not the haphazard affair that a freedman's son got in an American city like Baltimore.

Fortunately, the means for that were at hand. There were, by now, half a dozen missionary schools in New Antrim and at least three in Fort of 98. Sheff had already begun investigating them when to his relief—the Laird made the choice unnecessary. Arkansas' chief decreed that the army needed a school of its own, and he set it up within a week.

The teachers were all Christian missionaries, of course. But since the school was secular, most of the education concentrated on the practical business of reading, writing, arithmetic, and the like. That suited Sheffield just fine. He didn't need Bible instruction. That was the one book in the world he already knew. Pretty much by heart, thanks to his uncle.

The school was military as well as secular, because the Laird also decreed that officers who attended it needed to undergo additional instruction as well. He called it an officers college and asked Major General Ross to oversee it.

Ross did more than that, actually. He was the college's principal instructor himself.

Sheff liked Robert Ross, once he got the measure of the man. And Sheff had an admiration for the Laird that came

very close to outright hero worship, and one for Charles Ball
that wasn't much the slighter.

So, inexorably, he'd come to the second of his conclusions. Ambition needed education as a means, but it also
needed a channel to focus itself upon. In Sheff's case, that
would be the army. The only other alternatives were politics
and business, and Sheff didn't think he had any particular
aptitude for either. Or any real interest, for that matter.

But he thought he had the makings of a good soldier. And,
for what it was worth—which was quite a bit—he had the
encouragement of both Driscol and Ross to spur him on.
General Ball had had complimentary things to say, also,
which was something of a minor miracle.

So. Education, and a career. That left . . .

Sheff had no firm opinion of the customs that he saw
emerging around him in Arkansas. He didn't share his uncle
Jem's stern disapproval or his mother's ambivalence. That
was mostly because he saw the issue as being personally irrelevant.

Others could do what they chose. Sheffield Parker wanted
to rise as far as he possibly could in this life. And, looking
around him at the men he took for his role models, he saw
one characteristic in common.

They were all married. Even Charles Ball, although his
uncle would insist that the ceremony that had united him and
the notorious Laveau woman was more heathen than Christian.

Patrick Driscol was married. Robert Ross was married.
Sam Houston was a widower, now, but he'd been married.
Nor was it a race matter. The two outstanding leaders of the
Cherokees, John Ross and Major Ridge, were both married.
So was Ridge's son John—in his case, to a white girl he'd
met while he'd been in the United States pursuing his educa-
tion.

That was the way ambitious men conducted themselves in
the United States also, he knew. Sheff couldn't think of a
single man of any prominence in America who wasn't married, unless his wife had died.

So, he'd started turning his mind to that problem. No
sooner had he done so than the figure of Imogene Johnson
had come into very clear and sharp focus. Almost instantly,

she'd gone from being a very attractive but too young to being something completely different.

The girl was *important*. A girl to *aim* for. Her father was a United States senator. She'd been raised in wealth and privilege, even if the privileges had been somewhat constrained by her skin color.

But the latter, from Sheff's viewpoint, was what made the whole thing thinkable at all. John Ridge had married a white girl, and from what Sheff could determine the marriage seemed to be working out quite well. But Sheff couldn't even contemplate the idea, leaving aside whatever social barriers he might encounter. The idea of a white wife just made him nervous.

Imogene, on the other hand . . .

"Come on, Sheff." Cal jogged his elbow. "Let's mingle a bit."

Sheff made his decision. You couldn't be an officer unless you were bold, after all.

"No," he said, shaking his head. "But you go ahead if you want to."

With no further ado, he headed for Julia Chinn and her daughters, seated against one of the walls of the great hall. Behind him, he heard Cal mutter something. He wasn't sure, but he thought it had been "Damn hero! You'll get us both killed in action."

Sheff had to consciously restrain himself from adopting a quick march pace. It wasn't easy. By now, that had become his ingrained habit whenever there was something urgent and pressing to be done. He knew that Robert Ross was still critical of many features of the Arkansas Army, especially its small officer corps, but the one thing he would allow was that it was probably the best disciplined and best trained army in existence, when it came to a sergeant's basics. Certainly on this side of the Atlantic.

Imogene spotted him almost immediately. With a new feeling—plain warmth, instead of nervous excitement—Sheff realized that was because she'd been keeping an eye on him since the ball started. He didn't begin to understand why the girl was interested in him. But that she was, he was now quite certain.

In the uncanny way the two had, her twin's sudden interest registered on Adaline within a couple of seconds. Now she, too, was watching him come closer. Or, more likely—he thought he could hear Cal's footsteps behind him—his fellow officer.

After a moment, Adaline's gaze began sliding off and then back again, in the awkward way a thirteen-year-old girl tries to act demure in public.

Imogene didn't bother. Her eyes remained fixed on Sheff the whole time. So did the big smile on her face.

By the time Sheff was within twenty feet, their mother had spotted him also. The expression on her face made it clear that he was about as welcome as a tornado.

Fortitude, fortitude. He kept advancing fearlessly.

"The girls will not be dancing, Lieutenant Parker," Julia Chinn announced as soon as he came up. She stated the sentence with the same firmness a granite boulder might announce it was a real, no-fooling rock.

"Oh, certainly, Miz Julia. They're still a bit young for such carryings-on." He was quite proud of the smooth way he said that. Not a single stammer or waver anywhere in it, even with his hands properly clasped behind his back. "But it occurred to me you might need some refreshments by now, and—"

He nodded toward their chairs. "If you relinquish these seats, you'll never get them back, with this mob."

He said and did all that smoothly, too. With just the right smile: slight, sophisticated, relaxed, at ease. Fortunately, he'd had a better role model for such business over the past few months than he'd ever had in his life. Major General Robert Ross did *everything* with style, and he made it a point to correct his students' manners if they lapsed—which they often did—into the sergeants' ways of the older officers of the army.

He'd heard the Laird grumble once that Ross seemed determined to produce a pack of young officers who acted for all the world as if they were English gentry. Which he thought absurd, given that all but seven of them were black. But on this subject at least, Sheff was firmly in the British general's camp.

Julia Chinn was staring at him. The hostility was still there in full force—it didn't even lessen when Cal showed up alongside Sheff—but she now seemed a bit startled, also.

"I *am* thirsty, Mama," Imogene said.

"So am I. And you were just complaining about it yourself," her twin added.

Chinn glanced at the girls. Then, at the long table at the far end of the ballroom where the drinks were being served.

"Well . . ."

She rallied for an instant. "I'm not having these girls touching any liquor! Certainly not the blackstrap and applejack they're serving over there. No wine, neither."

"Of course not, ma'am." Cal unclasped his hands and motioned toward the table with his right. "But I believe there's some apple cider available, as well as tea. And I can probably rummage up some tea cakes, as well."

"I *am* a little hungry, Mama," Imogene immediately piped up.

The refrain from Adaline followed as smoothly as if they'd rehearsed it: "So am I. And you were just commenting yourself—"

"Enough!" Chinn nodded abruptly. "Very well, then. Some tea and cakes would be nice. And, ah, thank you, Lieutenant Parker. You as well, Lieutenant McParland."

Once the refreshments were brought to Julia Chinn and her daughters, Sheff didn't try to dawdle in their company for more than a reasonably gracious minute or two. Just an officer and a gentleman, doing his duty. If he'd learned nothing else from Robert Ross over the past few months, he'd learned the difference between a battle and a campaign, and a campaign and a war.

This was a campaign at the very least. He hoped he could avoid an outright war.

"You're still plotting, aren't you?" Cal grumbled after they left.

"Yes."

Sheff kept an eye on them throughout the next hour, maintaining proper position. Once he saw that Julia was finally taking the girls out of the ballroom, he moved to intercept them just outside the hotel. By now, Callender was no longer with him. He'd gotten distracted by the dancing, followed by a friendly argument with another artillery officer. The sort of argument that two young men get into, neither of them knowing much concerning the subject they were debating and both of them absolutely certain they were correct. A complete waste of time, so far as Sheff was concerned.

. He emerged out of the shadows just as the Johnson women came off the veranda onto the street.

"Miz Julia. What a surprise. I was just leaving for the barracks myself. I need to be up early tomorrow to see to the arrangements for the march." He gave the twins a courteous nod. "Imogene. Adaline."

Chinn was looking at him suspiciously. So it seemed, at any rate. The light shed by the two lamps on the veranda was poor, and the streets beyond were completely dark except for an occasional lamp in front of a tavern.

Sheff had come prepared for that, of course. He didn't think he was the smartest young fellow around, not by a long shot. But he was possibly the most methodical and systematic.

He held up the oil lamp in his hand, which he hadn't lit yet. "I've a lamp handy. If you'll give me a moment to strike a light, perhaps I could escort you home."

Julia had given up her rooms at the hotel six weeks earlier, foreseeing the prospect of an immense influx of Choctaw refugees. She'd rented rooms in one of New Antrim's few good boardinghouses, just four blocks up the street. The lodgings weren't as spacious as they'd enjoyed at the Wolfe Tone, but the boardinghouse was considerably quieter than the hotel, and the food was better. The black family who owned and operated the boardinghouse and its adjacent tavern were freedmen from New York, who had experience in the trade.

She hesitated for a moment. Quite obviously, torn between the impulse to refuse and the practical reality that walking in the dark down New Antrim's streets—the main street perhaps worst of all—was a chancy business without a lamp. Even in boots, much less good shoes.

"Well . . . I was thinking of hiring a carriage."

Sheff waited patiently, the very soul of politeness, while Julia worked out the arithmetic herself. True, New Antrim *did* have public carriages. Quite a few of them, in fact, since that was a trade that was open to black people in the United States. Mostly simple buckboards in the summer and booby huts in the winter—the ungainly sleighs that were sometimes called Boston boobies. An occasional shay or even a Dearborn here and there.

The problem was that the city also had, by now, a population as large as that of any in the United States outside of New York, Philadelphia, Boston, and Baltimore. And if the population was proportionately much poorer, that was mostly due to the absence of much in the way of a wealthy upper crust. The average resident of New Antrim wasn't probably any worse off than the average resident of New York or Philadelphia, certainly not the average immigrant. Most of them could afford a carriage, now and then, for special occasions.

Which tonight most definitely was. In a few days, Arkansas would be fighting for its very existence. The whole city was turning out to cheer on its army, whether they could get into the Wolfe Tone or not.

"Well . . ."

"Oh, *Mama*." That was Adaline, not Imogene, expressing simple impatience. Imogene was—probably wisely—keeping her mouth shut.

A strange little smile came to Julia Chinn's face. It seemed so, at least, to Sheff. More sad than anything else. He wasn't sure, though. The lighting on the veranda really wasn't very good.

"Very well, Lieutenant. And thank you for the offer."

On the way to the boardinghouse, Julia began questioning Sheff. Pointed questions concerning his own prospects, to his surprise, rather than the general inquiries he'd expected regarding the upcoming campaign.

"But why the *infantry*, Lieutenant Parker? It's . . . Well, I can only go by what my—the senator says—but Dick tells me the infantry is the lowest-regarded of the service branches. At least in the United States Army."

"That's true, ma'am. Engineers are held in the highest esteem in the American army, followed by artillerymen, cavalrymen—and, sure 'nough, infantrymen at the very bottom."

He gave her a smile that he hoped looked confident. Assuming she could see it at all, in the light thrown off by a single lamp. "But the thing is, Miz Julia, the U.S. Army is mostly designed for peacetime. The main thing they do is build dams and the like. And since that sort of civil engineering requires advanced mathematics—the artillery also, to some extent—it draws the best educated men."

He shrugged. "Which I'm not. But the Laird doesn't look at it the same way, in any event. Neither does General Ball. Arkansas is mountain country, from a military point of view."

"Most of the people don't live up there," Adaline objected.

"Yes, I know, Miss Johnson. Most people in Arkansas live in New Antrim, the Fort of 98, or somewhere in the river valley. But that's not where any big war will be decided. Our enemies can probably take the Delta and the lower river valley, if they try hard enough. Maybe even New Antrim.They can't take the Ozarks and the Ouachitas. That's where Arkansas lives and dies—and that's infantry country."

They'd reached the boardinghouse. "Arkansas has the best infantry in the world. That's our opinion, anyway—and we aim to prove it, sometime in the next week or so."

Sheff held the lamp a little higher to allow the women a good view of the short staircase. "It's been a pleasure, ladies."

"Be careful, Sheff!" Imogene blurted out. "Please be careful!"

In the dim lighting, right then, she looked much older than she was. A young woman instead of a girl. Sheff thought his heart might have skipped a beat or two.

Or three. Lord, she was pretty.

"Please be careful," she repeated.

"Imogene, stop carrying on," her mother scolded her. But there wasn't much heat in it.

"Thank you for the courtesy, Lieutenant. We'll be going in now. Please take our best wishes with you. And . . . Well. Be careful."

A moment later, she was shooing the girls into the boardinghouse. Sheff waited until the door closed, and then went on his way.

*   *   *

As soon as they got into the house, Imogene raced over to the small window that gave a view of the street outside. Within a second she had her nose pressed to the pane.

"Imogene, stop carrying on!"

"He's gonna get hurt, Mama," the girl whispered. "I just know he is. Maybe even kilt."

"It's 'going' to get hurt, not 'gonna.' And if I hear you say 'kilt' again, you'll be the one kilt. And take your face out of the window!"

Imogene's nose didn't budge.

"Oh, Mama, please. I really *like* Sheff."

Julia sighed. She wasn't really up for this battle. The problem was . . .

She liked Sheffield Parker herself. Quite a bit, in fact. He seemed like a very levelheaded and reliable young man. Quite well suited to Imogene, actually, who was a bit too high-strung.

But it just wouldn't do. Richard would have conniptions at the idea. And while Julia didn't have the same emotional reaction, she didn't really disagree with him. A person had to be cold-blooded about these things. The best chance Imogene and Adaline would have in this world, with everything else they had against them, would be to marry white men. Not a negro boy whose skin was almost literally as black as coal. It didn't matter what else might be true about him. Not until the afterlife, at any rate.

"He's going to get hurt," Imogene said. "Oh, Mama, I just *know* it!"

Under the circumstances, Julia decided to settle for the grammatical victory.

CHAPTER 33

The Arkansas River
Three miles downstream from Arkansas Post
JULY 22, 1825

Gloomily, Major General William Henry Harrison watched
men from one of the batteries of the 1st Artillery struggling
with a six-pounder whose carriage had gotten stuck in the mud
by the riverbank. They were having to manhandle the thing
up onto dry land—drier land, rather—because the footing
was so bad that trying to use horses for the purpose would
have been more trouble than it was worth.

"Wish we had some oxen." That came from Stephen
Fleming, one of the young lieutenants who served as an aide
to the general.

"And what good would that do?" Harrison almost snarled
the words. He pointed a finger at the battery, whose three
other guns and two howitzers had finally been dragged clear
of the muck on the riverbank. "That's supposed to be *field*
artillery, you—"

He bit off the rest. Then, after a moment to steady his temper, continued in a more even tone. "The whole point of
light artillery, Lieutenant Fleming, is to be able to maneuver
with it on a battlefield. Maneuver—with oxen! Do you know
how fast a team of oxen can pull a cannon? Any cannon,
whether it's a four-pounder or a siege gun?"

Abashed, the young lieutenant avoided his commanding
general's gaze. "Uh. No, sir. I don't."

"One. Mile. An. Hour." Harrison shifted his glare from the
hapless officer to the battery crew still struggling with the six-
pounder. "Which is just about what we're managing as it is."

He looked up at the sun to gauge the time, rather than taking the trouble to pull out his watch. It was already at least an hour past noon. No way to begin the assault on Arkansas Post until the morrow, at the earliest. They'd lost *another* day.

The whole campaign, thus far, seemed to be nothing more than one lost day after another. Silently, Harrison spent the next few seconds cursing Thomas Jesup and the Arkansas Delta in about equal proportions.

That done, he spent considerably more time cursing militiamen in general and the Georgia militia in particular. Their slack habits, near-constant drunkenness, and indiscipline had cost him at least as much in the way of lost days as fouled-up logistics and soggy terrain.

He'd been warned about them by Andrew Jackson himself, when he'd paid the Tennessee senator a visit at the Hermitage in mid-April. Harrison had decided he could afford to take the time to do so, since his supplies were so badly snarled it would be at least two weeks before anything got moving again.

Jackson had been cordial, and the visit had gone smoothly. There was no love lost between the two men, to be sure—never had been—but Jackson was being careful. The running stream of caustic and excoriating comments he was having published in the nation's newspapers concerning "Clay's War" were always aimed entirely at Henry Clay and John Calhoun and the politicians around them. Toward the U.S. Army itself, Jackson's stance was friendly and supportive. In public, at least—and in private as well, if the tenor of Harrison's visit with him was any gauge.

"No militia's worth much, of course, unless you've got time to train them thoroughly—which you usually don't, because their terms of enlistment are so short. But the Georgians are the worst of all."

They'd been standing in the front yard of the Hermitage when Jackson made the comment. He pointed to an aged hound lying in the shade by the wall of the house. "Old Hussar, over there, is no lazier. The difference is, he don't drink, he don't gamble, he don't steal—well, not much; nothing compared to what a Georgian will—he don't rape all the womenfolk he can get his paws on, he don't sass you, he don't argue every blasted thing under the sun"—Jackson took time for a breath—"and he don't run off in a panic if a rooster crows or a cat hisses at him."

"That bad?"

Jackson nodded. "That bad. The worst of it is they're also the biggest braggarts in the country. If you didn't know better, just listening to 'em, you'd swear that their forefathers whupped Alexander the Great and Julius Caesar, and their own martial accomplishments put those to shame."

Jackson barked a sarcastic laugh. "Southron valor, they call it. Bah. I wouldn't trade a whole company of Georgia militia for one Tennessean or two Kentuckians. Well. Three Kentuckians. You always got to subtract one Kentuckian on account of the whiskey consumption."

At the time, Harrison had thought Jackson was exaggerating. The man was notorious for his vindictive temper and his unrelenting feuds, after all. The stories of his clashes with Georgia militiamen during the war with the Creeks were well known.

Now, three months later, Harrison was more inclined to think Jackson had been light-handed in his condemnation. Evenhanded, for sure. The bastards *were* that bad.

He'd had the unit that committed the outrages on the Quapaws put under arrest as soon as he heard about the incident. But he was sure there'd still be Sam Hill to pay when the newspapers got hold of the story. Which they surely would, as many pestiferous reporters as the army had hanging around it, like flies on a horse.

Harrison took a few more seconds to silently curse newspapers and newspapermen. And the abolitionist maniacs and bedlamites who were egging them on. What had the world come to, when a military campaign against Indians and rebellious negroes had to worry about maintaining a so-called good press?

To be sure, any competent commander would punish soldiers who committed flagrant atrocities, even against savages. But that was simply for the purpose of maintaining discipline. Nobody actually cared that much about the incidents themselves. It wasn't as if any treatment was being visited on the savages that they didn't commit themselves, after all.

But . . . Harrison did have to concern himself over the business. He'd been given explicit instructions by the president. By the secretary of war, also, but for Calhoun that was obviously just a formality. Henry Clay, on the other hand, had been quite serious about it—and, for once, Harrison didn't think that had been purely a matter of maintaining his political reputation. The newly elected chief executive had seemed genuinely concerned that the conflict with Arkansas be waged according to civilized rules of war.

The idiot. Only a man who'd never gotten any closer to a battlefield than—

Harrison broke off his sour train of thought. The battery had finally gotten the last of the six-pounders clear of the mud. Thank the heavens. Now, maybe they could—

A different young officer was at his elbow, looking fidgety. John Riehl, his name was, if Harrison remembered correctly.

"What is it, Lieutenant?"

"Ah, sir, the commander of the Louisiana militia is complaining that his men aren't being fed properly. Well. The food's all right, I guess, but he's real peeved that the regulars and the Georgia—"

"Tell that fucking—! No. Never mind. I'll tell him myself. Where is he?"

Riehl looked more fidgety than ever. "Ah. Well, that's the other thing. He and the rest of the Louisiana officers went off afterward—after he chewed on me, I mean—to have lunch on the *Chesapeake* to get some relief from the heat, and . . . well."

"Don't tell me," Harrison said through gritted teeth.

"Yes, sir. She ran aground on a sandbar."

Lieutenant Riehl cleared his throat. "Again."

The Arkansas River
Missouri Territory
JULY 22, 1825

Some four hundred miles to the northwest, Colonel Zachary Taylor wasn't in any better mood. In his case, though, the source of dissatisfaction was far more concentrated. The Missouri militiamen he'd been saddled with weren't really that much of a problem, and he had no complaints at all concerning the terrain. The plains in that part of Missouri Territory that some people were starting to call Kansas were perfectly dry this time of year, even next to the river.

It helped, naturally, that the Arkansas River this far upstream from the Confederacy didn't bear much resemblance to the big river that passed through Fort of 98, New Antrim, and Arkansas Post before it emptied into the Mississippi. The Arkansas was the fourth longest river in North America, with its headwaters in the Rocky Mountains far to the west. But for most of its length—especially in midsummer, after the end of the snowmelt—it was a modest affair.

No, Taylor's foul mood was solely and entirely due to one single man.

Robert Mitchell. Plucked from obscurity as a junior state representative from South Carolina by the secretary of war personally, and foisted on Colonel Taylor's "Army of the Missouri" as a special commissioner to handle relations with the Indian tribes of the Great Plains.

It sometimes seemed to Taylor that John C. Calhoun's madness had no limits. Had the former senator from South Carolina suffered from simple dementia, the dementia itself would have conscribed his sphere of action. But Calhoun's disease was a mania, more than maniacalism as such.

So—Heaven grant mercy—it possessed theories. Notions. Schemes. Delusions of certainty, and convictions that were unshakable in direct proportion to their lack of bearing on reality.

All of which traits were concentrated in the person of Robert Mitchell to a degree that was genuinely breathtaking. As if the man were the distilled essence of lunacy, given two legs to walk about—and, alas, armed with the powers given him by the secretary of war and the president of the United States.

The division of authority was clear and simple. Colonel Zachary Taylor was in command of all U.S. military forces assembled under the somewhat preposterous name of the Army of the Missouri. To put the matter in less grandiose perspective, he commanded the 2nd and 6th Infantry Regiments and two full batteries from the 3rd Artillery—about fourteen hundred men, all told.

Special commissioner Mitchell, however, had been given full authority to treat with any and all Indian tribes west of the Mississippi, saving only those who were part of the Confederacy. He had the power to make whatever treaties and arrangements with said tribes he felt would be to the advantage of the mission of the Army of the Missouri, with no regard whatsoever for what the actual commander of that army might think.

It was sheer madness. The only thing Taylor could figure out was that Calhoun, having—very disapprovingly—seen the way in which, in years past, Sam Houston had transformed a similar special commission into something that bore a definite resemblance to a magic wand, had decided that the magic resided in the title, not the man.

Sam Houston had been adopted by the Cherokees as a teenager, was intimately familiar with their ways and customs, and was fluent in most of the languages of the southern tribes: Cherokee, Choctaw, and the major dialects of the Creeks. He also had a passing knowledge of some of the Plains Indians' tongues.

So, naturally, Calhoun had appointed a man to the post who spoke no Indian languages at all, had never in his life had any real contact with Indians, and was still confused by the fact that the chiefs of the southern tribes wore turbans instead of feather headdresses.

Sam Houston had also had a detailed and in-depth knowledge of the political factions and political issues in dispute among the Indian tribes he dealt with. Whereas it had never occurred to Robert Mitchell—still didn't, so far as Taylor could tell—that Indians had any "politics" to begin with. He seemed to think they behaved according to some mystical inner tribal essence, or something.

But that wasn't surprising, really. Mitchell was one of Calhoun's most fervent—say better, fevered—partisans. So far as he was concerned, the only people in the world who really deserved the term "people" at all were white men. All the other breeds weren't simply lesser ones. They were, in some fundamental sense, not really human to begin with. Semi-intelligent two-legged animals, basically, who managed with great effort and usually ridiculous results to mimic some of the simpler aspects of human society.

To make things worse, the only trait Mitchell shared as special commissioner with his predecessor Sam Houston was that he was scrupulously honest. So there wasn't even the hope—usually a near certainty, with Indian agents—that he'd soon be distracted from his Great Mission by the usual vices of peculation and swindling.

Not that his personal honesty did any good for Indians. Since Mitchell couldn't speak any of the indigenous tongues, he was forced to rely on the existing network of Indian agents to translate for him and to carry out the ensuing decisions and agreements. Which, of course, they did in their usual corrupt manner.

Houston had had to deal with them also, of course. The difference had been that Houston spoke the languages as well as they did, was approximately five times smarter, and had a network of his own in most of the major tribes that was better than that of his subordinates. He'd overseen them the way a great gray wolf oversees foxes. The foxes had been on their very, very best behavior.

But worst of all—worse than anything—was the man's temperament. Mitchell was so infuriatingly *chipper*.

"Splendid news, Colonel! The Kiowas have agreed to join our cause!"

With an air of great self-satisfaction, Mitchell plopped himself down onto one of the stools in Taylor's command tent. Taylor was still using the tent for his headquarters until the fort's construction was finished, even though he'd started sleeping in the commander's quarters of it. This was a big fort being erected on the Arkansas, since it would have to serve as the base of operations for the whole campaign. The noise from the construction work during the day was too much to allow for the conduct of business.

Mitchell bestowed a beaming smile on the colonel and his two medical officers, who'd been in the tent discussing the health issues facing the army. They were Surgeon John H. Bendel and Assistant Surgeon Charles Stewart.

Taylor had insisted on having a full medical unit attached to the expedition, all the way down to two ambulances staffed by each of the artillery batteries. He'd known Bendel for years and had specifically requested him. Stewart was a

Rhode Islander, new to the service. But in the short time since he'd been with the expedition, Zack had been pleased with his performance.

As he was again, that moment. He'd come to realize that Stewart had a very sly, very dry sense of humor. Quite different from Zack's own, but still one he could appreciate.

The assistant surgeon's eyes widened. "The Kiowas have expressed a deep concern over the prospect that an independent Arkansas might stir unrest among black slaves in the Carolinas? Who would have imagined?"

Taylor managed—barely—to choke down a laugh. Bendel didn't do quite as well.

Mitchell gave Bendel a quick glare, followed by a longer one aimed at his assistant.

"I fail to see the humor, Mr. Stewart. Of course the savages don't care about the maintenance of proper racial order in the United States. What difference does that make? The Kiowas have agreed to join our campaign against the Confederacy, which is all that matters."

There were so many errors in that last sentence that Taylor didn't know where to begin.

So he simply started with the subject. "*Which* Kiowas, Robert?"

"Ah. Well, two of their chiefs." Mitchell pronounced two names, neither of which meant anything to Zack. That was assuming that the special commissioner was pronouncing them correctly in the first place, which was about as likely as snow in July.

"I'm not actually sure which clans they represent," he admitted.

"Well, that part's easy enough," said Taylor. "They didn't represent any. The Kiowas aren't divided into clans."

"But . . . they have to be."

Clearly, Zack had contradicted one of Mitchell's certain pieces of Indian lore. He might as well have said the sun rose in the west. There were two things the special commissioner Knew To Be True. Indian chiefs all wore feather headdresses, and Indians all belonged to clans.

"Why?" grunted the surgeon. "We're not divided into clans."

"Leaving aside Scotsmen, Baltimore plug-uglies, and

opera enthusiasts," his assistant quipped. The Rhode Islander's derision for Mitchell, however, was momentarily overridden by simple interest.

"Is that indeed the case, Colonel?" he asked. "I confess I labored under the same misapprehension as the special commissioner."

Bendel answered before Taylor could. Like Zachary, he'd spent years serving on the frontier. "They're all called Indians. But the truth is, Charles, that's just a white man's notion. There's as much difference between the southern tribes like the Cherokees and the nomads on the plains as there is between a Frenchman and a Mongol. Their languages aren't remotely similar, their customs are different, their religion is different—native religion, I mean, insofar as the Cherokees still retain it—and the whole way they look at the world is different. There's no love lost between them, either, believe you me."

Taylor chimed in. "The Kiowas don't reckon descent through the mother, the way the southern tribes do. And, no, they don't have clans of any kind. They've got loosely defined ranks, instead. It's a nobility of sorts, except a man can move up or down depending on his accomplishments and behavior. The most important divisions, for men at least, are the six military societies. The Dog Soldiers, they're called."

Unable to resist the temptation, he turned back to Mitchell. "So, Special Commissioner. Which Dog Soldiers may we rely upon to augment our forces? And were these two 'chiefs' ranked Onde or Odegupa? It'll make a difference."

Mitchell just stared at him.

After a few seconds, Taylor gave up the momentary pleasure. "Never mind."

The special commissioner rose and headed for the entrance to the tent. Once he had the flap pulled aside, he gave Taylor a cheery look over his shoulder. "I don't see what difference it could make, Colonel. Once they receive the guns I promised them, they'll surely rally to our side."

Then he was gone.

"Marvelous," Bendel muttered. "Just what the world needs. Well-armed Kiowas. Do you know, Zack—just yesterday—the lunatic told me he was planning to pass out arms to the Comanches also. In the event they 'rallied to our cause,' of course."

"Oh, God help us."

"Yup. Comanches. Between whom and the Huns the only difference I can see is that the Huns were less barbaric. *Everybody* hates Comanches. Even more than they do Kiowas."

The assistant surgeon had been looking back and forth between them. "This is a problem, I take it? Forgive my ignorance. I'm from Rhode Island, as you know."

Bendel grunted. "Yeah, Charles, you could call it that. 'A problem.' Our blessed special commissioner has been making promises to provide guns and ammunition for every tribe of nomads anywhere in the area. The worst of it is, he'll likely manage to do it, too, with the backing he's got from Calhoun."

"For which," Taylor growled, "we'll get practically no help in our campaign against the Confederacy. No direct military help, for sure. The Osage and the Kiowas— certainly the Comanches—will raid outlying Cherokee and Creek settlements. Commit their usual depredations and outrages. That will have the effect of infuriating the southern Indians and making them cleave more tightly to the Arkansans—which is exactly the opposite of what we *should* be doing."

He ran angry fingers through hair caked with dust and sweat. "Best of all, when the war's over—which it will be, sooner or later—the idiot will have scattered guns all over the southern plains, putting them in the hands of the worst tribes I can think of. God damn the fucking bastard. The army'll be putting the pieces back together for years."

"Years and years," the surgeon agreed. "Trust us on this, Charles. A war between the United States and the Confederacy—Cherokees or Arkansas negroes, it really doesn't matter—will be a pretty civilized business." He nodded toward the tent entrance. "Which the wars we'll have with those nomad savages out there for twenty or thirty years afterward will be anything but."

Taylor was tempted to add a verbal damnation onto the heads of Henry Clay and John Calhoun, too. But he was a career officer, so he stifled the impulse. That would, after all, technically be insubordination. Even if the chances that either of the medical officers in the tent would report him were about as likely as snow in August.

*Some miles east of the Arkansas River
Missouri Territory*
JULY 22, 1825

"It's him, all right." Scott Powers lowered his eyeglass. "Now all we gotta do is figure out how to pry him out of there."

Lying next to him in the tall grass, Ray Thompson squinted at the distant bandit camp. "Why can't we just ride in there? You said his cousin was a friend of yours."

"Well . . . he is, in a manner of speaking. But by now he'll have heard about the reward offer. And, ah . . ."

"Right. He might suspect your motives."

Powers grinned mirthlessly. "About as likely as a rooster guarding hens, who spots a coyote coming. 'Well, hello there, my old friend the rooster. I just dropped by to pay a social call.'"

Ray went back to studying the bandit camp some hundred yards away. "Why hasn't *he* turned him in for the reward, do you think?"

Scott shrugged, insofar as a man could manage that gesture while lying prone. "Who knows? Eddie's another Georgian. You know the type. Walk around calling themselves Southrons and challenging their images in a mirror to a duel because of some slight nobody else noticed. Crazy bastards can find a point of honor in anything. There's no way he's going to let us have Andrew Clark without a fight."

Ray sucked his teeth. "You know, Scott, you *could* have maybe mentioned this little problem a few weeks back. Before we added horse stealing and card cheating to our track record."

"We let the horses go, and we didn't get *caught* cheating," Powers pointed out, reasonably enough. "And we would have needed the money no matter what. Besides, I got a plan."

"A plan. That'll somehow make it possible for two men—yeah, sure, we're the most dangerous desperadoes on the frontier—to win a gunfight with eleven bandits. *And* an assassin, even if we know he can't shoot straight. You got a plan."

The same grin came back to Powers's face. "Well, of course *that's* not the plan. Do I look like an idiot? But why bother? When—"

He rolled a little sideways to clear his left arm and pointed to the southwest. "When just over yonder we got two regiments of the U.S. Army to do the work for us. Even got artillery."

Ray's eyes widened. "You think—"

"Hey, look. Zack Taylor's in command. He'll remember us from when he commanded Cantonment Robertson at Baton Rouge."

"Sure he will," Ray said sourly. "He'll remember we tried to swindle his commissary."

"'Swindling's' an awful harsh way to put what I prefer to think of as frugal business practices. It's hard to keep meat from getting wormy in the Delta. Even if you try."

"It's the way *he'll* put it. Taylor's always been unreasonable."

Scott shook his head. "Fine. But it's beside the point. All we have to do is convince him we know where Mrs. Houston's killer is. For that, our perhaps unsavory reputation will work in our favor. 'Thieves falling out,' as they say."

Thompson thought about it for a moment. "You think?"

Scott did that awkward prone shrug again. "Worth a try, the way I see it. It sure beats eleven-to-two odds in a gunfight. Even ten-to-three, figuring that any dang fool who can't hit a man as big as Houston at point-blank range is likely to shoot one of his own."

"Well, that's true."

CHAPTER 34

Arkansas Post
JULY 23, 1825

By the time Sheff's 3rd Infantry got close enough to get a good view of Arkansas Post, the fort was already under siege by the United States Army. Had been, in fact, for at least two hours. They'd been able to hear the cannons from miles away.

Now that Sheff could actually see the Post, he realized that the U.S. forces had begun a mass assault. He'd been puzzled by the fact that the Laird had been moving them so slowly this morning until the quick march of the last two miles. The regiments had needed less than four days to complete the march from New Antrim to their camp upriver the night before. They'd been up and ready by five o'clock this morning and could certainly have reached the Post before the siege had barely gotten under way. Instead, the Laird had taken four hours to cover less than ten miles. For Arkansas regiments, except for the last stretch, that amounted to a leisurely promenade.

Now, fitting the sight with what he already knew of their battle plan, he understood. Sheff wondered if he'd ever learn to be that cold-blooded and calculating.

He wasn't sure. But he'd work on it.

It all made sense, of course. Half of the U.S. forces would be tangled up in the assault on the Chickasaws forted up in the Post when the Arkansas regiments got within fighting distance. Harrison would have to match an equal number of regiments against his Confederate opponents until he could call off the assault—which was a lot easier said than done.

By delaying the march, Driscol had partially nullified the Americans' numerical advantage.

It was tough on the Chickasaws, of course. But Sheff didn't see where the army of Arkansas was under any obligation whatsoever to sustain worse casualties in order to rescue them from their own pigheadedness. And he suspected the Laird's cold-bloodedness ran still deeper than that. The Chickasaws were notorious all over the frontier for their pugnacity and independence. Sheff was pretty sure the Laird had no problem at all with the idea of bleeding them half dry before letting them into the Confederacy.

Neither did Sheff, come down to it. The Chickasaws were also notorious—among black people, anyway—for being the one southern Indian tribe that had taken to slavery wholeheartedly. More precisely, they'd traditionally used lots of slaves. The only change in the past few decades was that most of their slaves were now black people purchased on the market instead of other Indians captured in battle.

With their ingrained warrior culture, much more akin to that of Plains Indians than tribes like the Cherokees or the Choctaws, Chickasaw men didn't do much work. Except for fighting and hunting, they thought the proper role for a man was to loll about while the women did all the real labor. So it was hardly surprising that Chickasaw women wanted as many slaves as they could get their hands on.

In short, as far as Sheff was concerned, the Chickasaws were the southern Indian equivalent of South Carolina gentry. Sheff was just about as likely to shed tears over their plight as he was to shed them over the difficulties of men like John Calhoun.

Let 'em bleed. Better them than the regiments. The Arkansan soldiers would bleed plenty enough before this day was over.

"Oh, God damn it," muttered General Harrison. "I didn't think they'd get here this soon."

From his vantage point on one of the artillery berms east of Arkansas Post, he'd just gotten a glimpse of the oncoming Arkansas forces. They were using the well-built military road that followed the north bank of the Arkansas, which placed them on the same side of the river as most of his own army.

He indulged himself in one of those moments of silent cursing that seemed thus far inseparable from the Arkansas campaign. Curses aimed, this time, at the American legislatures of times past.

Congress, in its infinite wisdom, had drastically reduced the size of the U.S. Army in 1815 and again in 1820. The reductions had cut infantry and artillery to the bone and had eliminated the cavalry altogether as an independent branch of service. Not even dragoon units had been kept.

The measure had seemed sensible at the time. Cavalry was expensive to maintain, and neither the War of Independence nor the War of 1812 had seen much in the way of cavalry action. The American military tradition was an infantry and artillery tradition, with cavalry as an afterthought.

That might be fine and dandy, fighting in the relatively cramped terrain of the eastern seaboard amidst a largely friendly populace. Here, fighting in the Delta across the Mississippi, in a countryside whose population was implacably hostile, Harrison was feeling a desperate need for strong cavalry forces.

He was *blind,* damnation! He had no way to determine what might be happening in the surrounding terrain, much farther than his own or his officers' eyes could see with an eyeglass. He'd learned quickly that sending out the small dragoon units he had in his command was pointless. They'd either get killed within five miles or be sent in hasty retreat.

The Delta here in Arkansas was still mostly natural wilderness. The thick woods and underbrush seemed to be crawling with Choctaws. They were quite at home in the terrain and were burning for revenge on the Americans who had just driven them out of Mississippi.

Brown's Raiders were out there, too, somewhere. Harrison's soldiers, especially the militiamen who were usually their target, had developed a real dread of the fanatical abolitionist irregulars.

"Should we call off the assault, sir?" asked Lieutenant Fleming.

Harrison's eyes went back to the fort. He'd spent the first two hours after daybreak bombarding the east wall of Arkansas Post with most of his artillery. Field guns, unfortunately, not one of them bigger than twelve-pounders, and only three of those. Still, they'd done an adequate job of clearing a way in for the infantry, once they got past the outer fortifications. The walls were wooden logs, after all, not stonework. Harrison had been able to move his guns up to what amounted to point-blank range for artillery, since there was no counterbattery fire coming from the Post. Either the Chickasaws didn't know how to use cannons, or—more likely—the Arkansans had taken them out when they'd abandoned the fort. No point leaving the valuable guns in the hands of savages who'd ignore them anyway.

The infantry assault was now in full steam, with both the 3rd and the 5th Infantries engaged. They'd suffered some casualties, but they'd gotten the fascines in place and were on the verge of storming into the fort through the breaches made by the artillery bombardment.

That would be bloody fighting, in there, against Chickasaws. But Harrison was quite confident the two regiments could manage the task. He'd had all of his howitzers raining shells into the Post during the artillery bombardment. Between that and the inevitable tendency of Indian forces to disintegrate into small units under pressure, the Chickasaws would not be able to put up a well-organized and centrally directed defense.

As individual warriors they'd be ferocious enough, as Indians normally were. But it didn't matter. It never had and it never would. Harrison couldn't think of a single battle between coherent and well-led white military forces and Indians in two hundred years that hadn't ended with a victory for the whites and enormous casualties for the Indians. Leaving aside cases of ambush or surprise, or poor leadership, or completely disproportionate numbers—none of which applied here.

"No, Lieutenant. We'll have Arkansas Post within two or three hours. I want that fort. We need a solid base from which to continue the campaign upriver, and it's far better to seize one of the enemy's—especially something this well built—than have to construct one of our own."

He turned to summon the commanders of the 1st and 7th but saw that Colonels McNeil and Arbuckle were already trotting up.

"You've seen them, I assume?" McNeil and Arbuckle had enjoyed a perch on the next berm over.

McNeil simply nodded. Arbuckle, as usual, was verbose.

"Two regiments, I figure, General. They'll be up to strength better than ours, they being so close to home and us so far away. Call it twelve hundred men to our thousand. But John and I can stand them off, long enough"—here came a sneer and a backward wave of the hand—"for that horde of militiamen to finally work up the nerve to join the fight. After that—"

Harrison disliked talkative officers in general, and Arbuckle in particular. "Spare me the obvious, please," he said impatiently. "The militias won't be much good, but there *are* three thousand of them. If you and Colonel McNeil can fix the enemy in place, Colonel Arbuckle, I can get the militias up soon enough to simply overwhelm the foe. I'll give you artillery support, also, once the 3rd and the 5th are into the fort. As much as I can, at any rate, keeping in mind that I need to hold most of the guns by the river in case the Arkansans bring down their steamboats."

Arbuckle opened his mouth, but Harrison cut him off. "Be about it, gentlemen. Now."

Sheff Parker was attached as a second lieutenant to the leading company of the 3rd Infantry, commanded by Captain Charles Dupont. And the 3rd was leading the march down the road to Arkansas Post, with the 2nd following behind. So he had as good a view as anyone of the evolutions of the American forces as they drew near Arkansas Post. He also had a better angle from which to examine the enemy now, since the military road curved to the north, here, just half a mile from the Post. Most of the American units were no longer out of sight behind the bulk of the fort.

They were . . .

Reacting pretty much the way the Laird had predicted. Driscol, either because of his own temperament or because of Robert Ross's coaching—both, most likely—was not in the habit of keeping his officers in the dark regarding his plans. He'd thought that Harrison would take the risk of dividing his forces rather than ignoring the Chickasaws altogether and concentrating everything against the Arkansans.

That was foolish. Concepts that had seemed abstract and half unreal in Ross's seminars now took on real life and concrete weight. It wasn't just simply that "division of forces" lowered the numerical strength of a military force. Now that Sheff could see an enemy actually doing it, on a real battlefield, he could fully understand something else Ross had told them.

Battlefields were incipient chaos, just waiting to happen. The noise alone—they were still hundreds of yards from the fighting—was numbing to the mind as well as deafening to the ears. Add to that the clouds of gunsmoke that would soon be obscuring everything, the shrieks and screams of injured and frightened men, the confused and half-heard orders of officers trying to maintain control in a tornado—

"Dividing your forces" meant doubling the demands on your brain and nerves at the same time as you lessened your ability to act. It wasn't *impossible,* as a tactic. In fact, the Laird was planning to do it himself if the opportunity arose. But it did require, as a supposition, that your army was not only well trained but also had an officer corps that was accustomed to working together and operating independently when needed.

The first might be true of the American regulars, here. They'd find out soon enough. But the second wouldn't be.

Couldn't be. Until a few months ago, these American regiments had been scattered in posts all over the country, and it was a country that filled a good part of a continent. Many of those officers had never worked together, and even the ones who had, hadn't done so since the end of the war with Britain ten years ago.

"Never forget something, gentlemen," Robert Ross had told them in one of the seminars. "When you read accounts of a battle written afterward, it all seems very primitive. The actions of men with, it would seem, not much more in the way of sagacity than a six-year-old child."

He stood, then, and began gesturing. His right hand straight out, forefinger pointing down. "You, remain here."

His left hand, forefinger pointing out. "You, move around to the left—that way—and go over there."

He brought both fingers together. "Then, attack the enemy together."

He dropped his hands and gave them a smile. "Doesn't seem like much, does it? Walk a straight line while rubbing your stomach. Any child can do as much."

There'd been a little titter of a laugh. Ross had shared in the humor for a moment. But the smile faded soon enough.

"Yes, very simple indeed. But you'll be trying to do it under the worst imaginable conditions. Conditions that are literally impossible to describe adequately in mere words. Conditions that will hammer your senses, hammer your body, and certainly destroy bodies around you, if not your own; conditions that will leave your mind grasping for sanity. And all the while, as officers, you'll be expected and required to think and act coherently. Not only for yourself, but as leaders of men. Imagine, if you will, trying to walk a straight line while rubbing your stomach, in the middle of a house on fire and collapsing around you—and making sure all the men following you are doing the same."

The British general resumed his seat at the table. "And now—O ye military geniuses—you propose to divide your forces as well. So you have *twice* as much to keep track of, and worry about, in the middle of all that."

The laugh that time had been more than a titter.

Ross shrugged. "It can be done, mind you. Even done brilliantly. But it's the sort of thing that requires a good, experienced army and very good officers—and all of them with the mutual confidence that comes from joint experience. To put it another way, it's no trick for amateurs, or even professionals who are no longer or never were in peak condition."

They were five hundred yards off, now. Sheff could see the lead companies of the nearest American regiment trying to form a line across the road, barring the Arkansans from coming to the fort's relief.

They weren't going to manage it in time, he didn't think. Colonel Jones would follow standard Arkansas practice of coming to within three hundred yards of the foe before ordering the regiment into line formation. That was something

General Ross had his doubts about, Sheff knew. But it was a tactical issue that the British general wasn't going to argue with a soldier of Driscol's experience if the Laird thought his army could move quickly enough to manage the risky maneuver. The Americans didn't have that much more in the way of cavalry than the Arkansans, after all.

The terrain wasn't bad, once you got off the road. Not soggy at all, this far into summer. There weren't any trees, either, and not much in the way of brush, since the garrison of the Post had kept the terrain clear within half a mile of the fort's walls. But it was still rough enough that not even the American infantry would be in a good position when the clash came, much less their artillery.

Sheff could see American artillerymen in the distance, struggling to move some of the cannons from the berms where Harrison had positioned them to bombard the Post. The enemy commander must have separated his artillery units from the infantry regiments they'd normally be attached to, in order to mass all of his guns for the assault on the fort. It had probably seemed like a good idea at the time. But he'd pay the price for it now.

"Quick march!" came Colonel Jones's piercing voice from behind. "Artillery, *up!*"

Sheff doubled the pace while he and Captain Dupont led the men off the road itself—Dupont to the left, away from the river, Sheff to the right—so the field artillery could pass through the ranks and take up position at the front. Even with their rougher footing, the 3rd was still advancing very rapidly. The Laird always thought like a sergeant. Whatever else his army could or couldn't do, the one thing it could do superbly was *move.*

Harrison was dismayed to see how quickly the two Arkansas regiments were coming into position. He'd been warned about that by Colonel Zachary Taylor—both in person, shortly before the colonel had left for Missouri, and in his written reports of the clash with Crittenden.

Harrison had discounted most of it. Taylor had a reputation among some circles in the U.S. officer corps—the ones who were concentrated in Harrison's own army, as it happened—for becoming obsessed with minutiae at the ex-

pense of the bigger sweep of things. That made him a superb
trainer of garrison troops, granted, as even his longtime an-
tagonists Colonels McNeil and Arbuckle would admit. But
they'd also pointed out to Harrison, when he'd discussed
Taylor's reports with them, that Zachary Taylor had not
much of a reputation as a *fighting* commander. Certainly
nothing compared with Harrison's own demonstrated skills.

Most of that latter, Harrison had also discounted as the inevitable flattery of subordinate officers to their commander.
Still, it was all true enough. Taylor's combat record in the
war with Britain had been respectable but hardly distinguished. Whereas Harrison had been the victor in two of the
major battles of the war, Tippecanoe and the Thames.

Today, watching the celerity and precision with which the
Arkansans were maneuvering their infantry and their artillery, Harrison was developing an uneasy feeling. He'd
thought of this war as being, in its essence, not much different from the campaigns he'd fought against the British and
their Indian allies in the northwestern theater during the War
of 1812. A mass of Indians—fundamentally undisciplined
and disorganized, even if fired with zeal by Tecumseh—with
a small core of British regulars who'd been as much exasperated as helped by the actions of their allies.

But he hadn't yet seen a single Indian since he'd arrived in
Arkansas, except for the Chickasaws who'd so foolishly gotten themselves trapped in Arkansas Post. That was, of
course, another predictable trait of the savages. No matter
how many times the United States proved to them
otherwise—you'd think Jackson at the Horseshoe Bend
would have settled the matter for all time—Indians still had
a near-mystical faith in the value of fortifications.

Which, admittedly, did well enough against militias—just
as the forts of settlers were usually good enough to withstand Indian raids. But against trained and disciplined regulars, supported by artillery, not even something as well built
as Arkansas Post could be held against a superior force.

That there *were* Indian warriors out there in the Arkansas
countryside around him, Harrison didn't doubt in the least.
If nothing else, he had the ambushes encountered by his
small mounted reconnaissance parties to prove it to him. But
that was how they were fighting—as irregulars, not as an in-

tegral part of the Arkansas Army. If the Americans broke and ran, their Choctaw and Cherokee allies would savage the fleeing troops. But so long as Harrison's men stood their ground, it would be a straight-up fight between regular armies.

Very much, in short, the sort of war that Jacob Brown and Winfield Scott had fought farther east on the Niagara front. And Harrison was now pretty sure, watching the oncoming enemy, that beneath Brown's claim of illness when he retired, and Scott's histrionic claims of political principle when he did the same, something much more darkly practical had been lurking.

They didn't think the Arkansas War was going to be anything but a bloodbath. The sort of bloodbath they'd faced willingly at the Chippewa and Lundy's Lane when they'd seen the survival of the nation at stake. But not something they felt the need or desire to go through again, for purposes that were considerably less sublime. As even Harrison—even President Clay, for that matter—would readily admit. Only John C. Calhoun, on the American side, thought this war was being fought over fundamental principles.

"Move it!" Harrison bellowed at the two artillery batteries he'd ordered out of the berms in support of McNeil's and Arbuckle's regiments. "God damn you, move it!"

CHAPTER 35

Being one of the few men in the Arkansas forces who was riding a horse, Sam had a fairly good view of what was developing, even though he was positioned behind the 3rd Infantry. So did Winfield Scott and William Cullen Bryant, who were riding next to him.

The reporters occupied a somewhat peculiar position. As

noncombatants—and technically enemy civilians—they wouldn't be privy to any of the Arkansas Army's battle plans, of course. On the other hand, given the importance to Arkansas of getting American newspaper coverage that was as favorable as possible, Driscol was bending over backward to accommodate them.

Naturally, he'd handed Houston the job of keeping the two reporters happy but ignorant.

Sam couldn't honestly complain, though. He wouldn't have much to do in this battle until and unless what they'd taken to calling the Georgia Run became possible. Colonel H. Spencer Street, the commander of the 2nd Arkansas Infantry, didn't need Sam to tell him how to handle the regiment in a battle.

If the Georgia Run took shape, things would be different. Meaning no disrespect to Colonel Street, but Driscol wanted a more experienced commander in charge in the event that a complex maneuver became possible. At that point, of course, keeping Winfield Scott and Cullen Bryant happy but ignorant would be a moot point. What was about to transpire would be blindingly obvious to anyone.

Street had been perfectly happy with the arrangement. Spence, as everyone called him except in the field, was an unassuming officer. One of Charles Ball's naval gunners from the Capitol, later the Iron Battalion at New Orleans, he'd steadily worked his way up the ranks in the Arkansas Army because he was immensely reliable and cool under fire. But he wasn't the man to pull off something that required flair and initiative, and he knew it himself.

The formalities were being respected, anyway. Street would remain in command of the 2nd. Houston would officially assume overall command of a maneuver that involved one of the batteries from the 3rd Battalion as well as Spencer's regiment. An impromptu miniature brigade, as it were.

He glanced over to make sure the battery was maintaining position. When he did so, his eyes met those of John Ridge. The newly commissioned Cherokee lieutenant had been assigned to the artillery, as had his cousin. Major Ridge had insisted on that. The way the Cherokee chief looked at it, if his oldest son and his nephew were bound and determined to put on the green uniform of Arkansas, then they'd damn well learn to use the big guns while they were at it.

Sam didn't blame him. Who could know what the future might hold? One of the biggest military weaknesses of any Indian tribe was that they had no artillery at all and wouldn't really know how to use it if they did. Soon enough, whatever else, that would no longer be true of the Cherokees.

John Ridge gave Houston a nod. Then he went back to paying attention to what Callender McParland was explaining to him. For this battle, as new as he was, John's rank was a formality. In practice, he'd be watching McParland to see how it was done. His cousin Buck Watie had an identical position with Lieutenant Thomas Talley, who commanded the other battery that had come with the expedition.

John would be the one who got all the excitement if the Georgia Run happened. His cousin Buck would be stuck with the unglamorous—and deadly brutal—business of slugging it out alongside the 3rd Arkansas against the American regulars.

Sam didn't envy them. That was likely to get purely murderous before it was over.

Movement in the distance caught his eye. Looking up, he saw what appeared to be three people scuttling through one of the little groves that dotted the plain. He thought they were black but couldn't really be certain. Perhaps sixty or seventy yards behind them, he could see two more people. Definitely Chickasaws, from the costumes. One of them appeared to be a woman; the other, an old man brandishing some sort of weapon. Sam couldn't tell what it was, exactly, this far away. Perhaps a spear, perhaps an antique long-barreled musket.

"What's that all about?" asked Winfield Scott. The former American general was squinting at the same distant little drama.

"At a guess, some of the Chickasaw slaves just ran off, figuring they could make it to New Antrim before the Chickasaw warriors in the Post could get on their trail." Sam nodded toward the woods. "Most of the Chickasaws are out there in hiding. The noncombatants, that is. They've got, at most, seven hundred warriors. That's enough in itself to pack the Post fuller of men than it should be. No room for women and children, so the Chickasaws sent them off into the woods. That means women and old men, watching over maybe a thousand slaves."

Sam gave his head a slight backward jerk. "With freedom and sanctuary not much more than a hundred miles upstream. You can figure out what the odds are that they'll be able to keep things under control."

"Ah." The general gave Houston a quizzical look. "You don't seem much disturbed by the prospect that your Chickasaw allies will soon be very disgruntled allies."

"Frankly, who cares?" Sam's face felt tight. "Everybody in Arkansas, including me, is sick and tired of Chickasaws. For over a hundred years, the bastards have picked fights with everybody and made slaves out of anybody they could. So fuck 'em if they're finally between the hammer and the anvil."

"Yes, I understand. But I'd think it would cause you a great deal of trouble. With the rest of the Confederacy, I mean."

Sam shrugged. "Yes and no. The Cherokees and Creeks are none too fond of Chickasaws, either. The Choctaws purely hate them, even if they do speak the same language. Besides, the Choctaws have never engaged much in slavery, not even their mixed-bloods. The Cherokees and Creeks have, but most of the ones who own slaves"—again, that little backward jerk of his head—"are way back there in Oklahoma. The Cherokees and Creeks who live in Arkansas—we figure there's now about six thousand and two thousand, respectively—don't own slaves to begin with. Besides, by now I think it's an open question which way they'd swing in the event of a real clash."

He looked over at Scott and Bryant. "Finally, there are all the pure-blood traditionalists. They don't own hardly any slaves, not even the Chickasaw ones. So what do they care if some rich mixed-bloods have to start working for a living?"

He started to add a comment about people like The Bowl and Chief Aktoka but broke off when he heard Colonel Jones's shout from ahead.

"Quick march! Artillery UP!"

"And here we go," he said.

*   *   *

Fifty yards behind Houston and the other battery, Lieutenant Buck Watie was feeling nervous. More nervous than he'd ever felt in his life.

He wasn't scared, exactly. But that was simply because fear seemed completely inadequate to the situation. Buck knew the battle plan—he'd been one of the officers at the back of the mess hall when Driscol and Ball explained it— and he knew what the role of his battery would be.

It wasn't complicated, to put it mildly. They'd stand with the 3rd Infantry and go toe-to-toe with the American regulars, while Houston and the 2nd Infantry—and his cousin's battery, talk about having all the luck!—kept an eye out for the Georgia Run.

A man got scared when he contemplated taking a risk. This wasn't a risk. This was that crazy white man's way of fighting a battle. Plant yourself—standing straight up, right out in the open!—in plain sight of your enemy, and then swap gunfire until one or the other of you quit. And the reason you quit was because you'd been bled dry.

Madness was what it was. There was no skill involved, no way a man could use his reflexes and cunning. The "risk" was no risk at all, but a certainty. Such-and-such percentage would die; such-and-such percentage would be mortally wounded; such-and-such percentage would survive but would be permanently maimed or disfigured; such-and-such percentage would suffer temporary wounds; and such-and-such percentage would somehow, miraculously, emerge entirely unscathed.

The only question was which one of those percentages you wound up falling into. Which was determined by nothing but pure, blind, stupid luck.

"You white people are insane," he muttered to his fellow lieutenant and instructor, Thomas Talley.

Belatedly, he remembered. Talley's answering grin was all the brighter because the white teeth stood out so sharply against skin the color of old coffee.

"You right," Talley said. "We is definitely crazy. On the other hand, we ain't color-blind."

Harrison was up on his horse by now. Everyone—except the Arkansans—was moving too slowly.

Much too slowly. He had the sick sensation a man gets while watching a carriage sliding off a bridge. Every moment of the disaster as clear as crystal, and seeming to take forever. But with no way to move fast enough to stop it from happening.

"God *damn* it! Get that artillery over there!"

The familiar clap of six-pounders jerked his eyes to the front. He saw two companies of the 1st Infantry staggering back from the enemy. McNeil *still* hadn't gotten them into a proper line, and already the Arkansan artillery had hammered his lead companies with a volley. Canister, from the looks of it.

Thankfully, Arbuckle's regiment was almost in position. Within a few minutes, that leading Arkansas regiment would be matched up against two American ones, and good ones at that. Coming around the fort the way they were, the Arkansans were hemmed in, too. Even with understrength regiments, McNeil and Arbuckle would have that leading enemy regiment outnumbered, without enough room for the Arkansans to bring their other regiment into play very quickly or easily.

It'd be brutal, though, if the Arkansans stood their ground. Brutal as all hell.

"Fire!" Sheff yelled, echoing Captain Dupont's command. He did his best to emulate that high-pitched, piercing tone that both Driscol and Ball had mastered on battlefields. With his natural tenor voice, he thought he did pretty well, too.

Not that anyone—including him—could possibly tell. The whole regiment fired the volley on cue, as if six hundred and fifty men had one single brain and one single trigger finger. Anyone's voice, in that incredible white-clouded thunderclap, vanished without a trace.

His ears were ringing, worse than he remembered them doing at the earlier battle at Arkansas Post with Crittenden's army. That was probably because he, now an officer, was standing slightly in front of the line of muskets instead of being part of them. A bit off to the side, of course, but that didn't compensate.

His brain felt muzzy, too. He shook his head to clear it,

squinting at the gunsmoke that obscured everything. They should be—

The answering clap came. Not as loud, perhaps oddly.

Sheff sensed a bullet whizzing by his head. Felt something—another bullet, maybe—that seemed to tug briefly at the uniform which was slightly bunched at his waist.

Other than that, he was quite uninjured. Glancing behind, he could see that at least three of his men had been hit. But looking farther down the line, he was relieved to still see his uncle Jem, now a sergeant in the company, urging the men forward as if he were Samuel himself.

These were no border adventurers they were fighting today. These were U.S. regulars. Wretched men, as a rule, taken one at a time. Recent immigrants, at least half of them, mostly from Ireland or Germany. Drunkards, gamblers, blasphemers; life's failures; flotsam and jetsam.

It didn't matter. They were professional soldiers, trained to do a job and able and willing to do it. Crittenden's men had crumpled under a single mighty blow. These wouldn't. The regulars would stand and fight.

The regiment had reloaded.

"Ten paces forward!" Sheff led them into the gunsmoke.

Houston was standing in the stirrups, straining to get as good a view as possible.

No use. The damn fort was in the way! Somehow, in all the planning, nobody had thought of that. He could see the two regiments of U.S. regulars that Harrison had brought out to meet the 3rd Arkansas on the road. And it was obvious just from the gunfire and the shouting and shrieking that the other two enemy regiments had broken into the Post and were fighting its Chickasaw defenders.

But he had no idea at all where the Georgia and Louisiana militias might be found. They were hidden from his view, somewhere behind that hulking fort.

Driscol and Ball trotted up.

Patrick had a wry smile on his face. "Never fails, does it, lad? Scheme all you want; the god of battles will roll his dice."

Ball was scowling. "Very funny. Patrick, we *can't* risk it without knowing. If they're too close to the regulars, we'll get torn to pieces. Especially after Harrison pulls the rest of the regulars out of the Post. Which"—Ball pointed at the fighting on the road ahead— "he will. He'll have to."

Sam was already studying that fight and had come to the same conclusion. The U.S. regulars were accounting adequately for themselves, true. No signs of panic, at least not yet. But they'd been caught off guard by the speed of the Arkansas attack, and they still hadn't recovered. Even as Sam watched, another perfectly timed Arkansas musket volley went off, followed by an almost equally perfect volley of canister from the six-pounders McParland had positioned slightly to the north.

Whichever that American regiment was, up in the front, it was being hammered very badly indeed. Its companion regiment had been partly shielded from the Arkansas muskets, but McParland was concentrating his guns on them.

The solution was obvious. It wasn't as if Sam really had any other duties, anyway, unless the Georgia Run was on.

"I'll reconnoiter," he said. He spurred his horse into a trot, not bothering to wait for permission from the two generals. He and Patrick and Charles went a long way back together, now. Ten years and counting. After a point, formalities were just silly.

Harrison's horse was shot out from under him by a volley from the six-pounders. Caught by surprise—he'd been looking at the Post, trying to gauge from the outside how well that fight was going—he couldn't free one of his feet from the stirrups in time.

Fortunately—great good fortune—the horse's knee crumpled under the carcass. Just enough to leave him room to kick his boot free.

He'd lost his sword. Where—

Lieutenant Fleming came up with it. "Here, sir." The youngster even had the presence of mind to proffer it hilt first. "Are you all right?"

He was helping Harrison to his feet as he asked the question.

"Never mind that!" Harrison pointed at the Post. "Get in there and find out—*God damn you, sir!*"

Fleming was staring at him empty-eyed. Empty-headed, too. A heavy three-ounce canister ball had caught him right in the forehead. Most of his brains were lying on the ground behind him.

Slowly, he toppled over onto his back. Falling as stiffly as a pine tree.

"Oh, *damn* you, sir," Harrison repeated. He looked for another aide.

He found Lieutenant Riehl a minute or so later. But John Riehl was equally useless. Another one of those deadly Arkansas canister balls had taken his left hand off at the wrist. Riehl was holding it in his right hand, just staring down at it. Completely oblivious, it seemed, to the blood pouring out of his left stump.

"Bind yourself up, you idiot," Harrison snarled. "Or you'll bleed to death."

Riehl turned puzzled blue eyes up to him. "My hand seems to be no longer attached, sir. What should I do?"

"Bind yourself—Ah! Here!"

Quickly—he was the commanding general, he had no business being distracted like this!—Harrison tore a strip of cloth from Riehl's uniform. That was easy because the uniform was torn. There was another wound somewhere on the lieutenant's ribs. Probably nothing serious, though, judging from the small flow of blood.

He tied the tourniquet roughly, crudely, and most of all quickly.

"Report to the rear, Lieutenant."

"Sir, my hand seems to be no longer attached. What should—"

"Shut up!" Harrison looked for another aide. He'd started the battle with three of them.

Sheff was a little amazed that he still hadn't been hurt at all. Not *very* amazed, but that was because only a tiny part of his brain was paying attention to the problem.

Which was just as well, since that part of his brain was gibbering like a monkey.

But he simply ignored it. Victory was all that mattered. The regiment was all that mattered.

He looked over and saw that Captain Dupont was lying on the ground. He was groaning and moving a little, so he was still alive. But from the looks of the wound—what Sheff could see of it, which was a coatee blood-soaked above the waist—he might very well not be in a few days. He'd probably been gut-shot.

That put Sheff in command of the company. He raised his sword and went at the enemy.

"Ten paces forward!"

By the time Harrison found a soldier, who could substitute for the missing aide, and sent him into the Post and got himself back to the front lines, he knew that the situation was rapidly becoming critical. Outnumbered or not—their other regiment still unused or not—that initial hammering blow from the leading Arkansas regiment had caught his own men off guard and off balance.

They'd been kept off balance ever since. The Arkansans were relentless, despite the heavy casualties they were suffering themselves. They kept coming forward, steadily—ten paces, fire; ten paces, fire—no matter how hard the 1st and 7th fought. By now, the battle was centered just north of the Post, with the Arkansans right and the American left anchored on the fort's wall.

McNeil was dead. He'd been killed just before Harrison returned, a musket ball right in the heart. Arbuckle was still in the fray. He'd even finally managed—God damn him, as well—to get his regiment into line.

McNeil had been succeeded in command of the 3rd by Captain Jeremy Baisden. The major who should have succeeded him had been killed in the same volley that slew the regiment's commander.

Just as well. Harrison had thought the major was an incompetent. Baisden seemed to know what he was about.

"You'll have to hold them, Captain!" Harrison shouted. "Until I can get the 3rd and the 4th out of the Post!"

Baisden waved his hand. Then, calmly, went back to his business.

Good man. Best of all, he didn't talk much. If Harrison

had to lose one of his experienced regimental commanders, it was really a pity the Arkansans hadn't killed Arbuckle instead of McNeil.

He needed another horse. Unfortunately, he seemed to have lost all of his young aides. One dead, one maimed—and God only knew where that useless Lieutenant Whatever-His-Name-Was had gotten off to.

The terrain in the Delta was generally flat, but there were small rises here and there. Sam found one of them within a couple of hundred yards that—finally—gave him a decent view of the entire battlefield.

He spotted the militia units right away. They were hugging the river, at least a third of a mile from the regulars, who were now completely tangled up with the 1st Arkansas or the Chickasaws in the Post itself.

"Oh, what a beautiful sight."

There was no need to stand on ceremony. Rising again in the stirrups, he could easily see Patrick and Charles. That meant they could see him also, if they were watching.

He laughed. As if they wouldn't be!

He swept off his hat—a proper one, not that blasted fur cap—and waved it around.

"Come and get it, boys! Dinner's on the table!"

CHAPTER 36

The first companies of the 3rd and 4th Regiments had just come out of Arkansas Post and were moving into position in support of the 1st and 7th when Harrison spotted the second Arkansas regiment coming forward.

He'd been expecting that, of course, and already had a battery of six-pounders in position to guard his right flank.

He'd take casualties from the coming assault, but for once the Arkansans had been sluggish.

"Get up there!" he shouted at the two captains leading the companies emerging from the Post. He stood up in the stirrups and pointed to the battery. "Take position! They'll be coming at our flank!"

It didn't occur to him until after they passed by that he hadn't inquired as to conditions within the Post itself.

Stupid. He might have a sally from the Chickasaws to deal with soon.

But, thankfully, it seemed there wasn't much chance of that. The battle was finally turning his way.

"No, sir." Captain James Franks took off his hat and wiped his brow with a uniform sleeve. That only replaced the sweat there with a smear of blood, because that whole side of his uniform seemed blood-soaked.

None of it his, apparently, judging from his demeanor.

"No, sir," he repeated. "There isn't much left, except a lot of bodies. I will say there wasn't no quit in them. There's probably two or three hundred live Chickasaws hiding out somewhere in there—the place is a maze—but they won't be doing no sorties."

There was a grim satisfaction in the words. The regulars had known of the Chickasaw reputation, and nothing that had happened in the two hours since the beginning of the assault on Arkansas Post had done anything to modify it. "No, sir. There won't be no Chickasaws coming out of there until we let them out."

Captain Franks was probably right. But Harrison had had to leave much of the artillery behind at the river, anyway, to guard against the steamboats that had finally appeared upstream. The same batteries could have two or three guns moved around to bear on the main entrance to the Post, as well as the breaches. If the Chickasaws did come out, they'd be met with a storm of canister.

Yes, indeed. The battle was finally—

"General Harrison!" He looked up, squinting to see who had called him. One of Arbuckle's officers. Captain . . . Whatever.

"General Harrison!" The captain was pointing to the north.

Harrison looked.

"What in the name of . . ."

The Arkansas maneuver made no sense at all. That second regiment was staying much too far to the north, as if it were simply evading Harrison's army. What was the point of that?

And they weren't even developing into a line. Instead, they were—

What *were* they doing?

"Oh, how splendid!" Winfield Scott exclaimed. He was standing up in his stirrups. As tall as he was, that gave him quite a good view of whatever the 2nd Arkansas was up to.

Bryant was considerably shorter, to begin with. Perhaps more to the point, the incredible din of the nearby battlefield had left his mind feeling numb.

"What are you talking about, Winfield?"

Scott pointed. He was genuinely excited, Cullen could tell. Not even making the slightest attempt to hide it under a patina of calm professionalism.

"I've never seen one! Read about them, of course."

The infernal cacophony had also left Cullen more than a bit irritable.

"What *are* you talking about?"

"It's a French column, Cullen! Right out of the Revolution and the early days of Napoleon. Don't think one's been used in a battle in years."

He might as well have been gibbering in Greek.

Well, no. Turkish. William Cullen Bryant's grasp of the Greek language was actually rather good.

He'd never heard it spoken. But he could read it, of course.

"Oh, dear God," Harrison whispered.

The bizarre formation finally made sense. That second Arkansas regiment was ignoring the American regulars altogether. They were sweeping around Harrison's regiments, keeping just out of musket range, and going for the militiamen.

Who were—

"God damn those bastards!"

Who were almost half a mile downriver. Figuring they'd

be completely useless in a close assault, Harrison had left them to their own devices while he handled the attack on Arkansas Post. Then, in the press of affairs and the chaos after the Arkansans launched their attack, he'd simply forgotten about them altogether, even though he'd originally intended to use them to reinforce the 1st and 7th. He'd simply been overwhelmed by too much happening, too soon.

Naturally, the wretches hadn't come to his aid on their own. If he knew militia officers, they'd have been dancing back and forth trying to decide what to do and spending most of their time quarreling with each other.

Well, they weren't going to have to decide anything, any longer. The Arkansans were going to make the decision for them.

For one tiny moment, before he suppressed it, Harrison found himself hoping the Arkansas maneuver would succeed.

At least it meant he could concentrate on fighting that one Arkansas regiment that had been gutting his army from the first moment of the battle. If nothing else, *they* would go under.

Sheff was still unhurt, but by now he was in command of the regiment's entire right wing. Anchored against the side of the Post the way they were, those companies had been unable to maneuver at all. Nor did they have any artillery support, as the left wing did. It had just been simple, straightforward, volley against volley. Moving closer and closer, until the distance separating them from the nearest American regiment was less than thirty yards.

"Reload!"

He wasn't ordering any further advance. Not unless the left wing came forward and Colonel Jones ordered a bayonet charge. Which Sheff didn't think was likely at all. The Arkansan and American lines had met at an angle. By the Post, not more than thirty yards separated them, but the distance between the Arkansan left and the American right was still almost a hundred yards. That enabled the Arkansan artillery battery positioned on the far left to bring what almost amounted to enfilade fire on their opponents.

Sheff didn't know whether it had happened by pure accident or by conscious design on the colonel's part. Either way, in effect, he'd used the companies on his right—Sheff's among them—to pin the Americans while the companies of his left and the artillery pounded them into pieces. Much the way a barroom brawler might use one hand to hold his opponent while he flailed away with the other fist.

It wouldn't have worked if the Americans had had guns of their own to bring counterbattery fire. But they didn't. Sheff was guessing, but he was pretty sure the American guns were still stuck in front of the Post or by the river, guarding against a sally by the riverboats upstream.

As battle tactics went, this one was dandy. But it was rough on Sheff's people.

"Fire!"

The musket volleys were starting to get a bit ragged, with as many casualties as they'd suffered. But not as ragged as the ones coming in return. Sheff was impressed that the one American regiment was still fighting at all. Tough bastards, for sure.

Sam joined up with Colonel Street after the 2nd Regiment had bypassed the U.S. forces tangled up at the Post and were heading straight for the militias. He'd bided his time, since he wanted to gauge how well the militia commanders would handle the sudden crisis they'd found themselves in.

Just about as he'd expected. Officers running back and forth, shouting orders most of which countermanded one another. The men, for their part, doing whatever struck their fancy.

Some of them had formed a line. Not much of a line, but a line. They'd even gotten two of their four-pounders into something that approximated a decent position.

Approximated, no better. The guns weren't far enough forward. That was typical of militia artillery. It took experience and confidence for artillery crews to be willing to position themselves far enough in advance of their infantry to do much good. Militias could almost never manage the thing properly.

Sam couldn't really blame them. Not only did the gun crews need to be confident that they had the skill to pull their guns back into the shelter of the infantry in time; also they needed to be confident that the infantry would be there to shelter them in the first place. More often than not, militia infantry would break, leaving the artillerymen they were supposed to protect high and dry. Ten years earlier, some of the men who were now serving in the Arkansas artillery had been cursing militiamen who'd left them exposed to the mercy of British regulars at the Battle of Bladenburg.

Another chunk of militiamen—several chunks, rather, and big ones—were obviously making preparations for a hasty retreat. "Rout," to call things by their right name.

Those were the complete idiots. They *had* to be idiots. There were two thousand Choctaw warriors out there, and at least two hundred men from Brown's Raiders. They'd been lying low, as instructed. But if the militiamen broke and ran, they'd be like rabbits at the mercy of predators.

Most of the militiamen, about half, were doing neither. They were just milling around in confusion, not sure what to do.

"It ain't complicated, boys," Sam murmured, kicking his horse into motion to rejoin the 2nd. "You can stand and die, or you can run and die. But either way, lots of you are gonna die today."

Sheff finally received his first wound. A small one, just a bullet that grazed his ribs. Barely even a flesh wound, and he was too busy anyway to take the time to bind it up. The uniform would be a ruin by the end of the day, but he didn't care anymore. He could barely remember the thrill of that first day he'd put it on.

Truth be told, he was a little relieved. His luck had been too good. Maybe this would even things out a bit.

Then, not fifteen seconds later, he saw a musket ball catch his uncle Jem in the throat and rip his neck open. Jem had been standing just in front of the line and slightly off to the side. He collapsed to the ground like a pile of rags, dropping his musket.

Sheff stared at him blankly for a moment. But there was nothing he could do.

Nothing at all. With that wound, his uncle would bleed out long before any aid could get to him—and no possible medical treatment could prevent his death, anyway.

Ruthlessly, Sheff stifled the spike of anguish that started to come. Only victory mattered. Only the regiment mattered.

"Reload!" he shouted, channeling the grief into his voice, bringing it to just the right high pitch for a battlefield. More like a shriek than a shout. It was the first time he'd ever really done it right—and he knew he'd never forget how to do it again, no matter how many battles he fought.

Harrison was just plain astonished. That first Arkansas regiment was *still* fighting. Staggering some, to be sure, especially the companies on their right. The volleys no longer came with their earlier crispness. But they were still recognizable volleys—and at the range the fight was now taking place by the wall of the Post, aiming was completely meaningless. That was sheer murder.

He'd never seen anything like it. The closest comparison had been that last charge on Tecumseh at the Thames. But that had been quick, however desperately fought. This was like fighting some sort of mindless machine. Black ants, wearing uniforms and armed with muskets.

"God damn you!" he shrieked at the Arkansans.

There came no response except another volley.

Sam found the final moments of the 2nd Arkansas' charge on the militias rather fascinating. The regiments had been trained in the tactic, and Driscol had predicted its success—so had Robert Ross—but Sam had wondered.

The term "column" was a misnomer, he now realized, applied to the fighting formation of the French armies of the Revolution. This bore no resemblance at all to a long, slender line of men marching down a road.

It was more like a sledgehammer. Or perhaps a very blunt spear. Fifty men across, at the front, firing as they came, with the rest of the regiment in close support. The formation relied on speed and impact, more like a cavalry charge than anything else Sam could think of.

Watching it in action, he could now understand why the formation had eventually been abandoned. Very well-trained and disciplined professional armies, formed into lines, could bring too much fire to bear on the front of the column. Hundreds of men against fifty.

But that presupposed the sort of professional armies trained and led by generals like the Duke of Wellington, or Napoleon and his marshals. Against levies raised by French noblemen—or Georgia and Louisiana gentry—the French column did very splendidly indeed.

It struck the Georgians like a hammer. An axe, rather, since the bayonets came down at the final moment.

The Georgians, not the Louisianans. The militia units had very distinctive and different colors, naturally, and the Arkansans knew what to look for. Any Louisianan or Alabaman who got in their way would get dealt with, to be sure. But on this day, July the 23rd of the Year of Our Lord 1825, Sam Houston and the 2nd Arkansas were looking to kill Georgians.

Another hybrid. Black people didn't actually have any reason to detest Georgians more than any other Southern militia. But the Cherokees and Creeks hated them with a passion. And, whatever strains might exist in the Confederacy between its different races and peoples, there was also much that united them. Some of those black men in uniform now had Cherokee or Creek wives or paramours—either way, usually with children in the bargain—and all of them had Cherokee and Creek neighbors.

The Georgians had made the mistake of coming· to Arkansas to commit their depredations. The nearest friendly jury was four hundred miles away as the crow flies—and not one of them had a pair of wings.

The Louisianans peeled away before the blow came and were already racing in a panic downriver. The Alabamans put up a bit of a fight before—very wisely—sidling out of the way and scrambling upriver for the shelter of the regulars.

The 2nd Arkansas let the Louisianans go. The Choctaws and Brown's men would deal with them. They wanted the Georgians.

David Ross was half fascinated and half appalled. Officially attached as an observer to the battery that was part of Houston's column, he had an excellent view of the fighting that erupted on the north bank of the Arkansas when the 2nd

Regiment struck the Georgians. He didn't even have any specific duties to keep his attention elsewhere. His status in the Arkansas Army was still unsettled, since no one was ready to accept him as a straightforward soldier except David himself. His father and the Laird—and Sam Houston, apparently—all felt the possible diplomatic complications were still too uncertain, should word get out that the son of a British major general was actively serving against the United States.

In practice, everyone understood that being an "observer" also meant that he would be getting informal training as an artillery officer. But since no one really wanted him getting underfoot in the furious fire that the battery was leveling on the Georgians, he spent most of his time just watching.

That was another massacre taking place down there on the riverbank. But the most fascinating—and appalling—thing about it was the lack of any apparent murderous frenzy. David thought he finally understood, deep in his bones, why the Laird had ordered that massacre of Crittenden's army the previous year. Many of the soldiers in the 2nd were veterans of that affair, and they'd imparted the lessons and the attitudes to the newer recruits. What resulted was an implacable determination to kill as many men as the regiment possibly could, today, coupled with the confidence that they *could*.

So, it was like watching craftsmen at their trade, even if the trade itself was murder. Almost all the fury and frenzy was being displayed by the Georgians. Many of them had fled, or were trying to, but many of them were fighting back. But it did them precious little good. They fought as individuals, for the most part, and poorly trained ones at that. Whereas the Arkansans they faced were maintaining order and discipline even now that the bayonets had been brought into play.

So was the artillery. The captain in command had positioned them on the left flank of the 2nd Regiment. To the fore, when the engagement began; now, perhaps two hundred yards to the rear. But they were firing balls, not canister, and two hundred yards for that shot amounted to point-blank range. The artillerymen were being careful to keep their fire well away from the regiment, but with the huge numbers of Georgians—some Louisianans, too—who were spilling down the Arkansas, that left them with plenty of targets.

The ground was even dry enough, this far into summer, to allow for the grazing shots that good artillery always tried for when facing infantry. The guns were trained low, so that the balls would strike the ground some yards before the enemy and then carom into their ranks somewhere around waist-high. A six-pound ball fired in such a manner could easily kill or maim half a dozen men or more if it caught them in a clump.

There were a lot of clumps down there: first of men, then of offal.

After a while, David looked away. For the first time in his now twenty years of life, he wondered if he really wanted to become a soldier.

He thought so, still. But he understood, better, something about his father that had never been very clear to him before. Robert Ross had always seemed strangely reticent about his exploits, given that there were enough of them to cover an entire wall at their home back in Rostrevor with the mementos.

David thought he understood now. The reticence was because many of those memories were not ones his father wished to dwell upon. The mementos were there to remind him—perhaps reassure him—that there had been a reason for them in the first place. A full-grown and very mature man's way of doing something that little boys often did. Make sure there was a light of some sort shining into a room at night, so that when a sudden nightmare-inspired waking came, the monsters in the room could be seen for what they were.

Sam didn't participate in the slaughter. Not directly, at least. But that was only because he felt duty bound to make sure the situation as a whole didn't get out of control. There was always the possibility that Harrison might send some of the regulars down to the aid of the Georgian militia.

Not much of a possibility, granted. Sam couldn't see enough of the fighting that was still raging around Arkansas Post to get a clear sense of the battle's progress. But for his purposes, all that mattered was the sound of it. There was no way, in the face of such ferocious and continuing gunfire, that Harrison was going to make the mistake of dividing his forces again.

Too bad for the Georgians. They were on their own. Sam had never met William Henry Harrison, but if the professional soldier from Ohio had a different attitude toward militias than almost any other professional officer Sam had ever met, he was certainly hiding it well that day.

So, Sam Houston didn't kill a single Georgian himself. But he watched with pitiless eyes. So far as he was concerned, each and every one of those men shot or bayoneted or clubbed to death on the banks of the Arkansas River was no different from the Georgian who'd murdered his wife. The whole state could burn in hell for all he cared.

And hundreds of them were killed before it was all over. The slaughter at the river wasn't as bad as the slaughter of Crittenden's army the year before, but that was only because the Georgians weren't trapped in a peninsula. A much higher percentage of them managed to make their escape into the countryside.

Where two thousand Choctaw warriors waited, with a very recent and burning grudge to settle. And if the Choctaw grudge was more with Mississippians or Louisianans, they'd settle for Georgians.

Brown's men were out there, too, and they didn't care at all about the fine distinctions between states. John Brown had agreed to abide by Chief Driscol's rules when it came to fighting U.S. regulars. But the militias weren't included in those prohibitions. So far as Brown and his people were concerned, those militiamen—be they from Georgia or Louisiana or Mississippi or Alabama, it made no difference—had come to Arkansas for the express purpose of reenslaving its citizens.

That made them damned in the eyes of the Lord, pure and simple, and as plain to see as the nose in front of your face. It was right there in the Bible. There was no good reason not to assist the Lord in his righteous work of sending them on their way to eternal hellfire. Indeed, it was a duty, and Brown was not the man to shirk his duty.

*   *   *

"All right, Charles, pull them out," Patrick Driscol commanded.

General Ball nodded and sent the order. He'd been waiting for the order for some time. Only a man as troll-blooded as the Laird could have held off that long. By now, the 3rd Arkansas was a bleeding ruin.

But not broken. Not even close. They'd gone head-to-head for as long as it took against two—and then units from three, and then four—regiments of U.S. regulars. Moving forward or standing their ground, never retreating an inch.

For years, the Iron Battalion had served the black people of Arkansas as a magic talisman. There hadn't actually been much reality to it for some time, since the Iron Battalion as such no longer existed. They'd had to break it up in order to use its men as the core around which to build other and larger units.

After today, it wouldn't matter at all. After today, Arkansas had the 3rd Infantry, which stood its ground, and the 2nd, which broke the state of Georgia.

And hadn't used the 1st Infantry at all—which might actually be the best.

This war might go on for years. Probably would, in fact. But it was already won where it mattered. Arkansans would have the stomach to fight forever, after Second Arkansas Post. The Americans had been dragged into this war by politicians and had no stomach for it at all outside of some of the Southern states.

From here on, it was just a matter of how long it would take the enemy to figure it out.

For all Sheff knew, he was now the commanding officer of the regiment. The companies on its right wing, for sure. Colonel Jones was gone. Wounded, not dead, although it might have been a mortal wound. He'd looked awful bad. Sheff didn't know what had happened to the major or any of the captains of the left wing. The captains of the three companies by the Post had all been killed or wounded by now. The gunsmoke was so thick you couldn't see much in any direction, except once in a while when a gust of wind cleared the air for a bit.

Sheff hadn't spent any time wondering about the colonel's fate. He'd stopped wondering about anyone's fate, including his own. He'd reached some sort of pure state of mind, he decided. Slogans that he'd once recited to himself as if they were prayers had become simple realities.

Only victory mattered. Only the regiment mattered. They'd fight until the last man shot the last bullet, and then they'd lower the bayonets.

"Pull out! Pull out!"

Sheff recognized General Ball's voice, but the words didn't quite register. He ordered another volley. Couldn't hardly call it a volley any longer—but the same could be said for what was coming the other way.

"Listen to me, Lieutenant Parker! Pull the men *out*! Move!"

That registered. Groggily—his brain really wasn't working too well anymore—Sheff tried to remember the orders for calling a retreat.

No. Fighting withdrawal. Big difference.

He got the first two orders out. Properly, he was pretty sure. But while he was still groping for the next evolution, a musket ball took him square in the shoulder and spun him around. Around, and down, taking all consciousness with it.

The last thing he remembered was a great sense of relief. He'd done his duty and could finally rest.

CHAPTER 37

For a moment, Harrison was tempted to order a pursuit. The Arkansas regiment his men had been fighting while the other one went after the militias was pulling back now. It was a fighting withdrawal, not a retreat—certainly not a rout. But that evolution was extremely difficult to manage properly, especially by a regiment that had lost so many of its officers.

If he brought enough pressure to bear, they might finally crack.

Easier said than done, though, in the real world where battles are actually fought.

His own 1st and 7th Regiments—the 1st, especially, which had taken the brunt of the fighting right by the Post— were too badly battered for the purpose. They'd stood their ground like good regulars, but they were in no shape to launch a pursuit. He'd have to use the 3rd and 5th.

Mostly the 3rd. Lieutenant Colonel Cutler had come out of the Post and, by now, had his regiment pretty well organized. But Harrison still hadn't seen the commanding officer of the 5th. He might be dead; he might be injured; he might just be too confused to understand what he was supposed to do. Whatever the reason, the 5th as such was still incoherent. What Harrison had available, right now, were maybe half of its companies for a pursuit. By the time the others finished their withdrawal from the Post and got into position, it would be too late.

Much too late. The gunsmoke had finally cleared away, most of it, and Harrison could see that the top commanders of the Arkansans had taken direct charge of the withdrawal, substituting themselves for the regiment's fallen officers. That regiment was pulling back in good order, even managing to take most of their wounded with them.

The moment passed. There was no chance, he realized. Especially since—

Belatedly, he remembered. Hurriedly, he trotted his horse to the rear, to one of the artillery berms where he could get a better view of what was happening downriver. What was that *other* Arkansas regiment up to? For all he knew, he might soon be fending them off.

On the way, he took the time to level silent curses on himself. He'd lost control of this battle from the very beginning, and he knew it. His plans had been too complex. He'd taken the risk of dividing his forces without enough of a staff and regimental officers who'd worked together and shaken themselves down. He hadn't even been able to remember the names of some of his aides, for the love of God.

So, now, here he was—forced to serve as his own scout because his staff had disintegrated around him and his regimental commanders were completely preoccupied with their own affairs.

He also cursed Henry Clay and John Calhoun. They'd lied to him, damn them. Reassured him that he'd simply be facing savages—better still, negroes who didn't even have the martial customs of the savages. And William Henry Harrison—he went back to cursing himself—had been too ambitious, too eager, to question their assurances.

He reached the berm. To his immense relief, he saw that the second Arkansas regiment had broken off their own pursuit of the militias and were returning. But they were back in that peculiar thick column formation and were angling away from the battlefield. Clearly enough, they'd be coming back the same way they went, avoiding his own forces until they could reunite with their fellow regiment.

In short, the battle was over—unless Harrison insisted on trying to continue it. Which he was no more inclined to do than he was to order a charge on the moon. He slumped in the saddle. He was exhausted. Mentally, even more than physically.

He'd suffered a wound somewhere along the way, too, he suddenly realized. The whole left side of his torso ached. Looking, he couldn't see any blood. But when he pulled up his tunic, he saw a huge bruise beginning to form over his rib cage. The ribs themselves weren't broken, obviously. With a rib flail, he'd have been completely incapacitated. But some of them might well be cracked. He'd find out by the morrow.

God only knew what had happened. He had no memory at all of having any injury inflicted on him. But it could easily happen in such a ferociously fought and confused battle—confusing for him, at any rate. The most likely cause was a glancing blow from a cannonball, although to the best of Harrison's recollection the enemy had used canister throughout the engagement.

His mind in something of a daze, he watched the second Arkansas regiment moving across the Delta to the northwest. That part of his brain that was still working professionally—which was no small part, given his experience—recognized that Taylor's report had been quite accurate in this respect also. The Arkansans could march like nobody's business. He'd remember that in the future.

Somebody was talking to him. Looking down, he saw that the commander of the 5th Regiment was there, standing atop the berm and looking up at him. Harrison groped for the man's name and couldn't find it.

"—do about the Chickasaws, General?"

Harrison had to grope for the meaning of the question, too. Fortunately, the colonel's pointing finger gave him the clue. Aided, a moment later, by the sound of six-pounders going off.

Looking in the direction the 5th's commander was pointing, Harrison could see dozens of Chickasaw warriors—hundreds, within a minute—pouring out of the Post. Some through the main entrance, some through the two breaches in the east wall, some by simply taking the risk of climbing over the walls and jumping.

The batteries by the river were firing on them, as Harrison had instructed them to do. Quite a few of the fleeing Chickasaws were being killed before they could get out of range. They were racing upriver as fast as they could run.

No danger there, in short—which, at the moment, was all Harrison cared about.

"Just let them go, Colonel."

Peters. That was his name. Lieutenant Colonel Curtis Peters.

"Just let them go, Colonel Peters," he repeated. He forced up the energy for a compliment. "You battered them badly, I take it. Very well done."

Peters nodded. "I estimate we killed four hundred hostiles in there, General. Well. Three hundred, for sure. At no great cost to ourselves. We were able to trap most of them in the mess hall and had four guns to bring to bear. By the time we sent in the infantry, they were too rattled to put up much of a resistance. But we couldn't catch all of them, of course."

Even as he spoke, Harrison could see soldiers from the 1st Artillery hauling a six-pounder out of the Post. No easy task, that, without horses. But they couldn't possibly have used horses to bring guns into a fort under assault. No matter how well trained, the beasts would panic.

"Just let the Chickasaws go," he said again. "For the moment, we need to concentrate on preparing a defense against the possibility of counterattack by the Arkansans. We've taken Arkansas Post"—he said that with more energy, it being the sole consolation of the day—"so let's make sure we keep it."

He pointed up the river. "I'd appreciate it if you'd bring your regiment into position just west of the fort, Colonel Peters. And tell Colonel Eustis to move his batteries up with you. Those Arkansas steamboats are still up there, and it'll be days—weeks, possibly—before we can finally get armored steamboats of our own."

The Arkansans hadn't ever used their steamboats. Harrison was pretty sure they'd never intended to. Simply having them there had immobilized a good portion of his artillery, the arm in which he had the clearest advantage over his enemy.

Grudgingly—he was not a man for which doing so came easily—Harrison admitted that his opponent had fought a considerably smarter battle than he had.

He didn't say it out loud, of course. "Be about it, please, Colonel."

Peters left. Harrison took a few more seconds to rally his spirits and energy.

He'd need them. The battle was over, but there was still the butcher's bill to be examined. There were dead and wounded all over the area. Small piles of them near the Post—and from what he could tell at a distance, considerably bigger piles of militiamen by the riverbank downstream.

Leaving aside the Chickasaws in the Post—that'd be a charnel house in there; his mind shied away from it for the time being—most of the dead and wounded outside the fort were Americans. But there were a fair number of Arkansans, too. The enemy had done their best to carry off their wounded, but there was only so much that could ever be done in that respect on a still-contested field of battle.

He'd better see to that immediately, he realized. The regulars would be furious at the casualties they'd suffered. Furious enough that they might not only ignore their training but ignore practical reality as well.

Of all the things Clay and Calhoun had lied to him about, the biggest lie had been the first.

A *short* war. Blithering nonsense. The fact that both the

president and the secretary of war had probably believed it themselves didn't make it any less of a lie. It just made them stupid liars.

Short wars can wash themselves away, along with their sins. Long wars require rules. Best to establish them immediately.

Fortunately, if nothing else, the regulars had been too exhausted to do anything but rest. Whatever other energy they'd had available had been devoted entirely to assisting their own injured. Their officers hadn't even started picking through the enemy soldiers lying about, separating the wounded from the dead.

So, Harrison found himself one of the first three American officers to start moving through the enemy bodies. He was accompanied by a captain and a lieutenant from the heavily battered 1st. The captain's name he remembered, thankfully. Trevin Matlock. The lieutenant's was unknown to him.

The Arkansans were lying in piles, too, especially near the Post. The first body Harrison came across was that of a young officer, lying slightly before his men. A second lieutenant. Arkansans used the same insignia as the American army, even if the uniforms were green instead of blue.

A very young lieutenant, he could now see, once he looked more closely. As always—being from Ohio, he was not very familiar with negroes—the racial differences had momentarily obscured lesser matters like age. Not even twenty, he thought. It was hard for him to be certain, however, since the lieutenant's skin was very dark and his features completely African. Very young, though, he was sure of that.

The Arkansas officer wasn't moving, but his chest was rising and falling. A very bad injury to the shoulder, that was. The sort of bone-shattering wound that usually rendered a man unconscious, even if it wasn't directly fatal. Especially if he was already exhausted, which Harrison had no doubt he had been. The battle had been ferocious as a whole, but nowhere more so than here right by the walls of the Post, where the two armies had met at point-blank range.

"Him," the lieutenant from the 1st Regiment said tonelessly. "Hadn't been for him, I think we could have beaten them here, at the end. I can't believe he's still alive, the bastard. I've half a mind—"

"Shut up," Captain Matlock said, just as tonelessly. "He did his job and did it well. And there's an end to it."

"Indeed," Harrison said firmly. "A most gallant foe."

He gave the lieutenant—very young himself—a look that was more harsh than he felt but as harsh as it needed to be.

"We shall be following the rules of war here, Lieutenant. I trust that's understood? And if I discover there have been any violations, I shall have the man—or officer—immediately court-martialed. Do I make myself clear?"

The lieutenant seemed suitably abashed. "Yes, sir. Ah. Sorry."

"I understand, Lieutenant," Harrison said in a milder tone. "Emotions always run high after a battle. But indulging yourself in them is a bad mistake, leaving aside any moral concerns. Do keep in mind that the day might come when you—or me, or Captain Matlock —might find ourselves in the very same position. You'll be thankful then that you weren't an idiot now."

That assumed, of course, that the enemy followed the rules of war also. Harrison was by no means sure of that, yet. Who knew what negroes would do? They'd been pure savages, by all accounts, in the small uprisings in North America and the huge one in Hispaniola.

But rebellions and uprisings were almost invariably savage, no matter the color of the men involved. The negroes he was fighting here were part of a regular army, established by a government that the United States had diplomatically recognized. Still did, for that matter, even if war had been declared. Harrison could only hope that they'd conduct themselves like white men.

Whether they did or not, however, he would. Civilized behavior and custom was determined by its own imperatives, not petty bargaining with breeds outside the law.

"See to it, Captain Matlock, if you would. I want any wounded Arkansans gathered where they can be given medical attention, whenever our surgeons can be freed from tending our own. There's probably a suitable area somewhere in the Post."

He started to move off but paused. "And place a guard over them, Captain. Reliable men, with a steady sergeant in command."

"Yes, sir."

An hour later, after he was sure the regular units were steady and Harrison was satisfied that they could repel any Arkansas counterattack, he went downriver to see how the militias were doing. He took Captain Matlock with him, since he no longer had any of the three lieutenants he'd had for aides at the beginning of the battle. Fleming was dead; Riehl would be retired from the service with that wound, assuming he survived; and he'd finally found the missing third lieutenant.

The lieutenant had been brought before him, rather. The youngster's wits were quite gone. He'd been found by soldiers from the 7th huddled in a ball some fifty yards from the lines, weeping uncontrollably. Harrison had a vague recollection of sending the boy with orders to Colonel Arbuckle. He'd never gotten there, apparently, his nerve having completely broken along the way.

Harrison still couldn't remember his name, and the young lieutenant had been too incoherent to provide it himself. No matter. He'd learn it when the time came to put together a court-martial. Which there had to be, given the circumstances.

Harrison would be demanding the death penalty, which was called for in cases of pusillanimity in the face of the enemy. He didn't care for the idea, but he simply had no choice. The nameless lieutenant who'd die in a few weeks at the end of a rope would be just one more casualty that could be properly laid at the feet of Clay and Calhoun, from Harrison's viewpoint. In a short war, sins could be forgiven as well as washed away. In a long war, they couldn't. Simple as that.

The commanders of the militias—those few of them Harrison could find, most having run away with their men—were livid.

But Harrison's energy was coming back, and he was no mild-mannered man himself.

"Shut. Up." He glared at the loudest of the Georgian officers. Insofar as the term "officer" wasn't a bad joke to begin with. The man was actually a Georgia state representative whose military experience was entirely limited, so far as Harrison knew, to having gotten himself appointed a "colonel" in the expedition for the sake of garnering some more votes. Georgians seemed to grow militia colonels with the same profligacy that they grew cotton. And they were just about as fluffy.

"You had three thousand men," he rasped, "to face not more than seven hundred. And you tell me the fault was *mine*? You ran like rabbits from a force a quarter the size of your own because *I* didn't give you proper support? Be damned to you, sir!"

Angrily, he pointed back at the Post. "My *regulars* defeated the forces we faced while taking the fort as well as preventing the enemy steamboats from coming into play."

That was taking some liberties, perhaps, but it was technically correct. By ancient custom, the army that held the field at the end of a battle was considered the victor, even if the term was more a formality than anything else. The fact that the Arkansans hadn't been "defeated," so much as simply choosing to withdraw from the field, could be ignored.

The American forces at Lundy's Lane had done the same, after all, whereupon the British had claimed to be the winners of the battle. In the world where professional soldiers dealt with each other, it simply didn't matter. Protocol would be respected, even if both sides knew perfectly well that, in all important respects, the battle had been something quite different.

The Georgian and his three fellows were glaring back. So were the two Louisiana officers present. One of them was also a state representative—also with the rank of "colonel." It seemed to be an iron law with militias that they had as many colonels as they did privates, with precious few majors or captains—and not a single paltry lieutenant—anywhere to be found.

They could glare all they wanted. What could they *say*? Even politicians playing at being soldiers had enough sense to realize that their forces had suffered a complete humiliation today.

Not that it would make a difference in the long run, Harrison was gloomily certain. They'd shut up today, sure enough. But in the months to come—half of them would be finding excuses to leave the campaign as soon as possible—they'd be back in their state legislatures and doing their level best to ruin Harrison's reputation. So would their fellows in the Congress of the United States. Unfortunately, while militias were rarely worth much on a battlefield, they were quite potent in the American political arena.

"So just shut up," he repeated. "And I'd recommend you get busy rounding up your men."

He waved a hand at the surrounding countryside. "Leave them out there for very long, and they'll be coming back in pieces."

The glares started to fade then, replaced by worry.

"I'll provide units from the Fifth and Third to help you," Harrison said, in a milder tone. "With some artillery."

That eased the worry from their faces some, but not much. These so-called officers weren't really concerned about the military aspects of the situation so much as the political ones. *They* would have to answer to their constituents directly, where Harrison would at least have the shield of the professional army. And all they had to do was look around to see that a lot of their constituents were now dead, an equal if not greater number were badly injured, and all the survivors would be blaming them for the disaster, no matter how much of it they tried to shift onto Harrison's shoulders.

So would their relatives back home. Especially those whose husbands and sons weren't coming back.

"And you'd better detail some burial parties right away," Harrison added. "Big ones. This is the Delta in July. That many corpses will stink like you wouldn't believe, give them any time aboveground."

The sergeant in charge of the guard over the wounded prisoners being held in a room of the Post was simply amused.

"Do ye now?" he asked, in a pronounced Irish accent. He glanced at his four men. "D'ye hear that, lads? These gentlemen from Alabama wish to wreak havoc upon yon niggers. Having failed the task miserably, mind, when the niggers were on their feet and had guns in their hands."

"It ain't funny, you fucking Irish—"

Click.

The Alabaman who was more or less the leader of the little group froze. The musket barrel held by one of the sergeant's men was now pushing under his chin. It was cocked, too.

"Hey, fella . . ."

"Oh, there's no point pleading with Private Aupperle," the sergeant said, still grinning. "Dieter doesn't speak but three words of English. The first two are 'fuck you.' The third is 'asshole.' He got off the boat not six months ago and joined the army straight off, that being the only trade he knows. How's your German?"

The six Alabamans stared at him.

"My German's quite good. Even if the dumb Krauts complain about the accent."

"Can barely understand him," the corporal growled. His accent was German, whereas the sergeant's was Irish, and even thicker.

His expression was a lot thicker than the sergeant's, too. "Fucking militia *scheisskopf.* You go home, two months. Maybe three. Half of you already running there now. We will be here long time. Get out."

He brought up his own musket and cocked it. "Get out *now.*"

"Best do as he says, lads," said the sergeant, as cheerily as ever. "Dieter's even-tempered, being from the Palatinate. Corporal Affenzeller, it grieves me to relate, is not. Juergen's a Swabian, alas. A surly breed; they're known for it."

After they were gone, a few seconds later, the sergeant chuckled. "Even in Alabama, now."

Private Dieter Aupperle uncocked his musket. He uttered several phrases in German that were most uncomplimentary on the subject of militias in general. So did Corporal Affenzeller, after he uncocked his own weapon. But, having considerably more knowledge of their adopted country as well as its language, he added details and specifics.

"—fuck pigs, being Creoles, no better than filthy Frenchmen. But at least the French have a few brains. Georgians can't figure out which end of a pig to fuck in the first place. Alabamans—"

* * *

Late in the afternoon, a delegation from the Arkansas Army showed up under a flag of truce. Harrison ordered them escorted into the Post.

Sam Houston, in the flesh. Harrison had never met him, but the man was one of those few in the world whose reputation genuinely preceded him. In the United States, at any rate.

To Harrison's much greater surprise—he'd known Houston was serving in the enemy colors—Winfield Scott came with him. Along with a poet whose name Harrison couldn't remember, even though he could remember reading two of his poems. One had been a gloomy thing, full of histrionics on death. Overwrought, the way poets will be about the subject and professional soldiers won't. But the other had been a poem about a man's thoughts watching a waterfowl flying in the distance. Harrison had been quite taken by it.

While he listened to Houston, Harrison's mind was at least half on Scott and the poet. They represented a real danger to him, which Houston didn't at the moment. He knew why they were there, of course.

"—the eighteen prisoners who are uninjured or walking wounded, we propose to exchange immediately against a similar number of our own. It's your choice, but we recommend that you permit us to continue providing medical attention to the other thirteen prisoners."

Houston glanced around the room in the Post that Harrison had chosen for his headquarters. He'd chosen it for the purpose partly for its size, but mostly because it had little in the way of the carnage that was being cleaned up elsewhere. Still, there were several pockmarks in the wall from bullets, and one bloodstain that hadn't quite been removed.

"I think we can do better for them at the moment than you could do here, General," he concluded.

Harrison didn't doubt it. His medical staff was exhausted already.

"All regulars?"

"Yes, sir. We have no militia prisoners."

Houston didn't bother adding: *We didn't take any.* The complete lack of expression on his face would have made that obvious, even if it hadn't been already. Just as it made clear there would be no apologies forthcoming for the fact, either.

Harrison had no intention of asking for them, anyway. His concerns for the moment, outside of his own professional prospects, were entirely for his regulars.

The terms of exchange seemed fair enough. But—

"Let's make it an equal exchange—within the usual parameters—but I'd prefer not to distinguish between walking and immobile wounded." He gave Houston a nod that was respectful, perhaps a bit on the embarrassed side. "We—ah—don't have but three walking wounded of your own. You didn't leave more than that."

"Fine. Select fifteen of our men that you think could manage the transfer without further injury, and we'll begin with that. We can do the rest later, as they heal."

"Terms of parole?"

"We propose an agreement not to fight on the same front—for a year, let's say?—but no overall prohibition against bearing arms in the current conflict."

Harrison thought about it. A complete prohibition—especially with no time limit—would better serve the interests of the United States Army. With their much smaller pool of manpower to draw from, the Arkansans could ill afford to have capable soldiers removed from service altogether.

But he was sure the Arkansans would never agree to that, for the same reason, so there was no point raising it. He could live with their proposal, and it was similar enough to various prisoner exchanges that had taken place in the war with Britain that no politician could yap about it.

Not that some of them wouldn't try, of course.

"Done." He extended his hand. "Please convey to your officers and men my salutations. You fought a most gallant battle."

Houston returned the handshake, an expression coming back into his face. Quite a friendly one, even an animated one. "And please accept our own compliments. Generals Driscol and Ball asked me to forward their admiration to your First Regiment and its commander, in particular. That was a bloody business by the wall."

Harrison nodded. "I'll certainly pass that on to the regiment. The commanding officer—that was Colonel John McNeil—fell in the battle, I'm afraid."

And then it was a round of handshakes between all the officers present. The fact that two of the three Arkansans were black caused not even a moment's hesitation, so far as Harrison could detect.

Not even on his part. He tried to remember if he'd ever shaken a negro's hand. He couldn't recall doing so, unless one were to count pressing a coin into a doorman's hand at a fancy hotel in Philadelphia and Washington.

Which would be an absurd comparison.

Scott and Bryant stayed behind, after Houston and the other Arkansan officers left to begin the prisoner exchange.

The first words out of Winfield Scott's mouth were the critical ones.

"The victory was yours, General Harrison, and Cullen and I shall so report it in our account."

Harrison nodded, stiffly, trying to let no sign of his relief show.

For a moment, he and Winfield stared at each other. They were not friends and never had been. Harrison resented the man, actually. Despite his victories at Tippecanoe and the Thames, Harrison's resignation from the army in 1814 as a result of his clash with Secretary of War Armstrong had inevitably removed some of the luster from his reputation. Scott, on the other hand, had suffered a dramatic wound at Lundy's Lane that had enabled him—in effect if not in name—to withdraw from the rest of the war with his great victory at the Chippewa untarnished.

Still, there were rules. And since Scott had made clear he would follow them, Harrison had no legitimate grounds for complaint.

He knew full well, of course, what sort of account Scott would be filing with the newspapers. Any discerning reader with any military experience who got past the headline— *U.S. VICTORIOUS AT SECOND ARKANSAS POST*— would understand that beneath the formality lay something completely different. An Arkansas Army less than half the size of its American opponent had completely outmaneuvered the U.S. commander; allowed a good portion of its

Chickasaw allies to escape a trap; fought a superior force of U.S. regulars to a standstill in a battle whose butcher's bill, proportionate to the size of the forces involved, was worse than Lundy's Lane; and practically destroyed the Georgia militia to boot.

A complete disaster, beneath the headline. A tactical "defeat" that was actually a strategic victory. A battle—never mind the formalities—that guaranteed that Henry Clay's short war was going to be a long and protracted one. With God-only-knew-what consequences would come out of it, at the end.

Still, Harrison had the headline. He clutched it for all it was worth.

Quite a bit, actually. Luckily for him—on this occasion—almost all the politicians in America with real military experience were on the other side anyway. Clay and Calhoun would clutch that headline even more tightly than he would. They'd have no choice.

"Please be seated, gentlemen." He indicated some nearby chairs. "This will be a long interview, I imagine. Some refreshments, perhaps? I believe—"

He cocked an eye at Captain Matlock, who gave him a quick little nod in return.

"We have some whiskey."

He'd start with Matlock to assemble a new staff. His regimental commander would protest, of course, but too bad for him. For the war that was coming, Harrison needed a staff. A real one, this time.

CHAPTER 38

New Antrim, Arkansas
JULY 26, 1825

Sheff would retain flashes of memory of what happened to him after he'd received his wound. But flashes were all they were. The last one, thankfully, was a hazy recollection of himself screaming while two men held him down and a surgeon dug a bullet out of his shoulder.

The one thing from that episode he did remember clearly was the surgeon grunting, "Well, he's a lucky one."

If he'd had any strength at all, he'd have hit him. As it was, he lapsed into unconsciousness again.

So, when his eyes opened and he saw the hand, he spent some time just looking at it, getting reacquainted with having a clear head. It was a delicious sensation, as enjoyable as one of the glasses of iced milk his mother made on occasion when she could afford ice.

Sheff had never drunk much whiskey, anyway. But he made a promise to himself then and there that he'd avoid liquor altogether henceforth, except when doing so would be socially ungraceful. He'd never appreciated before what a blessing it was to have an unfettered consciousness. Why would any sane man go out of his way to imitate an experience that a battle wound provided?

It was a small hand, quite nicely shaped. Female, clearly. The hand wasn't moving, just lying loosely on an open book. He couldn't see the thumb, just the fingers. They were spread out on the pages, curled up a bit. The book was the Bible, he realized after a while. From what he could tell, open to some passage midway through the Old Testament.

Eventually, it occurred to him that the hand belonged to an arm, and the arm belonged to a person. So his eyes began moving up along the forearm, then past the elbow. He couldn't see the arm itself, though, above the wrist. It was covered in the sleeve of a calico blouse, which seemed better made than usual. That didn't necessarily mean it was store bought, since there were women who could cut and sew that well. Sheff's mother was one of them. But he had the sense that this blouse was tailor made. The common everyday calico seemed more finely dyed than usual.

His eyes got as far as the shoulder, which was puffed out in one of the new-style gigot sleeves. What his mother called leg-of-mutton sleeves. Then, his eyes couldn't roll any further in their sockets. He had to decide whether he had the strength and interest to shift his position.

He was in a bed, he suddenly realized, covered by a thin blanket. He wondered how that had happened. There were no beds in the tents of army surgeons. You were lucky if you got a cot.

It dawned on him that he wasn't in a tent to begin with. This was a room. In a house of some kind.

For that matter—

His eyes rolled back, coming to bear again on the hand.

Yes, that was a woman's hand, sure enough. No chance of error. A young woman's, too, he was certain. But there wouldn't be any women in an army medical tent, either, certainly not young ones. Nursing wounded soldiers was a filthy business.

He was interested enough, and he thought he had the strength and energy. So, painfully—champing down a shout when he placed weight on the left shoulder and felt a spike of agony—he managed to shift position enough to be able to look up at the woman's head.

Which turned out to be pointless. The woman was asleep, her head slumped forward with her chin resting on her chest.

At least, Sheff assumed the chin was on the chest. He couldn't actually see any part of the woman's face. Her head was covered by a large bonnet with a flaring brim. Sheff thought the technical term for it was "cabriolet," but his mother just called them coal-scuttle bonnets. She had one herself, since they were handy out in the sunshine.

A thought finally occurred to him, then, and he experienced what might just possibly have been the single most frustrating moment in his life. Was this . . .

Tarnation, he couldn't *move.* No more than he had, anyway, and he'd almost fainted doing that much. And what good would it do, anyway? He couldn't very well shake the woman awake, even if he could have reached her.

Fortunately, his quandary was resolved.

"Stop fidgeting, young man! You'll reopen the wound, and I'll have to get the surgeon around again."

Well, he knew that voice. *Courage,* he told himself. He'd faced U.S. regulars, hadn't he? Hadn't even flinched, so far as he could remember.

Turning his head a little, he saw the dragon in the doorway. She was glaring at him as usual.

Well . . . not quite. The look on her face seemed more one of exasperation than outright hostility. So did the look she bestowed upon the mysterious woman sitting by his bed.

"The two of you!" he heard her mutter. The dragon came into the room and laid a hand on the leg-of-mutton shoulder. Then, gave it a little shake.

"Wake up, Imogene. Your precious captain's come around."

The head popped up. Yes, that *was* Imogene under the brim.

"Oh," she said.

Julia Chinn was now looking at the open Bible on Imogene's lap.

"I told you!" Firmly, she moved Imogene's hand aside and, more firmly still, closed the Bible. "You're too young to be reading that."

Puzzled, Sheff tried to remember what part of the Old Testament—

Oh.

Fortunately, he didn't say it out loud. He even managed not to smile. He could remember the time his own mother had caught him engrossed in the Song of Solomon the way no proper thirteen-year-old boy ought to be.

To cover the moment's awkwardness, he cleared his throat. "I'm not a captain, Miz Julia. Just a second lieutenant."

Julia gave him that same exasperated look. "I wish! Boy, I will say you are prob'bly the most tenacious critter I ever met."

But the tone in her voice didn't seem as chilly by the time she got to the end of the sentence as it had when she started it. She reached down and tugged his blanket back into position and said quietly to Imogene: "Five minutes, girl. Then I want you out of here."

After she'd left the room, Imogene burst into a smile so wide it looked to split her face in half. That expression, with her full lips, brought out the African part of her ancestry, which was normally overshadowed by her light skin and hazel eyes. More green than hazel, really.

For the first time, Sheff felt a surge of passion. No poetic abstraction, neither.

Fortunately, he was still too weak to embarrass himself. The hand that would have impulsively reached for her lay limp on the blanket. So did . . . well. Everything else.

"They promoted you, Sheff! All the way to captain."

"That's . . ." He tried to decide how he felt. Pleased, of course. But —

"I'm not even eighteen years old. Won't be, till next month."

The smile wasn't fading at all. "Don't matter! The whole town's talking about it. Oh, Sheff, I'm so proud of you!"

" 'Doesn't' matter," he corrected.

"You and Mama!" She waved a dismissive hand. Which, on the way back, somehow found its way into Sheff's. "Both nagging me."

He had enough strength to squeeze the hand. "You listen to your mama. Listen to me, too. She wants you talking proper. Properly. I'm trying myself."

The smile was replaced by a serious look. "Do—does it really matter, Sheff?"

"Yes, Imogene. It does."

In the corridor of the boardinghouse just outside the open door, where she'd been eavesdropping, Julia Chinn pressed the back of her head against the wall. It was either that or bang it against the wall.

The next three minutes weren't any better. She could have handled a rascal, easy as pie. This one . . .

"Imogene, that's been five minutes, for sure!" she shouted. "Mama!"

"You listen to me, young lady!"

Sheff's firm voice could be heard clearly, even through the wall. "Best do as your mama says, Imogene."

Julia had heard the talk herself. It couldn't be avoided, anywhere you went in New Antrim. Parker by the wall. For just that moment, she had a deep sympathy for the U.S. regulars who'd faced him. If only they'd . . .

But that thought led to a place Julia Chinn never wanted to go. There were limits. Whatever else, there *had* to be limits, or there was no point to any of it. She might as well sell Imogene to a slave brothel right now. Or herself, for that matter.

Sheff's mother arrived shortly thereafter. She was all solicitous concern, fussing over him, but Sheff thought that was mostly her way of handling the grief caused by her brother's death. Sheff was still trying to come to grips with it himself.

It was hard. He still had that iron shell around him. The battle shield, he'd come to think of it. As useful as it was— indispensable, perhaps—it was now getting in the way of normal emotions. He was pretty sure he'd have to be careful about that. Taken too far, or too long, it could rub a man's soul so hard it became just a callus.

But he wasn't ready to deal with it yet. So, the two hours his mother spent in the room before she had to go home were mostly taken up with practical concerns.

There, fortunately—in a horrible sort of way—his uncle's death had eased the strain.

"The bank says it's canceling the loan outright," his mother said quietly. "On account of Jem. Well, your uncle's part, anyway. We still got to pay yours off. But Mr. Crowell told me they'd take your service as being complete. So there won't never be no interest."

Sheff knew the bank had adopted a policy of canceling any loans secured by a soldier's pay in the event the soldier died in the line of duty. The chiefdom's legislature was also talking about providing some subsidies for widows and orphans, but Sheff didn't think anything would come of it. Arkansas was actually thriving, economically, on account of all the new construction and manufacture. The war hadn't even put a dent in it—probably stimulated it, in fact. But wages were very low, with the constant influx of freedmen, and there just wasn't that much money to throw around.

Still, between the increased pay that would come with his promotion to captain and the work his mother got as a tailor, they should manage. She was paid a real tailor's wage, too, not the much lower rate most girls got in the garment manufactories. He was pretty sure they'd even be able to let Dinah keep going to school instead of her having to go to work in the shops.

His mother was holding up pretty well, too. She had her own version of a battle shield.

"The truth is, Sheff, we're doing better than we were back in Baltimore, with your father and uncle bringing in whatever they could. Which weren't never much. So you just make sure when you can get about again, that you keep fighting for Arkansas. You hear?"

Cal McParland came to visit him later that day. He brought John Ridge and Buck Watie with him.

"Congratulations," Ridge said immediately after walking into the room. "You heard about your promotion, I take it?"

"You'll give him a swelled head," Cal chided. But he was smiling as he said it. "Jumped him a rank, even."

Buck Watie slid into a chair. "Gave you the Legion of Honor, too. Only one who got it except Captain Dupont."

Cal laughed. "My cousin says the Laird got the idea from Napoleon, but he's obviously going to be a lot stingier than the emperor ever was."

Sheff had been wondering what a Legion of Honor was. For the most part, the Arkansas Army was patterned after the American, since that was the experience of most of its veterans. The American army didn't have the custom of awarding decorations for valor or merit, as did most of the European armies.

But that thought was swept away for the moment. "How's the captain doing?"

The good cheer left the room. Buck Watie shook his head. "Captain Dupont didn't make it, Sheff. The Americans returned his body the day after the battle."

"At least he didn't die slowly from being gut-shot," Cal added. "The Americans think he must have bled to death before the fighting was even over. From what I heard, our surgeon who looked at his body agreed with them."

Well, that was something. Sheff had liked Charles Dupont, even if he'd found his heavy accent hard to understand sometimes. He'd been a lot less prone to judging people simply by skin color than most of the Creole freedmen from New Orleans were.

As a group, Sheff didn't care for them much. Some of them had even been slave-owners themselves, and they still retained a lot of the attitudes. If they hadn't been forced out of the city after the Algiers Incident, most of them would still be in New Orleans. As it was, they tended to cluster together in one part of New Antrim that people were starting to call the Creole Quarter.

But Sheff hadn't really been close to Dupont, so there wasn't any personal grief involved. Besides, he *was* still short of eighteen, and . . .

He tried to figure out how to ask without seeming full of himself.

Fortunately, Cal saved him the effort. "Yup. The Legion of Honor. The Laird established it right after the battle. Announced he would, before the day was over, even."

"Established" was a word that seemed a little absurd if they only gave out two of them. But that mystery got cleared up by Buck.

"He also established what he's calling the Arkansas Post Medal, and they're handing those out like candy. Everybody who was there gets one, except the steamboat crews, and they're complaining like nobody's business."

"Them!" Cal snorted. "They didn't get within half a mile—not even that—of a shot being fired."

He gave Sheff a big grin. "Don't get your hopes up too soon, though. What I heard, it'll be weeks before they can get around to actually making the things. There's a big squabble over who gets the contract."

That brought a little laugh to the room. The Arkansas

House of Representatives was even more notorious than its American counterpart for the fervent dedication of its members to advancing the interests of their constituents. If anything, the House of Chiefs was worse.

The next half hour was spent bringing Sheff up-to-date on what had happened in the battle after he'd been taken out of combat. It was a cheerful discussion until Sheff asked about the Chickasaws.

His three fellow officers exchanged glances, their smiles either fading or seeming frozen in place.

"Well," said Cal.

"That got a little sticky," John Ridge added.

His cousin Buck gave him a glance that was at least half angry. The rest of it seemed derisive.

"You talk! We were the ones had to do the dirty work."

John made a face. So did Cal.

"Give," said Sheff. "What happened?"

Cal provided the answer. The first part, anyway. "They got really hammered in there, Sheff. Near as we can tell, half the warriors in the tribe died in the Post—they never had but a little over six hundred, to begin with—and a fair number got killed or badly wounded during the escape. So . . . well, by the time they could pull themselves together, the Laird already had their slaves in custody. By then, Houston was back with the Second Infantry. And—ah—he'd already moved over my battery and the others from the Third."

"The women and old men raised Sam Hill, of course, but . . ." John Ridge shrugged. "Wasn't really much they could do to stop him. Houston was in no friendlier mood than the Laird. Neither was General Ball, of course."

They fell silent again. "So?" Sheff demanded.

Buck provided the rest. "So, the Chickasaw warriors finally got there and starting hollering and making threats. Real nasty threats, not just name-calling. And—" He took a deep breath. "We followed orders. Cut loose with both batteries. Canister—and we were targeting the Colbert clan."

"The Laird told us to spare as many full-bloods as we could," Cal added. "And we did. But they were pretty well mixed together, and canister's what it is. There ain't much left of the Colberts, I can tell you that."

"Oh . . . Jesu—Sam Hill," Sheff murmured, barely avoiding the blasphemy.

John Ridge's face was stiff. "Sam Hill is right. My father's furious. So's Chief Ross, although he's hiding it better. Even the Choctaw chiefs are hollering about it. The Creeks will be, too, soon as they hear."

"Sure, and nobody likes Chickasaws," Buck chimed in, "but . . ." He shook his head. "I did what I was told—well, watched, anyway—but I can't help think the Laird'll come to regret it. This could even start a civil war."

Callender McParland started to say something but broke off before he got a word out. From the quick look he gave his two Cherokee companions, Sheff had no trouble figuring out what he'd been about to say.

So he went ahead and said it for him. He was too weak to summon up the energy to be diplomatic.

"Fuck the Chickasaws. And fuck the Choctaws and the Creeks. And—sorry, fellows—but if push comes to shove, fuck you Cherokees, too. You got Sam Hill's nerve, as far as I'm concerned, expecting us niggers"—he rolled his eyes at Cal—"and some white boys to do your fighting for you while thinking you'll keep us in slavery."

Anger that had been quietly festering for a long time finally came to the surface. "Fuck you," he stated flatly. "Learn to work. I've been working since I was ten years old."

"Me too," said Cal. "My family's poor Scots-Irish—well, not poor any longer—from New York. We never owned any slaves. And sure as hell aren't gonna start now."

He gave Buck a look that had none of its earlier friendliness. "And I'd be real careful, was I you, Lieutenant Watie, making too many noises about 'civil wars.' You think we can't do the same thing at Tahlequah we just done at Arkansas Post, best you think twice."

So there it was: the threat naked and right out in the open. Strangely, perhaps, that was enough to start draining away Sheff's anger.

"Come on, now, Cal—there was no call for that. Buck was just expressing a concern. He wasn't making no threats."

Hastily, he corrected himself. "Any threats."

Their voices had gotten raised a bit. You never knew. Imogene might be somewhere close enough to overhear. Worse, so might her mother.

Cal took a long deep breath. Simultaneously—it almost made Sheff laugh, watching it—the two Cherokees did the same.

They let it out at the same time, too. Then Cal said: "Sorry. Didn't really mean it that way."

John chuckled. "Sam Hill, you didn't! Still . . ."

He sighed, and wiped a hand over his face. "The truth is, Buck and I don't really disagree with you. And I already told my father so. Our newspaper will have some criticisms of the way the Laird handled it, I imagine, but we're not going to make any bones about the rest of it. There's no slavery in Arkansas—that's established, right there in the Constitution—and since the Chickasaws sought refuge in Arkansas, they had to abide by Arkansas law. And the threats they were making went way beyond anything you could rightly call a petition in redress of grievances."

Sheff's anger was almost gone, now. Enough, even, for him to play devil's advocate. "Members of other Confederate chiefdoms *do* have the right to travel in Arkansas, with their slaves, without having them seized."

"For no more than two weeks, without a permit," Cal countered. "No way were all the Chickasaws—almost any of them, the shape they were in—gonna make it to Oklahoma in two weeks. And the chance that the Arkansas Chiefdom would have issued permits for a thousand slaves is exactly nothing."

John shook his head. "It doesn't matter, anyway. Nobody"—he managed a real smile, here—"not even us disputatious natural-lawyer Cherokees, thinks this is something you can settle in a courtroom. The Laird's been pushing for this ever since he brought out that separate Arkansas flag. Pushing it harder than ever, after Houston arrived and made clear he'd back him. Sooner or later, something like this was going to happen, anyway. May as well be now—when everybody knows there's another U.S. army sitting there on our northern border, and the second battle of Arkansas Post is fresh in everybody's mind."

He caught the look on Sheff's face.

"Oh," Ridge said. "Guess you didn't know about that, either, did you? The word just got to New Antrim yesterday."

"There's at least two regiments of U.S. regulars sitting on the Arkansas just north of the border," Buck added. "They're building a great big fort. Colonel Zachary Taylor's in command."

"They got us surrounded, in other words," Cal said. "The stupid bastards."

CHAPTER 39

Missouri Territory
JULY 29, 1825

Skeptically, Zack Taylor eyed the two men standing in front of him. "Explain to me why I should care in the least whether this Clark fellow stays alive or not."

He waved a hand at the rise in the prairie, beyond which lay the bandit camp. "I've got three companies here. I'll call for them to surrender, but . . ."

His shoulders shifted, too slightly to be called a real shrug. The movement was an accurate reflection of his attitude, which was that bandits were unlikely to just lay down their arms—and he was indifferent to the matter. With three companies of dragoons, he could afford to be.

"What do *you* care, for that matter? The reward—both of them—specify 'dead or alive.' I'd think 'dead' would make things easier for you."

The man on his left—that was Ray Thompson—shook his head.

"It doesn't work like that, Colonel. Sure, and the reward poster *says* 'dead or alive.' You believe that, you believe in paradise on earth. What'll really happen—"

His partner chimed in. "You bring in a dead body, the man offering the reward will look at it, shake his head, and tell you it's the wrong man. Dancing with joy the whole time. And how are you going to prove otherwise? Seeing as how your principal witness to the contrary is dead, on account of you killed him."

Scott Powers, that was. Taylor remembered them both quite well. The two scoundrels had had the effrontery to claim that the meat they'd try to fob off onto Cantonment Robertson's commissary hadn't really been wormy. Just "prespiced," in the Louisiana custom. To this day, Zack didn't think he'd ever encountered more bold-faced liars in his life.

He hadn't run into them since, but he'd almost had the two arrested, just on general principles, when they arrived in his camp a few days ago. But eventually he'd agreed to come look for himself. There was no good reason not to, after all. It was less than a three days' ride, even for a sizeable force of dragoons, and until he heard what had happened to General Harrison's first thrust up the Arkansas River Valley he'd had to bide his time in Missouri Territory anyway. If Mrs. Houston's murderer was within his grasp, he had the duty to seize him. Besides, he just couldn't figure out any way—any reason, rather—Thompson and Powers would be lying about this matter.

Taylor still didn't know if Mrs. Houston's killer was in that camp. But that it was a bandit camp, he didn't doubt at all. There was no reason in the world for white men who weren't bandits to be camped out here like this. Not to mention still be sleeping this late in the morning if they were doing honest work. The sun had come up over an hour earlier.

"The two of you are experienced bounty hunters, I take it?"

Thompson looked more shifty-eyed than ever. Powers just grinned. "Not exactly, Colonel. Be more accurate to say 'experienced bounty.' But we know what we're talking about."

He pointed a thumb toward the hidden camp. "Anyway, that's why we need Clark alive."

Taylor's patience had run out. "Fine. But you'll have to figure out how to do it, because I'm not about to risk any of my men for the purpose. I'll give you ten minutes to get into whatever position you think might do the trick for you. After that, I'm calling on them to surrender—and if any of them so much as wave too hard, I'll have 'em all shot down."

"Ain't this a mess?" Ray grumbled, nine minutes and maybe fifty seconds later. They'd found a place to wait in ambush in some switchgrass on the opposite side of the bandit camp. It was a good hiding place, sure, but switchgrass was no fun at all. It was almost like hiding in a thicket of razor blades.

"Shut up," Scott hissed. "It's worth ten thousand dollars."

"I think there's a *snake* somewhere in here."

"So bite him if he gives you any trouble."

"I hate snakes, you know that. What if—"

He was interrupted by the sound of distant shouting. He and Scott were too far away to make out the exact words.

It didn't matter, though. He'd heard words spoken in that official tone of voice often enough to know the gist of it. *We're the law and you ain't, so give up or we'll shoot you dead and not even have to skip lunch on account of it.*

Not five seconds later, the camp burst into activity, men spilling out of their bedrolls and running every which-a-way. Most of them were pulling out guns, and two or three of them were shooting at nothing.

The idiots. Ray and Scott could only hope that their quarry was at least a little smarter.

The company that Taylor had had hidden behind that rise came over it, just as crisp as you could ask for. Up came the muskets, and a volley went off. That took down at least three bandits. The rest started veering north, but another company was in front of them, and another volley went off.

This was about as uneven a contest as you could ask for. If their quarry was in that pack of dumb yahoos, he was a dead man, and they'd just have to hope Andrew Jackson and Henry Clay were more honest than most reward-posters. Given that one of them was a U.S. senator and the other was president of the whole country, Ray thought that was about as likely as getting a royal flush in an honest game of poker.

"Somebody's coming," Powers murmured. "Over there."

Ray followed the direction of Scott's little nod. Sure enough. Somebody was moving through the bluestem grass that covered most of the area. The stuff was tall enough for

a crawling man to stay out of direct sight, but not so tall that
his progress couldn't be followed by watching the grass
move, if you were looking for it.

"Two of 'em, I think," Powers added.

Ray thought he was right. He gauged the course of whoever it was crawling through the grass, maybe forty yards
off, and the pace they were making. Another volley went off
while he did so. He could hear men shouting and screaming
in the distance, but he ignored all that. The bandits who'd
been caught in the camp were as good as dead. Taylor
wouldn't be taking any prisoners, given that they'd put up a
resistance. Such as it was.

So he and Scott might as well assume that Andrew Clark
was one of the two men making their escape. There was no
point in doing anything else.

"Fancy or not?" Scott asked.

Damnation, there *was* a snake in here. Ray could hear it
slither.

"Fuck 'fancy.' I can run if you can't."

He was out of the switchgrass and running toward the
quarry not two seconds later. It didn't occur to him until then
that maybe the soldiers off in the distance would take *him*
for a bandit.

But he ignored the risk. The range was long for muskets,
and he really hated snakes.

He could hear Scott pounding behind him. As ambushes
went, this one was about as crude as you could ask for.

The men in the grass heard them once they were halfway
there. They rose up, each holding a pistol.

Sure enough, one of them was Clark. The other was
Scott's erstwhile friend.

"Erstwhile" being the operative term, Ray stopped and
shot him when he was ten yards off. The man returned fire—
tried to—but his gun didn't go off.

Ray's shot hit him somewhere in the ribs, turning him.
Scott's following shot hit him in the upper arm, knocking
him down.

They each had two pistols, the second of which they
brought to bear on Clark.

"You're under arrest!" That came from Ray's partner.

Clark fired his pistol. Scott yelped, clutching the top of his

shoulder. Too angry to think straight, he fired back. His returning shot must have come within a hair of Clark's head,
judging from the way the assassin flinched.

"We need him alive!" Ray shouted.

"The bastard hit me! He couldn't hit Houston right in front
of him—but he hit *me*."

"So what?" Ray might have had some sympathy, except it
was obvious Clark's bullet hadn't done more than graze
Scott's shoulder.

The assassin was now trying to reload, not paying any attention to Ray at all.

Ray shook his head. "Andrew Clark, you are one dang
fool." He stepped forward a few quick paces, leaned over far
enough to move the grass aside, aimed, and fired.

The shot was perfect, right through the top of Clark's
Blucher half-boots. Probably blew off a couple of toes. He
wouldn't be making any escape, for sure—and he wouldn't
bleed to death, either.

Clark screeched and threw up his hands. The pistol he'd
been reloading sailed off somewhere. He stumbled backward and fell on his butt.

Up close, with Clark howling the way he was, Ray could
see the scar where Houston had split his lip pretty badly. At
least three teeth were missing, too.

No reason not to subtract a few more. Ray kicked him in
the face, twice, and then clubbed him with the pistol butt.
That ought to do it.

"You stinking bastard!"

Looking over, he saw that Clark's companion was still
alive. In fact, he'd levered himself up on the elbow of his
uninjured arm.

Which was his left arm—and he was left-handed. In that
position, he couldn't fight a kitten. The world was full of
dang fools.

By then, Scott had retrieved the man's pistol and was
working at it. "Sorry 'bout that, Eddie," he said, "but ten
thousand dollars is ten thousand dollars."

"You stinking bastard!"

Scott flipped up the frizzen and shook his head. "You got
some dew in the primer. You should've watched for that, this

early in the morning, crawling through grass like you were doing." He scraped out the powder and reprimed the pistol.

"I'll kill you, you stinking bastard!"

"Oh, Eddie, that ain't likely at all." Scott cocked the pistol and shot the man in the head. At that range he could hardly miss, and he didn't.

He looked up at Ray and shrugged. "Sorta hated to do that, him being a friend of mine and all. But Eddie always was the unforgiving sort. I don't feel like having to look over my shoulder all the time, the next twenty or thirty years."

That was the main reason Ray and Scott had been partners for so long. They were both reasonable men, neither one of them given to silly fancies that might strain the relationship.

By the time they got back to the fort, three days later, word had arrived about Arkansas Post. The news was on the scanty side but enough for Taylor to know that he wouldn't be marching into the Confederacy any time soon. Victory or not—and Zack was sure that was a formality, in this instance—any army that had been battered that badly would need months to recuperate. Harrison wouldn't be moving out of the Post until winter came, and then he might very well decide to wait for spring. He'd need reinforcements— lots of them—before he could even think of marching up-river on New Antrim.

That meant Zack was effectively stymied also. The Confederates had the advantage of interior lines. If he and Harrison didn't move together, the enemy could simply switch forces back and forth between their southeastern and north-western fronts.

He took it philosophically enough. Zack had never thought this war would be over quickly, to begin with, and he'd had years of experience on the frontier. Just another six to twelve months ahead, building another fort and keeping his men in fighting condition. Nothing he hadn't done many times before.

Besides, there was at least one small benefit. He'd be able to make sure those two rascals were telling the truth.

"Send a squad down to Arkansas," he told his aide. Then, thinking about it, amended the order. "No, better make it a whole company. The way that luna—the special commissioner—has been throwing arms around to Indians in the area, a squad might get ambushed. Under a flag of truce, of course."

"Yes, sir. And they're . . ."

"What do you think? Sam Houston was really the only eyewitness. See if he's willing to come here and verify that we've got the right man."

AUGUST 22, 1825

"Yes, that's him. I'm quite sure of it, Colonel Taylor."

Sam had wondered how he'd react if indeed it proved to be the man who'd killed Maria Hester. Six months earlier, he'd probably have had to be physically restrained from attacking him.

Now . . .

The man glaring at him from a much-battered face just reminded him of a filthy rat. Not even a cornered one, but one caught in a trap, and knowing it.

He turned away, not ever wanting to see the man again in his life. Taylor's rough, honest features were a relief.

"And thank you, Colonel."

"My pleasure." Taylor looked to the guards holding Clark. "Get him out of here, and back into chains."

When he looked back at Sam, his face was a bit stiff. "Ah . . ."

Sam waved his hand. "Yes, I understand, Colonel. The crime was committed against an American citizen, on American soil. The prisoner will have to be returned there for trial."

Taylor nodded. "Personally, I'd be quite happy to hand him over to you. Or Arkansas, for that matter. But—"

He rubbed his heavy jaw for a moment. "I think it'd be best, all around, if we did everything by the book."

There was a slight stress on *everything*.

"Yes, I agree. Everything by the book."

Later that day, Sam met privately with the two men Colonel Taylor credited with the capture.

"I can guarantee you that Andy Jackson will pay his half of the reward, once he gets my letter. Clay's half . . ."

He shrugged. "Who knows? And even if Clay is good for it, I'm not sure where you'd need to go to collect. You can wait for Andy's money in New Antrim."

The two men looked particularly shifty-eyed in response to that.

"Well. Ah." That came from the one called Ray Thompson. It might even be his real name.

His partner, Scott Powers, echoed him. "Well. Ah."

Sam grinned. "Don't tell me you boys are in bad odor in the chiefdom of Arkansas?"

"Well. Ah."

"Well. Ah."

That was worth a chuckle. "What was it? Slave trading? Or were you part of Crittenden's crowd?"

That was worth an outright laugh. "Both, huh? Anybody ever suggest to you that you're not walking in the ways of the Lord?"

"Well. Ah." That was Thompson. Powers managed to return the grin. "Yeah. Started with my mother. I was maybe five."

A thought came to Sam. It was . . . intriguing, anyway.

"Tell you what," he said. "You come back to New Antrim with me. I'll guarantee your safety."

Those *had* to be the two most skeptical looks he'd ever gotten in his life.

"Safety out, too?" asked Thompson.

"Oh, relax, will you? Nobody'll lay a hand on you, all the way in and out of Arkansas. Fact is, I think the Laird's more likely to be amused than anything else. Charles Ball, for sure."

At the mention of Charles Ball, Sam thought they almost jumped.

"We'll probably have to keep you out of John Brown's sight, however."

At that, they did jump. Not more than half an inch, though. Tough fellows, obviously. Rogues, rascals, and renegades, too, just as obviously. But Sam was pretty sure he could find a good use for such. Several good uses, in fact.

It took two weeks longer than anyone expected to get Andrew Clark back to Washington, D.C. Not because of his bad foot, which none of his captors cared about in the least. But simply because the army soon realized it had to detail sizeable units to escort the prisoner every step of the way.

As it was, they almost lost him at Uniontown. The crowd that surrounded the company was more in the way of a small army than the lynch mobs they'd encountered in St. Louis and the Ohio river towns.

Fortunately, the governor of the state was there also, and Shulze finally managed to talk the crowd out of the hanging they'd been looking forward to.

He'd been there by pure coincidence, as it happened. News of Clark's capture and return for trial had spread all over the country by then, but Shulze hadn't paid much attention to the details. He'd had no idea the prisoner was coming through Uniontown when he planned to be passing through.

Word had spread all over the country about the Second Battle of Arkansas Post, too. "Word," in the form of extensive and detailed reports printed in every newspaper in the nation.

Not always the same reports in all the newspapers, of course. Most newspapers gave pride of place to the reports filed by Bryant and Scott, those being authoritative in terms of their authors as well as being the only really eyewitness accounts from all sides of the fray. But not all did. A considerable number of papers, especially in the Deep South, refused to run the Bryant-Scott accounts at all. Several of them went so far as to point to those reports as prime examples of the sort of pernicious abolitionist propaganda that the Georgian delegation to Congress had already announced it was going to demand be banned from being carried by the U.S. Postal Service.

Some newspapers emphasized one thing; others something else. *U.S. DEFEATS ARKANSAS* in one paper might be *MONSTER CASUALTIES IN ARKANSAS* in another. But there was enough commonality for one thing to be clear to everyone.

The Arkansas War was just starting, and it wouldn't be over any time soon.

In Washington, D.C., the president and the war secretary announced that they'd be presenting to the next Congress, convening over the winter, a plan for the drastic expansion of the American military in response to the threat posed by the Confederacy. Or Black Arkansas, as Calhoun referred to it, not being a man given to euphemisms.

In response, Senator Andrew Jackson called for the formation of a new political party, since there was clearly no longer room in the existing Republican Party for both him and—"the rascals" was the mildest term he used—Clay and Calhoun. And he invited several key political figures in the nation to meet with him in advance of the convening of Congress, so that a common platform for the new party could be forged.

And that's where Governor Shulze of Pennsylvania had been headed when he passed through Uniontown and, by pure accident, happened to be there at the right time to save Andrew Clark from a lynching.

At the Hermitage, in Nashville, another declaration of war was being prepared. A war, in this case, that nobody in the United States with any political sense at all thought would be over any sooner than the other one—and a goodly number thought would continue long after peace came to Arkansas.

Clark did eventually make it to Washington. The trial that followed was brief, as was the sentencing. Several congressmen from Georgia, at the last minute, made a somewhat bizarre attempt to persuade the president to commute Clark's sentence to life imprisonment. Bizarre, at least, in its contorted logic.

But other than a few Georgians, only John Randolph rose in the House to defend the proposal, and his logic couldn't be followed by anyone.

President Henry Clay turned them down flatly, even— very unusual for him—in a curt and almost uncivil manner. First, he said, because he had no proper jurisdiction over the matter. Granted that the District of Columbia was under federal authority, not being part of any state, murder was a local crime. So why didn't Congress act directly instead of trying to shuffle the matter off on the president? And what exactly had happened to John Randolph's principles concerning states' rights and the ever-present danger of an overweening executive branch, by the way?

That last, with a sneer, which Clay did very well also.

Beyond that, he told them, even if the courts ruled that he could intervene, he would under no circumstances do so anyway.

"The bastard murdered an innocent young woman! Who might very well have been pregnant with child. Right there—not a mile away—on the steps of the Capitol! What in the name of God is wrong with—"

He broke off abruptly and resumed the seat behind his desk. "No, gentlemen," he said. "The answer is no. Let the murderer hang by the neck until dead, and good riddance. And now, I'm sure you have other business to attend to. If not, I do."

The murderer did hang, on January 23, 1826. But by the time the noose finally took his life, Congress had convened, and no one was paying much attention any longer.

No politician, at any rate. One observer at the hanging was a visiting plantation owner from South Carolina. When it was all over, he was heard by some of the guards to curse Andrew Clark with vehement bitterness, ending with "You dang fool! Why did you have to *miss*?"

PART V

CHAPTER 40

The Hermitage
Nashville, Tennessee
OCTOBER 12, 1825

"—not budging an inch on the subject of the Bank! No, sir, Mr. John Quincy Adams. Not—one—inch." Andrew Jackson broke off his angry stalking back and forth in the living room of the Hermitage. Planting his bony hands on his hips, he leaned over and, from a distance of not more than two feet, bestowed his patented Andy Jackson glare on the short, chunky man sitting in the chair in front of him.

Who, for his part, was glaring right back. Watching the two of them from the far side of the room, Jackson's old friend and confidant John Coffee didn't even try to hide his grin.

You had to tip your hat to Quincy Adams. The whole Jackson style just plain aggravated him, but he'd soon learned how to deal with it. The man might have the mind of a scholar, but he could be just as pugnacious as anyone in Jackson's camp, including Andy himself.

"—don't care about all that fancy economics prattle," Jackson was continuing. "The issue's not finances in the first place. It's politics! A national bank with the authority of the federal government behind it is a mortal threat to the republic. You might as well put a viper in a baby's crib."

Standing by a window not far away, Thomas Hart Benton cleared his throat noisily. Noisily enough, in fact, to break off Andy in mid-tirade and intercept the harsh riposte that Quincy Adams was obviously about to launch.

"Got to say I agree with Andy here, John," the senator

from Missouri said, in a mild tone of voice. He then gave the Tennessee senator a look of deep reproach. "Though I can't see where there's any call for him to get so rambunctious about it."

Thomas Hart Benton! Complaining that someone *else* was being "too rambunctious." Coffee still had vivid memories of the gunfight in the City Hotel, not more than a few miles away though a considerable number of years back in time. It'd been a fistfight and knife fight, too, no holds or weapons barred.

"But he does cut to the heart of it, I think." Benton took a few steps forward, placing himself in front of most of the men gathered in the room. The senator was a natural orator of the rip-roaring school, and he began lapsing into the sort of speech he might give on the Senate floor.

"I plain can't see why, in a confederacy of such vast extent, so many independent states, so many rival commercial cities, there should be but one moneyed tribunal, before which all the rival and contending elements must appear."

Sure enough, his left hand was slipping into his waist, and the right was beginning to wave about. "What a condition for a confederacy of states! But one single dispenser of money, to which every citizen, every trader, every merchant, every manufacturer, every planter, every corporation, every city, every state, and the federal government itself must apply, in every emergency, for the most indispensable loan!"

He was in full roar, now, the right hand no longer waving about but pointing—no, thrusting—the forefinger of denunciation from a mighty thick fist of righteousness. Fortunately, at a blank spot on a wall, beyond which lay defenseless farmland, rather than at John Quincy Adams.

Though, to be sure, Adams was not far from the line of fire. Benton had only to lower the hand perhaps a foot and shift it three inches to the left to bring the man from Massachusetts directly into the accusatory finger's aim.

"And this!—in the face of the fact that in every contest for human rights, the great moneyed institutions of the world have uniformly been found on the side of kings and nobles, against the lives and liberties of the people!"

Adams clapped his hands together. Once, twice, thrice.

"Splendidly said, Thomas! And I can assure you that

should I ever choose to forgo the barren soil of New England for the fertile vistas of Missouri, I shall certainly cast my vote for you upon every possible occasion."

That brought a laugh to the room. A booming one from Benton.

Coffee laughed, too, but his laugh faded quickly. Choked off at the source, so to speak. Adams had turned his head slightly, and Coffee finally spotted the little gleam somewhere in there.

Uh-oh. Belatedly, he remembered. Adams had so few of the overt political skills of most of the men in that room that it was easy to start underestimating the rest of the man. Even Andy Jackson, by now, would allow—not often, and then only grudgingly, true, but he'd still admit it—that John Quincy Adams had probably the finest political brain in the nation.

That didn't mean he was necessarily right on any given issue or dispute. He had his own biases, his own sectional and class views and interests, as much as any man. Not to mention that stiff Puritan way of looking at the world, so different from that of the Jackson camp, all of whom were certainly Christians but few of whom belonged to any church or regularly attended services.

But you underestimated that rapier intelligence at your peril.

"Fine, gentlemen," he said firmly. "We've argued this matter long enough. Clearly, I'm in a small minority on this issue, in present company. A minority of one, to be precise."

Sitting on a divan nearby, Governor Shulze waggled his hand. "Say one and a half, John." With his German accent, it came out more like "vun-und-a-haff."

Shulze gave the room at large a mildly apologetic glance. "I understand—even agree, for the most part—with the points made by the senators from Tennessee and Missouri. Still, mine is a state with much industry and manufacture. I should not care to return to the financial chaos of previous times when it comes to the nation's banking system. I have also seen poor men—even thrifty German ones—stripped of all they own because a wildcat bank collapsed, and through no fault of their own. That is a form of tyranny, also."

Adams gave him a nod. On the opposite side of the room,

so did Jackson. Shulze was raising the practical and financial side of the problem, which not even Andy would deny existed so long as the basic principle was retained.

But John Coffee barely noticed all that. His attention was riveted on Adams. There was a great big giant trapdoor opening here somewhere. He was sure of it.

Adams cleared his throat, almost as noisily as Benton had done a few moments ago.

"So I shall concede the point, while not restricting myself from saying what I believe on the issue as a representative from my state. In the event I should be elected, of course."

Normally, that would have brought a laugh, too. That Adams would be sitting in the House—in less than two months, not even having to wait for 1826—was now a foregone conclusion. As soon as John Quincy had announced his intentions, the sitting congressman from the Massachusetts 11th District had offered to resign his seat—on the condition that the governor of the state would appoint Quincy Adams to serve out his term.

The governor was no great friend and admirer of Adams, but no one expected him to do otherwise—for the simple reason that, whatever his personal inclinations, refusing to appoint Adams would pretty well guarantee his own removal from office at the next gubernatorial election. The Arkansas War had all of New England hopping mad, no state more so than Massachusetts. In the fray that was coming, the Bay State wanted its best lance in the tournament.

Coffee saw that Jackson wasn't smiling any longer, either. Andy had spotted the same gleam.

"But having done so, I must advance a demand of my own. It strikes me as grotesque for the senator from Missouri—as well as the senators here from Kentucky and Tennessee—to be making orations on the subject of the dire threat posed by a national bank to the foundations of our democracy."

Adams cocked an eye at Jackson. "A 'viper' in the crib of the republic, as I recall you putting it. A very nice turn of phrase. But having conceded the viper, I must now insist that my colleagues here explain to me how they can tolerate— decade after decade—the presence of a dragon in that very same crib. That great ancient reptile that is called slavery."

Coffee blew out his cheeks. So. There it was.

The elephant in the middle of the room, that they had all been doing their level best to pretend wasn't there.

Jackson sighed and looked away, staring out of one of the windows. Through whose panes he could easily see some of his own slaves—his many slaves—working in the fields beyond.

His lips quirked slightly. "Tarnation, John Quincy, the Republican Party managed to get all this way without ever much talking about that."

"Yes. I know we did. Quite successfully. But that was because the dragon was asleep."

For the first time since that day's session began, Adams rose from his chair. Unlike most of the politicians there, he was not given to perorations. But, clearly enough, his time had come. John Coffee didn't doubt for a moment that Adams had planned it this way from the opening of the informal session.

Not today's session, either. From the beginning. From the day he arrived at the Hermitage—or, more likely, weeks earlier when he'd accepted Jackson's invitation.

"It is time to face reality, gentlemen. We did not ask for the Arkansas War. Indeed, we opposed it. But the war is here, and none of us expects it to be over any time soon. Not before 1826, at the very earliest, and most likely not until 1828."

He pointed a finger of his own toward the west. Not a finger of accusation, simply that of a scholar, in college, instructing students.

"The Arkansas War changes everything, gentlemen. Whether you like it or I like it. Whether you ever intended to deal with the matter, or I did."

Adams paused long enough to finish composing his stance and expression. That Puritan rectitude business, whose self-critical honesty was perhaps even more annoying than the critical nattering at others. "And I will state here, for the record, that I never had any intention of doing so, either. Like you, I decided long ago to let the dragon sleep. As did George Washington, our first president. As did my father, who succeeded him. As did his successor, Thomas Jefferson—for all his public histrionics on the subject."

The last was said with a sneer. The whole Adams family, even those like John Quincy who had abandoned Federalism, had a corrosive detestation of Jefferson stemming from the campaign of 1800.

But his sneer was no greater than Jackson's. For all that the Republican Party—movement, say better—was sometimes called Jeffersonian, Andy Jackson despised Thomas Jefferson. So did the majority of the men in that room.

"As did James Madison and James Monroe, who succeeded them," Adams went on. "And you can be quite certain that our sixth president, the estimable Henry Clay, will be moving heaven and earth to do the same. Not that Calhoun will allow him the luxury."

He paused again, to sweep the room with a hard gaze. "Oh, no. In John C. Calhoun, you can *see* the dragon, gentlemen. Erect and breathing fire. Henry Clay will sacrifice the virgin to the beast, or the beast will devour him whole. It has come wide awake. A dragon that might well have continued sleeping for decades, had things been otherwise. Slept long enough, indeed, for all of us here to pass on to the afterlife, never having dealt with the monster. Although I suspect our descendants would not have thanked us for it, two or three generations hence. And I have come to do much more than suspect that the God we will all someday answer to will most certainly not thank us at all. In that, if nothing else, I think the scoundrel Jefferson was stating the simple truth."

He sat down abruptly. "So. There it is. I have some proposals of my own. I am most willing to listen to proposals from anyone else. But this much I will not budge on. I will give you the bank, Senator Jackson. We have already compromised on the tariff and internal improvements, in which I conceded more than I gained. I will probably concede much else. But I *will not*—ever again—participate in a political party that does not at the very least have the simple honesty—the simple virtue, if you will—to be able to call a reptile a reptile. If it can't even manage that much, it can't manage anything worthwhile."

Silence followed. Coffee looked around the room.

Andy was still staring out the window. Benton was giving Adams a look that was half a glare. Only half, though. Shulze was obviously trying not to look smug. Martin Van

Buren, over in the corner, had an unreadable expression. But that was a given with the senator from New York. If there was any politician in the country slicker and smoother than Henry Clay, it was the Little Magician. The former Radical Republican's first and immediate reaction to anything was to start calculating the votes, once he was assured that states' rights would be respected. And no one thought Adams was challenging that principle.

Coffee then looked at Richard Johnson. The senator from Kentucky was giving Adams a look that Coffee couldn't interpret at all. Well . . .

He could, actually, he thought. If you remembered that Johnson was a man as well as a politician.

Finally, he looked at the two men who, in the end, were perhaps the most important ones of all. They were sitting side by side in a divan angled to the one holding Shulze.

William Carroll, governor of Tennessee. Joseph Desha, governor of Kentucky. There was no one here representing the state government of Missouri, because the elected governor had just died a couple of months earlier and his successor wasn't known yet.

Both men looked more like rabbits paralyzed by the sight of a viper—or a dragon—than anything else he could think of. Coffee couldn't really blame them. In the United States of America, in the year 1825, the states were more often than not the battlefields upon which the political wars were fought. A proposal—not even that yet, just a question—that frightened presidents and senators and congressmen could be downright petrifying for a governor.

Jackson spoke first, still looking out the window. His tone was quite mild. "Let's start with this, John. Under no conditions will I support outright abolition. Not even on a state level, much less a national one. First, because I detest abolitionists. Second, because I don't think it would work anyway. Third, because"—he had a crooked smile, now—"fine, I'll be honest. I can't afford it myself."

"Agreed," said Adams immediately. "To make something clear, Senator Jackson—or anyone here—I have no fondness for abolitionism myself. Never have had, despite what some people insinuate." He shrugged heavily. "The truth is, being blunt, I don't care much what happens to negroes.

They are not my race of men, and I've never seen much evidence that leads me to question the general assessment of their capabilities. But that's not the point. The problem with slavery, so far as I am concerned, is not its effect upon negroes. The problem is its effect upon *us*. It is corroding the republic, gentlemen. Like venom from a viper. Sooner or later, it will sweep the republic under, in all but name, or it will tear it apart."

Carroll started to protest. "I think that's more than a bit—"

"No, he's right," said Jackson quietly. He still hadn't taken his gaze from the countryside beyond. "I didn't use to think so, either, Bill. But John's right. Arkansas changed everything. Or maybe it's better to say that Arkansas stripped away the blinders. Where do you want to start? States' rights? Calhoun and his people are already demanding that the federal post has to be closed to abolitionist literature."

"But you said—wasn't but—"

Jackson waved his hand impatiently. "I know what I said. Didn't seem like such a bad idea to me, once. Stinking abolitionists. But haven't you been paying attention? Now they're claiming that even the reports being filed by Cullen Bryant—even Scott!—are 'abolitionist.'"

Finally, he turned away from the window. Some fury was coming into his eyes. "And don't that cap the climax? Winfield Scott, who whipped the British at the Chippewa and almost lost his life at Lundy's Lane, has to shut his mouth and not tell the country the truth about its military affairs— so that John Calhoun, who never once in his life put himself in harm's way for the sake of the republic, isn't discomfited on his plantation. No different, I tell you—no different at all!—from those damn traitors in New Orleans!"

He gave the room a sweeping gaze much like the one Adams had just given it. Allowing for a fifty-degree increase in temperature. "No, sir! Be damned if I'll support that!"

His eyes met those of John Quincy Adams, then, and the two men exchanged a quick, hard nod.

So, it was all over but the shouting.

* * *

Well, all over but the dickering. There'd be days of that, still.

John Coffee thought about his own reaction and was a bit surprised at what he found.

Simply relief. A man could live with a reptile, even place his own well-being in the creature's care. That wasn't easy, but it could be done. What was truly hard—exhausting, after a while—was the need to keep insisting the scaly damn thing was warm and furry. As if it were a pet instead of a vicious wild beast that could turn on you at any moment.

By midafternoon, two days later, they finally agreed on a modification of New York's method of gradual emancipation. Quincy Adams dragged the negotiations out for at least half a day, all but calling them a pack of cowards. New York had taken longer to free its slaves than any of the Northern states except New Jersey. In fact, they still weren't all free. There were hardly any negroes remaining who were affected by those particular curlicues in a set of laws that was riddled with curlicues, true enough. But, technically, the last slave in New York wouldn't be free until 1827.

But Coffee knew—everybody knew—that was just Quincy Adams's way of applying the goad. Fine for him to advocate the Vermont or Massachusetts approach, when slaves had never featured significantly in those colonies and states to begin with. The legislative program they were trying to develop had the border states as their principal target, and slavery was prominent in those states.

So, they felt the New York model would be more palatable, given that New York had had a large number of slaves through most of its history. In fact, until very recently, there had been more slaves in New York City than in any city in the nation, including Charleston, South Carolina. Nor was that simply a reflection of the fact that New York was by far the largest city. It was estimated that, as late as the end of the century, one out of four households in the city had owned slaves.

There was the further advantage, using the New York model, of having Martin Van Buren's expertise—no small thing, when it came to what would surely be bitter infighting in Congress.

Not that the issue would really be decided in Congress.

Jackson, a firm advocate of states' rights, was adamant that no emancipation program of any kind could be applied to the nation as a whole. The new party could legitimately use Congress only as a podium from which to expound its views. The battles themselves would have to be won in the separate states, one at a time.

In practice, that meant Tennessee and Kentucky within a year or two, with Missouri to come later. The issue of slavery was still a sore point in Missouri because of the Missouri Compromise. Benton warned them that it would take, in his estimate, at least four years before any Missouri legislature would be willing to seriously contemplate the notion.

You never knew, though, he added. More and more German immigrants were coming into the state, and wherever Germans went, support for slavery was sure to drop. Drastically, at times. What was perhaps more important, however, was the uncertain variable of the Arkansas War.

Arkansas had forced the issue—and Arkansas might very well continue to set the pace and determine the parameters. If for no other reason than the simplest and crudest. The longer and more successfully a mostly black nation could defend its independence, the more difficult it became for any white man in America—even John Calhoun—to persist in the claim that black people were incapable of managing their own affairs.

That was the ancient formula, even older than the dangers of a Praetorian Guard. A nation might produce no poets, no philosophers, no inventors, no scientists, no statesmen, no theologians, no sculptors—no barbers and butchers and bakers, for that matter. But if it could beat down anyone who tried to conquer it, no one could claim that it didn't produce men.

Poets and philosophers might weep over that crude arithmetic. But Andrew Jackson was neither, whatever John Quincy Adams's pretensions might be. He had no trouble with it at all. He had subscribed to the formula in full since the age of thirteen, when he told a British officer who commanded him to shine his boots that he'd not do it. He still had the scar on his forehead from the officer's ensuing saber cut—but he'd never shined the boots.

CHAPTER 41

On the following day, having settled the core question, the founders of the new National Democratic-Republican Party—such was the title they decided upon—were seized by a bolder spirit. Or perhaps it was simply that they could calculate a different arithmetic. That was certainly true of Van Buren.

With the political authority gathered at that founding convention of the new party, its leaders were quite confident that they could win in Tennessee, Kentucky, and Missouri. Not easily, no, but win they would. And they'd win Delaware, too, perhaps even sooner than Missouri. The Quakers and Methodists were influential in that state. The Quakers had long been antislavery, and the Methodists had been moving steadily in that direction. Arkansas Post—the whole Arkansas situation—was turning the Methodist drift into a powerful current.

That aside, the new party's program of gradual emancipation was sure to lose them all of the South itself, with the possible exception—over time, not quickly—of Maryland and the Old Dominion. That was sure to be true, even though the rest of their program would generally appeal to the poorer classes of white Southerners.

That meant, whatever else, that they needed to seize and keep the allegiance of New England—and New England would chafe at too many compromises. Outright abolitionism was growing by leaps and bounds in the region after Second Arkansas Post. A current in Delaware, it was a tide in New England.

The same was true in Pennsylvania, perhaps even more so. If Pennsylvanians were not given to Puritan posturing,

they were considerably more iron-headed than New En-
glanders. Abolitionists might pour into meetings at Faneuil
Hall in their thousands. Pennsylvania had already sent a
Lafayette Battalion to Arkansas. A small one, granted, according to the news reports. More in the way of a company
than anything a military man would call a battalion. But
there would be more coming, if the same accounts were accurate.

Needless to say, countermoves were being planned, beginning in South Carolina and Georgia. Calls had already been
issued for the formation of Cavalier Brigades to show
Brown's Raiders and the so-called Lafayette Battalions what
was what on the field of valor. Even allowing for the usual
Southron bombast, no one had much doubt that private military forces from Southern states would be entering the fray
by next year. "Bleeding Arkansas" would soon be more than
an abolitionist's histrionic slogan.

So, for the rest—with the obvious exception—they swung
over to the Vermont road. The "high road," as Quincy
Adams persisted in calling it, much to the irritation of his
colleagues.

No disenfranchisement due to race or color.
No restrictions of property due to race or color.
*No restrictions of movement or residence due to race
  or color.*

In short, in one fell swoop—with the obvious exception—
they proposed to eliminate the middle ground between slavery and freedom. Strike down any and all forms of exclusion
laws. A black man might be a slave, or he might be free. But
if he was free, he would have—legally, at least—the rights
of any white citizen.

The work done, they basked in self-esteem.

For perhaps three minutes, until Richard Mentor Johnson
finally spoke after days of almost unbroken silence.

John Coffee had been afraid he would.

"Gentlemen, I can't go along with this any longer." The
Kentucky senator's face seemed more homely than ever. But

it was also set as stubbornly as any mule's. "Not without the rest. It just sticks in my craw."

Jackson was back at the window. The others were in their usual seats.

No one said anything. Their faces were stiff, wooden. With the exception of the two border states' governors, anyway. Their expressions were back to that rabbit-staring-at-a-viper look.

"To Sam Hill with all of you," Johnson said tonelessly. "I don't care what you think. I've been in love with my wife since I was eighteen years old. She's the mother of my two children. And I find, when all is said and done, that I just don't see where all the rest means a good God-damned thing if a man can't marry his own wife and claim his children for his own. Which I would surely like to do some time before I die. Let that hypocrite Tom Jefferson explain Sally Hemings and his bastards to the Lord when his time comes. I don't want to have to do the same."

"Well said," stated Quincy Adams. "My salutations, sir."

Coffee looked to the window. After a moment, Jackson turned around. "Yes. I agree. Add it to the list."

Carroll threw up his hands. "Andy, for the sake of— tarnation! We throw in amalgamation, we may as well just fold up our tents right now."

"Oh, bullshit." Jackson nodded at Johnson. "He's been married in all but name to a nig—negress—for a quarter of a century. And if there's anybody—any voter—in the state of Kentucky who don't know it, I'd like you to show me where they're hiding. And how many times has he gotten elected, Bill? And reelected?"

The governor of Tennessee tightened his jaws. But they weren't any tighter than those of the state's senator. The next words from Jackson almost came through gritted teeth.

"Besides, it doesn't matter. The thing that separates our party from—whatever you want to call that pack of scoundrels who don't agree on much of anything except they want power—is this, before it's anything else. You figure out what you think the republic needs. First. Then you figure out how to get enough people to vote for you. What you don't do—ever—is go at it the other way around. Leave that to the Henry Clays of the world."

"Well said, also," stated Quincy Adams. "In fact, I'd like to propose a drink to that statement. Manifesto, I should rather call it."

He bestowed the first real smile on his colleagues he'd given them since he'd arrived at the Hermitage. "Whiskey, of course."

Even Carroll chuckled at that. But he made one last stab at it.

"How about—"

"*Add it,* tarnation," Jackson growled. " 'No restrictions on marriage due to race or color.' To Sam Hill with the whole business! I've just gotten sick of it. And the longer we argue about it, the sicker I get. In the end, you've got to ask yourself a simple question. What kind of democracy have you got when a man can't make such a basic decision on his own as to which woman he marries? And if the decision he makes is one that you or me think only a lunatic would make, so be it. Every man in this room"—he gave Adams a semi-skeptical glance—"except maybe the blasted Puritan over there, believes staunchly in the separation of church and state. And marriage is a matter between a man and a woman and their God. So what business has the state got sticking its nose into it?"

He waved his hand, more or less in the direction of the nation's capital. "You know and I know what the real issue is here. It's the same issue that's underneath every single blasted one of these points. It's not about marriage, just like"—here he gave Adams a frosty eagle's look—"the Bank quarrel's not about banking. It's about *power.* You give black people that last opening—give it three generations, who's to say what's black in the first place?—and you throw overboard John Calhoun's precious so-called 'positive good.' Slavery's just a thing, then. A machine to make money. Nothing more, nothing less. And no machine lasts forever. Never has, never will."

Carroll took a very deep breath, and let it out slowly. "Well . . . all right. We'll take a beating, though, Andy. Don't think we won't."

"Yes, I know," Jackson replied. "I've taken beatings before."

He grinned then. "But the worst one I ever took in my life came at the hands of that bear-sized bastard Benton sitting right over there. So why am I supposed to worry about what a skinny pipsqueak like Henry Clay might do?"

That brought uproarious laughter, and the whiskey came out. And stayed out, for the rest of the day and well into the night. The work was done. No one could say it wasn't, any longer.

Toward evening, Governor Carroll approached Senator Johnson, who had joined Jackson and Coffee at the window.

"Look, Dick, I don't want you to think there was anything personal about that. It's just—"

Johnson smiled and shook his head. "Oh, I know that, Bill. I couldn't hardly get too self-righteous about it anyway. Seeing as how I didn't make up my mind until yesterday. And the truth is, it didn't so much involve Julia in the first place. Not really."

He seemed to be a bit embarrassed then. "What I mean is, she and I have managed well enough for a long time now. We could have gone on the same way. But the thing is . . ."

His voice trailed off, and his eyes went back to the window. Beyond, there really wasn't much to be seen except the sunset over the Tennessee countryside. And black people walking slowly back to the slave quarters. Their day's work was done, too.

"I got another letter from Julia two days ago," he said. "Longer one than usual."

"How's she holding up?" asked Coffee.

"Pretty well, actually." He chuckled, very softly. " 'Course, she spent the first page of the letter goin' on and on about how much she misses me. Which I don't doubt. But it's pretty obvious New Antrim agrees with her quite well."

He paused, watching the slaves. Their pace was picking up as they neared the quarters. Faster, the closer they got. That was because the word was spreading, not because they were all that eager to return. Their quarters were decent enough, as slave quarters went. Andy wasn't the sort of plantation owner to force his slaves to live in shacks. But they were still considerably more modest—certainly more cramped—than even a frontier family's log cabin.

"How much whiskey are you passing out?" he asked.

"As much as they want," Jackson replied, "so long as they don't get rowdy. Not the good stuff, of course. And I told the overseers to give them the day off tomorrow."

A thin sort of grin came to his face. "And I'm prepared to be charitable about how I define 'rowdy.' So don't be expecting too much in the way of quiet rest tonight, gentlemen. But to go back to the subject, I can't say I'm surprised that she finds New Antrim agreeing with her. She *is* a black woman, Dick, even if she's got twice as many white ancestors as black ones and her skin's no darker than most Indians. And New Antrim is a black city. Bigger than any in the United States, now, according to the newspaper accounts, except a handful."

He shook his head slightly. "I got to admit, I'm surprised. I wouldn't have thought you could pack that many black folks in one place without them burning it down. Just by accident."

"It's pretty orderly, actually, what Julia says. But the main thing about the letter was that she turned to Imogene. It seems my daughter has formed a certain attachment to a young fellow there. Pretty serious, Julia says, even if Imogene's still too young for any such thing."

Jackson frowned. "Your twins are . . . what, Dick? Not more than fourteen, if I remember right."

"Not even that. Thirteen. And the boy involved just turned eighteen. Julia don't approve, of course. But . . ."

Johnson sighed. "Imogene's always been the more rambunctious of the two, and she's stubborn like you wouldn't believe. The main thing, Julia tells me, is that he's a nice boy. Quite a decent sort, and not one to take advantage of a girl so young. In fact, it seems he's leaning on her to pay more attention to her studies, and she's even obeying him. And ain't that a laugh? I couldn't ever do it with a stick!"

"So . . ."

"What's the problem? The problem is that Julia went on for another two pages about what a splendid young fellow this here boy was. Courteous, level-headed, responsible. He's even an officer already, in their army. Just got promoted to captain, in fact."

"At *eighteen*?" Jackson's brow was close to thunderous. "What kind of army promotes an eighteen-year-old—? Oh."

Johnson squinted at him. "Oh what, Andy?"

Jackson's frown was fading quickly. "Didn't you read Scott's account of the battle?"

"Well, sure, but—"

"Dig it up and read it again. You'll find your Imogene's swain. I can even tell you his last name, though I don't remember the first. Parker."

He shook his head. It was one of those odd sorts of headshakes, though. Admiring more than disapproving, mixed with something of just plain wonder. "That's quite some boy, I can tell you that. But I see your problem."

Carroll and Coffee were both lost, now. They'd also read the accounts of the battle, of course. But they hadn't subjected them to the sort of fine-tooth-comb scrutiny that Andy had. Not that Jackson actually expected he'd ever be leading an army against Arkansas. But . . . you never knew, and an old general's habits die hard.

Seeing their looks of confusion, Johnson got to the point. "Oh, come on, fellows. You both know Julia, as many times as you've visited Blue Spring Farm. When was the last time—or the first time—you ever heard her showering praise on *anybody*? Much less two pages worth in a letter?"

Coffee smiled. "She's astringent that way, no doubt about it."

Johnson was staring out the window again, his expression gloomy. "There's only one possible explanation. This Parker boy might be a veritable paladin. But I can tell you for sure what else is true about him, that Julia just somehow never got around to mentioning in her letter. He's black as the ace of spades, too. Only reason she'd be carrying on like that."

"Oh." That came from Carroll.

"Yeah. Oh."

"Yes, Scott mentions that in his account," Jackson added. "As negro as they come."

He twisted his head to bring his eyes to bear on Johnson. That same frosty eagle's look he'd bestowed on Adams earlier. "Also as valiant as they come, in whatever color. Read Scott's report. So what do you propose to do about it, Dick?"

Johnson chuckled humorlessly. "Well, first I'll try to talk the girl out of the foolishness. Whenever I can manage to see her next, which is Sam Hill knows when. Knowing Imogene, though . . ."

The sun had almost set by now. "But that's actually why I got stubborn in the end. To go back to where we started. What it all comes down to is that I just can't really see where anybody except the Creator who made us all has the right to pass the sins of the fathers onto their children. I hope Imogene gets more sensible about it all when she gets older. But whatever she does, I don't ever want her having to live the lie I did. Not ever again. I wouldn't wish that on anybody."

There was silence for a bit, until the sun finished setting. Then Jackson called for another round of drinks.

Later that evening, when Coffee had a moment alone with Jackson, he leaned over and said quietly: "I'm not all that surprised, now that I've had time to think about it, that you swung over to John Quincy on the matter. But I'm still surprised you did it so fast and easy."

Jackson's responding smile was a bit rueful. Coffee might have even called it a bit of a guilty smile. Except that "guilt" fit Andy Jackson about as well as feathers fit a bull. Whatever else Old Hickory might be, he was surely the most self-righteous man in America.

"Well . . . That was Houston's doing. I've gotten letters from him about every week for months now." He nodded toward Adams. "So's John Quincy, he tells me. When Sam puts his mind to something, that blasted youngster can be awful persuasive."

Coffee thought about it. That was true, up to a point. Sam Houston's silver tongue was famous all over the country, and although Coffee had never read any of his correspondence, he didn't doubt that the man's pen was just as silvery. Still . . .

"Andy, you could teach stubbornness to a mule. Nobody who ever lived can be *that* persuasive."

Jackson's smile broadened and lost any trace of ruefulness. "Sure he can. When he's got Arkansas Post on his side—and he's writing letters to a general. Think about it, John. The question Sam kept posing was as simple as it gets.

As long as Arkansas stands, the issue of slavery just can't be ignored any longer. And did I think—really think—that Arkansas could be driven under? And if so, how? Blast that conniving youngster!"

Coffee wasn't quite following him. "And your answer was . . . ?"

"Of course I could whip Arkansas! The first time he asked, I sent back a short summary of how I'd do it. Pretty much the same plan Zack Taylor tried to talk those idiots in Washington around. It ain't complicated. Stay out of that death trap in the river valley after seizing as much of the Delta as we can. Threaten them on the south, doing whatever it takes to secure a route up the Red. Then make the big thrust from the north, down the Arkansas, splitting off the Indians from the negroes. It'd all end with a siege of Fort of 98. Bloody damn business, for sure, but I'd win."

He took a self-satisfied sip from his whiskey. "It'd work, sure as the sunrise. There just aren't enough negroes and Indians in Arkansas—I don't care how tough they are—to stand off eight million white Americans."

He fell silent. Coffee frowned. "And . . . ?"

"And what do you *think*? Sam right off sent back a letter congratulating me on my perspicacity and posed a few more questions. And did the same in all the letters that followed, until I gave up."

Now, Coffee was completely lost. "*You* gave up? Why?"

"Figure it out, John. You've fought wars, too, right along-side me. Sit down when you get home, and start writing down everything you'd have to do to make that plan work. Figure the size army you'd need. Figure the logistics you'd need. That part's not too hard. Then—Sam never let me off the hook, not once—start figuring out all the *political* changes you'd need to back all that up. By the fifth letter, I'd had martial law declared all across New England and Pennsylvania. And how do you finance the business? Nothing in the world's as expensive as a war, especially a big one that goes on for years. By the time I got to the seventh letter— maybe the eighth—I was starting to contemplate the virtues of a national bank. So help me God, I was."

Jackson drained the rest of his whiskey. "And there's your answer, which Sam Houston wouldn't let me slide away from. Yeah, sure, I *could* conquer Arkansas. But was I willing to pay the price? And for what?"

He waved the empty glass at the window, beyond which the slaves could be heard at their festivities. "So I could keep my slaves? Tarnation, I came into the world without a slave to my name, and the day I'll destroy my republic in order to keep them is the day my name stops being Andrew Jackson. I can figure out ways to emancipate slaves without going broke in the process. Not easily, but I can. What I can't do is figure out how to keep them—not for all that long—in a world that has Arkansas in it. Without gutting and skinning the republic. It just ain't worth it, John. Simple as that."

Now he waved the empty glass at Adams, who was in a corner talking with Van Buren. "I imagine Sam did exactly the same to that poor bastard. Except—being a pigheaded Massachusetts scholar—it probably took John Quincy twice as long to admit he was cornered as it took me. How about another drink?"

The slaves did push the limits of "rowdy," although nothing important actually got broken. But on both occasions when the overseers came to Jackson for instructions, he sent them away.

The masters were pretty rowdy themselves by then. His pious wife Rachel, much disapproving, went early to bed. They were even beginning to blaspheme quite openly, laughing all the while.

Especially after John Quincy Adams, no longer even remotely sober, proposed an alternative title for their new party: the National Illegitimate Party. With its clear and simple fighting slogan: *Better a Plain Black Bastard in Office than a Fancy White-Striped Skunk.*

CHAPTER 42

"It's definite," said Adam Beatty. He laid a copy of the *National Intelligencer* onto the president's desk. "Today's edition. It has the full text of the program of the new party. The 'Declaration of Principles,' the silly bastards are calling it."

At Clay's courteous nod, Beatty took a seat in one of the chairs surrounding the desk where Clay's other political advisers were already seated. Fortunately, not adjoining Porter's. By now, Peter's dislike for the Kentucky legislator had grown into pure loathing.

"Everything's there, Henry," Beatty continued, grinning. "And—believe me—it's every bit as insane as any of the rumors. Ha! The bedlamites might as well have cut their own throats and been done with it!"

Clay already had the newspaper spread in front of him and was starting to read the first-page headline story. Most of the advisers—all of them, actually, except Porter himself—were craning their necks. Josiah Johnston, sitting the closest, had half risen out of his chair.

Beatty rummaged in his satchel. "No need to strain yourselves, gentlemen. I obtained plenty of copies. Enough for everyone."

A moment later, Porter had a copy of the *Intelligencer* on his own lap. He didn't give it more than a cursory glance, though, for the same reason he hadn't craned his neck with the others. He'd already read it before coming to the meeting this morning.

Twice. All the way through and back again.

"They're madmen, I tell you!" exclaimed Beatty, still with that grin. "They're even advocating amalgamation!"

Porter cleared his throat. There were limits, and he had finally reached all of them.

"No, actually—and I'd advise you to be careful how you phrase that. They are not *advocating* amalgamation. They're simply calling for the removal of all laws that regulate marriage by criteria of color."

Beatty was giving him that look that Porter had come to detest. Half frowning, because he was stupid. Half jeering, because his stupidity had no bottom.

"If you can't understand the difference, Representative Beatty, it's the difference between advocating divorce and allowing for it in the law. I do not advocate that you divorce your wife."

Not that the poor woman probably wouldn't thank me.

"I do, however, propose to make it legally possible for you to do so, should that be your choice."

He didn't bother disguising the underlying sneer.

Clay spoke a bit hastily to keep the matter from escalating. "Yes, yes, Peter, of course you're right." He gave Beatty a veiled look from under lowered brows. "Do be careful about that, Adam. We don't want to be accused of outright fabrication."

Porter had become all too familiar with that veiled expression, also. More and more, Clay was separating his lines of action and using different advisers for different purposes. He might just as well have said: *By all means throw the charge around, Adam—with wild abandon—just make sure it can't be traced back to me.*

Granted, Clay had always been a rough political fighter, even if he wore gloves. Porter had admired the trait in times past, and he wouldn't have objected if the gloves came off. The problem was that Henry was doing the opposite as time went on. He was adding more gloves at the same time his blows were getting lower.

It was becoming . . . filthy. There was no other word for it.

Johnston spoke next. "We shouldn't have any trouble, now, getting Congress to pass the military appropriations bill. None at all, I'd think."

Porter levered himself upright. That issue was his principal concern. "Henry, I want to advise you again that I think it would be a mistake to present that bill to Congress."

The other advisers were looking either pained, in the case of Johnston, or derisive, in the case of Beatty, or something in between. Clay's face had no expression at all.

Porter knew this was his last chance, so he decided to use whatever leverage he had. What little leverage he had any longer.

He pointed to the *Intelligencer*. "Let the ramifications of that settle in for a bit. In a month or two, I think you'd be able to get the appropriations bill passed that we *need*."

"Oh, for the love of—" Beatty broke off the incipient blasphemy. Clay didn't approve of such, and at least part of his disapproval was actually genuine.

Beatty slid forward, perched on the edge of his chair. "We've been over this more often than I want to remember. Mr. Porter, no one except you thinks it will take an army the size of the Russian tsars to squelch a pack of rioting negroes. A simple doubling of the regiments—"

Weeks—months—of simmering doubts and frustration boiled to the surface. Without realizing he'd done so, Porter was on his feet.

"Mr. Beatty, have you ever gotten any closer to a battlefield than you have to the moon? Because I *have*." He pointed a slightly shaking finger at the newspaper. "Did you read the account of the battle, every detail of which was published in that same newspaper? And many others. They were *outnumbered,* and they still held off half the existing U.S. Army while inflicting worse casualties than almost any battle in the war with Britain and routing several thousand militiamen. And you—you—you—propose to call them rioting negroes, as if we faced nothing more than a minor civil disturbance?"

Clay was saying something, but Porter was simply too angry to pay attention. "Blast you! Gentlemen, we are dealing with a *war,* here. A very real, no-joking, *war.* That means we have got to mobilize the same way—"

"*Peter!*"

Porter broke off at that half shout. He saw that Clay was on his feet. The president's expression was just short of a glare.

"Peter," he said sternly, "I'm afraid I shall have to ask you to leave. And please do not return until and unless you have regained your composure."

Porter stared at him.

"Now, please."

There was—

Nothing to say, that he could think of. Any longer. Explosively, he let out a breath that he hadn't even realized he was holding in.

"Yes, of course, Mr. President. My apologies." He gathered up his own satchel and made for the door.

On the way out, he heard Clay saying: "For that matter, gentlemen, I think we should leave this whole issue out of our discussion altogether. It is now properly a matter for the Cabinet."

The Cabinet. That meant John Calhoun, first and foremost. Who had also never in his life come closer to a battlefield than he had to the moon. And who, while he favored as big an expansion of the army as possible, had a contempt for black people so deep that it blinded him.

But as he passed through the door, Peter realized it was no longer any of his concern. There were limits. There *had* to be limits, and he was now past them.

Outside, on Pennsylvania Avenue, he looked down at the Capitol. Trying, for a moment, to remember how many years he had spent in the republic's service, doing his best to help guide it.

Enough. He had his own affairs to tend to, which he had long neglected. What would happen would happen, unfolding according to its own grim logic. A war begun by happenstance—some scheming, too, to be honest—would now be fought by men who thought they could do everything by half measures, supplanting the other half with schemes. The half measures would fail, succeeded by fuller ones—but those, too, would be stunted by that same cleverness, which was too clever by half. Until, in the end, they found themselves in a roaring rapids, in a rudderless raft they'd thought to be a steamboat, with the falls ahead.

Be damned to them all. Peter Porter owned no slaves and never had.

He was finally able to laugh, a bit. And never would own any, of course. Not now.

New Antrim
NOVEMBER 7, 1825

Sheff Parker was surprised when Julia Chinn ushered Winfield Scott into his room. He knew who the man was, of course, and had even seen him a time or two on the streets before his injury. But they'd never exchanged so much as a single word.

He lowered the newspaper he'd been working his way through, with some relief. He'd have preferred reading an account of the new National Democratic-Republican Party's program in an article written by Cullen Bryant and Scott. But Bryant had left a few weeks ago. He'd decided to remain in Arkansas for the duration of the war. But, that being the case, he had no desire to remain separated from his wife and daughter, so he'd gone to get them and bring them back with him.

From what Sheff had been told by Julia, Scott had considered the same course of action. But either because his family was larger—five children in all—or because his wife came from Virginian upper crust, or because he was apparently planning to cover the war from both sides of the line, he'd decided otherwise.

Unfortunately, from Sheff's point of view, that meant the analysis of the new party's program was being written by John Ridge and Buck Watie. And they tended toward a far more flowery style of prose. Sheff's ability to read was improving rather quickly, now that he had so much time on his hands. But this was a strain.

Scott came to the bed and leaned over to see what Sheff was reading.

"Oh, dear Lord. I don't envy you that. I leave aside the fact that their assessment misses the mark wildly, and on at least three counts."

"Why do—ah, please have a seat, General."

"Thank you. Why do I think that?" The tall former officer drew up a chair. "Let's start with the most basic. If you took that seriously, you'd think the entire program of the new party—well, let's say nine points out of ten—was essentially a fraud. Then let's consider the fact that the estimable Ridge and Watie can't decide whether that's good or bad. Which is understandable enough, given their predicament. The Ridge family estates in Oklahoma have more slaves working them than all but the wealthiest plantations in the South. After that, we can move on—"

"Is it true that most of the slaves will never see freedom?"

"Oh, yes, Captain Parker, that's quite true. The same thing will happen in Tennessee and Kentucky—and Missouri, though perhaps not Delaware—that happened in New York and most of the Northern states that adopted gradual emancipation. Before the time limit expires, most slave-owners will have sold their slaves to masters somewhere in the South. I'd be surprised if more than one out of five people who were scheduled for manumission ever receive it. The black populations of most of those states dropped precipitously in the years prior to emancipation—and I can assure you they didn't move to Canada, the most of them."

He nodded toward the southeast. "They—or their children—are laboring on a plantation somewhere in the Carolinas or Georgia, or perhaps working as stevedores on the docks of Savannah or Charleston. As I say, Delaware may be an exception. The Quakers and Methodists will be vigilant, and they may be able to keep that to a minimum. In any event, Delaware already has the largest freedmen population of any state in the nation, at least in percentage terms. The people of the state are fairly accustomed to it by now."

Sheff studied the man's face. For all the cynicism that rested on the surface of Scott's expression, something else lay underneath.

"Please explain," Sheff said. He lifted the paper a bit. "Why that goes against what they're saying."

"Because they're like men on a battlefield who see only the casualties and don't consider the fight. In the long run, Captain Parker—yes, I know this will sound very callous to you—it doesn't matter what happens to those people. Give it two generations, three at the outside, and slavery is dead. Jackson knows that, Adams knows that, and you can be quite sure that John Calhoun knows it, too."

Scott waved a dismissive hand at the newspaper. "Those lads—they're very young, so I'll grant them the excuse—are approaching this as if it were simply a moral issue. Which it is, of course. But battles are not won with moral splendor. They're won by the brute force of the clash of arms."

Sheff just waited, patiently. Sooner or later, he figured the man would get around to it.

After a moment, Scott smiled at him. "You *are* smart. Patrick told me you were."

He lifted one long leg and crossed it over the other. Then, folded his hands in his lap.

"Here's how it is, Captain Parker. Slavery expands, or it dies. For two reasons. First, because the agriculture involved is frightfully wasteful of the soil. Within a much shorter time than you might think, so-called King Cotton will look like a bedraggled down-at-the-heels little robber baron. As it already does in the northern tier of slave states. The truth is—my father-in-law dislikes to admit it, as do most of my native state's gentry—Virginia's main crop nowadays is slaves themselves. Whom they breed like so much livestock in order to sell to cotton growers in the Deep South."

A sneer came to his face. "Remember that, the next time you read one of John Randolph's perorations on liberty. But you can see where I'm going. How are slave-owners in Georgia and Alabama to make the same transition—from King Cotton to King Negro—when there are no new slave territories into which cotton production is expanding?"

Sheff thought about it. "Well, there's Texas."

Scott chuckled. "Yes, indeed. And—remember I told you this—I expect within ten years we'll be seeing a war down there, too. But Texas alone, even if the South can seize it, won't be enough. Once Kentucky and Tennessee and Missouri are closed to slavery, it begins to die in its own waste. But it won't come to that, anyway. Because the *other* reason slavery needs to expand is political. The population of the North and the West in the United States grows much faster than that of the South. Because of immigration, if for no other reason. No immigrants except wealthy ones—and they're but a handful—want to live in a slave state. Slavery depresses wages, and it stifles opportunity for small enterprise. So they move to the North and West. And now—"

He pointed to the newspaper. "—*this* is the essence of that program, which the estimable Ridge and Watie managed to miss completely. The border states have finally decided they are part of the West, not the South."

"They haven't actually decided yet," Sheff said mildly. He wasn't trying to be disputatious, though. He was just deeply interested in the former general's assessment and wanted to draw it out as far as he could.

Winfield Scott really did have quite a magnificent sneer. Sheff was impressed.

"Ha! With *that* band of brigands leading the charge? My dear captain! Should the legislature of Tennessee be so bold as to defy Andrew Jackson, he's quite capable of ordering the militia to train their guns on the state capitol. I believe he still holds the rank of major general in the militia, which remains fiercely attached to the man. By 'guns,' I include twelve-pounders. There are precious few slave-owners in the Tennessee militia, and those not major ones. One or two slaves, more like family servants than the chattel labor on big plantations. Hired hands, once they're freed, which is an easy enough transition for all parties involved."

Once again, he waved his hand dismissively. "No, no. With Jackson and Benton and Johnson and Carroll and Desha calling for it, the border states are lost to slavery. Not immediately, but they're lost. And once they're gone, the South will slide further and further into political impotence. The slave states have already lost the House, and the imbalance will grow deeper every year. Now, soon enough, they'll have lost the Senate. And I doubt if you'll see more than—at most—one Southerner ever sitting in the president's house again, so long as slavery lasts, where the first four of five came from the region. Five out of six, if we count Clay. Which I suppose we must, given that he's thrown himself into Calhoun's clutches. The blithering idiot."

Sheff studied him for a moment. "And that doesn't concern you?"

"Oh, of course it does. But it concerns me as a soldier of the United States, not as a Virginian. My loyalty is to the nation, Captain Parker. It always has been. I have no use for men with divided loyalties. On that if nothing else, I've always agreed with Andrew Jackson. So . . . I imagine I'll be returning to the colors one of these fine days."

The handsome patrician head looked very much like one of the Roman busts Sheff had seen in the Wolfe Tone Hotel. He'd wondered, a bit, why the Laird had gone to the trouble and expense of having them shipped there all the way from Philadelphia. He was normally quite frugal.

He figured he finally knew, now.

"You think there might be a war over it."

"That's . . . putting it too strongly," Scott mused. "But it's a possibility, yes. Although I think it's more likely to take the form of a series of armed clashes than what you could properly call a war. Either way, I expect I'll have work to do. My real line of work, so to speak."

He said that last with a smile. "Which, actually, brings me to the purpose of my visit. Patrick insisted I come. I didn't dare refuse him, of course. Him being my old master sergeant and a troll of most frightening proportions."

They shared a laugh at that. Sheff decided he liked Winfield Scott. Not that he could imagine ever being what you could call a real friend of the man, given the chasm of their origins. Although . . . who could say what the future might bring? As each year—each month—passed, Sheff was finding the future less and less predictable.

It was an enjoyable sensation, even a thrilling one, for an eighteen-year-old who could well remember how the future had looked not more than two years earlier. Extremely predictable, indeed. A life—probably a short one—filled with hard labor and poverty, ending in a grave. A pauper's grave at that.

There was a little commotion at the door. "Ah, that'll be the workmen," said Scott. He gave the small bedroom a quick inspection. "We'll have to move that dresser to another room. I'll let Julia figure that out."

He rose and went to the door, leaving Sheff to frown at the dresser.

Why would they need to move—

The answer came within five seconds. Two men entered, carrying between them a very large oak bookcase. It was bigger than any bookcase Sheff had ever seen, except the one in the parlor of the Wolfe Tone. Behind them came two more men, each bearing boxes. From the strain in their shoulders, heavy ones.

The next few minutes were simply confusing. Scott didn't seem to feel that explanations were needed. But when it was all done, the dresser in the corner was gone, and the bookcase was in its place. Filled with books, now.

Sheff could hear Julia talking with the workmen in the corridor beyond. Trying to decide where to put the dresser, he imagined, but he didn't spend any time worrying about that. None of his own clothes had been in it. All of his clothes, even the two uniforms, fit into the locker that was shoved under his bed.

"There you are, Captain," Scott said, presenting the bookcase with an outstretched hand. "Mind you, it's only on loan, and I'll want it back when my peregrinations are finished. Since my partner chose to leave for a few months to fetch his family, I'll let him handle the American side of the reporting. I'm off—tomorrow, in fact—for the first of several tours of the Oklahoma front. Colonel Taylor has agreed to give me an interview. I expect I'll be visiting the Red River region as well. But by the time that's all done, you should be fit for active duty again."

He wagged a finger at Sheff. "Mind you, I'll expect them all to be in the same good condition. Some of these books took me years to track down."

Sheff's expression must have finally registered on Scott.

"What?" he exclaimed. "Patrick didn't *tell* you? What a troll!"

But he was smiling, quite widely. "It's my famous military library, Captain Sheff. Patrick felt that it was time you applied yourself to your work seriously instead of lolling about in comfort and ease. General Ross agrees, with the caveat that he expects to be able to borrow from them himself. And now, I must be off. Good day."

He paused briefly at the door and looked back. "I spoke with the surgeon, by the way. Your wound seems to be quite similar to my own. The one I acquired at Lundy's Lane. If so, Captain, expect it to hurt off and on for the rest of your life. But there shouldn't be any other problem of any consequence. And if pain is a major concern to you, then you'd best start looking for a different line of work."

He was gone.

Ten seconds later, his head reappeared in the door. "One last thing. If you're still struggling with your reading, I'd recommend you start with the biographies. The technical manuals can be quite dismal."

Gone again. Sheff stared at the bookcase.

After a while, defying the surgeon's orders, Sheff levered himself out of bed and began to examine the titles.

Eventually, he decided on Julius Caesar's *The Gallic War*. He had no idea who the Gallics had been, but at least he'd heard of Caesar. Now that he thought about it, in fact, that might be one of the busts in the hotel.

But maybe not. It was always hard to know with the Laird. Being as he was a man who hated tyranny, but never seemed to have any trouble being a tyrant himself when he thought he needed to be.

Not that Sheff cared. Like almost everyone in New Antrim, he'd seen tyranny at its most naked. No nebulous abstraction that someone like John Randolph might declaim against, but the real faces that had murdered his father.

So if it took a tyrant to deal with that tyranny, he'd surely be the tyrant's legionnaire. Not hesitate for an instant, not though he waded through an ocean of blood.

He'd only gotten through the first few pages, though, when there was another commotion at the door. Julia Chinn came in with a white man Sheff had never seen before.

"Will this do?" she asked.

The man shook his head vigorously. "Impossible, Mrs. Johnson. Not for what you want. We really need a much larger room, where we can place at least three chairs."

Julia nodded and gave Sheff a quick inspection. "Can you sit upright, Captain? For—" She cocked an inquiring head at the stranger.

"Two hours at a stretch, Mrs. Johnson. Though I'd prefer three."

Julia turned back to Sheff. "Can you manage that?"

"Oh, sure, Miz Julia. Truth is, I'd find it a relief. I get real tired of lying in bed, no matter what the surgeon says."

"Splendid. Let's begin at once then, since Mr. Wiedeman has the day free, and that's hardly ever true."

Wiedeman gave Sheff a curt nod and left. Julia moved over to help Sheff out of the bed. "That's Lyle Wiedeman, Captain Parker. He just arrived in town less than two weeks ago. Everyone's thrilled, of course. First real artist we've ever had in New Antrim. Well, painter, at least. But for this purpose, a wood-carver like Antoinette simply wouldn't do at all."

It was odd hearing Miz Julia talking so properly. Not that she couldn't when she wanted to. She always did, in fact, on the frequent occasions when General Ross's wife, Eliza, came to visit. But Sheff wasn't accustomed to hearing her talk like that when just he and the girls were around.

After she helped him to his feet, she shook her head, smiling widely, and indicated his bedclothes with a finger. "And that won't do at all, either. Can you manage to put on your uniform, Captain? The dress uniform, I mean."

"I might need some help with the coatee, Miz Julia, but I can do the rest. If you give me just a few minutes."

"Certainly. But there's one other thing, Captain, I'd much appreciate."

"Yes, Miz Julia?"

"*That.* It won't do all, either. Not any longer. So I must insist."

The words were said sternly—whatever they meant—but she was smiling more widely than ever.

"I don't understand, Miz Julia."

"Mrs. Johnson, Captain. That's my name. Please use it, henceforth."

CHAPTER 43

By the time Sheff got into his uniform, Mrs. Johnson helping him with the coatee, and made it out into the boardinghouse's salon, he discovered that the whole room had been rearranged. Lyle Wiedeman had an easel set up to one side, with a large blank canvas, and paints of various kind on a small table next to it. The divan that normally occupied pride of place in the room had been moved against one of the walls. The boardinghouse's owner, Susan Wilson, was perched on its edge watching the activities, with her grandchildren—all six of them—filling the rest of the divan.

Fortunately, it was one of the crudely made but sturdy pieces of furniture produced by the McParland Furniture Company in Fort of 98. The young children were rambunctious, climbing all over the thing, and Mrs. Wilson was not being her usual stern taskmistress self. The widow's dark eyes were bright with interest at the unusual goings-on in the rest of the room. Clearly enough, she was giving only a small part of her mind to the matter of the youngsters.

Sheff thought that might get sticky before too long. Literally sticky, what with all the paint bottles on Wiedeman's little table—which was not sturdily built at all. He hoped that nothing disastrous would happen before the children's two mothers and their uncle got back from work.

That would be a while yet, though. Susan Wilson's daughters worked for one of the larger of New Antrim's garment manufacturers, which, like all such, had long hours. The uncle, a partly disabled veteran since Second Arkansas Post, enjoyed one of the secured jobs set aside for such by the army's commissariat. His hours of work were not particularly long, but he was sure to dawdle after work in one of the military saloons before finally wending his way home.

The husband of the younger of the Wilson daughters wouldn't be returning for two weeks at the earliest, since his unit was on patrol somewhere in the Ouachitas. The husband of the older daughter would never be returning at all. He'd died at Second Arkansas in the fighting at the wall, not more than fifty feet from the spot where Sheff had been struck down.

But Sheff didn't give the matter of the children much of his mind, either. First, because he was too fascinated and puzzled by everything else. And second, because Imogene was in the room and wearing a fancy dress he'd never seen on her before. It looked brand-new and store-bought.

She was grinning at him and seemed to be on the verge of jumping up and down with excitement like a girl half her age. Sheff wouldn't have thought much of it a year ago, when he'd first met her. She'd seemed so young, then, that the difference between a twelve-year-old and a six-year-old would have been minor.

But he couldn't help notice it today. It was odd, really, the way the girl seemed to age, since he'd been moved into the room upstairs and got to see her all the time. As if she were a month older for every day that passed. Sheff would swear that was true, except he was pretty sure it was just his mind playing tricks on him.

He'd asked Cal about it, just the week before.

"You wish!" had been the unkind response.

Mrs. Johnson clapped her hands. "All right, everyone take their positions! Mr. Wiedeman's time is valuable, and we can't waste any of it."

She pointed imperiously to one of the three chairs lined up in a row. "Captain Parker, you take the seat on the left."

No sooner had he done so than Mrs. Johnson took the seat next to him, in the middle. The other seemed destined to remain vacant.

"Mama!" Adaline exclaimed. "Cal's not here yet!"

For the first time, Sheff noticed the twin. It might be better to say that her presence registered on him. He realized now that she'd been in the room all along, wearing a dress very similar to her sister's except in small details of color and trim. But, as often happened when Imogene was there also, he simply hadn't paid any attention to her.

And there was another oddity. Sheff kept hearing people comment on the identical appearance of the two girls, leaving aside whatever clothing they might have on. Sheff would have thought they were insane, except he had a vague recollection of having once thought the same thing himself.

That was hard to imagine now. He could tell them apart instantly at any distance, rain or shine. He'd never had to test the matter, but he was just as sure he could tell them apart in pitch darkness, just from the sound of their voices. For that matter, just from listening to them breathe.

But he forced that last thought aside. Best not to dwell on the thought of listening to Imogene breathe, in the here and now. He had time to do that—and did, and would—every night that passed. In a bed covered by a blanket, where he didn't have to worry about the possible indelicacy posed by the tight-fitting trousers of his dress uniform.

"Hush, Adaline!" her mother scolded. "Lieutenant McParland will be along soon enough. Something must have detained him. In the meantime, we can get started. Mr. Wiedeman tells me he'll be concentrating on one part of the portrait at a time. So he can start with Sheff and Imogene. Be still, I say!"

Imogene came to stand behind him, and just to one side. A moment later, he felt her hand coming to rest on his shoulder.

He stiffened slightly, casting a nervous glance at Mrs. Johnson. He'd been careful—very, very careful—not to engage in any sort of physical contact with Imogene. That would get him pitched out of the house in an instant, he was quite sure. And as much as he sometimes found the temptation difficult to resist, he managed. Whatever else he was, Sheffield Parker was patient and methodical. If it took him longer to get somewhere than it might take someone else, he'd get there all the more surely.

But, to his relief—and surprise—he saw that Mrs. Johnson was simply giving the hand on his shoulder a calm assessment.

"Not so close to the neck, Imogene. And keep your fingers still."

That was it. Sheff had to tighten his jaw to keep it from dropping altogether.

"Begin when you're ready, Mr. Wiedeman. Susan, I would recommend that you not allow that rascal to stand on the arm of the divan."

"Oh!" Mrs. Wilson tore her eyes away from the tableau in the center of the room. "Andrew, you sit down! Right now, or I'll smack you!"

"Everybody please be still," Wiedeman commanded.

"Where's Cal?" Adaline wailed.

Some part of Callender McParland felt like wailing, himself. The mission that the Laird had recruited him for as he'd been on his way to the boardinghouse—"recruited" as in "press-gang"—was now successfully completed.

They'd found Sam Houston, missing since the night before. He was sprawled on a pew in the city's big Catholic church, just underneath the wall where the new painted carving of his wife was suspended.

Drunk as a skunk, as the saying went—except no skunk who ever lived would get this drunk. He was almost comatose.

The Laird took a deep breath. "What I figured," Cal heard him mutter.

Standing next to Driscol, Charles Ball shook his head. "Like old times, isn't it? Tarnation, he hasn't had hardly a drop of whiskey in . . . how many months has it been, Patrick?"

"Twelve," he replied stonily. "Exactly. God damn me for a fool, I plain forgot. His wife was murdered a year ago yesterday."

On the Laird's other side, Charles Crowell sighed. "Oh, Lord. I forgot, too."

He heaved his massive shoulders and moved toward Houston. "Old times, Charles, as you say. I carried him before; I'll do it again."

"Wait," said Driscol, putting a hand on the huge banker's arm. His eyes were on the carving.

"For what?" asked Ball.

The Laird didn't answer for a moment. Then he shook his head.

"No. The boy will have to deal with this soon enough. Not often, I'm hoping. Sam made it through a widowing, and moving his son to a new home, and fought and won a battle. But it'll happen again. You know it and I know it. So go to the Wolfe Tone and bring little Andy here. It's the best place to begin."

Ball nodded. Crowell hesitated. "Are you sure—"

"No, he's right," said Ball. "You stay here with Patrick and watch over him. I'll get the boy."

"Tiana'll have your hide, Patrick, when she finds out," said Crowell.

"No, she won't. She'll not say a word. Times like this, she's pure Cherokee."

Driscol turned to Callender. "Thank you for your assistance, Lieutenant McParland, but it won't be needed any longer. My apologies for detaining you."

Cal left with Ball. At a dignified enough pace, until they got out of the church and went their separate ways. Then he starting walking as fast as he could.

Adaline would have *his* hide, for sure. And the worst of it was, he still couldn't figure out exactly how he'd found himself in this fix. As close friends as they'd become, he understood what drove Sheff to his fixation on Imogene. But what was *his* excuse?

The girl was only thirteen! Cal wasn't any sort of Puritan, sure, but some things a man just didn't contemplate. And he wasn't looking for a wife of any age. Not yet, anyway. Most men didn't get married until they were ten years older than he was. He'd figured to do the same.

He still hadn't come to any conclusions by the time he reached the boardinghouse. Except the dim, growing, horrible sense that things just happened because they did. Whether a man planned them or not, or wanted them or not, they just went right ahead and happened all on their own.

Then he was ushered into the salon by Mrs. Wilson, and Adaline squealed the moment he came in, and the next thing he knew she'd raced over and was hugging him and—sure enough—her mother was fit to be tied.

"*Adaline!* You come back here right this instant! And stop behaving disgracefully!"

After about three seconds, Adaline obeyed. Cal was pretty sure that had been the most thrilling three seconds of his life.

The dragon's glare now got leveled on him. Tarnation, he hadn't done anything!

"Lieutenant McParland."

But he'd look on the bright side. Might as well, since it was obvious the world would toss him however it would.

"How nice of you to come."

An ice cream parlor had finally opened for business in New Antrim. Wildly popular, of course, with Cal as much as anyone. Whenever it was open, the line went around the block. But it wasn't open very often, because ice was so hard to come by.

"Sit. Here. Please."

Not any longer. Just bottle that voice.

When Adaline put her hand on his shoulder, he liked to fly out of the chair. But, to his astonishment, the dragon didn't say a word.

Of course, if you could bottle the look in its eyes, you could probably freeze the whole chiefdom of Arkansas. And whenever Adaline so much as twitched a finger, the monster's hiss was enough to freeze your blood.

Still. It was an awfully thrilling two hours, with that hand there the whole time. By the end of it, Cal was halfway reconciled to the inescapable chaos of existence.

"Mrs. Johnson," said Sheff, sounding a bit timid.

"Yes, Captain Parker?"

"Ah . . . If I might ask, what's the—I mean. What are we doing here?"

She bestowed on him a look that was a *lot* warmer than anything she'd given Cal in at least two months. Just another example of life's essential unfairness.

"Oh, that's simple. I told my husband I'd have a portrait of us made up. Since it may be quite a while before we see him again. Mr. Wiedeman assures me he can have it shipped safely to Kentucky."

"Oh, certainly," said the artist. "Might be a problem a few months from now, of course."

Cal almost choked. He leaned over a bit to get a good look at Sheff.

Sure enough. Amazing that a face that black could manage to look that purple at the same time.

"Ah . . . am *I* going to be in the portrait?"

"What a ridiculous question. Of course you are, Captain Parker. Why else would you be sitting here?"

"But . . . ah . . ."

"*Imogene!* I told you! Not so close to the neck! For that matter, the session is over. Remove the hand, please. At once."

All the ice cream you'd need for everyone in New Antrim, dawn to dusk.

"Is Daddy all right? He looks real sick."

Driscol shifted the boy a bit farther into his lap. "He's fine, Andy. A little sick, yes. But he'll be fine by tomorrow. It might happen again, mind. You needn't worry about it though, lad, because we'll take care of it. Your father has many friends."

The boy looked up at him uncertainly. Then, just as uncertainly, swiveled his head to look up at the carving.

"That's Mommy, isn't it?"

"Yes, it is."

There was silence for a time as the boy settled his head on Driscol's shoulder and stared up at the carving. Houston's gentle snores were the only sound in the church.

Antoinette really had done a splendid job. It was Maria Hester, almost to the flesh.

"Will she go away again?"

"No, lad. She will not." All the weight of the Ozarks and the Ouachitas was in that voice. Ireland, too, and the mountains of Spain.

"Not today. Not tomorrow. Not ever."